One car. Four journeys.

A CONTEMPORARY REVERSE HAREM

ADDISON ARROWDELL

Road Trip

ISBN: 9781800681774

BEFORE YOU READ...

This book has references of emotional abuse, descriptions of moderate violence, offensive language, homophobic slurs and graphic sexual content, including same sex couplings.

If any of these things offend or upset you, please do not continue.

If you're okay with all of the above, buckle up and enjoy the ride . . .

1

I'm aware that running away to Las Vegas is a cliché, but it isn't my first choice. It probably isn't even my second choice. Or third. I'm beginning to think the I-90 will never end, and Chicago feels like a lifetime ago. Glancing at my watch, my stomach dips as I realize, it's only been eight hours. My stomach rolls for the hundredth time, and I crank down the window, hoping the summer evening air will stem the doubt suffocating my thoughts. A road sign looms overhead, and I squint, trying to figure out how much further until Sioux Falls.

"Shit! Shit! Shit!" I pump the breaks and swerve, just making my exit.

Luckily, the roads are quiet, and a solitary truck is the only witness to my erratic leap across the turnoff. I blow out a shaky breath, my heart hammering its way out of my chest as the interstate fades into the distance behind me. I could have driven straight to Vegas. In fact, I could have flown there direct. Booking a flight would have required planning, though. There had been no planning early this morning when I left Brent's apartment for the final time. Instead, I threw everything I thought I might need, or miss, into three gym bags, tossed them in the back of my car, and started driving.

My big sister, Stacey, owns a bar in Vegas. It's only a small place, but when I called and told her I was leaving Brent, she insisted I come and stay with her for a while. She says I can tend bar to pay my way. I haven't tended bar since college, but I remember it being okay. It was how I met Brent. He was a regular at the bar, drinking after his shifts as a beat cop.

My hands grip the steering wheel a little tighter at the thought of my boyfriend. My *ex*-boyfriend. I blow out a slow, calming breath. He'll know I've left by now. I've deleted and blocked him on everything imaginable and he's only met Stacey once, three years ago, so he'll find it hard to get hold of her. If he does manage to, I almost feel sorry for him, knowing how my sister feels about him.

An hour outside of Chicago, I decided it might be fun to turn the journey into a road trip. The thought both thrills and terrifies me—to the point where I'd pulled over and vomited on the side of the road. Although, part of that might have been anxiety from quitting my job and running away from my partner of five years. I swallow the bile rising in my throat.

I've always wanted to drive to the West Coast, but Brent always found a reason not to. Five years and we never had a single vacation. This is the first time I've left Chicago since college. I can just about afford it. If I keep to budget motels, it's doable. When I stopped for a coffee a few hours back, I made a rough plan, hitting all the places I want to see on the way. First on the list is Mount Rushmore.

I smile at the 'Welcome to Sioux Falls' sign, my shoulders feeling a little lighter. I've done it. I've made it to my first destination. I'm not a complete waste of space. My teeth grit at the words that have been branded into my heart, and I grip the steering wheel, the leather warm under my grasp. *I'm not a waste of space.* Focusing on the road ahead, I keep an eye out for the motel I found online. It's part of a small strip mall and looks dodgy as hell, but it's cheap. I'm kind of hoping that the fact it has a couple of stores and a bar next to it means it's a little safer. No one can murder me when there are people everywhere, right?

Why would anyone want to murder you?

I can practically hear Brent's sneering tones. His disdain for me has underscored my life for so long, it's like having my own personal narrator.

Bright neon signs flare up ahead and I slow the car. The motel looks even worse in person, but the green sign says there are vacancies, and I'm too tired to drive any further. Pulling into a parking spot right outside, I glance over my shoulder at the three gym bags on the backseat. In my haste to get on the road, I hadn't even put them in the trunk. People are milling around outside the bar, and I eye them warily. If I move the bags now, people will see. If I leave them in the car, they might get stolen. I only really need my backpack, sitting on the passenger seat.

A wave of sadness washes over me. My entire life—all twenty-five years—contained in three battered gym bags. Reaching into the backseat, I pull two bags down onto the floorboard and drape my black jacket over the one on the seat. Hopefully, they'll be okay. Honestly, if someone bothers to steal them, they'll be disappointed. There's nothing inside but clothes, photographs, and my childhood teddy bear. I'm wearing the only things of any value I own. My watch, my grandmother's silver necklace and my mother's opal stud earrings. Someone once told me opals are bad luck unless they're your birthstone. They aren't my birthstone. Maybe I should stop wearing them.

Heaving my backpack over my shoulder, I climb out of the car and head to the front desk. A painfully thin woman with folds of skin hanging from her bones sits behind the desk, a cigarette in her hand and black mascara smeared beneath her bloodshot eyes.

"Good evening," I say, offering a smile. "I'd like to book a room, please."

The woman stares at me for a second, then puts out her cigarette. When she looks back up at me, she smiles to reveal a mouth full of nicotine-stained teeth.

"Sure thing, honey. We've got one room left, but it's a twin. That okay?"

I frown. "The website says you have singles available."

"The website is wrong."

My heart sinks. "How much is a twin?"

"Twenty dollars more than the single."

I huff a sigh. I know from my research this morning that the next cheap motel is far enough away that it would cost me almost twenty dollars in gas to get to.

"Fine."

More yellowed teeth appear. "Great. You'll be in room twelve. I'll get it ready for you in the next hour. That okay, honey?"

I blink. "Next hour?"

The woman nods. "Yep. Why don't you go wait in the bar? If you're staying here, you get one free drink. Just tell Barry that Mylene sent you."

After eight hours of driving and leaving my entire life behind, all I want to do is collapse on a bed and go to sleep. I'd rather walk to the next motel than go and hang out in a bar in the middle of nowhere. Mylene stares at me expectantly.

"An hour?" I repeat.

"An hour."

Trying to keep myself from crumpling, I hoist my backpack up onto my shoulder and head back out into the rapidly cooling evening. The bar is only a few steps away, music leaking out onto the street. A few people stand outside chatting and smoking, with bottles of beer in their hands, but no one spares me more than a second's glance as I move through them to the door.

It's a small place. Dark, with neon signs behind the bar and scattered high tables around the sides. Two pool tables are busy at the far end of the bar and an empty stage takes up the other. Posters advertise live music on weekends. I'm relieved it's a Monday. If it had been busy, I would have turned right back around and waited in my car.

Perching on a barstool, I rest my backpack on my knees and eye the selection of bottles behind the bar. I'm not a big drinker. Brent says it's not ladylike. We had a poker night with friends once, years ago, and I got a little bit too drunk. He didn't talk to me for a week afterwards, saying I was an embarrassment.

"Hey there. What can I get you?"

I look away from the rows of booze to find a middle-aged man with sparkling eyes and a bushy beard watching me. Although his chin is covered, his head is completely hairless and gleaming under the neon lighting.

"Mylene sent me," I say. "Are you Barry?"

He grins. "Sure am. You can have a single house spirit or any bottled beer from that fridge there."

"Can I have a bottle of . . ." I pause, overwhelmed by the choices. "Whatever beer you'd recommend, please?"

"You want a glass?"

I shake my head and take the bottle he offers me. I'm not even sure I like beer. It's been so long since I've had one. Holding the ice-cold drink in my hand, I try to drown out the constant derisive narrative running through my head. Brent isn't here. He has no control over me anymore. If I want to drink a beer, I damn well will.

Taking a swig, pleasantly surprised by the crisp, cool taste, I turn away from the bar to survey my surroundings. The place is fairly empty. Most of the patrons are playing pool, but a small group of men stand around a high table laughing loudly, looking like they've come from an office. I frown. Are there any offices near here? I haven't seen any.

I take a second swig and start to relax a little. If anything, I feel a little giddy. I hold up the bottle and squint at it. Surely beer doesn't work that fast.

"You okay?"

I swivel on the chair to find Barry watching me, his eyes narrowed in concern.

"Yeah, fine. Thank you."

And I am. I am fine. If someone had told me this morning that in eight hours' time, I'd be sitting in a bar in Sioux Falls drinking a beer, I'd have laughed at them. Anticipation fizzes in my limbs. I'm free. I can do whatever I want. Go wherever I want. Well, maybe not wherever I want. I have a budget. But still.

Laughter from outside infiltrates the bar as someone opens the door, and I turn my head toward the noise. A man walks in, his expression probably as wary as mine was when I first stepped inside. If it wasn't already clear he's not a regular, the large duffle bag gives it away. He turns toward the bar, and I freeze, my beer halfway to my lips. He's gorgeous. Not just better looking than average. Gorgeous.

Shit. I realize too late that I'm staring and turn back to the bar, studying a coaster like it has the answers to life written on it.

"Hey," Barry says. "What can I get you?"

I keep my attention on the beer-soaked coaster, aware that the gorgeous man has come to stand just two seats down. He's so close, I can smell him. The scent reminds me of those Abercrombie shops but with a little more pine. It takes all my self-control not to lean towards him and inhale. I squint at my drink. How strong is this beer?

"I'll have a vodka coke, please."

I stare at the coaster for so long, I could draw it blindfolded. Should I look up? Should I say something? It's like I've forgotten how to be human. No. I should turn away. Talking to strange men in bars is asking for trouble.

"Is it always this quiet in here?"

It takes me a second to realize that Barry has moved to the far end of the bar to serve some of the pool players, and the question is directed at me. I look up, cheeks burning and eyes wide.

"Erm, I don't know. I've never been here before." I gesture to the backpack on my lap. "I'm waiting for my room at the motel to be ready."

Gorgeous Man smiles and my limbs melt. He has light blue eyes that are so vivid, they remind me a little of a husky. Or a wolf. Picking up his drink, he moves over a chair.

"My name's Carter," he says. "Mind if I join you?"

I shake my head. "Hailee."

"Hi, Hailee." He sits down on the stool next to me and leans on the bar. "So, you're just passing through?"

"Yep." I take a sip of my beer, trying to be subtle as my eyes roam his face. He has dark brown hair styled like he's spent the day messing it up, which contrasts beautifully with the neatly trimmed stubble lining his jaw. I swallow. *That jaw.*

"Sorry," Carter says. "I didn't mean to pry. I mean, rule one-oh-one, right? Don't talk to strangers in bars."

I laugh. "It's not that. It's just new."

He takes a sip of his drink. "How so?"

"I sort of only decided to take this trip this morning."

His dark eyebrows rise. "Spontaneous. I like it."

"Something like that."

I haven't been spontaneous since high school. I'm not sure I had been even then. I plan. I like safety. Security. Maybe that's why I stayed as long as I did.

"Sorry if I'm prying," Carter says. "I've been on the road for a while, and this is the longest conversation I've had with someone that wasn't behind the counter at a diner."

"Oh?" I say. "Where are you from?"

"Washington D.C.."

My eyebrows shoot up. "That's a lot of driving."

"I wish." He huffs a laugh. "Most of it's been by Greyhound."

I wince. "How did you end up here, then?"

"I made friends with a couple of tourists just outside Wisconsin. They were heading to see Mount Rushmore, so they gave me a ride."

"I thought you said this was the longest conversation you'd had with someone?"

Carter grimaces. "The couple were Brazilian. They barely spoke any English, and I definitely don't speak Portuguese. We got by on hand gestures and pointing."

I laugh. It's the first time I've laughed openly in a long time and the sound takes me by surprise, ending far too soon.

"So, where are you from?" Carter asks. "I'm guessing not far if you only started this morning."

"Chicago," I admit. "Funnily enough, I thought I'd go see Mount Rushmore. Perhaps I'll see your friends there."

Carter smiles, the corners of his eyes crinkling. "Is that the reason for the trip, then? Sightseeing?"

I press my lips together, considering a lie. Is there any point? I'll never see this man again after I finish my beer.

"I decided to run away."

Carter's eyebrows shoot up. "Run away? Well, you look old enough to leave home by yourself, so dare I ask what you're running from? If it's the law, I don't want to know. Guilty by association and all that."

I smile ruefully. "No. Nothing as exciting as that. Running away from my boyfriend."

Carter snorts and lifts his drink in a salute. "Me too."

I stare at his raised drink for a second too long before remembering what to do, clinking my bottle against his glass. He's gay. Of course, he is. Immediately, I chastise myself. What difference does it make? It's not like I'm going to make a move on him. I left my boyfriend *this morning*. I haven't even thought about being with someone else. *Oh god*. A wave of nausea rolls through my gut and I place my beer down on the bar.

"Are you okay?" he asks. "Was he just a dick, or are you *literally* running away?"

"A little of both?" I admit. "I mean, he never physically hurt me, if that's what you mean."

"I'm sorry you're in that situation," Carter says. He notes my almost empty bottle and nods toward the bar. "Can I get you another one?"

A glance at my watch tells me that Mylene won't be finished for another half an hour. "Sure. Thank you."

As Carter flags down another round of drinks, I take the opportunity to sneakily check him out. He might be gay, but a girl can dream. He's wearing fitted dark jeans and an olive-green t-shirt beneath a grey jacket. Almost as if hearing my curious thoughts, he stands and shrugs off the jacket, placing it on the stool next to him. I almost groan. His t-shirt stretches across his toned chest, the rolled sleeves show-casing muscular arms. He's not huge, but he's defined enough that I'd bet my last dollar he looks incredible shirtless.

"What about you, then?" I ask, nodding my thanks for the replenished beer. "Why are you running from your boyfriend?"

Carter frowns at his drink. "He was a dick. Plain and simple. It took me far too long to see it, though."

"Yeah, I get that. It took me five years."

"Ouch." Carter shakes his head. "Three and half for me."

I lean back against the bar. "Sounds like you had more sense than me, then."

He places his drink on the bar and slides off his bar stool. "It doesn't matter how long we stayed. It only matters that we left."

I nod thoughtfully, and he winks before heading to the restrooms at the back of the bar. A smile creeps onto my face. He's a nice guy. Hope begins to blossom in my chest. I can do this. I left. I got to my first stop and now I'm drinking beer in a bar with a gorgeous man. Things are going better than expected.

"Can I buy you a drink?"

I look up in surprise, finding one of the disheveled suited guys standing beside me.

"Erm, I'm okay, thank you." I gesture to my full bottle. "My friend just bought me one."

The man smiles, leaning against the bar. His eyes are slightly unfocused, his top two buttons undone. I suspect a tie is shoved in a pocket somewhere.

"I haven't seen you in here before," he slurs. "What's your name?"

My smile tightens. I don't want to be rude, but I also don't want to encourage conversation. Shooting a look in the direction of the restrooms, I clutch my backpack a little tighter on my lap.

"I'm leaving in a minute," I say. "Thanks for the offer of the drink."

He leans a little closer, the smell of alcohol enough to make my eyes water. "Don't be like that, gorgeous. Why don't you come and say hello to my friends?"

I frown, glancing over at his table. His friends are all watching, laughing, and jeering. Is this a dare?

"No, thank you."

He pouts, clutching at his heart. "You wound me. Come on. Just a quick hello."

"No."

I look over my shoulder again, but there's no sign of Carter, and Barry is deep in conversation with a couple of the pool players. I open my mouth to shout for him when a hand closes around my wrist. As the drunken man pulls me off my barstool, I twist, trying to balance myself. My backpack falls off my legs and I stoop, trying to catch it, but the momentum of the man's tug keeps me falling forward. There's no time to react as my head smacks into the edge of Carter's barstool. When the floor rises up to finish the job, the world goes black.

2

Shit. I step out of the restroom just in time to see some asshole drag Hailee off her chair and onto the floor. The barman that looks like he belongs in a log cabin is already rushing out from behind the bar, but I sprint across the room, arriving first, and dropping to my knees beside her.

"She fell, I swear!" the asshole protests.

Leaving Barry to deal with him, I focus on Hailee. Leaning down, I gently lift the long brown curls from her face. There's no blood, thank fuck. I shake her shoulder.

"Hailee? Are you okay?"

She groans, and I roll her over, easing her head onto my lap. Somewhere behind us, Barry is kicking out the suits and threatening to call the police. It's a good thing too, because it means I don't have to knock that asshole out.

"Is she okay?" Barry asks, crouching beside us.

"I think so." I wince as my fingers find a lump on the side of her head. "She banged her head pretty hard."

"I'm okay," Hailee mumbles, trying to sit up.

"Hey, take it easy," I soothe. "How are you feeling?"

She squints, raising her fingers to the lump just above

her forehead. "Like some dickhead knocked me out."

"I'll call an ambulance," Barry says, standing and backing away toward the bar.

Hailee straightens, her big brown eyes wide. "No! Don't do that. I'm okay, I swear."

I get to my feet, trying not to grimace as my fingers stick to the floor, and hold out a hand to help her up. "You were out cold. You really should get checked out."

"I'm honestly fine. I blacked out for like, a second. It's only a small lump. I don't feel sick or dizzy."

Barry shares a concerned look with me. I know what he's thinking. If something happens to her and he didn't call it in, he could get in trouble.

"I swear, I won't sue," Hailee says, returning to one of the barstools and picking up her beer. "Stop looking at each other like that."

I try to stop it, but a smile pulls at my lips. "You're that tough, huh? Get knocked out and you just pick up your beer and carry on drinking?"

Hailee makes a face and presses the beer to her head. "It's cold."

I laugh as I sit down beside her. "It's still pretty badass."

"I got pulled off a barstool. It's not like I won a fight." She turns to Barry who's lingering, his forehead wrinkled in concern. "Seriously. I'm fine."

"Look, I deal with enough head injuries to know you should still be careful," he says. "If you don't want to get it checked out, you need to make sure someone keeps an eye on you. Don't go to sleep for a few hours and have someone with you in case you start vomiting or get dizzy."

Hailee's mouth falls open, her eyes wide in protest, but I lift my drink from the side and raise it in salute. "No problem, Barry. I've got her."

With visible relief, the bartender goes to serve the patrons peering curiously at us from the far end of the bar. I turn back to Hailee to find her watching me with raised eyebrows.

"What?"

"How have you 'got me'?" she says. "You just lied to the poor man."

I shake my head and take a sip of my drink. "You didn't want him to call for an ambulance, so I took care of it. And I didn't lie. I'll look after you."

"You'll what?"

My smile widens at her perplexed expression. "I'll look after you. You know? Make sure you don't choke on your own vomit in your sleep."

Her nose wrinkles. "I am not going to vomit in my sleep."

"Good," I say. "Because that sounds disgusting."

I watch as her mouth twitches, fighting a smile. She's really pretty. The kind of pretty that you notice right away, but the more you look, the brighter and clearer it becomes. Her long copper curls, big eyes and light brown skin drew my attention the second I walked into the bar, but it took a few minutes for the details to come into focus. Like how there's a faint smattering of freckles across what might possibly be the most adorable nose I've ever seen. How plump her lips are, and the fact her eyes aren't just brown, but somewhere between copper and hazel.

"And how exactly are you planning on looking after me?" she asks, taking a sip of her beer.

I grin, and she splutters on her mouthful of beer.

"I didn't mean that the way it sounded," she gushes. "Oh my god. I honestly . . . Oh, for fucksake."

Laughing, I hold up my hand. "I know you didn't. It's fine."

"I'm going to blame that on the head injury." She shakes her head. "What are your plans, anyway? In a non-creepy way. You said some tourists dropped you off here. Why here?"

I lean my elbow against the bar and draw a long breath. "I'm trying to get to Vegas."

After a few too many seconds of silence, I turn to find Hailee watching me through narrowed eyes. "What?"

"I'm going to Vegas too. I was just trying to remember if I told you that."

My eyebrows shoot up. "You told me you were going to Mount Rushmore, not Vegas."

"Yeah, well the end destination is Las Vegas. I just decided this morning to make a little road trip out of it—see a few things along the way."

Reaching up, I tug my fingers through my hair. "That's quite the coincidence. The couple I hitched with decided to drive through the night, but I didn't want to go that far out of the way, so they dropped me here. I figured I'd just make my way to the nearest bus station in the morning."

Hailee's attention is focused on the rows of spirits behind the bar, and I watch her with open curiosity. Why is she going to Las Vegas? She's running away from an ex, but why there? I want to ask, but I'm aware we're still barely more than strangers.

"Where are you staying tonight?" she asks, her eyes fixed on her beer as she pulls a finger through the condensation.

It's my turn to look at her through narrowed eyes. Curiosity fizzes beneath my skin. "I was going to book into the motel next door. Last I saw, the vacancy light was still on."

Hailee takes a long drink of her beer, and I almost hold my breath, waiting for what I think she might suggest.

"The woman at the desk said they only had twin rooms left, so I booked one. I mean . . . If you . . ." She takes another swig of her drink.

I hide my grin behind my hand. I'm sure that if it wasn't for the dark bar and the glare of the neon lights, her cheeks would be flushed.

"Are you very kindly offering me the separate and empty bed in your room so that I can make sure you don't choke on your own vomit?" I ask.

Her shoulders sag as she exhales. "Exactly."

"It's very kind of you to offer," I say. "I feel like the gentlemanly thing would be to say no, but I did promise Barry I'd take care of you, and splitting the cost would certainly help me out."

Hailee smiles and places her empty bottle down on the bar. "Great."

"You guys leaving?" Barry calls. "Hang on."

I slide off my stool and shrug on my jacket as the bartender lifts four bottles of beer onto the bar.

"An apology for what happened," he explains. "Two of them are non-alcoholic, though. You really shouldn't be drinking if you've got a concussion."

The look on Hailee's face is priceless, and my grin widens as I grab the bottles and shove them in one of the end pockets of my bag.

Hailee heaves her backpack onto her shoulder. "Thanks, Barry."

I grab mine, and we head out into the night. It isn't the nicest of places, and I was a little annoyed when Christiano and Ana left me here. I tried to get them to drop me off before we reached Sioux Falls, but whether they didn't understand me or didn't want to, I can't be sure. I've stayed in some questionable places since leaving D.C., but this is in the top three for sure. I can almost hear Andrew's 'I told you so'.

"Looks like it would have been me or the street," Hailee says, pulling me back to the present.

I blink, following her pointed look to see that the 'vacancies' sign has swapped to 'no vacancies' in blaring red. What's more concerning is that the reception light is off, the entire motel looking as though it's turned in for the night. I follow Hailee as she pushes open the door and heads for the desk.

"You've got to be kidding me," she mutters.

I step over to see what the problem is. A key for room twelve has been left on the desk with a note saying, 'Curly girl. Pay in morning.'

"That's ridiculous," Hailee says. "Anyone could have come and taken this key."

"Good thing they didn't, Curly Girl," I say, using my shoulder to push open the door leading to the rooms. "Do you have any other bags?"

"This is the only bag I need for now." She smiles in thanks as she moves past me, striding down the corridor peering at numbers on the doors. "Here we go."

The room is a decent size, and in better condition that I expected considering the outside. Two neatly made single beds take up most of the room, with a television perched on a small desk at one end and a small bathroom at the other. Hailee drops her backpack on one of the beds and kicks off her shoes.

I shuck off my sneakers and jacket and grab two of the beers from my bag. I twist off the caps and hand the non-alcoholic one to Hailee.

She accepts with a small wrinkle of her nose, lifting her bottle to mine. “To shitty ex-boyfriends.”

“To escaping them,” I clarify, knocking my beer against hers.

Hailee hums in response, and I sit down on my bed, stretching my legs out in front of me.

“So, what do you do, Hailee? When you’re not driving across the country.”

She peers at the label of her beer for a second, considering. “I worked in a grocery store.”

There’s something in the way she says it that tells me she isn’t particularly pleased about it. “One of those fancy organic ones? Or one of the big chains?”

Hailee turns to me, her face pinched. “You don’t need to feign interest. It was boring as shit, and definitely not a lifelong dream.”

“What is the dream then? Something in Vegas?”

It’s the wrong thing to say, because she closes her eyes and leans back against the headboard with a groan.

“No. I don’t know what the dream is anymore. I got a fine arts degree at college. I wanted to be an artist, I guess.”

“What happened?”

“Life happened,” she says dismissively. “What about you? What do you do when you’re not convincing tourists to take you across the country?”

I smirk, letting the change of topic slide. “I’m a high school geography teacher. It’s summer break, so . . .”

Hailee’s eyebrows shoot up. “Yikes. I wish my teachers had looked like you when I was in high school. I bet the girls are gutted you’re gay.”

In answer, I take a deep swig of my beer. This is where I should tell her that I’m not gay. I mean, I’m not straight, either. Andrew made me feel ashamed of being bisexual. He thinks it's disgusting, and in the end, it was the thing that broke us. Every time I smiled at an attractive woman, he'd accuse me of trying to sleep with her. I wasn't allowed to have female friends. I mean, I could have. It just wasn't worth the stress.

My grip tightens around my drink. His jealousy was not a sulking, petty thing. He never raised a fist to me, but whenever he got jealous, he'd make it his mission to fuck it out of me; making sure he was the only one I would think about. *Could* think about.

"You okay?" Hailee asks. "Did I say something?"

I shift on the bed and take a drink of beer. "No, not at all. Sorry, I just spaced out."

"Want to see if there's a movie on?" she asks, reaching for the remote.

"Sure."

I half-watch the screen as Hailee flicks through channels, trying not to spiral down the dark hole of memories I've accidentally opened.

"What about this?"

I blink, re-focusing on the screen. It's some action movie from the nineties, and I'm pretty sure I've already seen it. "Sure. Looks good."

Hailee swings her legs off the bed and stands. "I'm going to get changed, because I'm not going to lie, I'll probably fall asleep halfway through this movie."

"You're supposed to stay awake for a bit, just in case."

"I'll stay awake as long as I can. Honestly, my head barely even hurts."

I shrug, picking at the label around my beer. "Your funeral."

"You know the only reason you're here is because you're supposed to be preventing me from dying."

The way her words sound muffled causes me to look up. I swallow. Standing with her back to me, watching the television, Hailee hasn't bothered going to the bathroom to change. She's pulled her sweater up over her head to reveal a tight white tank top with thin straps. I pause, my beer halfway to my lips, unable to look away as she reaches around to unclasp her bra. She slides the straps down her arms and pulls it through the front of her top in an impressive maneuver that means she doesn't need to take her top off.

My throat is suddenly as dry as the Nevada desert. She has a great figure. A little toned, but the swell of flesh around her hips and ass is soft in a way that makes me want to sink my fingers into it—grip it. My dick twitches, and I bite my lip, looking away.

I shouldn't have looked away.

A long strip of mirror lines the wall behind the television, and I realize I can see Hailee perfectly in the reflection. My first thought is that she's seen me watching her, but a quick glance tells me she's engrossed in the film. Maybe she hasn't seen it before. I try to look away, but I can't. I don't know where to look other than at my hands, which I try a couple of times, but my gaze always drags back—back to where I can see her dark nipples straining through the thin white fabric of her top. My jaw tightens as I fight against the uncomfortable pressure of my hardening dick. Is there a way I can adjust myself without her noticing?

I tell myself repeatedly how depraved I am as I watch her unfasten the button of her jeans and slide them down over her hips. *Fuck*. She bends over and my cock pays full attention, straining against my zipper. Her ass. It's perfection encased in adorable pale pink underwear that look a bit like briefs. My fingers tighten against my bottle of beer as I imagine squeezing it with both hands, leaving imprints of my fingertips as I slide inside her. *Fuck.*

I'm officially the worst. I force myself to stare at my hands, the knuckles white. It seemed like a good idea in the bar, sharing a room with Hailee. I mean, I said I'd look after her, but now the reality of the situation is beginning to hit home. *Hard.* I know the real reason she offered to share her room with me is because she thinks I'm gay. I should have corrected her. It didn't seem important at the time, but now, sitting on the bed less than two feet away with a dick like fucking stone, I'm realizing my mistake.

My heart races. What will happen in the morning when she wants a shower? I don't think I'll be able to cope with her walking around in a little towel all wet. I have to be smart. I can get through one night.

"I'm going to take a shower," I say, the words barely formed in my head before I blurt them out. "That way we're not both fighting for it in the morning."

"Good idea," she says, flashing me a smile over her shoulder.

The bathroom is on my side of the room, so I slide off the bed, managing to keep my back to her as I lug my entire bag in with me. This was a fucking awful idea.

I strip off and turn the shower to the coldest possible setting. It does nothing to deter my traitorous cock and I end up taking matters into my own hands, coming hard against the sad, gray motel shower wall to thoughts of Hailee's supple, golden skin.

Tomorrow, I plan on being up and out before she can even think about walking around in her underwear. I lean against the shower wall, breathing hard as the cold water splutters against my skin. After tomorrow, I'll probably never see her again.

3

Carter is gone when I wake up. I stare at the ceiling, wincing at the lump on my head. It's probably a good thing Barry swapped me onto non-alcoholic beer, or the headache would be a lot worse. I didn't make it to the end of the film. I don't even remember falling asleep. Stretching out, comfortable and warm beneath the sheets, I marvel at how different my life is this morning from the one before.

Yesterday, I woke to an empty bed, but under very different circumstances. Brent had gone to a poker game, and the fact that he wasn't back by eight the following morning meant one of two things: he'd either lost a shit-ton of money and passed out somewhere drunk and dejected, or he was still playing. Neither were options I was happy about. Especially when he was gambling my money.

Every muscle tenses, my breathing quickening. I'm not sure why yesterday morning had been the one to break me. There had been so many before it. It was as though I was sleepwalking. I just picked up a gym bag and started packing. Then another. And another. Before I knew it, I was in my car with Stacey on speakerphone.

I wonder what he'll do without my money to gamble away. The thought should make me happy, but it fills me with ice cold dread. I exhale. He can't find me. He won't.

I look over at Carter's bed. He's made a half-hearted attempt to make it, and it looks like his stuff is gone. It's hard not to take it personally. He could have at least said goodbye.

Reluctantly sliding out of the warm bed, I pad over to the window and pull the curtain back. The sun assaults my eyes, and I withdraw with a hiss. When I try again, I find the deserted parking lot looking even more dilapidated in the morning sunshine. My car is still outside; with no signs of breaking or entering, I note with relief.

I lean a little further forward and spot a lone figure standing by the side of the road, a phone pressed to his ear. *Carter.* I watch for a moment, my brain warring with itself. Part of me wants to get dressed and try to catch him—to find out why he left so quickly. Did I do something wrong? The other, possibly more rational, part of me knows I should just let him go. He clearly wants nothing more to do with me after last night. He kept an eye on me and now we're done. My lips press tightly together as I watch him for a second longer, then I close the curtains and head for the bathroom.

I take my time. The shower is appalling. More of a drizzle. But I wash my hair, sure I can still feel the stickiness of the bar floor pressed into my curls. According to my weather app, it's going to be a hot day, so I select my favorite pair of stonewashed denim cutoffs and a dusky pink linen shirt. It's creased to fuck from being shoved in my backpack, but after staring at it for a moment, I remind myself that I'm not out to impress anyone. I have no idea what to expect at Mount Rushmore, but it's a mountain, so thinking it probably does what it says on the tin, I opt for sensible sneakers instead of sandals.

Feeling refreshed, and certain that Carter is long gone, I head to the front desk to pay for the room. There's no sign of Mylene. Instead, a teenaged boy sits behind the desk, a greasy mop of hair obscuring half of his face.

"Good morning," I say. "I'd like to pay for room twelve, please."

I have no idea whether Carter had already paid his half. Perhaps that's why he sneaked off. Maybe he wanted the free room. An uncomfortable twinge pulls in my stomach as I wait for the boy behind the desk to respond.

"It's already been paid for," he mutters, not glancing up from his phone.

I frown. "By whom?"

"Some guy."

Carter paid for the room? Shucking my backpack higher on my shoulder, I step out into the parking lot. It's no surprise that he isn't by the road any longer. It's been at least an hour since I peeked at him through the curtains. I wish we'd exchanged numbers. At least then I could text him and say thank you.

"Morning."

I jump at a voice behind me. Turning, I find Carter sitting slumped against the wall of the motel, his bag at his side. He's wearing a navy t-shirt this morning and it makes his eyes look impossibly blue. Like a summer sky.

"You're still here."

His mouth quirks to the side. "I am."

I shake my head, trying to gather my thoughts. "You paid for the room. I need to give you half."

Carter winces, scratching his chin. "I was kind of hoping you could pay me back in another way."

"Oh?"

His eyes widen for a split second, then he grins as he

gets to his feet, dusting off his jeans. "I've been trying to get a ride to the nearest bus station all morning, but it's hopeless. I was wondering if you could help me out."

I stare at him, wondering whether I should ask why he left this morning. If he'd managed to find a way to the bus station, he'd be long gone. Is he using me again? My head throbs. He hasn't used me at all. He paid for the room. Shaking my frustration from my head, I swing my backpack around so I can fish my car keys from the front pocket. "Of course. No worries."

"Thank you." Carter sags with relief and picks up his bag.

I unlock the car, shoving my backpack onto the backseat with my other bags, before opening the trunk for Carter's bag.

Silence falls over us as we buckle up, and I back out of the parking lot. For almost five minutes, the only sound is the monotone voice of my map app, but I have no idea what to say.

"I'm sorry for bailing this morning," Carter says, his gaze fixed on the fields passing outside the window. "I'm not great with goodbyes and I wanted an early start."

"It's okay." Relief tickles along my limbs. "I thought perhaps I snored and kept you up all night."

"No. No snores that I heard. Pretty sure I fell asleep right after you."

I glance at him with a grin. "You were supposed to make sure I didn't choke on my own vomit."

"You didn't," he says sheepishly. "I said I'd look after you, but I didn't say I'd be any good at it."

"So it seems." I laugh, glad that the tension has finally lifted. "How long will it take you to get to Vegas by bus?"

Carter gives a half shrug. "Like, two days. I think it said thirty-eight hours or something like that."

"Thirty-eight hours?" I grimace. "It would be a lot faster to drive."

"It would be, but I don't have a car."

"Why don't you come with me?" The words tumble from my lips before I can stop them, and my cheeks flame. "Sorry, I mean—"

"I couldn't," Carter interjects. "I wouldn't want to hijack your road trip."

I nod, keeping my eyes fixed on the road. The offer leaped from my mouth before I had time to consider it, but it isn't the first time it had occurred to me. The second he told me he was heading to Vegas; the thought had entered my head. Carter is so easy to be around. And easy on the eye, too. As much as I'd like to try and be a fierce, independent woman, I haven't travelled this far by myself before and I would feel safer having a man with me. I cringe inwardly at the thought. So much for female empowerment. I make a promise to myself to invest in martial arts and self-defense classes when I get settled in with my sister.

When my phone announces loudly that the turning for the bus station is in two miles, I grip the steering wheel a little tighter. "You wouldn't be hijacking my road trip," I say carefully. "If you wanted a ride all the way to Vegas, I'd appreciate the company."

Silence fills the car once more and my fingers itch to switch the radio on. I can feel Carter's attention on me, and my skin heats under his gaze. It suddenly occurs to me that perhaps I'm putting him in an awkward situation and my throat runs dry.

"I'm sorry. I shouldn't have pushed it," I rush. "You said no and I should have left it at—"

"If you're sure you don't mind," he says, cutting my frantic ramble in half, "I'd really appreciate it."

I exhale, leaning back against the seat. "Well, that wasn't awkward at all."

Carter laughs, the sound deep and warm as it fills the car. "I'll go halves on gas and everything else, of course. Plus, if you change your mind, just drop me off at the next bus station we come to with no hard feelings. Deal?"

I smile, reaching for the radio. "Deal."

4

"Maybe it makes me unpatriotic, but visiting Mount Rushmore has never been on my list of things to do." I squint up at the vast gray rock face, trying and failing to be as impressed as I'm sure I'm supposed to be. It's strange standing before something that's so incredibly famous. It doesn't feel real. I can see veins of silver glinting high in the rock, and the sheer size is mind-boggling.

Beside me, Hailee pushes her sunglasses up on her head. "It's weird seeing it in real life. I'm not quite sure how I feel about it."

"You want to do the tour?" I ask.

Hailee drags her teeth over her plump bottom lip as she stares up at the four enormous faces and I can't tear my eyes away from the simple gesture. I'm not sure what I was thinking when I agreed to go with her to Vegas. I mean. I do know. Travelling with an attractive woman whose company I really enjoy is the clear winner when the other option is a crusty seat on a crowded bus. I shouldn't have said yes, though. With each passing hour, my unintentional lie burns hotter in my chest.

"I think I'm done," she says. "Black Hills National Forest looked pretty nice when we were driving here. It must have some scenic spots. Why don't we grab some food and have a picnic? I think I'd rather spend my lunch appreciating nature than these old, dead white guys."

"That sounds like a great plan," I say, surveying the surrounding food trucks and cafe. "Let's do it."

Hailee grins and heads toward a truck selling wraps. I hang back, shamelessly taking in the view. She's wearing shorts today and they are fucking sinful. They're not those little booty shorts where the ass cheeks show, and on paper, they're perfectly respectable. But there's something about the way they cling to her curves, the teasing rips, showing tantalizing glimpses of golden skin. My dick shifts as I stare, and I swallow, forcing myself to catch up.

I haven't been with a woman since college. I broke up with my last girlfriend for Andrew. He swept into my life and eclipsed everyone else with his confidence, claiming me for himself. It had been an addiction, knowing that someone wanted you so badly they couldn't keep their hands off you. I got so lost in that feeling, I never stopped to question it.

"See anything you like?"

Hailee's voice pulls me to the present. *Yes, I definitely do.* "Sure," I say, studying the chalkboard menu. "Spicy chicken wrap sounds good to me."

As Hailee orders, I lean against a signpost and pull out my phone. I blocked Andrew last week and deleted him from everything I could think of, but it still makes me nervous. If he wants to get in touch with me, he'd find a way. The fact that he hasn't, leaves me unsettled. He didn't take the breakup well. I had the forethought to move my stuff out first, arranging to meet him in a quiet café before he could get home from work. Even with the public setting, he'd still caused enough of a scene to get kicked out. The café owner had offered to call the police. He wouldn't have hit me, though. I'm bigger than him, but even so, he's not a fighter.

Hailee comes over, the receipt in her hand as they prepare our order. "You okay?"

I smile and nod, sliding the phone back into my pocket. "Great. You?"

"I got us a couple of packets of chips and some muffins too," she says.

I reach for my wallet. "How much do I owe you?"

"Don't be silly." She bats my hand away. "We're going to be eating together for the next couple of days. You can get lunch tomorrow."

My stomach flips. *Tomorrow*. Another night in a hotel. Will she want to share a room again? This is such a bad fucking idea. Maybe I can fake a headache and go to bed early. Maybe I can just keep my eyes closed.

"Are you sure you're all right?" Hailee asks, reaching out and laying her fingertips on my forearm.

My skin tingles under her gentle touch, and I'm torn between pulling away and hauling her into my arms. What the hell is wrong with me? I rub my temple and shake my head. "I think I might have gotten a bit too much sun yesterday," I lie.

Hailee squeezes my arm, opening her mouth to say something, but the guy in the food truck calls out to her and she turns to collect our food.

"Do you have a license?" she asks as we start the walk back to the car.

I nod. "Yeah. Why?"

"My insurance covers other drivers if I'm in the car," she

explains. "So, we can share the driving, if you're down with that."

"Of course! I'd like that. I was already feeling guilty at the thought of you doing all the driving."

Hailee smiles and my chest tightens. It's such a warm and beautiful smile. Like a fucking hug for the soul or something. I'm screwed.

"What else is on your itinerary?" I ask. "Now you've seen Mount Rushmore."

"I want to see the Four Corners Monument and the Grand Canyon."

"Interesting choices."

She looks up at me. "Are they?"

"Well, not the Grand Canyon. But why the Four Corners Monument?"

She shrugs. "I don't know. You're the geography teacher. If anyone was going to understand, it should be you."

I huff a laugh. "Fair enough."

It's so easy being around Hailee—like we've known each other for years. I try and fail to remember the last time conversation flowed so easily with someone.

"Are you okay with that?" Hailee asks, her lip disappearing beneath her teeth again.

"Okay with what? Your weird fascination with American geographical phenomena?"

She reaches out and shoves me playfully. "With not going straight to Vegas."

I shrug. "I'm not in a rush, and the Grand Canyon is on my bucket list, so why not?"

Her shoulders relax a little, her lips curling into a smile. "Great."

5

"Remember, if you feel at any point that I'm ruining your road trip, just drop me off at a bus station," Carter says as we join the sprinkling of tourist traffic exiting the park.

I grin. "It's not like this was planned. This trip is a last-minute decision, probably stemming from my desire to prolong the inevitable."

"The inevitable?"

"That I'm going to end up living with my sister and working at a bar in Las Vegas when I should be," I shrug, trying to find the words, "more."

"Don't be so hard on yourself."

Carter reaches out and squeezes my leg, but as soon as his fingers tighten against my flesh, he whips it back as though burned. It takes all my willpower not to turn and look at him, keeping my eyes on the road instead. I mean, I suppose it crosses a boundary, but it's not like it was inappropriate.

"Thank you," I say. "It's just not where I pictured my life being at twenty-five."

Carter huffs. "I don't think many people are where they pictured being."

"Do you enjoy teaching?" I ask. "Is it what you always wanted to do?"

"It's not what I dreamed of doing when I was in high school if that's what you mean. But I enjoy it. It's steady money and it's not boring."

I nod thoughtfully. The road is curved, with rich green forest on either side and I'm terrified that a deer, moose, or something will come sprinting out in front of the car. Every now and again, a car zooms past, passing me impatiently, and causing me to wince.

"You okay?" Carter asks. "Don't let those assholes make you drive faster than you feel safe doing. They'll be sorry when they smack head on into a deer and wreck their car."

I smile at my own thoughts being echoed. "I'm fine. I'm used to city driving, that's all. The forests are much prettier than buildings, though."

Carter leans forward, pointing to a sign up ahead. "Look, I think there's a turn off. Want to check it out and see if there's somewhere to park and eat?"

I flick on the blinker and turn off the road, grateful to avoid the car-rattling truck that's been gaining on me over the last minute or so. The road is little more than a dirt track, and the car rumbles and jolts over the uneven ground, the forest growing denser around us.

"You realize," I say, "this is where you'd take me to murder me, right?"

Carter chuckles, low and deep, and the sound lights up parts of me it has no business doing. Not when he's gay.

"If I wanted to murder you, I could have just done it at the motel."

"Nuh-uh," I reply, shaking my head. "You'd have left an

easy trail. There are security cameras and stuff. Out here, it would take forever to find my body."

Carter shifts in his seat to face me. "Are you trying to convince me to murder you?"

"No!" I laugh. "Oh, my god. No. Please don't."

"I'll try not to." He shakes his head, his beautiful mouth curving into a grin.

The trail becomes rougher, and I can feel the car struggling, so I pull off to the side and park up.

"How's this?" I ask, peering out the window at the forest.

In answer, Carter opens his door and climbs out. I follow, a small gasp escaping my lips as I take in our surroundings. The forest completely encircles us—a dome of rustling, rich emerald greens peppered with streaks of sunlight. The scent of pine fills the air, accompanied by a serenade of birdsong.

"It's beautiful," I breathe.

"Yeah," Carter says. "It is."

I frown at the tone of his voice and turn, but he's already rooting in the back seat for our lunch. Grabbing the bag of food, he places it on the hood before moving to the back of the car and popping the trunk. I watch curiously as he rummages in his bag. When he closes the trunk, he has two bottles of beer in his hands.

"We never finished our beers from the motel," he says, holding them up. "They're not exactly cold, but they're not hot either."

He moves back to the front of the car, climbing carefully up onto the hood and leaning back against the windshield. I fold my arms, raising my eyebrows in mock judgement.

"Seriously? You're just going to defile my car like that?"

Carter grins and pats the space next to him. "Come on. The food's getting cold."

"They're deli wraps. They're already cold."

He pats the hood one more time, then pulls food from the bag. With a roll of my eyes, I climb up as gracefully as I can to join him. It feels weird and it's not particularly comfortable, but I try to allow the quiet bliss of the forest to soothe my reservations.

"You do that a lot, don't you?" Carter says between bites of his wrap.

I raise my eyebrows in question. "Do what?"

"Doubt yourself. There's always a pause before you do something, like you're weighing up the pros and cons."

"You say that like it's a bad thing."

Carter's eyes widen and he shakes his head. "Not at all. It's just, it's for the small things. Like sitting on the car."

My body tenses and I can feel myself shrinking inwards. I hate that he noticed. It isn't my own doubt. It's Brent's voice in my head.

Carter reaches over and rests his hand on my shoulder, his eyes soft with apology. "I didn't mean to upset you. I'm sorry."

"It's fine," I say, my gaze fixed on the half-eaten wrap in my hand. "It's just . . ."

I shake my head, the words sticking, thick and heavy in my throat. In the years I was with Brent, I never told anyone what he was like. At the time, I told myself I was being loyal. Plenty of my friends verbally bashed their partners behind their backs, and I thought of myself as above it. The reality is, I hadn't wanted to admit what he was like; what he was doing.

"Hey."

I look up to find Carter scooting closer. The concern etched onto his face causes my chest to tighten, and I look away, my eyes burning. When he loops his arm over my shoulders and pulls me to him, I allow myself to fall, fighting back the tears as I inhale his woodsy scent.

"You don't have to tell me what's wrong," he says softly, rubbing my arm with gentle, soothing strokes. "But if you want to, I'm all ears."

I nod against his shoulder, drawing a shaky breath. "My ex had an opinion about everything," I explain quietly. "What I should do, where I should go, what I should look like. It didn't bother me at first because I was so head over heels. We met while I was in college. He was a little older and had just joined the police force. I was smitten. It was only years later that I realized, his opinions had left me no friends and no life of my own. With nothing of my own."

Carter's grip tightens on my arm. "Sounds like a real asshole."

"We were happy for a while, I think." I reluctantly pull from the embrace and offer a grateful smile. "Sorry for ruining the picnic."

"Don't apologize," he says, his bright blue eyes scanning my face. "Nothing's ruined. And if you ever want to tell me the rest of the story, I'm here. Okay?"

"Okay." I look away, feeling exposed by how much he seems to be able to see right through me. "How about you?"

He takes a swig of his beer. "What about me?"

"What's your sad story? Maybe if you tell me about your ex, it'll make me feel better about mine."

Carter lets out a long sigh, and I wonder whether I've pushed too far. It feels so natural talking to him, it has me second guessing myself—not wanting to push too far too fast. I'm painfully aware that if I piss him off, he'll be hopping out at the next bus station, and I'll be on my own again.

"He was jealous," he begins slowly, his frown deepening.

"He had very strong ideas about things, and he liked things his way."

My eyes narrow at the way each word is carefully measured, as though he's worried, he might trip himself up.

"You can tell me," I reassure him. "I won't judge you. There's no pressure either. Like you said to me, I'm all ears when you're ready."

Carter gives me a grateful smile, but it doesn't reach his eyes. "No, I should tell you. I should have told you before . . ."

I watch as he picks at the label of his beer bottle, a nervous bubbling rising in my gut. "What should you have told me? Are you actually going to murder me?"

He winces at my lame attempt to lighten the mood. "My ex, Andrew, he's been out since he was a teenager, and has very strong opinions about people who aren't honest about who they are. When we met, I was just out of college and still figuring it out."

He takes a deep breath and I reach out and touch his arm. "You don't have to tell me if you don't want to. If it's too difficult—"

"No. I need to." Carter closes his eyes, pinching the bridge of his nose. "Andrew was my first boyfriend. I'd made out with guys in college, but he was most of my firsts. Even though we were together for three years, he was convinced that I never fully embraced my sexuality."

I watch him, his eyes still closed as he takes another breath. Dread builds in my gut. Has something horrible happened to him? Did Andrew do something?

"You were in a relationship with him for years," I say carefully. "If that's not embracing your sexuality, what is?"

Carter grimaces again, tapping the lip of his beer bottle against his forehead. "I'm not gay, Hailee. I'm bi."

6

I CAN HARDLY BREATHE AS I WATCH MY WORDS SETTLE OVER Hailee, her entire body freezing up beside me. Shooting her a sideways glance, I hope she can read the regret and apology on my face as it courses through my veins. "I should have said earlier. I'm so sorry."

"But you didn't say anything," she says slowly. All the warmth from her voice has gone. "You knew that if you told me, there was no way I'd have let you share my room with me. I got undressed in front of you for fucksake!"

I claw a hand over my face. "I know. I'm sorry."

"Stop apologizing!" she shouts. "Just *stop.*"

The sound is stark against the silence of the forest, and I slide off the hood to give her some distance. I try not to look at her as I clear away the remnants of our lunch, shoving wrappers into a bag to dispose of later. I know it would have come out sooner or later, but it still hurts.

"There's a bus station in Rapid City," I say quietly. "If you could drop me there, I'd appreciate it. Although I understand if you want to just leave me at the side of the road. I deserve it."

Hailee lifts her head and stares at me, wide-eyed. "Can you just . . . I don't know . . . Give me a minute to process?"

I nod, shifting from foot to foot under her gaze. "I would never have done anything. In the room last night. I really did just want to make sure you were okay."

Her eyes widen. "That's not why I'm angry. I haven't assumed you'd want to make a move on me just because you're bisexual. I'm angry because you clearly omitted it on purpose. And sure, I probably wouldn't have undressed in front of you if I'd known."

Despite begging my brain not to go there, my skin heats at the memory of her nipples through her white tank, and the soft swell of her hips. I shove my hands in my jeans pockets to hide my growing semi. The effect she has on me is ridiculous. I feel like a goddamn teenager.

She slides down off the hood and walks around to where I'm leaning against the passenger side door. "Why didn't you tell me?"

"Like you said. If I had, you probably wouldn't have let me share your room, and I promised I'd look after you." I look down at the ground, scuffing at the layer of pine needles with my sneakers. There's another reason too. A reason that squirms uncomfortably in my gut and I can't bring myself to voice it, so I squash it down. "I really enjoy spending time with you. It was a selfish decision to prolong it."

"If that's the case, why did you sneak off in the morning without saying goodbye?"

Tensing, I chance a glance at Hailee to find her watching me with a frown.

"Well?" she presses.

I exhale. "If I tell you, you're really going to want to leave me at the side of the road."

"I promise I won't leave you at the side of the road," she says, tightening her grip around herself. "However, I can't promise I won't be dropping you off at the bus station."

There's no way out of it. I have to tell her the truth. There's no lie I can spin that she won't see through, and I know layering another lie on top of the one I've already told will weigh too heavily on my heart. She deserves better. She deserves the truth. Even if it means I'll be making the rest of the journey alone.

I take a deep breath, my cowardly gaze focusing on a pinecone near Hailee's pale pink sneakers. "I left this morning because I knew I wouldn't be able to handle seeing you getting ready this morning. If you'd walked around in your underwear, you'd have seen the effect you have on me, and you'd have known I hadn't told you the whole truth."

The silence is deafening, and after an agonizing minute, I look up to find her eyes wide as the meaning of my words sink in. My gaze dips to her mouth, lips parted in surprise. *That mouth.* I want to suck on that plump bottom lip so badly it hurts.

Tearing my attention from her sinful mouth, I open the passenger door. "Like I said, if you can find it in your heart to drop me at the bus station instead of leaving me here, I'd appreciate it. Although, if you want to leave me in the woods, I'll understand."

"Has anyone told you, you're a bit of a drama queen?"

I turn around, eyebrows sky high. "Excuse me?"

"I'm not going to leave you in the fucking woods," she huffs, walking to the driver's side, and opening the door. "Get in."

Stowing the collected trash on the floorboard, I drop into the passenger seat. "Thank you."

Hailee mumbles something under her breath as she

buckles up and begins turning the car around. I sit silently, contemplating the many ways I could have played things differently. What if I'd told her from the start? What if I'd fudged the truth a bit and told her I was running from an ex-girlfriend instead? What if I'd just made a move on her at the bar? It's a pointless exercise. I didn't do any of those things. I shoved the full truth under the rug and now I've pulled it out from under her.

Glancing at her as subtly as I can, I try to gauge what she's thinking. When she first suggested that I join her trip, I should have tried harder to say no. I really like Hailee, but she literally left her boyfriend yesterday. She needs time to heal. *I* need time to heal. I tried not to spend too much time thinking about the scars Andrew has gouged into my soul as I'd stared past my reflection during the countless hours on the Greyhound.

Sadness settles in my chest. Spending time with Hailee is fun. It's effortless being around her. Ever since I sat next to her in the bar, it's felt like being with an old friend. An old friend whose legs I can't stop picturing wrapped around my neck. I attempt to halt my thoughts, but almost in desperation at the thought that these are our final minutes together, my brain hurtles down the track before I can stop it. Hailee's ass in those shorts—my hands slipping beneath the waistband to clutch at her cheeks. Her hard nipples against my tongue, her body arched in pleasure. My fingers gripping at her soft edges, almost hard enough to bruise, as I slam myself into her. My brain throws image after image at me until my dick is throbbing painfully against my jeans. Shifting in my seat, I try to rest my hand in my lap to hide the evidence of my arousal. Hailee has my body reacting like a horny teenager and I bite my lip to hold back the groan building in my throat. What is wrong with me?

The car skids to a halt on the dirt path, and I clutch the door, turning to Hailee in question. She sits, hands gripping the wheel and her gaze fixed forward.

"Are you okay?" I ask, my skin like ice as I try to figure out whether she's noticed. Maybe she's going to kick me out and leave me in the forest after all.

"What am I supposed to do?"

It feels like a rhetorical question, so I wait.

"I should take you to the bus station," she says, her fingers flexing and unflexing against the steering wheel.

I watch, trying hard not to imagine those long, delicate fingers wrapping themselves around my cock. *Get a grip, Carter. What the fuck?*

"I know that's the sensible thing to do," she mutters, almost to herself.

"Isn't that what you're doing?" I venture.

Hailee turns to me, the frown on her face melting away into something else. "I don't want to," she says. "What kind of woman does that make me?"

It's my turn to frown. "What are you talking about?"

"You," she says, waving a hand in my direction. "You lied to me, and I know I should take you to the bus station, but I don't want to. I enjoyed today."

I blow out a slow breath. "I enjoyed today, too. I don't want you to take me to the bus station, either."

Hailee turns off the ignition and leans forward, resting her head against the steering wheel.

"You should take me to the bus station, though," I say, running a hand through my hair. "If we're being honest with each other, I might as well tell you that today has been fucking torture, and I don't think I can do another couple of days of it."

Hailee turns her head and stares at me. "Torture? You said you enjoyed today."

My neck heats as I prepare to throw myself off the proverbial deep end. "Torture because I find you ridiculously attractive," I clarify. "Torture because ever since last night, all I've been able to think about is touching you. Which is exactly why you should take me to the bus station."

She stares at me, her brown eyes lined with gold as they scan my face. "What if I want you to touch me?"

I swallow, hyper aware of every molecule between us. Before I can second guess myself, I unfasten my seatbelt and reach for her, sliding my fingers into her hair, and pulling her toward me. I pause for a second, her breath warm on my face, as I give her a chance to back out—to realize what an awful mistake this is. I'm a fucking mess. She really shouldn't kiss me.

Hailee closes the gap, pressing her mouth to mine, and drawing a rumbling groan from my chest. Her plump lips are perfection, and as she parts them, brushing her tongue against mine, all my resolve evaporates. I can barely think, see, as I pull away and wrench open my door. Striding around the car, breathing hard, I reach Hailee's door and yank it open. She stares up at me, her beautiful eyes wide, and her body tensed against the seat as though she has no idea what's going on. Ducking down, I reach across and unfasten her seatbelt before pulling her to her feet. Then, she's mine.

I grasp her face with both hands and push her back against the car, my body pressed to hers as I claim her lips, her tongue. Every inch of me lights up at the sensation of her warm, soft body against mine. She's the first person I've kissed since Andrew. The first woman I've kissed since college. It's not that it feels different because she's female, it's that she kisses me like she's craving me. When Andrew kissed me, it was a fierce claiming, as though he was trying to stop me from thinking about anything other than him. Hailee doesn't even have to try. My brain is nothing but blissful fog as she winds her fingers in my hair, her tongue caressing mine with gentle strokes filled with promise.

At the thought of that clever tongue against my cock, my blood ignites, and I rock my hips against hers, taking her bottom lip between my teeth. Hailee breathes a whimper, and my hands drop to her waist, kneading the soft flesh I've been fantasizing about since the bar. She's driving me crazy. It's all I can do not to strip her naked and claim her on the hood of the car. The very thought of her spread out for me in the open, has my dick rock hard, straining against my jeans.

I pull back, breathing heavily as my fingers slip under her linen shirt. Hailee stares up at me, her beautiful lips pink and swollen. Her skin is a little red from my stubble and I wonder whether she likes it. If she doesn't, I'll get rid of it. Fuck, at this point, I'll do anything for her.

Her tongue darts out against her lower lip, and I watch, transfixed, as she grabs the waistband of my jeans and pulls me back to her, hunger lighting her eyes.

Fuck. I'm in deep, deep shit.

7

I'VE NEVER BEEN KISSED LIKE THIS BEFORE. WHEN CARTER GOT out of the car, I panicked, thinking I'd done something wrong. I'd watched, frozen, as he strode around the vehicle, and when he pulled me out and pushed me up against the door, it was like an out-of-body experience. Things like that don't happen to me. My life is boring and quiet. It isn't being kissed senseless by gorgeous men on secluded forest roads.

A small part of me says it's probably time to stop before things get out of hand, but my self-control and resolve are melting like an ice cream on a hot summer's day, and I can't find it in myself to care. Carter's fingers massage my hips, turning my brain fuzzy with desire as I will him to move them up to my aching breasts. My heart pounds at the feel of his arousal, hard against my stomach, and I move my hands under his t-shirt, letting my fingers explore the firm slopes of his stomach. He presses against me, sliding a thigh between my legs, and I moan, sucking his tongue as heat pools between my thighs.

I'm not sure whether it's my mouth or my fingers that

cause Carter to dip, sliding his hands under my thighs, and lifting me up. I gasp, wrapping my legs around his waist.

"I want you so fucking bad, Hailee," he groans, as he kisses his way down my neck, his teeth grazing my collarbone.

Tipping my head back, I grind my hips against him, desperate for friction where I need it most.

"I want you too," I breathe.

I do. I can't remember the last time I felt need like this. Brent and I had a decent sex life for the first year or so, but as drinking, gambling, and staying out late became the winning choice for him, our intimacy faded away to dust. Even when things were good, it hadn't been like this. This is sparks and flames, burning heat filling my lungs.

Carter's hands move under my shirt, his thumbs grazing the underside of my breasts and I lose it. Lust wins. I don't care that someone could drive past, or that this is a man I just met. All I care about is the burning need for his hands and mouth on my skin before I combust. Pulling back slightly, I take the hem of my shirt in my hands, buttons be damned, and pull it off over my head, dropping it on the roof of the car.

Carter stares at me, his eyes dark with lust, and his beautiful mouth curved in a devilish grin. Wrapping his arms tight around my back, he steps away from the car and carries me to the hood, where he sets me down. I can't get enough air into my lungs, my head dizzy as he reaches around and unfastens my bra. At the exposure to the air, my nipples harden further and Carter groans, leaning forward to take one into his mouth, his thumb flicking over the other.

Leaning back, my arms shake as Carter's tongue and teeth work my sensitive flesh. He lifts his head, his bright blue eyes wolf-like as he kisses me again, pushing me down against the warm hood. I reach for the button on his jeans, but he takes my hands in his, holding them above my head. Moving his mouth down my body in a series of kisses, licks, and teasing bites, he holds on until he reaches low enough that he has to let go.

"These fucking shorts," he says, his voice thick as he hooks his fingers on my waistband. "These have been driving me crazy all day."

I push up on my elbows, barely breathing as he unfastens the button and pulls down the zipper. A whimper escapes my lips as he slowly tugs my shorts and underwear down my legs.

His heated stare flicks to mine, and he licks his lips. "You're already wet for me, aren't you?"

My ability to form coherent words has long since vanished, so I nod. Carter grins slowly, his ice-blue gaze never leaving mine as he reaches between my legs and feels the evidence of my desire. His eyes flutter shut as he draws a breath.

"You're soaked, Hailee," he says, opening his eyes and bringing his fingers to his lips.

My body pulses and I press my thighs together as I watch him suck my juices from his fingers with a moan. It's only then that I realize I'm naked, save my shoes and socks, out in the open.

My heart manages to find a new gear and I gasp. "What if someone comes?"

"I'm hoping someone will," Carter replies with a smirk.

I bat at him with my hand, and he looks up and down the deserted dirt track. For a second, I worry he'll suggest we stop, but instead, he takes hold of his t-shirt and pulls it up over his head.

He places it beside me with a wink. "There you go. If anyone comes, you can cover yourself up with that."

I nod, but my attention has already moved on. I thought in the bar that he probably looked great shirtless, but seeing it is a whole other ball game.

"Are you okay?" he asks, running his hands down the inside of my thighs, and gently spreading my legs.

"Yes." I gasp as he runs his fingers down my center. "It's just a lot."

"What is?"

I wave my hand at him. "This . . . whole thing."

Carter's eyes flash. "Oh, Hailee. You have no idea. If you could see what I'm seeing."

He groans, lowering his head between my legs, and at the first long lap of his tongue, I gasp, arching against him. It's all the encouragement he needs, as he starts to work me with his mouth, until my breaths are nothing more than whimpers. Just as I feel my body tensing, Carter pushes two fingers inside me, curling and stroking as he sucks against my clit. My body shakes, and I cry out his name, the exhilaration morphing into laughter as I clench, trembling around his fingers. He keeps licking, even after I still, and I squirm against him.

"I'm not done yet," he murmurs, his stubble tickling the inside of my thighs as he trails kisses on the sensitive flesh there. He adds a third finger, causing me to cry out as he stretches me, plunging hard and fast. I grip at the hood, trying to find purchase as he watches me writhe.

"Fuck my hand, Hailee" he grinds out, leaning forward and flicking his tongue against my nipple. "Ride my fingers until you come."

I thrust my fingers into his hair, pressing his mouth against my breast as I work my hips against his fingers.

"I want you inside me." I whimper, desperate for the feeling of his naked body against mine.

Carter sucks my nipple hard before rolling it with his tongue. "I know. You have no idea how badly I want to be inside you. I don't have protection though, so we're going to have to wait."

I press my lips together, so desperate with need for him that I'm willing to say I don't care—that I'm on the pill. But I swallow the words. I can wait. I can wait for a bed to feel him inside me. Just the thought pushes me over the edge, and I cry out, trembling as Carter captures my moans with his mouth, his fingers gently coaxing the last burning embers of my orgasm from me.

He kisses me slowly and purposefully until I find the strength to sit up. I reach for his jeans, his erection straining against the denim, but he steps back out of my reach.

"I'll wait," he says. "I don't have any protection on me, and if you touch me now, I won't last more than five seconds. When you touch me, I want enough time to savor every moment."

My heart somersaults, my blood vibrating at his rumbling tones. I watch, my brain still numb with pleasure as he stoops and picks up my shorts and underwear, working them back up over my shoes and socks. I reach for my bra as Carter tugs his t-shirt back on.

With each passing second, I can feel the tension seeping back between us. Less than half an hour ago, I was driving him to the bus station because he'd lied to me. Now, I've fucked his hand on the hood of my car. Trying not to wince, I slide off onto the ground and fasten my shorts. When Carter hands me my shirt, I avoid his gaze as I pull it on over my head.

"Hey," he says, reaching for me.

He tips my chin, and I raise my gaze to meet his. I'm not sure what I expect to see there, but I find concern.

"Are you okay?" he asks, his thumb stroking my cheek. "Please don't tell me you're regretting that, because I'm certainly not."

I open my mouth to speak, but I don't know what to say, so I shut it again.

"Hailee," he says softly. "What are you thinking? Tell me."

"I don't know," I admit. "I mean, what do we do now?"

Carter drops his hand to my waist, a small smile tipping his lips. "Well, I suppose you have two choices. Take me to the bus station, or we carry on to our next stop and find a hotel."

I swallow. He's giving me an out. A way to never have to see him again. Even though we're both headed to the same place, I know Las Vegas is big enough that the chances of us ever running into each other are slim to none. Is that what I want, though?

Pulling away from him, I turn around and press my fingers to my temples. Why can't I make a simple decision? Why do I have to second guess everything? Anger builds, filling my chest. Not at myself, or Carter, but at Brent. Over the years we spent together, he disabled a vital part of me. He scrubbed doubt into every corner of my being, making me so dependent on him, I can't make a simple decision without checking with him first. I almost laugh. What would Brent say if I called him now and asked whether I should leave the hot guy at the bus stop or take him to a motel and let him fuck me senseless? My fingers itch at my side, wanting to check my phone. Wondering whether he's found a way to contact me. Perhaps he hasn't even noticed I've gone yet.

"Hailee," Carter says, his voice painfully gentle. "If you want, there's a third option. We can carry on but pretend this never happened. Honestly, I like being around you and I'd really like to get to know you better. We can go back to the beginning, as friends. No pressure."

As if it would be that simple. Maybe I could call my sister and ask her what I should do. I close my eyes, berating myself. I shouldn't need to ask anyone. It should be simple. What do *I* want? I want to get out of the forest. I want to not have to make decisions. I want a goddamn hug. My shoulders slump at the thought, and I fold my arms around myself, feeling emptier and more alone than ever.

8

Watching Hailee fold into herself, my chest tightens to the point of aching. I've kept my distance, knowing she needs space to sort out her head, but I can't stay back any longer.

Closing the distance between us, I take hold of her arms and gently turn her round, pulling her to my chest. I'm ready for her to push me away, but she sinks into me, her arms wrapping around my waist, and I sag in relief. Pressing a kiss to the top of her head, I rub my hands up and down her back.

"It's okay," I say. "Can I make a suggestion?"

She nods against my shirt, and I give her a gentle squeeze.

"Why don't we just get out of this forest? I can drive if you want. Let's head to the next stop on your list and you can make up your mind on the way. You don't have to decide everything right now."

Hailee tightens her grip around my middle. "That sounds good. I'll drive though. It helps me think."

"Sure thing."

It feels nice, holding her in my arms. She fits perfectly against me, and I rest my cheek on top of her head as I breathe her in.

"I'm sorry for being such a mess," she mumbles into my chest. "You're probably regretting ever sitting down next to me at that bar."

"Hailee, I—"

"No." She groans, pushing away from me. "I didn't just say that. That's fucking lame. I rescind your invitation to my pity party. Let's go."

I watch as she walks back to the driver's side and opens the door. My head is a mess. Is she taking me to the bus station? Are we heading to a hotel? Are we just friends now? She probably doesn't know herself. It's fine. We have time to figure this out.

"You coming or not?"

I snap out of my thoughts and climb into the passenger side, buckling up and swallowing my questions, as Hailee starts the ignition. The forest thins out around us, revealing silver tipped peaks and an endless winding road. I know I should probably take in the view, but my mind is too busy running over what just happened, playing a revolving slideshow that has my breath hitching. The whole thing had me lightheaded—almost like feeling high. I'm not used to being the one in control. I picture Hailee's face when I pulled her out of the car, the lust in her eyes when she took her top off, the way she looked, naked and laid out for me on the hood. I swallow, sending a mental apology to my neglected cock.

I think of how Andrew would often drag me from rooms, shoving me against walls and into dark corners, claiming me. Is this what it felt like? The high of taking charge? Although, it's more than just taking the lead with Hailee. It's also the way she feels against me. Her vulnerability has woken something in me. Maybe it's some sort of caveman instinct, but I want to protect her. I promised beardy Barry in the bar that I'd look after her, and I'm not done fulfilling that promise. Every now and again, I get a glimpse beneath Hailee's doubt filled exterior—a shadow of who she probably was before her dickhead ex got hold of her. I want to coax that part of her out into the sunlight. I want to see who she really is. Closing my eyes, I lean my head against the window. Who am I kidding? I have no business trying to fix her when I'm still broken myself.

"So, I never told you the whole plan," Hailee says, checking her rearview as a SUV roars up and passes us. "You've signed up to this road trip and you have no idea where I'm taking you."

"Hopefully Las Vegas."

Hailee makes a show of rolling her eyes. "Ha ha."

I sit up, something lightening in my chest at the topic of conversation. Surely, if she's telling me the itinerary, it means I'm still along for the ride. "Sorry. Cheap shot. Go on."

Hailee shoots me a quick smile before returning her eyes to the road. "So, I thought I'd be spending more time at Mount Rushmore, so I planned to stop over in Rapid City tonight. Then in the morning, I was going to head toward Denver. Like I mentioned before, I want to make my way to the Four Corners monument, and then finally on to the Grand Canyon. Does that sound okay?"

"This is your road trip," I say. "I'm down for anything."

"You said the Grand Canyon was on your bucket list, but have you been to any of the other places before?"

"No. I've never left the East Coast," I admit. "I always meant to. I wanted to travel after college."

"Why didn't you?"

I knew the question was coming, but it still manages to take me by surprise. Why haven't I travelled? The answer is a single word that rockets right to the front of my mind. *Andrew.*

"Sorry." Hailee's voice is soft. "You don't have to answer that."

I lean my head back against the seat. "I haven't really talked to anyone about Andrew before."

"Is that the ex-boyfriend?"

I nod. "I think I knew on some level that things weren't normal or healthy. But if I talked to my friends about it, they'd say as much, and I'd be forced to do something about it."

Hailee says nothing, giving me the space and time I need to decide whether to talk. She's told me about her ex—about how he made her question every decision. I know a lot about controlling boyfriends.

"We went on a trip once," I start, taking a steadying breath. "New York City. He splurged on a fancy hotel overlooking Central Park. I was so excited, even if it was only a three-day trip—it was more than enough."

I swallow, my stomach tying itself in knots. This is a bad idea.

"What happened?" Hailee presses, her voice tender with concern. "I won't judge you. I promise."

She reaches over, resting a hand on my knee, and I cover it with mine, relishing in the comfort of the simple gesture. When she doesn't pull back, I take another breath and continue.

"We had a stupid long list of touristy things to do. The

first day, we went to Central Park, with plans to visit the Empire State Building at sunset. It was going great until Andrew went to buy us some ice cream. While he was ordering, I waited on a bench. Two women came over and asked for directions. I told them I had no idea because I wasn't local, and we started chatting."

My heart speeds up at the memory, my face burning. Hailee must sense me tensing because she flips her hand and laces her fingers with mine. I want to turn back, pull the words back in, but it's too late. Andrew's face has already filled my brain. The way his eyes look almost black when he's jealous. My body begins to go through the well-practiced slew of emotions that look would bring forward. Fear. Doubt. Remorse. Anticipation. Acceptance. Guilt.

"I knew they were flirting," I admit. "They were really good looking, and who doesn't like to be flirted with, right? I didn't really know what Andrew was like at that point. It was still early on. I knew he got jealous easily, but I thought it was cute. When he saw me talking to those women, he lost it."

I shiver and Hailee gives my hand a squeeze. At the time I was mortified. He'd stormed over and told the women they shouldn't be wasting their time on a gay guy. Then he'd dropped the ice creams at their feet and dragged me away.

"He made us go back to the hotel," I say. "I tried to reason with him, thinking it was funny how he was overreacting. The whole way there, I tried to placate him. Apologizing. We didn't leave the hotel for the rest of the trip."

I pinch the bridge of my nose, color staining my cheeks at how naïve I'd been. How I'd just accepted his possessiveness. Andrew had tried to make it seem romantic. Ordering room service and running baths. Any time I'd suggested leaving to see the sights, he'd initiated sex, making it last long enough that there was no time to do anything else. I'd let myself enjoy the attention, ignoring the glaring problem. If you ignore something for long enough, you can convince yourself it's not there.

"And you thought *you* were hosting the pity party," I mutter, releasing her hand.

"I'm so sorry you had to go through that." She shakes her head, returning her hand to the steering wheel. "He sounds scary."

"I didn't see it," I say. "I told myself it was romantic at the time—that he wanted me all to himself. It was like he couldn't get enough of me, and it was addictive, knowing I had that effect on someone. It took me way too long to realize that he used sex as a weapon—a way to control me."

"How did you figure it out?"

I sigh. "Andrew invited a couple over for dinner. We played drinking games and the conversation got dirty real quick. It was only when they were talking about what they did together, that I started to question things. It's hard to know what normal is when you don't know any better."

Hailee signals and I frown as she pulls over to the side of the road, her hazards blinking. She unfastens her seatbelt and leans across to me, pulling me into a hug. I huff a laugh in surprise, but gratefully accept the embrace. Burying my face in her soft hair, I take a deep breath that pulls at every crack inside my battered heart.

"Thank you for telling me," she says against my neck. "I know that wasn't easy for you. I hope you feel better for sharing."

I squeeze her tighter. I'm not sure I do. Reliving the memory has brought fresh pain to the surface and I feel raw and exposed. When Hailee pulls back, she brings a hand to my face and strokes my cheek, her eyes glistening with sadness. I look away.

"Come on," she says, pulling at her seatbelt. "Let's go find a bar."

I laugh, her simple comment making me feel instantly lighter. "That sounds like a fucking brilliant idea."

9

"ARE YOU SURE THIS IS RIGHT?" I ASK, FROWNING AT THE buildings as we pass them.

Carter chuckles. "I think the massive sign saying, 'Welcome to Rapid City' was a clue."

"Yeah, but it says *city*. This isn't a city. Surely it should be Rapid Town or something."

Carter snorts and pulls out his phone. "Not everyone uses Chicago as their blueprint for a city."

"Yeah, yeah, yeah. Where am I going?"

"Straight ahead for another mile or so and then take a right onto North Street. There are like four different places we can choose from."

Ever since Carter opened up to me about his ex, things have felt more relaxed between us. After what happened in the forest, I've struggled to imagine us being friends, but we've fallen back into an easy rhythm, reminding me why I asked him to come on the trip in the first place. He has such a comforting presence. It's easier to breathe in his orbit.

"There! That one!"

I jolt as Carter leans across me and points at a two-story

hotel on the side of the road. Quickly checking my mirrors, I just manage to make the turn, the wheels kicking up gravel as I swerve into the parking lot.

“Fuck, Carter. A bit more warning next time, please.” I sink back against the seat, my heart pounding. “I thought you were looking at the map?”

“I got distracted by Instagram.” He gives me a sheepish grin. “Sorry.”

Playfully whacking his shoulder, I peer up at the hotel he so enthusiastically pointed out. It doesn’t appear to be anything special, but maybe I’ve missed something.

“It’s cheap and cheerful,” Carter explains. “But the best part is, there’s an award-winning cocktail bar next door.”

“Award-winning,” I repeat, my mouth twitching at his obvious excitement. “What award?”

“Like it matters. You said let’s go find a bar and I found us a bar.” He points at the barely visible lump on my head. “Unless you want me to find a bar where you can get assaulted again?”

“Nope. Cocktails sound great.” I turn off the ignition and grab my bag from the back seat. “Shall we check in?”

Carter pauses, his hand stilling on the passenger door.

“What?” I ask.

“We haven’t really talked about what we’re going to do,” he says carefully. “I’m going to guess you want separate rooms.”

My stomach flips. Less than two hours ago, I’d been desperate to get him somewhere with a bed. The memory of him taking off his shirt, of his head between my legs, of the way he’d groaned how much he wanted me, has heat pooling between my thighs and my breath quickening. That moment has gone, but I still want him. Badly. I’m just not sure what’s going on between us.

"I mean, if you wanted to save money," Carter continues, his gaze turning to the hotel. "We could get a twin room again."

Just like that, the offer is there. Separate beds. If we want them.

I shrug. "Well, I don't have a lot of money, so . . ."

"Frugal," Carter confirms. "It's the sensible choice."

With a smile on my lips, I get out and head up the path to the front door, locking the car over my shoulder when I hear him close his door.

A middle-aged woman with platinum blonde hair that looks as though it might have been solidified by several cans of hairspray is sitting behind the desk, sifting through a stack of paperwork. She looks up as we approach, her face lit up with a beaming smile.

"Well, hello," she says, taking off her glasses and setting them down in front of her. "Do you have a reservation?"

"We don't," I say. "We were hoping you might have a twin room available?"

She picks up her glasses and turns to a computer that looks about twenty years out of date. "I'm sure we do. Let me just check here."

I smile in thanks and take the opportunity to look around the lobby. It's like it's been decorated by a team of little old ladies in their eighties. Lots of creams and tiny flowers.

"What do you want to bet, the beds have flowered comforters on them?" Carter whispers in my ear.

I elbow him, despite thinking the exact same thing.

"Room thirty-six," the woman says, looking up from the screen.

"Can I pay cash?" I ask.

The woman smiles and folds her hands together. “You can pay cash, but I’ll need a card to secure the room.”

My ears burn, and even though I know I won’t find one, I root in the pockets of my bag as I try to think of a way out of this situation.

“Here,” Carter says, handing over his card. “I’ve got it.”

I flash him a grateful smile; certain he can see the supernova that is my burning face. “Thanks. It’s in here somewhere.”

The woman prints out the bill on a painfully slow printer and pushes it across to me. Carter has chosen well. It’s almost as cheap as the strip mall motel, but much nicer.

The woman holds out an old-fashioned brass key with a large wooden tag. “It’s just up the stairs and along the hallway on your left,” she says. “Enjoy your stay.”

We’re halfway up the narrow staircase when Carter breaks the silence.

“What do you want to do about paying for the room? Do you want me to transfer the cash?”

My heart stutters and I grip my backpack tighter. “No, it’s fine. You can get the next one. Or pay for drinks tonight.”

I can practically feel his frown burning into my back as I push open the door at the top of the stairs. Ignoring him, I stride down the hallway, eyeing the numbers of the rooms until I find thirty-six.

The lock is a little stiff, but after a few seconds of jiggling, the door opens to reveal a room larger and much nicer than the one we shared in Sioux Falls.

“Told you,” Carter says, throwing himself down on a cream comforter covered in sickly pink roses. “It’s like a retirement home.”

“You chose it,” I remind him, placing my bag down on the other bed.

As soon as the bag leaves my shoulder, the air seems to thicken. We're alone in a hotel room. I look at where Carter is sprawled on the bed, his arms behind his head and his eyes closed. His shirt has ridden up a little where he's thrown himself down, exposing a delicious slice of stomach. I let my gaze drink in the swell of his biceps and the way his jeans mold to his thighs. Then, I push my desire down, tucking it away out of sight.

"Do you think the bar is open yet?" I ask.

Carter opens an eye and peers at his watch. "Five o'clock. I'd say so. If we're lucky, it'll be happy hour."

"Awesome. Do you want to take the first shower? I need to grab something from the car."

Not giving time for a response, I grab my backpack and head for the door. I didn't really pack anything suitable for a cocktail bar, but I'm assuming it won't be like the bars in Chicago. The woman looks up from behind the front desk and I give her a small wave as I hurry past. When I reach the car, I open the back door and slide onto the seat beside my bags. It doesn't take me long to locate a pair of dark jeans and an off the shoulder top that should look smart enough with a pair of dangly earrings. My jewelry is in my backpack, so I don't need to root for that.

My evening outfit secured, I sit back against the seat and exhale. I don't want to go back up to the room and face Carter fresh from the shower in nothing but a towel. I only have so much willpower. Instead, I reach into my backpack and pull out my phone.

The screen lights up, revealing no new notifications and I'm not sure whether I'm disappointed or relieved. Even though I've blocked Brent on everything I can think of, I know there'll be something I've forgotten. Cutting someone out of your life after five years isn't as easy as snapping off a branch. It's a complicated surgery that involves severing nerves and slicing through diseased tissue.

I flick through my social media, but no one has reached out to me. This is nothing new. I called and quit my job at the grocery store, spooling a lie about a terminally ill grandmother and how I couldn't work my notice because I needed to go and look after her in California. I specifically avoided saying Nevada because I know Brent will go and ask Sal, my manager, what I said. He'd tell him too.

Everyone likes Brent. He's an all-American boy. Blond hair, blue eyes, and a bright white smile. He was even the quarterback on his high school football team. If I had parents to take him home to, I'm sure they would have loved him. Of course, no one saw the other Brent. The Brent that lurked just beneath the surface of his porcelain smile, hiding in the politeness of his words and the assuredness of his touch. He was something that sneaked, smothering and suffocating, until you realized, too late, that you were trapped.

I suck in a desperate breath, scrambling for the door. The car, the hotel—the world—feels too small. As if I'll never be free of him. 'You're overreacting, Hails,' he'd say. 'Calm down. You know you get like this sometimes. Don't embarrass yourself'.

My eyes sting as I make my way back to the hotel, my clothes clutched to my chest, fighting to get myself back under control with every step. I'm fine. Everything is fine.

I push open the door, hoping the bathroom is free so I can hide away for a few more minutes. If Carter presses, I know I'll crumble.

"Hey." Carter grins from where he's laid on the bed, his phone in his hands. "Bathroom's all yours."

I barely glance at him, shooting him a quick smile on my

way to the small ensuite. I lock the door behind me and lean against the sink, wishing there was a way I could chisel Brent's voice out of my brain.

The bathroom is still humid, the mirror a little foggy, save for a patch where Carter must have rubbed it clean. It smells incredible. His cologne permeates the air with a musky scent that has me closing my eyes and breathing it in.

Fifteen to twenty minutes. That's all I need to get ready. I just hope it's enough time to pull myself back together.

10

I'm not sure if something happened, but Hailee looked upset when she got back from the car. I know there's a good chance it was an excuse not to be around me while I got ready, but I have to admit I'm glad of it. After what happened in the forest, there's no way I wasn't knocking one out in the shower, and it was a lot easier knowing she wasn't waiting on the other side of the door.

My gaze flits from my phone to the closed bathroom door. I'm still not sure whether my suggestion of a twin room was a good one or not. Things seem to have gotten back on track since I bared a slice of my fucked-up soul to her in the car. Where that leaves us now, however, I have no idea. Are we just friends? We need to be. I want us to be. As much as I'd consider selling a vital organ to get her into bed, I don't want sex to mess things up. And isn't that what sex always does?

The bathroom door opens, and I lock my phone, sliding it into my pocket. *Shit.* She looks fucking gorgeous. The shorts have been replaced with dark skinny jeans that hug her legs like a second skin. Her white top hangs off one shoulder, the bare skin brushed by long golden earrings. I swallow. "You look beautiful."

"Thanks," she says, giving me a smile. "You look beautiful too."

Laughing, I get to my feet, pretending I don't see the way she checks me out as I do. I definitely haven't put on my favorite jeans and my best black button-down shirt just for her.

I open my mouth to ask if she's okay, but after a beat, I close it. If she wants to talk to me, she knows I'm here and that I'll listen. We might be a bit of a mess, but we know that much about each other.

"Ready to go?" I ask.

"Before we do," Hailee says, her attention on everything in the room but me, "I want to set things straight."

I frown. "What do you mean?"

"Like, between us."

"Ah."

I cross the room and take her hands in mine. She stares up at me, her eyes wide in question, and I smile. Sometimes she reminds me of a cartoon deer.

"I've been thinking about that too," I say. "Things got a bit heated between us, but above everything else, I want to be your friend."

"My friend," she echoes.

"I'm not saying that's all we are." I squeeze her fingers. "Things don't have to be strictly platonic. Just that I don't think either of us is in any state for anything more than that, right?"

Hailee exhales. "Definitely not."

"So, why don't we just take things as they come and try not to worry about it. No matter what happens, friends first."

"That sounds," she takes a deep breath before blowing it out slowly, "really good, actually."

"No pressure," I reiterate. "Okay?"

She nods and I squeeze her hands one more time before gesturing to the door. "Let's go try some award-winning cocktails."

If this place has won awards, it was a very long time ago. Despite the late afternoon sun outside, it's dingy inside, and I can't quite figure out what the place is trying to be. There are tall tables scattered around, and massive fake potted plants in between, which only serve to block the light more. My nose itches and I rub at it, trying to hold back the sneeze building there.

There are four or five people tucked away in the corners, drinking beer, not cocktails. A couple of women are near the bar giggling over the menu and speaking a language I don't quite recognize. *Tourists.*

"What is this place?" Hailee asks, bumping me with her shoulder.

"I have no fucking clue."

The music is a whole other thing. When we walked in, it was playing something recent by the Chainsmokers, but now it's morphed to 'Like A Prayer' by Madonna. This place is a trip.

We head to the bar, and I take the opportunity to admire Hailee's ass in her tight jeans. It wasn't enough in the forest. My fingers ache to touch her. I haven't wanted something so badly in a long time.

Perching on one of the shiny leather stools, Hailee reaches for a couple of menus and hands one to me. I try not to wrinkle my nose at the sticky plastic as I take a seat beside her.

"Happy hour is from five until seven," she says, wiggling her eyebrows. "Two for one. How many of these do you think we can make our way through in that time?"

I lower my menu. "Oh? Are we getting drunk, drunk?"

"I believe it was you that said we should take things as they come. So, why don't we see which cocktails come and take them."

I wonder for a second whether my comment in the hotel about being friends has bugged her, but there's nothing but mischief flickering in her copper-flecked eyes, so I return her grin.

"Any preferences?" she asks, frowning at the long list of names.

"I mean, I usually go for a Long Island iced tea," I admit.

Hailee rolls her eyes. "Okay, East Coast."

"Ha! No, because it's usually the same price as the other cocktails but it has three times the amount of alcohol." I point to it on the menu and watch as Hailee's eyes widen.

"That's ridiculous," she says. "Let's go for it."

I laugh and shake my head. "Let's work up to that one. Remember, we haven't eaten since lunch."

"They have bar snacks," Hailee says, pointing at a list of fried food.

The bartender appears, a young woman dressed all in black, with thick dark eyeliner curved almost out to her ears. She gives us both a smile, her gaze lingering a little longer on me than it needs to, and my answering smile tightens.

"Hey, folks. What can I get you?"

Hailee smacks the laminated cocktail menu down on the bar decisively. "We'll have two tequila sunrises, two cosmopolitans, two portions of fries and some mozzarella sticks please."

The woman behind the bar blinks, then mutters something and moves away to fix our order.

"You can choose the next two," Hailee says, taking the menu from my hand.

It's nice seeing Hailee relaxed and I watch as she takes in the room, her lips twitching at the bizarre, mismatched décor.

"Why would anyone think a life-sized Betty Boop would be a good addition to a cocktail bar?" she asks.

I shrug. "I mean, that's a good addition to any room, surely?"

"Oh? Is that your type? Small waist, big boobs?"

My withering response is halted by the sliding of two tequila sunrises in our direction.

"Why these?" I ask, peering at the red seeping through the orange juice.

"You said we hadn't eaten," Hailee explains, giving her own drink a stir. "So, I figured, orange juice."

Laughter shakes my shoulders again and I realize, as warmth spreads across my chest, that I've laughed more since meeting Hailee than I have in a long time.

"Orange juice is not a meal." I take a sip and wince. "I think my grandma used to like these."

Hailee smacks my knee and raises her glass. "Quit whining and start drinking."

11

My nose wrinkles at the sourness of the cosmopolitan. I'm sure it isn't supposed to taste like this, but it's two for one and quite cheap. Despite inhaling most of my order of fries, the alcohol is coursing through me, spreading warmth and a comforting fuzziness. The fuzziness isn't enough to distract me from how goddamn hot Carter looks, though.

I liked his worn, pale jeans, but these dark, fitted ones only serve to highlight his strong thighs and pert ass. I'm a sucker for a guy in a black shirt, and although I prefer a long-sleeved tee to a button down, Carter is making it work. He has the top two buttons undone and the sleeves rolled back to display his forearms. He looks gorgeous and I'm not the only one who's noticed. The two Italian women further down the bar haven't stopped looking at him since we walked in, and the server is checking on us way more than she needs to.

"Okay," Carter announces, placing down his empty glass. "For our next round, I'm voting for amaretto sours and margaritas."

I down the rest of my own cocktail and grimace. "We are going to feel like shit tomorrow."

Carter grins. "Yep."

"I'm voting for Long Island iced teas on my next round."

"Only if you order more food. I don't want to have to carry you back to the room."

The statement is innocent enough, but I find the smile sliding from my face. Carter stares back at me, and I watch his throat bob as he swallows, his bright blue eyes burning into mine. My mouth suddenly dry, I lick my lips, and his gaze tracks the movement.

"Ready for another round?"

I'm not sure whether I want to hug or punch the woman behind the bar for breaking our stare, but before I can decide, the sound of loud laughter pulls my attention.

A group of around fifteen people pour into the bar, clearly already a little tipsy. Leaving Carter to order our next round, I grin as I watch them take in the bizarrely decorated bar. Most of them appear to be middle-aged or older. It looks like a tour group, perhaps for retirees. There's a lot of khaki. They spread out, some claiming tables as others seek out menus, and the atmosphere shifts with their joy-filled chatter.

As they separate, one member of the group pulls my attention. Even standing with his back to me as he surveys the mismatched array of framed prints on the far wall, I can tell he's clearly a lot younger than the rest of them. With broad shoulders and a slim waist, his dark hair is tied up in a neat bun, his hands in the pockets of his charcoal dress pants. I start to wonder whether he's actually with the rest of the group at all. Perhaps he's just wandered in with them. I watch, intrigued, as one of the group—a lady who looks to be in her fifties—walks over and shows him a menu, pointing at something. Whatever he says in response causes her face to light up and she trots away to where others are waiting at the bar. I frown. So, he is with them. He turns around and my breath catches in my throat.

"You okay there?" Carter asks, pressing an ice-cold glass into my hand.

I reluctantly pull my gaze away, blinking. "Yeah, sure."

Carter frowns, looking across at where the guy has taken a seat at one of the tall tables. "You know him?"

"Nope." My gaze drifts back despite my best efforts.

He's beautiful—a masterpiece of high cheekbones, full lips, and dark eyebrows. I can't take my eyes off him. Carter touches my chin and I jolt.

"You're drooling," he says, a teasing grin stretching his lips.

I open my mouth to deny that I've been staring but stop myself. We're just friends. I don't have to justify or defend my actions. Besides, Carter doesn't seem bothered. In fact, I notice with amusement that his attention keeps wandering to the same place.

"Is he really with that tour group?" Carter asks, staring as he sips his amaretto sour.

I shrug. "If he's not, he seems to know them all. Maybe he's on a trip with his parents."

Carter snorts. "Can you imagine?"

Pressing my lips together, I decide not to answer. My parents have been dead so long, my memories of their faces are built on faded photographs. Bringing up dead parents is a conversation killer at the best of times, so I decide to let his flippant comment slide. I turn back to Carter, but the question I was going to ask evaporates from my lips as I find him staring at the beautiful stranger with more than general curiosity.

"Do you want a napkin?" I ask, nudging him with my knee.

He blinks. "What?"

"Now *you're* drooling."

Instead of denying it or showing any sort of embarrassment, Carter gestures at the man with his chin. "Have you seen him? Who wouldn't be drooling?"

"Oh?" I glance between them, my interest piqued. "Is he your type?"

Carter shakes his head. "I'm not sure if I have a type. I mean, he looks nothing like Andrew, and other than a few kisses, it was mostly women before him."

"But that guy ticks your boxes?"

"Come on," he says, shooting me a glance. "He'd tick anyone's box."

"Do you think he's gay?"

Carter shrugs. "No idea. Why don't you go and ask him?"

I snort with laughter and turn around to lean on the bar. Already halfway through my third cocktail, my cheeks are numb, and I'm buzzing.

"Back in a sec," Carter says. "Try not to get knocked unconscious while I'm in the restroom."

I make a face at him, and he laughs as he heads to the back of the bar.

Someone has turned up the music and the eclectic mix of songs has prompted some of the khaki crew to get up and dance near the life-sized Betty Boop. Their smiles and laughter have my own lips curving into a grin. I stare down at my drink before taking a sip. I'm kind of having a great time too. As awkward as things have gotten between Carter and me, they always seem to even out. It's like we're two broken pieces trying to convince the world we're whole, but when we're together, the cracks don't seem to matter as much.

"Any recommendations?"

I turn, my mouth still full of cocktail, to find the beautiful man standing beside me, a shockingly blue drink in his hand.

"My friend bought me this one, but it tastes like mouthwash," he continues. His eyes glance over our collection of empty glasses, yet to be cleared away. "Looks like you two are in the know."

I swallow, trying to remember what words are.

"I'd recommend the margarita," Carter says, slipping back onto his seat and raising the now empty frosted glass. "The amaretto sour was subpar, and if I ever have a tequila sunrise again, it'll be too soon."

Beautiful Man smiles an equally beautiful, white smile. Up close, his eyes are as dark as espresso and framed by thick, long lashes. It really is criminal for someone to be so attractive.

"What about you?" he says, looking at me. "What do you recommend?"

My brain fumbles, trying to remember what I've been drinking. "They're all a bit shit, to be honest. We're moving on to Long Island iced teas next, though."

Beautiful man nods in approval. "It's quite hard to mess up a Long Island iced tea. I mean, you just shove a ton of alcohol in with cola and hope for the best, right?"

"Want to join us?" Carter asks.

I turn to him, my eyes wide, but he ignores me, watching Beautiful Man over my shoulder instead.

"If you're sure I'm not intruding?" he says.

I turn back to him, feeling suddenly desperate for my next drink. "Not at all."

He pulls up a stool as Carter tries to flag down the woman behind the bar. "I'm Lincoln, but people call me Linc."

"Hailee," I say. "And this is Carter."

Carter turns and shakes Linc's hand before returning to flagging down the irate server. I have a feeling she'd been expecting a quiet weekday evening.

"So, what brings you to this award-winning establishment, Linc?" I ask, unsure what to do with my hands.

"I sort of got adopted by a tour group," he says, pausing to wave at a cluster at a nearby table. "I'm making my way across the country and when I ran into this lot in Niagara Falls, they insisted I join their tour. I mean, how could I say no?"

I press my lips together to hold in my laugh. "You could have."

Linc raises his dark brows. "Of course; but *look* at them."

Carter mutters something about having more staff working, and stands, leaning against the bar to try and get her attention. My gaze flits to his ass for a second in appreciation, before returning to Linc. My eyebrows raise as I find his attention focused on the same spot.

"It's a nice view, isn't it?" I ask. Instantly, my cheeks heat, and my breath halts at my alcohol-fueled brazenness.

Linc turns to me, his full lips curved in amusement. "It certainly is. Apologies for ogling your boyfriend."

"Oh, we're just friends," I correct, my skin burning so hot, I'm sure it's going to melt off my face.

Carter returns to his seat, having finally ordered our next round, and looks at us, eyebrows raised. "What did I miss?"

"I was just about to ask Hailee whether you two are local," Linc says, without missing a beat.

"No," Carter replies. "It's a bit of a funny story, actually."

I stare at him. "Is it?"

"You know it is."

"Oh, now I really want to know," Linc says, his grin warm and infectious.

Carter reaches for the new round of cocktails as the bartender pushes them towards us. "I hitched a ride with a Portuguese couple who couldn't speak English, and they dropped me off in Sioux Falls. I met Hailee in a bar there, and when we got chatting, we realized we were heading in the same direction. Then some asshole pulled off her stool and knocked her unconscious."

Linc almost spits out his drink. "Wait. What?"

"I offered to look after her and make sure she didn't have a concussion. We made it through the night, and she offered to let me join her road trip, so I didn't have to catch the bus."

"So dramatic," I mutter.

"A solo road trip?" Linc asks, his dark eyes searching mine. "Self-discovery?"

I take a deep sip of my drink to mask my unease. "I'm not sure. This is only the second day."

"Oh." Linc's eyebrows rise again as he looks between us. "So, you two have only known each other a day?"

Carter glances at his watch. "Twenty hours to be precise."

My head spins. Has it really only been that long? How is that possible?

"Wow," Linc says, shaking his head. "The vibe between you two. It's like you're really close."

Carter winks at me. "It does feel like that. We just sort of clicked."

"Yeah." I smile, my heart swelling. "It feels like I've known him a lot longer."

"There's no better feeling than when you meet someone who speaks to your soul," Linc says. "It doesn't happen often, but when it does, it's like finding a missing piece of yourself."

Carter shifts on his chair, and I feel my skin heat again. I'm not sure what I feel for Carter, if anything, but the talk of missing pieces of souls feels a little too deep, even after four cocktails.

Linc looks between us. "Sorry. I didn't mean to make you uncomfortable."

"No, it's fine," I say. "Uncomfortable is our default setting."

Carter's eyebrows shoot up. "What do you mean?"

"You know exactly what I mean. We only manage 'comfortable' for an hour or so, and then it gets awkward."

As soon as the words leave my mouth, I regret them. Carter's relaxed expression falters, and I can almost see him questioning everything between us.

"You fibbed," Linc says, pulling my attention.

I turn to him. "Excuse me?"

"You said you two were just friends, but I think that line got a little blurred in the last—what was it? Twenty hours?"

Carter downs the last of his drink and places the empty glass down on the bar a little more forcibly than required. He raises a hand to signal the server. "I'm ordering another. Shall I make it three?"

"Sure," Linc says as I nod. "So, what happened?"

I open my mouth to say it isn't really any of his business, but Carter turns from ordering the drinks with a frustrated sigh. "It was entirely my fault. I let her think I was gay."

My mouth falls open and I draw a breath to tell him to stop talking, but Linc cuts me off.

"And you're not?"

"I'm bisexual."

I look between the two of them, my annoyance fading as I wonder whether I'm fast becoming the third wheel. What if they want to hook up? Will I end up with the room to myself? Will I have to find another room? My heart speeds up at the thought, the reaction surprising me. I've never really thought much about two men together, but there's something about the idea of Carter and Linc, skin on skin, that makes my heart beat erratically. At the same time, I realize that despite my denial, part of me expected to have sex with Carter when we returned to the hotel. The idea that it might not happen weighs my stomach with disappointment.

"Judging by your appreciation of Carter's ass," I say, breaking their heated stare. "I'm assuming you're either gay or bi?"

Linc stares at me for a moment, his dark eyes assessing. "I'm neither and both. People's souls—their essence—attracts me. People put so much weight on sex, when they should just see it as what it is: enjoyment and pleasure."

"Is that an enlightened excuse for random hookups?"

Linc laughs. "If you wanted a dessert, would you debate about it? Feel guilty after it?"

"Probably," I admit.

Carter snorts and Linc rolls his eyes.

"You know what I'm getting at. Sex is like the best dessert. It can be decadent and luxurious. It doesn't need to be anything more than that. People ruin perfectly good sex by trying to label it, hooking responsibility and additional meaning to it." He holds my gaze, and I try not to squirm under the intensity of it. "Sex is pleasure. It's fun. Why does it need to be anything more?"

My heart is a steady drumbeat in my chest, echoing

between my thighs. Linc is right. Why am I trying to put so much weight on sleeping with Carter? It isn't like I'll have to marry him afterwards. From the taster I had in the forest, I know it would be great. Why the fuck am I denying myself?

"That's a great philosophy," Carter says, his voice little more than a rumble. "What do you think, Hailee?"

His gaze is fixed on Linc, but he places a hand on my thigh, his thumb stroking slowly. I grip my drink, staring at the ice cubes floating in the dark liquid, hoping I don't fall backwards off my stool. What the fuck is happening? When I raise my eyes, both men are looking at me expectantly.

"Can someone please explain what's going on?" I ask.

"I think," Carter gives a slow, sexy smile, "Linc is asking us whether we want dessert."

12

It honestly wasn't my plan. Of course, I noticed the attractive couple at the bar as soon as I walked into this weird-ass place, but I swear, subtly propositioning them had not been on the cards.

I consider ordering a couple of shots to play catch up, as they're clearly a little looser than I am. Not drunk, but definitely tipsy. Tucking a stray lock of hair behind my ear, my skin tingles with anticipation. Behind us, I know Brenda, John, and the crew will be watching with blatant curiosity. I've been honest with them from the start, and for a bunch of mostly white Americans in their fifties, they are pleasantly open minded. If anything, they've been curious about the concept of pansexuality. John says it sounds like everyone in the sixties and went on to grumble that kids these days act like they invented sex. Even still, they've spent most of our bus trip from Wisconsin to Rapid City trying to get me to explain why I don't have a partner.

There are a few reasons, and two of them are sitting in front of me. Why would I want to settle down, when the world is my oyster, and I'm not done sampling it yet? I'm aware that the sampling comes a little easier for me than most. Carter and Hailee probably wouldn't have accepted such a daring proposition from just anyone.

I know I'm 'gorgeous'. My mom is Sri Lankan, my dad Sicilian, and they signed me up for my first modeling job when I was nine months old. I've grown up with people telling me I'm beautiful; like I'm something to be revered and stared at like a portrait in a gallery. The way Hailee and Carter are eyeing me like I'm a steak? This is my normal.

By the time I was sixteen, I was landing regular shoots with major brands. The fact that I was a pretty successful model worked in my favor in high school, because I was around fourteen when I realized that I was crushing, not only on one of the cheerleaders, but the lacrosse team's male goalkeeper too. No one really cared who I wanted to kiss. Because I was going to be famous.

I down my drink, my heart pounding a little faster as Carter's eyes roam slowly and appreciatively over my body. The last time I hooked up with a guy was about a week ago, right before I joined the tour group. This guy, though. There's something in those ice-blue eyes that makes me nervous in the best way. Even though I usually go for guys a little older than me, it always seems to work out that I end up in charge once we find ourselves alone. Carter looks to be about my age, but my dick is already waking up at the thought of him taking the lead.

Tearing my attention away from him, I look at Hailee. She's watching us with a mix of awe and desire. No fear. I'm relieved. If either of them starts to show the smallest flicker of doubt, I'm out. Doubt, regret, and fear are three ingredients that ruin a dessert.

"What do you think?" I ask. Lifting my hand, I brush my

knuckles against Hailee's collarbone and down her exposed shoulder.

She trembles a little under my touch and licks her lips. My dick shifts at the movement. Hailee has a beautiful mouth. Her lips are plump and pink, and I'm consumed by the thought of tasting them. I drag my attention to her eyes and find her watching me with an awestruck Bambi expression that makes me want to do wicked, wicked things to her. *Fuck.* This could be a lot of fun.

"Sure," she says.

I reach up and tuck her thick curls over her shoulder, tracing fingers down her neck, smiling as her breathing quickens. "I'm not convinced. Tell me what you want."

Her gaze flits to Carter, who's watching her like a starving wolf, then she looks back to me, her eyes a little less wide. "I want dessert."

I smile. "Your place or mine?"

Carter stands and fishes out his wallet, signaling at the stressed-out bartender. "We're just next door."

My gaze snags on the crotch of his dark jeans, his cock visibly straining against the denim. "Good. How much do I owe you for the drinks?"

Carter waves me off with a frown, handing his card over. I'd have gladly paid for all their drinks but paying for people's drinks before you fuck them is a weird balance of etiquette. I stand and give Brenda and John a wave, and they wave back, grinning and giggling like fourth graders. I roll my eyes with a smile and turn back to find Hailee and Carter waiting.

It's colder outside than I expected, which gives us an excuse to hurry a little down the street to their hotel. It's a long, two-story white affair that looks nicer, but older, than where I'm staying. Barbara and John would love it.

We stride purposefully past the front desk, where a very blonde woman looks at us as though she wants to say something, but before she can, we're gone. My blood thrums under my skin in anticipation, and as Hailee digs out a ridiculously large key from her purse, I can't hold back a second longer.

Pressing my palm against Carter's broad, firm, chest, I push him against the wall and kiss him. He stills for a split second, his heart thudding against my splayed hand, but then he claims my mouth like I hoped he would. He tastes of cola, rum and citrus, and my fingers tighten against his skin, gripping his shirt as he strokes my tongue with his. I push my hips forward, pressing against his rock-hard cock, and he groans, sucking my lower lip.

Stepping back, I find Hailee standing by the open door, her big brown eyes wide, and her pupils dilated. My lips curl into a grin. This is one of the reasons I have high hopes for this threesome. Some women love the idea of having two guys, but not two guys together. After a very awkward experience when I was younger, I vowed only to entertain the idea of a threesome if everyone wanted all parties equally. This means threesomes are a rare and wonderful thing; a perfectly crafted chocolate souffle at a Michelin star restaurant.

Reaching out, I take the key from Hailee's limp hand and pass it to Carter, folding her fingers with mine. I lead her into the room and gently cup her face. Those big brown eyes give her such a look of innocence, I'm dying to know just how innocent she really is. I dip my mouth to hers and kiss her softly. She melts under my touch and as I feel her relax, I slide one of my hands to her waist, pulling her closer. Her lips are as soft as they look, and I lose myself in the kiss, enjoying the sensation. I wonder what Carter is doing. The idea of him stroking himself as he watches us has me deepening the kiss and sliding my hands down to her ass. Hailee moans against my mouth, and I open an eye to find Carter standing behind her, his mouth working her neck.

I pull back and watch Carter's hands as they cup Hailee's breasts. She leans her head back against his chest, her eyes closed, and lips parted, and I take a slow breath, calming myself. There's no need to rush this. Dessert is to be savored.

Keeping my eyes on them, I untuck my shirt and tug it off over my head. The movement draws Carter's attention and I watch as he drinks in the sight of me with a wolf-like hunger that has my heart slamming against my chest. Taking my cue, he takes hold of Hailee's top and pulls it up over her head before turning his fingers to his own buttons. I tug Hailee to me and press kisses to her shoulders as I unfasten her bra, letting it fall to the floor. A small gasp leaves her lips as I turn her around, pulling her back against my chest. She arches against me as I roll and stroke her peaked nipples, my lips and tongue caressing her neck.

In front of us, Carter unbuttons his shirt, his chest rising and falling heavily. He's in good shape and clearly hits the gym. His body is firm but not ripped. I like it. A lot.

"Pants off," I demand, locking eyes with him as Hailee leans her head back against my shoulder, her breaths uneven.

Carter swallows, and my eyes narrow as I wonder whether I've judged him wrong. Maybe he isn't as confident as I first thought. *Interesting.* My hands move to the button of Hailee's jeans, and I unfasten them, sliding a hand down beneath the waistband and cupping her over her underwear. She gasps, moving her hips as I flex my fingers.

"Are you wet for us, Hailee?" I ask, tipping her head to look at her.

She moans against me, and I swallow the sound with my mouth before gently taking her chin and turning her to face Carter. His pupils are large and dark in his pale blue eyes, as his gaze flits between Hailee's heaving chest and my hands and fingers. It's as though he doesn't know where to focus his attention.

"Didn't you hear me?" I squeeze Hailee's nipples hard enough to draw a gasp. "Pants off, Carter."

His hands drop to his jeans, flicking open the button, and I watch hungrily as he unzips his fly. He hooks his thumbs in his waistband and pulls down his jeans and underwear, his thick, hard cock slapping against his stomach as it bobs free. I swallow, my mouth salivating at the sight.

"Help Hailee out of hers," I rasp.

Carter toes off his shoes and socks and steps out of his jeans. I wish I could see Hailee's expression as he closes the gap between us, but I can feel her trembling against my chest, her breaths almost like whimpers, and I push my erection against her ass. Carter sinks to his knees and tugs down her jeans and panties, working them down over her feet until she's naked between us.

I lick and nip Hailee's collarbone, my fingers still working her breasts as I watch Carter press kisses to her hips, his hands sliding up between her thighs.

"Is she wet for us, Carter?" I ask. The hoarseness of my voice surprises me, and I swallow, trying to calm my pounding heart.

He reaches between her legs with a groan and Hailee whimpers against me.

"So, fucking wet," he rasps.

Taking Hailee's hand, I lead her over to the nearest bed, pushing her gently until she lies back. I'm torn. I want to dive between her legs and taste her—have her writhe against my mouth—but I also want to watch Carter. My dick is aching to be released, and I bite my lip as I consider my options.

"Pants off," Carter rumbles against my neck.

My heart leaps in surprise as he presses against my back, his hand palming my straining cock through my pants. I gasp at the sensation and feel him smile against my neck as he nips the flesh there. I can't figure him out and my curiosity is adding fuel to the fire igniting my blood.

Carter moves around me and sinks to his knees at the foot of the bed, grabbing Hailee's legs and pulling her to him. I bite my lip hard as he runs his tongue through her folds, and she cries out, arching off the bed. My fingers tremble as I unfasten my pants and shed my final layers. A deep, rumbling groan builds in my chest as I watch Carter feast on Hailee, his fingers stretching her as he flicks his tongue against her clit. I grip my cock, stroking, as my breathing quickens.

Hailee cries out, her hands gripping the bedsheets, as Carter brings her to climax and it takes every ounce of self-control not to quicken the pace of my stroking, my dick already aching for release.

Carter gets to his feet, his lips glistening, and I pull him to me, attacking his mouth with a kiss that is in no way gentle. I lick and suck the taste of her from him, and he grips me tight against his chest, trapping our dicks between us. Bucking my hips a little, desperate for friction, he moans against my mouth. I can't think straight. My head is spinning, I want them both so badly.

Carter breaks the kiss, his eyes wild. He turns to look at Hailee, who's kneeling on the bed watching us hungrily. She reaches for me, and I let her pull my face to hers. I sink into her kiss, my fingers tracing her soft golden flesh until they find their way between her legs. She whimpers, her hands exploring my body as I slide two fingers inside her. I open an eye to see what Carter is up to, and my heart stumbles as I find him on his knees in front of me, his eager gaze focused on my straining cock.

13

It's too much. Never has the phrase 'you can't have your cake and eat it too' felt truer. Linc's body is insane. He's ripped in the way you only ever see in magazines, complete with the vee of muscle that frames the path to his long, hard cock. I feel like a kid at an amusement park with not enough time to go on all the rides. I want to fuck Hailee so badly it hurts, but I also want to lay Linc down and lick my way between his abs before letting him claim my ass.

Kneeling on the floor before him, I take hold of his cock, smearing the bead of precum with my thumb. It's a beautiful fucking cock. I look up and find him watching me, his breathing ragged and his eyes hungry. On her knees on the bed, Hailee leans against Linc, her eyes half closed as he fucks her with his fingers. Holding his gaze, I take his cock in my mouth, swirling my tongue around the head, and he groans, his free hand fisting my hair. I close my eyes and swallow him deep, grabbing his ass as he bucks his hips, fucking my mouth in a gentle rhythm. I know he's holding back because this isn't the end game, so after a minute, I pull off him, running my tongue along his length one more time before reaching for my discarded pants.

Digging in the pockets, I pull out one of the condoms I bought at the dispenser in the men's room at the bar and tear it open. I slide it onto Linc's cock, and he raises his eyebrows in question as I get to my feet. My heart is hammering so hard I think I might pass out. I've never experienced anything like this, and part of me wonders if perhaps it's all an elaborate dream. Maybe I've fallen asleep in the backseat of Christiano's car and none of this has happened.

Linc watches me, his eyes slightly narrowed, as if he's trying to figure me out. I almost wish him luck. I'm still trying myself. Perhaps after years of being submissive with Andrew, I've learnt a thing or two. Both Linc and Hailee seem to like it when I take charge, so I push down my nerves and do what I want to.

With one hand working Linc's cock with firm strokes, I slide my other hand into Hailee's curls and pull her to me, claiming her mouth. She wraps her arms around me, her fingers gripping my hair, and I groan, tugging her lip between my teeth. Stepping back, I climb onto the bed, kneeling at one end.

"On all fours, Hailee," I command. "Facing me."

Her eyes widen as she realizes what I have planned, but then she places her hands on the bed and raises her glorious, supple ass in the air. My knees are weak with want, and I swallow hard as Linc climbs up on the bed behind her, his fingers smoothing over her curves.

Hailee's hand grips around the base of my cock, and I watch, hardly breathing, as she runs her tongue along my length. When she slips me between her plump lips, my eyes drift shut, and I exhale with pleasure. My hand grabs a fistful of curls to steady myself and it takes all my self-control not to push deeper into her mouth.

I open my eyes, my breathing heavy with want, to find Linc's gaze fixed on Hailee as her head bobs on my dick. Linc grips his cock with one hand, his other on her hip as he lines himself up. His dark eyes lift to meet mine at the same time he pushes into her, and Hailee's moan vibrates against my dick. I gasp, reaching back and gripping hold of the headboard to steady myself. Linc pulls out a little, then slams back in, causing Hailee to whimper, sucking me harder.

Every inch of me is burning with desire. I grip Hailee's soft curls, trying to stay still as Linc sets a relentless pace that soon has her choking on my dick.

"Are you okay?" I murmur, stroking her chin.

She pulls off me, panting and whimpering. "Yes."

Linc slows, but Hailee pushes back against him, causing him to breathe in sharply.

"Don't stop," she moans, taking me into her mouth again.

Linc reaches around, fingering her clit as he thrusts into her, and I watch, mesmerized by the way Hailee's soft flesh ripples with the movement. My gaze drags along Linc's taut skin, glistening with sweat, the sight of his coated cock sliding into her, and I swallow hard. The room is filled with the sound of skin on skin, whimpers and moans, and I feel as though I could die from the sensory overload. Nothing should feel this good.

Hailee's whimpering increases as she reaches the edge and I feel myself going too.

"I'm going to come," I grind out.

I let go of her hair in case she wants to pull off me, but she reaches up and cups my ass, her nails digging into my flesh as I empty into her mouth with a shuddering groan. When Hailee pulls off me, Linc picks up the pace of his thrusts as his fingers tip her over the edge. I watch, transfixed, as he chases his own release, his muscles clenching and his eyes screwing shut. I wish I was close enough to lick the sweat from his straining throat as he throws back his head with a deep groan.

When he stills, I scoop Hailee's boneless body up against my chest, brushing a damp curl from her cheek.

"That was fucking incredible," I whisper.

She mumbles in agreement, her arms wrapping loosely around my waist. Linc pushes stray strands of soaked hair from his face and winks at me before heading to the bathroom to get rid of the condom.

"Are you okay?" I ask.

Hailee pulls back enough to look me in the eyes and smiles. "More than okay."

I grin and kiss her, tasting myself on her tongue.

"Where's Linc?" she asks.

"Here," he answers, heading for his clothes.

"Whoa, there," Hailee says, reaching for him. "Do you have somewhere you need to be?"

Linc pauses, then smiles and steps toward her outstretched hand. I grin as she pulls him to her, pressing her lips to his. He instantly deepens the kiss and, despite its recent release, my dick twitches at the sight of him tasting me on her tongue. Linc reaches for me, his hand gripping my shoulder and moving up to my neck. I turned my head and grip his hand, pressing a kiss to his palm.

"Right," I say. "Off the bed."

Hailee and Linc pull apart, matching looks of bemusement on their faces, but do as they're told. I climb off and walk to the other bed, pushing the two together. Despite the carpet, it makes a racket that causes me to grimace.

"Doris isn't going to like that," Linc says, watching me with a smirk.

"Doris?" Hailee asks.

"The woman at the front desk. She looks like a Doris."

Stepping back, I admire my handiwork, before pulling down the sheets and climbing in. Hailee giggles and climbs in beside me, but Linc watches, indecision on his beautiful face.

"Don't tell me I almost put my back out for nothing," I say.

"It's not that," Linc says. "It's just—"

"You don't have to stay the night," I interrupt. "Just chill with us for a bit."

Linc shakes his head, a smile ghosting across his lips, and climbs in on Hailee's other side. I exhale a quiet sigh of relief, and I hope it isn't obvious. Just as I desperately grasped at the chance to keep Hailee longer than I should have, I wasn't ready to let this god of a man out of my life. Not yet.

14

MOVEMENT WAKES ME, AND I GROAN, THE LIGHT MORE THAN bright enough as it filters beneath the heavy cream curtains.

"Here."

I push up onto an elbow, my head throbbing, as a glass of cold water is pressed into my hand. Looking up, I find Linc fully dressed and standing over me. My stomach flipflops as the night comes back to me. I had a threesome. A fucking threesome. I realize a second later that I'm still completely naked, and I'm pretty sure I can feel Carter, hard against my ass. A quick check over my shoulder tells me he's still fast asleep.

"Don't," Linc says.

I sit up and take a sip of water, clutching the covers to my chest. "Don't what?"

"Spiral," he says. "It's just the hangover. Last night was fantastic."

I exhale. It had been unbelievable. I watch Linc as he reties his hair and I wish I'd seen it when it was loose. The alcohol hadn't exaggerated his looks. In the cold, sober, light of day, he's still stunning. My heart dips to my stomach at the memory of his sculpted body. This absolute god of a man fucked me last night. Hard. I swallow.

"It was pretty incredible," I say. "Thanks."

Linc laughs, the action lighting his dark eyes. "You don't need to thank me. That was the hottest threesome I've had in years."

I raise an eyebrow. *Years?* "So, what? Your journey across the country is some sort of... sexpedition?"

"Sexpedition?" Linc laughs loud enough that Carter stirs behind me with a groan. "That's brilliant. I'm using that. No. It's not. Instigating threesomes with strangers is not my go to move."

A small part of me purrs at that, and my grumpy, hungover internal voice punches it in the face.

"I've got to go," Linc says, stepping closer. "My phone died, and I need to get back to the bus or they'll leave without me. Even though they party hard, they're still early risers."

I grin at the thought of the khaki-clad group drinking until the early hours. "Where to next?"

Linc shrugs. "I think the next stop is Yellowstone. Eventually I'm hoping to get to San Francisco."

Carter groans and pushes up onto his elbows behind me. I pass him the glass of water and he takes it with a wince, downing it in one go.

"You sneaking off?" he asks, rubbing a hand over his face.

"Not sneaking," Linc says. "Clearly, or neither of you would have woken up."

I reach out and touch Linc's hand. "If you miss your bus, let us know and we'll give you a ride to catch up to them. I'd hate it if you got left behind because of us."

"If I do, it was worth it."

He leans down and presses a gentle kiss to my lips. All too soon, he pulls away and leans across me to kiss Carter.

"I hope the rest of your road trip goes well," he says, backing towards the door.

I smile, although my heart hangs heavy in my chest at the sight of him retreating. "You too," I offer, hating how no words I could say would feel right.

Carter stays silent behind me, and as the door closes, I turn to him. The disappointed look on his face has me reaching for his cheek. He closes his eyes and leans into my palm.

"You okay?" I ask.

He gives a halfhearted shrug. "He was really nice."

"Yeah." I sigh. "He was."

"It felt right, you know?" Carter says, opening his eyes. "Like, I thought it would feel super awkward afterwards, but it didn't."

I chew my lip as I consider his words. Although my stomach rolled a little as the night came back to me, I don't feel regret. Even as Brent's disgusted sneer crawls its way into my brain, it's not enough to make me want to take back what happened.

"Hey," Carter murmurs, reaching for me. "Are *you* okay?"

"Same as you, I think. A little sad that he left, but I know he had to."

Carter trails his fingers up my leg and across my hip, circling my stomach. "What about us? Are we still friends?"

My breathing quickens as his fingers trail higher, brushing the underneath of my breasts. "Yes."

"Good," he says, bending his head and pressing a kiss to my shoulder. "I like being friends with you."

His touch wakes me, my body aching for more, and I

brazenly reach across and take hold of his hard length, causing his jaw to clench. "I can tell."

Carter leans to kiss me, but I duck backwards.

"Morning breath," I explain. "I must stink."

"I don't care," he says, taking one of my breasts in his hand and circling my nipple with his thumb. Then he pauses, frowning. "Wait. Is mine really bad?"

Before I can answer, he pulls back the covers and gets out of bed, striding to the bathroom. I watch in bemusement, taking the opportunity to admire him. He looks great naked. His body isn't as defined as Linc's, but it's firm and hard and he has a great ass. He has a faint smattering of hair on his chest that leads down to his . . . I feel my cheeks heat as I watch his erection bob with each determined stride. Although he's gone down on me twice, and I gave him a blowjob last night, we haven't actually had sex yet, and the thought has my thighs clenching in anticipation.

"Are you brushing your teeth?" I call.

"Yep."

"Well, then let me use the bathroom while you do it."

Carter steps back into the room, his toothbrush already in his mouth.

I slip out of bed, my face heating as he slows his brushing to watch as I walk past him to the bathroom.

"Thirty seconds," he says around his toothbrush.

I roll my eyes, but the hunger in his eyes and the command in his voice has my heart thundering. It takes me twenty-three seconds, and as soon as I open the door, Carter chucks his toothbrush to the floor and scoops me up in his arms. I squeal as he carries me back to the bed. As soon as my head hits the pillow, he slides a hand behind me, gripping my neck as he claims my mouth. His minty tongue sweeps my mouth with an urgency that has me arching against him, desperate for his touch.

Climbing on top of me, he trails a hand down my body, his fingers squeezing my hips and ass so hard it draws a whimper from my lips. He pulls back, his wintery eyes wild as he moves down my body, his mouth nipping, licking and sucking at my breasts. The mint has my nipples painfully hard against the morning air and Carter flicks them with his tongue until my hips buck beneath him, begging for him to fill me.

"Please," I whimper. "I need you."

In answer, he slides a hand down between my legs, stroking fingers between my folds and I throw my head back, grinding my hips against the movement.

"Carter." I gasp, inhaling sharply as he tugs a nipple between his teeth at the same time he flicks his thumb against my clit. "Fuck me. Please."

Carter stills, his throat bobbing as he holds himself over me. Before I can ask if something's wrong, he rolls off me, searching for the pants he abandoned last night. He holds up a condom and tears it open, but there's something in his expression as he rolls it on that makes me push myself up onto my elbows, my eyes narrowed.

"Carter? What's wrong?"

His gaze snaps to mine. "Nothing."

"Are you sure? We don't have to—"

He drops over me, stealing my words with his lips and tongue, kissing me until I'm breathless. Only then does he lift himself up just enough to look at me.

"You have no idea how badly I want this," he says, pressing a soft kiss to my lips. "I've wanted this since the moment I sat down beside you in that bar."

He kisses me again as he settles between my hips,

nudging at my entrance. I slide my hands into his hair, lifting my hips as my heart thunders against his. His ice-blue eyes hold mine as he pushes tantalizingly slowly inside me, and I whimper, arching into the movement, guiding him deeper.

Carter drops his forehead to mine, his eyes fluttering closed, and he pulls out before thrusting back in. I lift my legs, wrapping them around his hips and tug his lower lip with my teeth.

"Harder," I murmur.

A low groan vibrates in Carter's chest, and his eyes fly open. Shifting his weight onto one arm, he reaches down with the other and hooks it around my leg.

I cry out as he slams into me, hard and fast, the muscles in his neck straining as he clenches his jaw. The animalistic way he claims me has me writhing and grinding against him in a frenzy. He sets a relentless pace, alternating between pounding into me so hard it shifts us up the bed and grinding against my clit. My whimpers grow frantic, my fingers clawing at his shoulders as he pushes me closer to the edge. His name flies from my lips as I tense around him, waves of pleasure flooding my body. Carter presses his mouth to my neck, picking up the pace as he chases his own release, but then his teeth close over my flesh as he trembles with a soft groan, his body stilling.

The room fills with the sound of our labored breathing, and I run my fingers up and down his heated back. I'm not sure if it's just the afterglow from the orgasm, but everything feels so wonderfully right. The way he fits around me—in me. The weight of his body on mine. I inhale his scent, and even the faint hint of sweat calls to me on some primal level. It feels like we've clicked. But even as I wrestle with the thought, Linc's face rises to the surface. It should have felt uncomfortable, being that intimate with a stranger. Carter might be barely more than a stranger, but I spent all of an hour with Linc before inviting him into my bed. It doesn't feel strange though, and the thought that I'll never see him again causes my heart to clench with sadness.

As much as I enjoyed every second of Linc's luscious mouth, clever, long fingers, and impressively large length, I equally enjoyed watching Carter with him. Watching Linc push him up against the wall had sent a jolt of heat straight between my thighs. And the sight of Carter on his knees with Linc's cock in his mouth . . . I bite my lip, my heart racing.

"Hailee," Carter says against my shoulder, pulling me from my thoughts. "You . . ."

I place my hands on his chest, pushing him up a little so I can see his face. "What?"

His eyes scrunch shut for a second, then he pulls out of me and presses a kiss to my lips. "You're fucking incredible."

I laugh. "All I did was lie here."

He huffs in response, nudging my nose with his. "I'm getting in the shower. Want to join me?"

"Yes, but I'm not going to. I'm not washing my hair this morning. It's a whole thing and we don't have time. Check out is in like half an hour."

Carter frowns, raising his hand to look at his watch. "How the fuck is it that late?"

I grip his face and kiss him before pushing him away again. "Hurry up. I still want a shower, just not the kind of shower you're suggesting."

He rolls out of bed, a look of mock hurt on his face. "Are you suggesting I won't be able to keep my hands off you?"

I raise my eyebrows and he laughs.

"Yeah, there's no chance I'd be able to keep my hands to myself."

The laugh fades from his lips as he stares at me, lying naked on the bed, his eyes travelling the length of my body and back up again. I try not to squirm under his gaze.

"It's a good thing that was the last condom," he says, backing towards the bathroom. "Doris downstairs would be breaking the door down to kick us out."

I grin and throw a pillow at him. "Hurry up!"

15

I'M A FUCKING IDIOT. WHEN I GOT BACK TO THE HOTEL, Barbara and John were herding everyone onto the bus. I had enough time. I could have gone back to my room, grabbed my bag, and I even know that they would have waited long enough for me to change my clothes. But I didn't. Instead, I gave them both a hug and told them I might catch up to them up later.

Sinking down onto the pavement, I stare at the disappointing yellow slither of battery on my phone. It charged a little while I showered and changed, but then I had to check out. Why didn't I get on the bus? I squeeze the bridge of my nose, my gut churning. I know why. And that's exactly why I'm an idiot.

Last night was immense. I've had more sex than a twenty-three-year-old probably should have, but I've never connected so much with two people in such a short space of time. Hailee and Carter intrigue me. We chatted a little before we fell asleep, but I still know almost nothing about them. That's the biggest mind fuck. I fall asleep occasionally after sex, but not like whatever last night was. I never stick around and *cuddle* after sex. Hailee had lain on my chest, her fingers tracing small soothing circles, while Carter slung an arm over us both, holding my other hand. It had felt . . . Nice. So, fucking nice.

Usually, the last thing I want to do is get to know the people I take to bed. I mean, why bother? I learned from a very early age that beautiful people make other people feel special. My mom used to say that being around me is like being in the sun. I was sixteen when I realized that when you're the sun, no one really cares what you want or how you feel, they only want to bask in your glow. Hailee and Carter took me up on my offer for that very reason. They're probably halfway to their next destination by now, laughing about what a great one night stand it was. I'm nothing more than a fun story to tell friends about when they get drunk. My eyes burn.

This is why I tagged along with Barbara and John. No one in that tour group wanted to sleep with me or befriend me on Instagram. No one wanted selfies. They were almost all older than my parents and treated me like a son or nephew, taking me under their wing. It had been so refreshing to talk to people, knowing they didn't want anything in return. And now, I've given it up. For what?

Blowing out a long sigh, I swipe at my screen. I need to decide where I'm going next and how to get there. Common sense tells me to get to an airport and take a flight straight to San Francisco. I don't want to, though. If I do that, this small pause in my life is over. I mentally kick myself again for not going with Barbara and John.

When a car slows, pulling near to the curb, I shuffle back, frowning at the exhaust fumes as I swipe through my apps.

"Linc?"

My head snaps up to find Hailee peering down at me from the passenger side of a silver sedan. I stare, speechless.

"Did you miss your bus?" Carter calls, leaning across from the driver's side.

"Yeah," I lie.

Hailee points her thumb at the back seat. "Get in. We'll give you a ride."

My heart hammers in my throat as I glance between my suitcase and their car. Isn't this what I wanted? Well, not quite. They're just giving me a ride. I'll catch up with the tour group and things will be back to normal. I swallow down the bitter taste of reality and get to my feet.

"Sure. Thanks."

Opening the door, I go to get in, but three massive bags take up most of the back seat. I stare at them for a second, before closing the door to try on the other side.

"Shit," Hailee says, unfastening her seatbelt. "Sorry."

She opens her door and walks around to pop the trunk. I watch, still a little bewildered, as she starts to lug one of the massive bags out. It's only as she grunts with the effort that I snap out of my daze.

"Here, let me," I say, grabbing hold of one end.

Another bag is already in the trunk, which I assume is Carter's. Once the other bags are added, there's barely any room, so I heave my small suitcase into the back with me.

"We were just going to go for breakfast," Carter says, locking eyes with me in the rearview mirror. "You want to come? Or are you in a rush?"

"Sure," I say, trying not to read too much into the way my mouth goes dry under his intense icy gaze. I swallow, remembering him on his knees, those same blue eyes darkened with lust as he took me in his mouth.

"Did you say the bus was heading to Yellowstone?" Hailee asks, turning around to look at me.

Her expression is so warm and trusting. My gaze flicks to her full lips and I look away with a noncommittal shrug. "I think so. Their end destination was Seattle, and there were a lot of stops on the way. I wasn't sure how long I was going to stay with them, so I just took each day as it came."

"Do you have a number for any of them?" Carter asks. "We were planning on heading to Denver after this, but we can take you as far as we can."

"Just a regular bus station is fine," I say. "I really appreciate the ride, thank you."

"Are you sure?" Carter asks. "I'm sure we can catch up to them."

I shake my head. "No, it's fine. I probably overstayed my welcome with that crowd, anyway."

Hailee turns around again, laughter dancing in her eyes. "It looked like they all adored you."

"How about here?" Carter says, slowing the car.

He pulls into the gravel parking lot of an old-fashioned diner. It's pretty empty, but I suppose it's a weekday and late for breakfast but too early for dinner.

"Looks good to me," Hailee says.

The diner is a mass of turquoise and red leather, complete with little jukeboxes on each table. There are only three other people, so we have our pick of the booths. Carter slides onto one side and I the other, expecting Hailee to sit next to Carter. Instead, she slides in next to me. She looks gorgeous in a different way to last night. Last night, she was sexy in her tight jeans. Today, dressed in white denim shorts and a loose-fitting pink t-shirt, she looks like summer personified—pure joy. I smile at her, and she grins back, blushing a little under my appreciative stare.

A waitress comes over, brandishing a coffee pot, and handed us large, sticky menus.

"Mornin' folks. My name's Sheila, and I'll be your server today. Coffee?"

We all mumble a chorused 'yes please,' which has Hailee giggling.

As soon as she has her filled coffee mug in her hands, she inhales with a groan. "Is there anything better than freshly brewed coffee?"

Carter and I catch each other's eye, and I find my mouth curving into a smile.

"I can think of several things," Carter says. "Shall I list them?"

Hailee rolls her eyes. "Oh, my god. Get your mind out of the gutter, I haven't even eaten breakfast yet."

"Fuck it," Carter says, smacking his menu down on the table. "I'm having pancakes."

I glance at Hailee, who's still studying the menu, her eyes narrowed and her teeth tugging her bottom lip. What is it about her that makes me want to touch her? I press my hands between my legs to stop myself from pulling her to me and kissing the top of her head.

"You ready to order?" Sheila asks, appearing with her pen and notepad poised.

Hailee waves her hand in Carter's direction, still focused on the menu.

"I'm going to have the house pancakes," Carter says. "Bacon, extra crispy please."

"Okay," Hailee says slowly. "I'll have the tuna melt please, with a side of fries."

"For breakfast?" Carter scoffs.

"I'll have the fruit salad please." I smile as I hand the menu back, and despite looking as though she might be in her late forties, her cheeks color pink as she collects the remaining menus and hurries to the kitchen to hand in our order.

"Okay," Carter says, looking between us. "Explain the food choices. A tuna melt? Seriously?"

"I'm hungover," Hailee hisses. "Someone thought it was a good idea to drink copious amounts of cocktails last night."

Carter barks a laugh. "Yes. You!"

Hailee wrinkles her nose and turns to me. "I guess you didn't drink as much. Are you feeling okay this morning?"

I notice the way she shyly drops her gaze, and I almost reach for her, but stop myself. "Yeah. I'm fine."

"What's with the fruit salad?" Carter presses. "Are you vegetarian? Vegan?"

"When I'm on the road, it's rare I manage to get to a gym." I gesture at my torso. "You don't maintain a physique like this with waffles."

Carter blinks, his gaze dropping to my chest as though he can see right through my sand-colored t-shirt. Then his face falls into a frown. "Why do I feel like those pancakes aren't going to taste nearly as good now?"

Hailee laughs. "You want pancakes, you eat pancakes."

"I'm sorry," I say. "I wasn't trying to be a dick, it's just the truth. Besides, you've got a great body."

A flush creeps over Carter's face, and I find myself grinning. He looks sexy as hell today in a fitted dark blue t-shirt and grey shorts. I let my gaze linger, enjoying the way his bicep flexes as he lifts his coffee.

"So, will you just head straight to San Francisco if we take you to the bus station?" Hailee asks, peering at me over her mug of coffee.

"I guess so. I mean, I'm not in any rush, but it probably

makes sense to just head there. How come you guys are heading to Denver?"

Carter looks at Hailee, who shrinks a little into the seat, her hands clasping the coffee mug like a lifeline. Before I can stop myself, I reach out and touch her arm.

"You don't have to tell me if you don't want to."

She shakes her head, her curls sliding over her shoulders. "It's fine. It's just . . . I'm still trying to figure it all out."

Hailee places her mug down on the table and places a hand over mine. I tense, thinking she's going to move it, but instead she links our fingers. The simple action lifts a chunk of weight from my shoulders, and I try not to stare at her delicate digits, dwarfed by mine.

"I'm kind of on the run."

Her big brown eyes flick up to mine and I raise my eyebrows in response.

"Not like, from the law or anything," she clarifies. "Well. Sort of."

"Wait, what?" Carter asks, leaning across the table. "What does 'sort of' mean?"

She winces and I squeeze her fingers. "Hailee?"

"My ex, Brent, he's a cop," she explains. "He's not a nice person, and after five years, I finally had enough. So, I left."

My mind flits to the three large bags in the trunk of her car. This isn't a vacation.

"So, you didn't actually break up with him?" I clarify. "You just packed your stuff and left?"

Hailee hangs her head, her curls shielding her face, and I let go of her hand, reaching around her shoulder and pulling her to me instead.

"It's okay," I say. "I'm not judging. I'm just trying to get the whole picture."

Carter reaches across the table and peels her hand from

her mug, linking his fingers with hers. "Has he tried to contact you since you left?"

Hailee shakes her head. "I blocked him on everything I could think of."

My heart aches in my chest. The guy must have been a monster for her to have had to pack up her life and run away without a word. Before I can form my next question, Sheila returns and places our food in front of us. She casts a questioning glance at where Hailee is curled up against my chest, but I give her a small nod to let her know everything is okay and she leaves.

"You know, you can tell us as much as you want to," Carter says. "We won't push."

His words have my gaze snapping to his. He doesn't know the full story either. My mind buzzes with curiosity. It seems it's not just me who's been sucked into this strange orbit. I press a kiss to the top of Hailee's head, expecting it to feel weird, but all it does is cause her to grip me tighter.

"There's this woman that works at the grocery store with me," Hailee says, her voice small. "She always seemed so sad and quiet, so everyone kind of left her alone. Then one day, I found her crying in the storeroom. We got talking and she said that she'd been suffering from depression for a while. Her friends coaxed her into seeing a therapist and after a few sessions, the therapist had suggested that she was in an abusive relationship."

Hailee draws a shaky breath, and my arm tightens around her shoulders, my fingers stroking her upper arm. I don't like where this is going, and my jaw ticks at the possibilities.

"I'd met her husband before," Hailee continues. "He picked her up most days. He seemed so nice. Kelly, the woman, told me she was leaving him, but she was scared. I couldn't get much out of her, but once she'd stopped crying, she gave me a leaflet that her therapist had given her.

"It was like every word had been written to describe mine and Brent's relationship. Mental and emotional abuse. He was all smiles and laughter, but the layer underneath was poison; sugarcoated so no one saw. Apparently, not even me."

She sits up out of my embrace and pulls her hand away from Carter. He keeps his hand out on the table, his brow creased with concern that I'm certain mirrors my own.

"He would call me names and make me feel stupid. He'd pick me to pieces, and if I ever told him to stop, he'd remind me that everything I had was because of him. But he'd taken everything without me even realizing. I had no friends. No one to turn to but him."

My fingers tighten into fists, and I realize my breathing has quickened. I want to wring this guy's neck.

"Anyway," she says, taking a breath and straightening. "Long story short, I left. I have a sister in Las Vegas, so I'm going to go and stay with her."

I share a look with Carter. There's so much more to that story, but it's clear she isn't ready to share. The thought of some fuckwit calling Hailee names and making her feel anything less than the beautiful, funny woman she is, has me seeing red. The intensity of my anger takes me by surprise.

"So, Las Vegas?" I say with an exhale, trying to calm the flames of rage in my chest. "You been before?"

Hailee shakes her head. "I've never really left Chicago until this trip."

"And you're headed to Vegas too?" I ask Carter.

He gives a tight smile, his concerned gaze still on Hailee. "Yeah. It was a weird coincidence."

"So, what's your story?" I ask him.

His blue eyes snap to mine, but I can't read the emotion in their icy depths.

"Honestly?" he says, sitting back and running a hand through his messy, dark brown hair. "It's a similar situation. I'm running away from a bad relationship too. Although, I told him I was leaving before I did."

"I take it you're not running from anyone?" Hailee says, giving me a sad smile.

I shake my head. "Not a person, no. In fact, I've never really been in a relationship."

My own confession takes me by surprise. It's not that I haven't wanted a relationship. It's just that my job takes me all over the world, and when you're surrounded by horny models all day, why would you settle down? I know there's a layer deeper than that, though. I've never trusted anyone enough. There was a female model eighteen months ago who I almost tried with. We'd been sort of seeing each other, but then I figured out that she was only dating me because of the media attention it got. She gained fifty thousand Instagram followers in the time we spent together. It hurt enough that I was in no rush to try again.

Fingers curl around the hand I'm gripping my coffee mug with, and I find Carter watching me with the same concerned look he gave Hailee. Fingers grip my other hand as Hailee links her fingers with mine.

My chest tightens. What is it with these two? Why do they look like they actually care about me when they barely know me?

"You know," Hailee says, looking shyly up at me through her long dark lashes. "If you're not in a rush to get to San Francisco, you could join us. We can get you as far as Vegas."

I stare at her. Every internal thought is screaming yes,

but I stomp the voices down, casting a glance at Carter. He gives me a warm smile that looks hopeful.

"You don't know me," I say carefully. "I could be an axe murderer."

Carter snorts. "It must be a very small axe. We've seen your little suitcase."

"Are you an axe murderer?" Hailee asks. "I mean, if you are, you kind of missed your opportunity last night when we were asleep."

"No. I'm not." I smile and shake my head, internally cursing the excited beating of my heart. "And, if you're sure it's okay, I'd love to join your road trip."

Hailee and Carter beam at me in a way that has my own happiness lighting my face. They let go of my hands with a squeeze and we wordlessly dig into our food. I have no idea what I'm getting myself into, but I haven't felt this excited about something in a long time.

16

My attention flits between Linc and Hailee as they eat. I want to know more about Hailee's asshole ex-boyfriend, and questions push and pull against my tongue. I can tell she found it hard to tell us about it, so I won't push, but it doesn't stop the anger from bubbling beneath my skin. How could anyone be anything other than nice to Hailee? She's the sweetest person I've ever met. Just the thought of someone purposely filling those beautiful copper-flecked eyes with sadness has my blood boiling.

My eyes turn to Linc, who devoured his fruit salad in seconds and is on his third coffee. I'd still been half asleep when he left this morning, and part of me had wondered whether he was actually as good looking as I remembered. Now, in the cold light of day, if anything, he's better looking than I remember. His thick, dark hair is tied back like it was last night, looking soft and shiny in a way that makes me want to thread my fingers through it. His eyelashes are long and brush his razor-sharp cheekbones when he blinks. I shake my head, trying to snap myself out of it before he notices me ogling.

Relief flooded my chest when Hailee invited him to join us. I'd wanted to, but it isn't my trip. It took a lot of coaxing to convince Hailee to let me drive this morning, and even then, she only agreed on the proviso that we'd swap after a couple of hours.

I watch, chewing on a satisfying mouthful of bacon and pancakes, as Linc stares out of the window at the sporadic traffic. Every time I look at him, my heart does a painful leap at the memory of kneeling before him, his huge cock hitting the back of my throat. I let my gaze trail down over his broad, muscled shoulders, admiring the way his t-shirt stretches across his chest and around the tops of his arms. My attention settles on the veins trailing down his forearms, the skin so smooth it makes me want to run my fingers along it. My chewing slows as I replay the image of him slamming into Hailee while she swallowed down my release. I shift slightly in my seat, my balls tingling. God, she felt incredible this morning. We fit together so perfectly and effortlessly.

I almost chickened out. The very thought is ridiculous. But that's what Andrew has done to me. Sex was both a reward and a punishment to him. In the beginning, if I did something that particularly pleased him, he'd suck me off. That hadn't happened in over eighteen months. My mind circles back to Hailee's plump lips around my cock, the swirl of her tongue . . .

"Carter?"

I blink to find Hailee looking at me questioningly. "Sorry, what?"

"I was asking what you think about Yellowstone?"

It takes me a full five seconds to pull my head out of the lust-filled corner it's buried itself in and try to remember what words are.

"The National Park? Why?"

Hailee glances at Linc with a smile. "Well, I chose to go via Denver because it was the quickest route, but if no one is in a big rush, we could add an extra day or two on and take in some more sights."

"I mean, I'm sure Denver is lovely," Linc says, his dark brown eyes teasing. "But I have a feeling Yellowstone might be a little more scenic."

My heart rate quickens as I realize what they're really asking. Would it be okay to extend our trip—to spend more time together?

"Sounds good to me," I say. "I've got time."

"Carter's a teacher," Hailee explains. "When does school start back for you?"

"Not for another three weeks or so."

It's technically true. The school I quit in June will start back in August. Just without me.

Linc pulls out his phone and opens a map app. I note that his phone is the latest model. His suitcase is a designer brand too. He's avoided telling us what he does for a living, but it's clear he isn't short of cash. Even though his clothes don't appear to be labelled, the quality is obvious. Maybe he's one of those trust fund kids. He looks around our age, but we haven't asked. Well, if the trip is being extended, it'll give us plenty of time to get to know him.

"It's seven hours' drive from here to Yellowstone," Linc says, frowning at the screen.

"Pick a nearby town," Hailee says. "We'll stay the night there and then get up early and go explore the park tomorrow."

Linc puts the phone down on the table between us and zooms in on the map. I lean forward, staring at the mass of green.

"What about that one?" I point at a dot on the screen. "Cody."

Hailee nods. "Looks good to me."

I sit back in the booth and down the dregs of my coffee. "Sounds like we have a plan."

"Before we get back on the road," Linc says, pocketing his phone. "It might be a good idea to discuss how this is going to work."

My breath halts in my throat. He's really just going to go there.

"Well, Carter's going to drive first," Hailee says, completely missing the point. "Can you drive? We could do two-hour shifts."

Linc catches my eye, his mouth tilting in a lopsided grin. "Sure. That does sound like a plan. It's not what I was talking about, though."

Hailee looks between us, and I watch with a smile as her gorgeous eyes widen.

"We had a chat yesterday," I offer. "We said that we'd take things as they come and try not to worry. Above everything else, we're friends first."

Linc nods. "That sounds good to me. It's a little different with three people though."

I can practically feel Hailee's skin burning from across the table, and I long to put her out of her misery, but Linc's right. It's a good idea to sort this out before we hit the road. It's either now, or in six hours when we check into a hotel. I think of how she struggled with the decision of what to do with me when we were in the woods. This discussion is probably tying her in knots. I reach across the table for her hand.

"I know this is weird to talk about," I say. "It's an unusual situation, but we're going to be spending a lot of time together, so it's better in the long run if we iron out some ground rules."

Hailee struggles to meet my eye and I can see the worry burning there. If we aren't careful, she'll end up leaving us here. I grip her hand with both of mine, rubbing with my thumbs.

"Option one is we just do this as friends. We had a lot of fun together, but nothing has to happen again." I pause glancing at Linc, who smiles encouragingly. "Option two is we . . ."

My nerve fades and I find my own skin heating. What *is* option two?

Linc reaches over and places his hand on top of ours. "Can I make a suggestion? I agree with the first option, and it's definitely on the table, but if we want to move forward on this trip as more than friends, we need to be realistic."

I swallow as Linc squeezes our hands. He could suggest anything, and I'll be down for it. A huge part of me is worried that Hailee is going to say we should just be friends. I know I told her it's an option, but I'm not sure it is. Not really.

"What do you mean?" Hailee asks.

Linc runs his long fingers over the backs of our hands, leaning closer. "I mean, I find both of you extremely attractive. We need to decide whether this is an 'only when it's all three of us' situation, or we can be together separately too."

Hailee's gaze drops to the table, and although my own stomach somersaults at Linc's words, I can't help but grin at her embarassment.

"I mean," he continues, "I'm assuming you two had sex this morning after I left. I don't have an issue with that happening again, but we all need to be okay with it."

Hailee's face falls into a frown as she considers the

options. I stare at our joined hands, waiting. Being together, all three of us, would be great, but I really like the idea of being able to have them all to myself too. Of course, that means that at some point it might be just the two of them, without me. Would I be okay with that? My mind reels at the idea that this is a conversation I'm actually having.

"I think it's unrealistic to only be together as a three," Hailee says carefully. "If you two were together without me, I don't think I'd be jealous, as long as you were honest about it. And you'd have to promise to tell me if you decided you only wanted each other. I don't want to be some pity fuck that hangs on and outstays their welcome."

My eyes widen and I open my mouth to speak, but before I can utter a word, Linc takes her face in his hands and kisses her.

"You could never be a 'pity fuck'," he says, brushing a soft kiss against her nose. "You're right though. Honesty is vital. Even if it hurts."

"I can do honest," I say, trying not to cringe at the half truth. "So, are we doing this?"

Hailee gives me a small, nervous smile. "I guess so."

Linc kisses Hailee again and I wait for the jealousy to kick in, but it's like my brain can't pick a side. Who am I jealous of? I want to kiss both of them. That said, I have to remind myself that we aren't on the East Coast anymore. Leaning across the table and launching myself at Linc might end up in us getting kicked out. He pulls back, pressing another kiss to the tip of Hailee's nose before turning his gaze to me. The promise that flickers in his dark eyes has my dick stirring. *Fuck.* We're really doing this.

17

I CRANK UP THE RADIO AND LEAN BACK, ENJOYING THE WARM breeze whipping through the window. After Carter drove the first two-hour shift, I took over when we stopped for gas in Gillette. Linc is currently sprawled out in the back, his long legs to the side. I offered to shift my seat forward, but he insisted it was fine. My mind reels at how things have changed in such a short space of time. This trip started out as a frantic dash for freedom, turned into a pitiful road trip for one and now . . . Now I'm not even sure what it is. I'm travelling with two gorgeous men, and I've had sex with both of them.

My gaze flits to my backpack between Carter's feet. I haven't turned my phone on for a while. It's not realistic to think that Brent won't find a way around my blocking him. He's the kind of cop that isn't afraid to bend the rules if it benefits him. The first chance I get, I'll try to buy a new phone. Of course, there's a chance he doesn't care that I've gone. Maybe he's glad I packed up and left.

"How old are you, Linc?" Carter asks, looking over his shoulder.

"Why? Worried I'm a minor?"

Carter laughs. "You think you look seventeen?"

"Are you saying I don't?"

My shoulders relax at their easy banter and once again I'm struck by how effortless it is being with the two of them. The only time I feel anxious is when I let Brent's sneering face and words into my mind. *You're such a soft touch, Hailee. What do you have to offer them? Don't think so much of yourself. You're nothing special.*

"Twenty-three."

Linc's voice pulls me from my thoughts, and I grip the steering wheel, blowing out a slow breath as I push Brent's words from my mind.

"You're twenty-five, right, Hailee?" Carter reaches over and squeezes my leg. "Same as me."

I nod. "Yep. Quarter of a century and all that."

"So, what do you do for work, Linc?" Carter asks. "Or are you still at college?"

There's something about his tone that makes me think the age question was only a way to get to this line of questioning. I have to admit, I'm curious too. I glance up at the rearview to find Linc frowning.

"It's pretty boring. I'm a photographer."

I raise my eyebrows. "That's not boring. What do you photograph?"

"Fashion."

Carter hums in response. "That makes sense."

"Oh, does it?" Linc's frown melts into a smile. "Why's that?"

"The way you dress."

"What's wrong with the way I dress?"

Carter turns around in his seat. "I didn't say there was anything wrong with it. I like it."

"Oh?"

A snicker bursts from my lips, and I catch his eye in the mirror. "Stop winding him up, Linc."

Linc holds his hands up in mock surrender. "Okay fine. Hailee said you were a teacher. What do you teach?"

"High school geography."

Linc leans forward, resting his arms on the back of my seat. "High school? How do the kids manage to pay attention when you're their teacher? I bet they can't name half the state capitals."

I glance over to see Carter flushing at the compliment. Despite his outward confidence, I've seen him disappear inside his head several times as flashes of doubt cloud his face. I have a feeling there's a lot more about his relationship with Andrew that he hasn't shared.

"Do you have just the one sister, Hailee?" Linc asks.

I nod. "Yeah. Stacey's eight years older than me. She pretty much raised me."

Linc's fingers find my shoulder, rubbing tender circles. "What about your parents?"

"They died in a car accident when I was twelve," I explain. "The state tried to put me in foster care, but Stacey was twenty, and along with our grandmother, they convinced the state to let me stay with them. Our grandmother was already in her eighties and died a couple of years later. So, it's just been me and Stacey ever since."

Carter turns in his seat to face me. "That's really rough. I'm sorry."

"Shittier things have happened to people," I say. "It's fine. I haven't seen her in a couple of years, so I'm looking forward to it."

I try not to think about the reasons I haven't seen her. My cheeks heat at how stupid I've been. Every time I picked up the phone to call her, Brent would say: 'she's probably busy' or 'are you sure she'll want to hear from you?'. At first, I ignored him, but the seeds of doubt had been sown, and before I knew it, I was in a forest so dense I couldn't see a way out, and I hadn't spoken to Stacey in months.

"Tell me about your families," I say, desperate to change the subject.

"Mine's pretty standard," Carter says with a shrug. "Mom's a dentist, Dad works in finance. I've got an older brother who's a vet and a younger sister who's still in college. They're good people."

"Are they all in D.C.?" I ask.

Carter nods. "Pretty much. Scarlett's in Florida but the rest are there."

"No siblings here," Linc says. "Only child of two immigrants. Mom's a nutritionist and Dad's a programmer."

"Where are they from?" I ask. "Were you born in the U.S.?"

"Mom's Sri Lankan and Dad's Sicilian. They met in London and moved to New York. That's where I was born."

I sigh. "I'd love to go to New York one day."

"It's not that different from Chicago," Linc says, his fingers stroking the sensitive skin at the base of my neck. "When you've seen one big city, you've kind of seen them all. Tall buildings, busy sidewalks."

"Thanks for trying to make me feel better." I throw a grin over my shoulder.

"Want to pull over into that rest stop?" Linc says, glancing at his watch. "It's time to swap for the last leg."

Nodding, I pull over. As soon as I put the car into park, both men open their doors and get out.

"Front or back, Hailee?" Carter asks, stretching his arms over his head.

My eyes linger on the expanse of skin across his stomach where his shirt lifts. "I'll go in the back," I say, climbing out. "There's more room up front for your legs."

Linc reaches for my hand and pulls me to him, wrapping his arms around me. The embrace takes me by surprise, and it's a couple of seconds before I relax into it, resting my cheek against his hard chest and inhaling his scent.

"What's this for?" I ask, my voice muffled against his t-shirt.

He pulls back and smiles, dipping his mouth to mine for a slow, tender kiss that has my toes curling in my sneakers.

"Does there have to be a reason?" he murmurs against my lips.

"I suppose not."

The sound of Carter closing the passenger door as he gets back into the car has us pulling apart, and I squeeze Linc's arm before climbing onto the backseat.

"Hey," I say to Carter, hoping he isn't annoyed at me.

He turns around, eyebrows raised, but there's no sign of annoyance on his face. I must look relieved because a small smile tips his lips.

"Don't worry," he says. "I'm not jealous. I am, however, calling first dibs on that mouth when we get to the hotel."

My cheeks heat, and he winks at me before reaching across to clasp Linc's thigh. I fasten my seatbelt and try to calm my thundering heart. What will happen at the hotel? The thought of another threesome has me clenching my thighs together in anticipation. I rest my head back against the seat and close my eyes. The summer air is warm, and between the radio, the rumbling of the road and my trailing thoughts, I find myself drifting off to sleep.

. . .

"Hailee? Wake up, sleepy head."

I blink awake, my mouth thick with sleep. "Where are we?"

"We're about half an hour outside of Cody," Linc says, "but we figured we'd stop for something to eat."

I sit up, rubbing my eyes. "Sure."

Looking out of the window, I can see we're in a quiet parking lot, but I can't tell where. I open the door and stretch, stifling a yawn. Carter wraps an arm around my waist, and we cross the gravel concourse toward a quaint-looking pizza restaurant. The front is decked in green and red, and Italian music leaks out from the open windows.

"It's cute, right?" Carter grins.

"It's something. I might appreciate it more when I've had a coffee."

Carter pulls me in tighter to his side. "Aw, someone's grumpy when they wake up from a nap."

I elbow him, and he releases me with a laugh. We've just reached the front door when a cold shiver runs through me, and I stumble backwards.

"My backpack." I gasp. "I need my backpack."

Carter glances at Linc. "It's a pretty quiet place, it should be fine."

"No," I say, shaking my head as I hold out my hand for the key. "I need it."

He shrugs and hands me it. My heart pounding, I jog back around the restaurant to the car. It isn't their fault. They don't know. I haven't told them that everything that's important to me—every cent I own—is in that backpack. I drag it out from the front seat and sling it over my shoulder, already feeling calmer.

It's with a heavy heart, I realize I should probably turn my phone on for a bit. I told Stacey I'd be in Vegas in a couple of days, but with the new detour, it'll take longer, and I don't want her to worry. She's probably already tried to call me several times, and my stomach clenches at the thought. Stacey is more nervous than me about driving, after what happened to our parents.

I round the restaurant to find Carter waiting for me, his blue eyes narrowed in concern.

"You okay?" he asks.

"I'm sorry. I didn't mean to overreact."

I go to move past him, but he takes hold of my elbow, halting me.

"There's nothing to apologize for," he says, his eyes searching. "And you didn't overreact. I'm just concerned. Are you sure you're okay?"

"I'm fine. Where's Linc?"

"He went inside to get us a table."

Carter lets go of my arm and I force a smile. I can tell he wants to press for more of an explanation, but he lets me walk past him into the restaurant. We promised to be brutally honest with each other, but there are some truths that are still too painful to speak.

18

SOMETHING ISN'T RIGHT WITH HAILEE. SHE LAUGHS, JOINING in with our conversations as we eat our pizza, but it doesn't feel right. Forced almost. Shadows lurk in her smile. If I felt protective of her before, after our car journey, the feeling has tripled. My heart aches at the thought of her growing up without her parents. I'm also even more angry at her jerk of an ex-boyfriend. He took her vulnerability and exploited it. She doesn't have to tell me that much. I know in my gut, the reason she's not seen her sister in a couple of years is down to him.

Five years she's spent being mentally and emotionally abused by that fucker. I don't know how long we have left together, but I vow to bring as much joy to her in the limited time we have as I can. Every smile, every laugh, is a 'fuck you' to her ex, and I plan on there being a lot.

As the waiter clears our table and Carter asks for the check, I watch as she pulls her backpack onto her lap and fishes out her phone. I haven't seen her use it once since we met. Carter is on his regularly, and I've been actively trying not to use mine as much as I usually would. My curiosity piques as I realize she's turning it on. Is she that scared of her ex contacting her? Or does she just not use her phone?

The waiter places the check down, and I snatch it up, handing over my card.

"Hey," Hailee and Carter protest at the same time.

"It's a couple of pizzas," I say, rolling my eyes. "Chill out."

"Thanks." Carter reaches under the table and places his hand on my thigh.

Hailee frowns at me a little longer, but then shakes her head. "Thank you. I guess we can take turns or something."

I open my mouth to tell her not to overthink it, but snap it shut. That's probably the kind of thing her ex said. I swallow my words and watch as she slides out of the booth, her phone in hand.

"I've got a load of missed calls from Stacey," she says. "I'm just going to let her know I'm okay. Do you want to wait here, or shall I meet you at the car?"

Carter's hand is still lingering on my thigh, and my breathing quickens as it moves a little higher, his fingers circling.

"We'll meet you in the car," he says.

She nods, and slinging her backpack over her shoulder, heads for the door. I turn to Carter, already knowing what I'll find. His eyes have taken on a predatory stillness that makes my breath catch, and he licks his lips as his hand slides a little higher.

"You look hungry," I rasp.

Carter smiles slowly, the intensity of his gaze burning hot. "I'm starving."

I swallow and slide out of the booth, hoping the bulge in the front of my shorts isn't obvious as I toss a couple of bucks down on the table for the tip. Carter strides out of the restaurant with purpose, and I follow, anticipation setting every nerve ending alight. He unlocks the car and opens the back door, jerking his head in a silent command to get in. There's not a lot of room back there, but considerably more since we rearranged our luggage, so it all fits in the trunk.

The parking lot is quiet, with a few cars scattered around, but none parked near ours. I climb in and shut the door, bemused by my own trembling fingers as I turn to Carter. He holds my gaze for a moment, his chest rising and falling, and then he launches himself at me.

We meet in a clash of tongues and teeth that tears a moan from my throat. Carter pushes me back against the seat, his fingers sliding up under my shirt before dipping down and hooking on my waistband. I lift my hips in response, urging him on.

"Fuck." He moans against my neck. "I want to lick every damn inch of you."

I slide my hand down and palm his erection through his shorts, eliciting a hiss from between his lips. "There's not enough room or time," I say. "I can think of a specific few inches you could lick if you wanted, though."

Carter chuckles against my skin, his teeth nipping before claiming my mouth once more. "Oh, don't worry. That's what I was planning."

I start to tug at his shorts, but he pulls back, shaking his head. "You first."

Before I can argue, he yanks my shorts and briefs down to my knees. A low growling noise rumbles from Carter as he crouches, his hungry eyes on my cock, where it rests, hard and ready against my stomach. He wraps his hand around the shaft and sticks out his tongue, lapping at the bead of precum that's formed at the tip. Looking up at me through dark lashes, he slides his hand up and down my aching cock, his lips and tongue teasing, until my head falls back with a groan.

"Carter," I warn.

The word has barely left my lips when he leans forward and takes me entirely into his mouth. My eyes roll back in my head, and I sigh, losing myself in the sensation of his hot, clever mouth. I sink my hands into his thick brown hair as I thrust my hips up, forcing myself deeper. He moans in response, gagging a little, and the vibrations have me clutching his hair tighter. He slides his hands underneath me, gripping my ass as he works me relentlessly with his tongue, his cheeks hollowing with the effort.

All I can do is stare. He looks so fucking hot. He does something with his tongue and teeth that feels beyond incredible, and I suck in a breath. I had a taste of Carter's skills last night, but only briefly. Now, knowing he wants me to fuck his mouth, that he wants to taste me, has me panting with need and my balls tightening.

I gasp, my hands sliding to his cheeks and neck, feeling how his Adam's apple bulges at the motion of my cock thrusting down his throat. I keep my hands there as I come hard, my fingers tracking the movement as he swallows me down.

"Fuck." I gasp, leaning my head back against the seat.

Carter chuckles, rising level with me. "I wish."

I grab a fistful of his shirt and haul him to me, kissing him deep, tasting myself on his tongue. Carter's hands move to pull my shorts back up and I lift my hips to help him. After tucking myself back in, my hands move to his shorts once more, but he leans back.

"You don't have to," he says, his fingers tracing my jaw.

"I know I don't *have* to. I want to."

Something unreadable flashes across his face and I

claim his mouth once more, pushing him back onto the seat. I'm six foot three and Carter's only a couple of inches shorter, so it's uncomfortable as fuck as we attempt to make it work. I try not to think about the possible bruises my legs will have after this, but it's so worth it. I pull his shorts down, watching as his cock springs free.

"I've been thinking about this all day," I breathe as I lower myself between his legs.

Carter says nothing, and I glance up to find uncertainty flickering in his wolf-like gaze. I can't figure him out. He's so dominant at times, but then equally scared and unsure. Both wolf and wolf cub.

"Do you want me?" I ask.

His blue eyes widen. "Yes. So much."

I flick out my tongue, circling the head of his cock, and he inhales sharply. "Carter. Do you want to fuck my mouth?"

His dick twitches against my lips, and he swallows audibly.

"Yes," he gasps.

Swirling my tongue over his swollen flesh, I take him into my mouth, relishing the groan I coax from him. He's hesitant, his hips barely lifting as I take him deeper. After a minute, I pull off him, taking him in my hand instead.

"You won't hurt me," I reassure him, pressing a kiss to his hip as I work his dick with long, firm strokes.

Breathless, Carter looks down at me, doubt etched on his handsome face.

"You won't," I repeat. "Let go, Carter. I want this."

Without waiting for a response, I take him back into my mouth. I want the wolf. I want the hungry, feral way he looks at me; like he isn't sure whether he wants to fuck me or eat me. His fingers gently trace my jaw, his thumb stroking my cheek, and I try to push down the disappointment. Maybe it's me. I've never had complaints, but maybe he just isn't enjoying it.

Then his fingers slide into my hair, gripping around the base of my neck. He thrusts his hips, and as his cock hits the back of my throat, I groan around him. Spurred on, he bucks again with a grunt that has me opening my eyes and looking up at him. If I could manage a smile with his fat cock down my throat, I would. There's my wolf. His pale blue eyes flash as he grips my head, fucking my mouth with abandon. If I hadn't just come, the sight would have made me hard again. Even so, I feel my spent cock shift, regardless. As Carter picks up the pace, his grunts and groans shift to whimpers, and I stare up at him through watering eyes. His head is thrown back and his eyes are closed, his mouth open. I decide his breathy whimpers are my new favorite sound, and I hum around his dick as I wonder what noises he'll make when I get the chance to fuck him.

"Fuck. Fuck. Fuck. Linc!"

I swallow down his release, my fingertips tracing the warm skin of his stomach as I watch his labored breathing. His hands release my head, falling limp to his side.

"Fuck," he pants. "That was incredible."

I pull his shorts back up, ghosting a kiss against his hip, and when I straighten, his blue gaze is fixed on me.

"*You* are incredible," he says, dragging a thumb along my cheek and across my bottom lip.

I lean forward and kiss him softly. "So are you, Carter. I just wish you believed it."

His hands still, and I wonder whether I've said too much. But then he tips his head and kisses me.

It's awkward, half leaning, half lying on the backseat,

making out like a couple of teenagers, but I love every second.

A knock sounds at the window, and we fly apart, straightening clothes. The car windows are steamed to the point we can't see a thing out of them, and I wonder just how careless we've been. It's broad daylight outside. I got so lost in Carter, we could have had a full audience and I wouldn't have noticed. But then the passenger side door opens, and Hailee throws in her backpack.

"Is it safe to come in?" she asks.

"Yeah, sorry," Carter says, running his hands through his messed-up hair.

She sits down and turns to look at us. I can only imagine what we look like. Carter's lips are swollen, his skin flushed. I can tell the skin around my mouth and neck is raw from his beard. I tug at my t-shirt, trying and failing to straighten it.

Hailee's mouth twitches. "Did you two have fun?"

"*So* much fun." Carter exhales, sinking back against the seat.

I lean forward and cup her face. "We'll make it up to you tonight at the hotel."

She rolls her eyes. "Come on. We've still got another hour to go."

Giving Carter another kiss before opening the door, I climb out and hop into the driver's seat. I glance over at Hailee as I buckle up, trying to gauge how her phone call went. She looks worse than she did before. More jittery. I start the engine, wondering how to find out whether she's okay without pressuring her. In the end, it's Carter who rips off the Band-Aid.

"Are you okay?" he asks, leaning forward. "How's Stacey?"

"She's fine," Hailee answers. "I told her I was taking in a few more sights along the way."

I try to catch Carter's eye in the rearview, but his attention is fixed on her. We both know there's more. I only hope she'll tell us when she's ready.

19

My eyes are wide as I stare at the expanse of lush green forest and multicolored rocky outcrops in front of us. It's breathtaking. A huge blue lake fills the gap between the emerald hills, the surface clear and sparkling like a mirror. It's so peaceful. Despite seeing several tour groups on our way into the park, right now, there's no one in sight.

"How big *is* this place?" I mutter.

"Over three thousand square miles," Hailee replies. "It's bigger than Delaware and Rhode Island combined."

I turn to find her squinting at the leaflet we bought on the way in. A smile curves my lips and I walk over to her, sliding my hands into her back pockets and resting my chin on her shoulder. Being allowed to touch her will never get old.

"I can't believe you're wearing these shorts again," I murmur, pressing a kiss to her neck.

She steps out of my reach, folding the leaflet, and shoving it back into her backpack. "There's nothing wrong with these shorts."

"Oh, there's nothing wrong with them," I agree.

Linc chuckles, lifting his sunglasses up as he runs his dark brown gaze over her appraisingly. "Definitely nothing wrong with them."

Hailee groans. "Not you too."

"Hey, if you could see how delicious your ass looks, you'd understand." I turn her around and kiss her, my hands gripping her ample cheeks.

Last night we checked into a hotel, but after her phone call with her sister, Hailee remained distant. She said she was tired from the drive, but Linc and I both know it isn't just that. We watched some chick flick with Jennifer Lopez in it and fell asleep in the king-sized bed, Hailee between us. As much as I was looking forward to being with both Linc and Hailee again, it felt nice waking amidst their warmth.

"Come on," Linc says, clapping his hands together. "Let's keep going. We've got an hour to find the perfect spot to stop for lunch."

"Do you think we could find our way down to that lake?" I say, nodding toward the expanse of blue.

He shrugs in response. "We've got time to try."

Linc is wearing dark blue basketball shorts with a white t-shirt, and it's everything. I take the opportunity to admire the hard muscle lining his thighs and calves. He's built like a Greek god. It took more self-restraint than I thought I possessed this morning not to lick my way down his body. Even if I'd tried, it wouldn't have been right. Like me, he was too distracted by Hailee's quiet demeanor.

We head back to the car, and I pull the key from my back pocket. It's only after I close the door that I realize Hailee is still lingering, her brow furrowed as she stares at her phone. I can count on one hand, with fingers to spare, the times I've seen her look at her phone, and the sight fills me with dread. What's on there that's causing her to look so worried?

"Hailee?" Linc calls. "You coming?"

Her head snaps up and she fumbles with the phone, switching it off and shoving it in her weathered backpack. "Yeah. Sorry."

Linc gives me a look as Hailee slips onto the backseat, and I press my lips together. I know I shouldn't push, but I need to know. When we stop for lunch, I'm going to try and get some answers.

The lake isn't too hard to find. Before we left this morning, we stopped at a grocery store in Cody and stocked up with snacks and stuff for a picnic. I grin, recalling the cashier's wide eyes as Linc brazenly threw in a massive box of condoms, and both a bottle and some wallet-sized packets of lube when we got to the counter. My stomach flips at the thought.

"Carter?"

I tear my gaze from the crystal blue waters of the lake to find Linc watching me with raised eyebrows. "Sorry, what?"

"Pass the chips."

We've spread the food out on a towel Hailee produced from one of her bags, and I pick up the packet and hand it to him, ignoring his questioning stare. Instead, I turn my attention to Hailee, who's picking at a sandwich, her brow furrowed.

"Are you going to tell us what's wrong, or is this just how you're going to be until we get to Vegas?"

Linc chokes on a chip as Hailee's eyes widen in that infuriatingly endearing way.

"Excuse me?" she asks.

I swallow down the nausea rising in my gut at being so damn rude. The words hadn't sounded so harsh in my head. There's no point treading on eggshells, though. We don't have months to work through this. We have days. A handful of days until we all go our separate ways. Perhaps it's selfish to push her, but I want things to go back to the way they were before. Seeing Hailee like this only reminds me that perhaps it's the way I should be, too. My gut twists. As much as I try to convince myself that I'm pushing her for the right reasons, I know it's more selfish than not.

"I want to know what happened on the phone with your sister." I force myself to hold her gaze. "You've not been the same since."

"Back off, Carter," Linc warns. "It was only last night. If Hailee needs time to deal with stuff, she gets time."

I snort, painfully aware that I'm acting like an ass. For some reason, I can't stop myself. I know it's more than just her sister. If she'd just tell us, maybe we could help. I want to help.

"Did Brent contact you?" I ask, not even trying to sugar-coat it.

She drops the remains of her sandwich onto the towel, her eyes shuttering. Even as my words hang heavy in the air around us, part of me already wishes I could suck them back in.

"Carter." Linc's voice is gentle but firm. "I know you're concerned, and you're not the only one. But you need to back off."

Guilt weighs my chest as I look at Hailee's face, her expression on the verge of crumbling. *Fuck.* If I make her cry, I'll lose it. That's the last thing I want to do.

"Sorry." I groan, dragging a hand over my face. "I'm just worried. I know what it's like to be scared, and I don't want you to feel that way."

She looks at me, and I hope she realizes the small piece of myself I've given her. After a moment, she gives a small nod and I exhale.

"So, where to after this?" Linc says. "There's a giant geyser somewhere."

"That sounds like fun." Hailee gives him a grateful smile.

"How far away is it?" I ask. "Could be like six hours. This place is so fucking huge. Where's that map?"

I reach for Hailee's bag, unzipping the side pocket where I saw her stash the map. She gasps and dives for the bag, wrenching it from my grip, but it's too late. I stare at her, eyes wide.

"Hailee? What's with all the cash?"

She stumbles to her feet, clutching the bag to her chest as she zips it closed.

"Hailee?" I press. "There's got to be thousands in there. You can't just carry that shit around."

At least I know why she's so damn protective of that ratty backpack. Why the fuck does she have so much cash? My heart hammers in my chest as I realize perhaps she's hidden as much of her real story as I have.

"It's none of your business," she says, backing away.

"It is my business," I reply carefully. "We had a deal. We're in this together as far as Vegas, right? If you're in some kind of trouble, we deserve to know."

"Our deal was to be honest about who fucked who," she spits, her eyes shimmering with unshed tears. "I didn't invite you on this trip to interrogate me or make me feel like shit. That's exactly what I'm trying to leave behind."

Her words hit me like bullets, and I stagger to my feet, my chest aching, as I grasp at words to explain. I'm nothing like Brent. Before I can string a sentence together, she turns and strides off towards the trees. Linc puts out a hand, stopping me from following.

"Let me," he says. "Just keep an eye on our stuff, okay?"

Although he doesn't say it, and his tone is neutral, the disappointment in his eyes is clear as day. I've fucked up.

Sitting heavily back down on the grass, I fist my hands into my hair, gripping tight. I've done it. I've broken the only good thing I had going on in my life. But then, isn't that what I do best?

I watch Linc disappear past the dense tree line after Hailee and hope that he'll be able to put the pieces back together.

20

Tears blur my vision as I stomp through the long grass, the blades brushing against my bare calves. I have no idea where I'm heading; I just know I need to get away from Carter. It's not that I'm hiding anything. There's no deep dark secret. The truth of it is, I'm ashamed. Ashamed of the fact I'm a twenty-five-year-old woman who's never had a bank account. Of the fact I can't make a fucking decision without questioning everything—without questioning my own self-worth. Over the last five years, I've been whittled down to nothing—a thin, brittle twig, ready to snap. The second I left Chicago, I tried to pretend that's not who I am. I tried to remember who I was before—who I could be again. I hoped if I pretended for long enough, it might start being true.

My backpack weighs like rocks against my shoulders. My whole pathetic existence shoved into one tattered bag. It's the backpack that saw me through college, and I know every hole and tear like I know my own skin. Perhaps that's why I've kept it. It's as ripped and broken as I am. The money inside it weighs more than the burden on my soul. Even though I hid it at the bottom of my closet, I think Brent knew. And ever since I left Chicago, I've been waiting for the other shoe to drop. Without me—without my income to fund his gambling . . . A sob escapes my throat.

"Hailee, wait."

I wince at Linc's deep, soothing tones and slow my pace. There's no point ignoring him. At some point, I'll have to get back in my car and face them. Face Carter. I stop, staring at the mossy ground. Sunlight dapples the blades of grass through the thick trees, and the only other sound is that of birdsong. It should be paradise, but instead it feels like a prison. Everywhere does. I don't think I'll ever feel completely free again.

"Hailee," he repeats, stopping just behind me, giving me space.

I draw a deep, shuddering breath and turn to face him. "Sorry."

He closes the gap between us, taking my face between his large, slender hands. "Please don't," he says. "Don't apologize for your feelings. Carter was way out of line. If anyone needs to apologize, it's him."

I drag my gaze to meet his, ever surprised at how beautiful he is. "I know he means well. It's just . . ."

Linc drops his hands to my shoulders and pulls me gently towards him, enveloping me in a hug.

"I didn't steal it," I mumble against his chest.

His arms tighten around me. "The thought never crossed my mind."

I sigh. Both Carter and Linc have my best interests at heart. I know that. I can feel it in my bones. But where Carter is intense, Linc is calm. I know he won't press the matter. He'll hold me for as long as I need, and then we'll go back to the lake. He'll probably hold Carter off if I need him to. I'm grateful for it.

"It's my money," I say.

Linc presses a kiss to the top of my head. "You don't have to tell me."

Taking a deep breath, I step back and look up at him. "I want to."

He glances around the dense woods, his eyes narrowed. After a second, he takes my hand in his and leads me over to a fallen tree. I sit down and he perches beside me, taking my hand in his, waiting as I collect my thoughts. My heart pounding, I take a breath and try to explain as best I can.

"I've never had a bank account," I explain. "I used my sister's when I was at college because it was easier. I was still using it when I met Brent, and when we moved into his apartment, he said there was no point in me having one. His wage paid our rent and bought our food. If I needed any money, he'd approve it and give it to me. When I got a job, he convinced me I still didn't need one. Somehow, he managed to convince the store manager to pay me in cash. Brent could convince anyone to do anything.

"My wage was what he used for gambling. He said it was the least I could do, considering he put a roof over my head and food on the table. He's always gambled, but it got worse over the last couple of years. He'd go out and not come back until the next afternoon, and usually with most of my money gone. I tried to speak to him about it once and he disappeared for two days, refusing to answer my calls.

"After it happened the third time, I started taking a little of my wage and saving it. I had an old shoebox I kept hidden in the bottom of my closet. I didn't even know why I was doing it. I wasn't planning on leaving him. Until I did."

I blink and silent tears escape down my cheeks. Linc

slides from the tree trunk and kneels in front of me, brushing the traitorous drops from my skin with his thumbs.

"I'm so sorry you had to go through that," he says softly. "Do you have any idea how brave you are?"

Huffing a laugh, I shake my head, causing his hands to drop to my knees. "I'm not brave. When he didn't come back from his poker night, I packed up my stuff and ran, without even leaving a note. I'm a coward."

Linc shakes his head, tipping my chin until I look at him. "You are anything but. I know you've only told us the bare minimum of what he did to you, Hailee. I can't imagine what five years of being made to feel inadequate is like, but you did the only thing you could. Even I know that if you'd tried to talk to him, he'd have convinced you to stay."

I swallow, wincing at the lump in my throat. He's right. There's no way he'd have let me leave. I wouldn't have put it past him to hide the car key.

"Are you worried he'll try to find you? Because you know we won't let anything happen to you."

I offer him a weak smile. "Until Vegas."

He frowns, something flickering briefly over his features, but he blinks, and it's gone. "Does your sister know about him? What he was like?"

"I think she suspects. He doesn't know she's in Vegas. Once I get there, I think I'll be okay."

Linc looks anything but convinced. I know he's thinking about what Carter said—about what happened with my sister. The truth is, it's nothing to do with her. My bag burns where it rests against my spine, every lump and bump painfully pronounced. I swear I can feel my phone searing into my skin through the worn canvas pocket. If I didn't need it to contact Stacey, I'd have thrown it into the lake.

Forcing my attention away from the weight at my back, I look at Linc.

He worries his plump lower lip as he studies me, and I watch the movement, wishing I could go back to yesterday and try again. Things were going great. We only have so many nights before this is over and I've wasted one already. It was lovely falling asleep between Carter and Linc, but I'm painfully aware that we could have spent the evening a lot more creatively.

Maybe I'm looking at the situation wrong. Our days are limited, so why am I holding back? My body and the truth. I'll never see Carter and Linc again after this trip, so what is there to gain by trying to hide the ugly parts of my story? I know Carter has just as many ghosts as I do. Perhaps I should just give myself to this experience, allowing myself to drift recklessly and freely towards our final destination.

A small smile tugs on my lips, and I sigh, my heart feeling a little lighter. I'm not sure what I did in a previous life to deserve the two gorgeous men who've chosen to spend the next few days with me, but I'm going to enjoy every goddamn second from now on. The next time they ask me something, I'll tell them.

"What is it?" Linc asks, a bemused smile curving his mouth.

In answer, I take hold of his chiseled jaw and pull him to me, slanting my mouth to his. He leans forward, bracing himself on the tree trunk, answering my request. As he deepens the kiss, his tongue gently moving with mine, I slide my hands into his hair, tugging the black elastic free.

He pulls back, his eyebrows raised as I run my fingers through his dark locks. His hair is longer than I thought, brushing his shoulders in loose waves.

"I've never seen it down," I offer in answer to his questioning expression. "I like it."

"Yeah?"

I hum in response, pulling his mouth back to mine. He kisses like he has all the time in the world. But we don't. I slide my hands down his chest, suppressing a groan as my fingers snag on his muscles. Real people aren't built like this. I wonder just how much time he spends in the gym when he isn't joining impromptu road trips. My fingers dip beneath the waistband of his shorts and his mouth stills against mine. I slide my palm inside his briefs, smiling against his lips when I find him half hard. I gently wrap my hand around him, and he inhales sharply.

"Hailee," he whispers against my mouth. "What do you want?"

"I want to forget," I reply honestly, sliding my hand along his hardening length. "For just a little while."

Linc sighs, his breath warm against my skin, still smelling of the lemonade we bought for the picnic. I wonder for a moment whether he'll say no—that we need to head back. But then he reaches up and tugs my backpack from my shoulders.

His mouth finds mine again, kissing me deeply, before moving to trail warm kisses along my neck while his hands slide up underneath my t-shirt. My grip tightens around his length, and he rocks his hips into the movement.

Reaching down, he gently pulls my hand away, but before I can question it, he lifts my shirt up over my head and places it down on the log before removing his own. I swallow, drinking in the sight of his taut golden-brown skin. He places his shirt down on the grass beside the log and then takes me in his arms, laying me down on top of it. My heart pounds against my ribs. We haven't seen anyone since we arrived at the lake, but that doesn't mean it'll stay that way. I move my head to check our surroundings, but as Linc lowers himself over me, pulling down the cups of my bra and taking one of my nipples into his mouth, my concerns evaporate instantly. I sigh a moan as he moves to my other breast, his hand snaking down my stomach to unfasten my shorts.

I arch off the ground as he tugs them down over my legs, laying them on top of my t-shirt. He leaves my pale pink thong, which he pushes aside, his fingers running through my center. His eyes flick to mine as he slips a long finger inside me, and I press my lips together, my hips lifting, urging him deeper. His eyes look almost black as he licks his lips, adding a second finger, curling them with each gentle thrust. I whimper, wanting more, and he reaches into his pocket, pulling out one of the condoms we bought earlier.

Linc leans over me, kissing my mouth before trailing kisses down my body, his soft hair brushing against my skin as he pays each breast attention. Then he moves lower, spreading my legs as he dips between my thighs. I gasp as he runs his tongue over my aching core, swirling around the most sensitive spot until I whimper. He stops and I open my eyes to find that he's pulled down his shorts, his hard length already sheathed as he lowers himself over me. I run my hands over his firm body, lifting my hips to meet him as he drags his cock between my legs.

"Please," I moan. "Linc."

He dips his mouth to mine, kissing in the languid, all-consuming way he does, as he continues to tease me. My fingers dig into his buttocks, trying to push him into me, but he smiles against my mouth.

"So impatient," he murmurs against my lips.

Shifting his balance onto one forearm, he moves a hand

to my breast, flicking my nipple as he runs his tongue along my neck. I inhale sharply, arching into him, a plea on my lips. But before I can utter the words, he lowers his hips, burying himself inside me in a single hard stroke.

"Linc . . ." I groan, my fingers grasping at him as I revel in the feeling of him filling and stretching me.

His hair forms a dark curtain around my face, his eyes fixed on mine, as he pulls out before thrusting back in torturously slow.

My whimpers increase as he continues his unhurried pace, and he smiles, enjoying the delicious torment he's inflicting. Desperation builds as I buck my hips, but he ignores my pleas, lowering his mouth to my breasts and sucking hard on each nipple.

Grabbing hold of his shoulders, I push hard enough that he looks up in surprise. I keep pushing, wrapping my legs around his as I try to roll us. His eyes flash as he realizes what I'm doing and he grabs hold of me, flipping us so I'm on top.

I sink down on his long, hard cock with a moan far too loud for being out in the open, but I don't care. My hands grip his chest as I look down at him, his dark hair splayed out on the forest floor. He looks like some sort of mythical creature I've managed to ensnare as he stares up at me, a mixture of lust and awe on his beautiful face.

He reaches up, running a thumb along my lower lip before dipping his index finger into my mouth. I suck it, holding his gaze, and he repeats the action with his other hand. He takes hold of my breasts, swirling his wet digits over my nipples and I gasp at the sensation, rocking my hips. He hisses, arching a little, and I increase my pace. Linc's hands drop, one gripping my hip as I ride him harder, the other moving between my legs. I throw my head back as he strokes my clit, the feel of him inside me almost too much to bear. I'm so close, but I don't want this to end.

Falling forward, I brace myself on either side of his head, and he lifts his mouth to my breasts, taking my hips in his hands as he thrusts up into me. Gone is his leisurely pace as he bucks hard and fast, his breathing melting into guttural grunts.

My own breathing is little more than moans and whimpers as pressure builds in my core, and I clench around him as my mouth falls open, my body shuddering through my orgasm. Linc slows, his thrusts deep and purposeful as he coaxes tremor after tremor from me. Then his hands tighten on my hips, his body tensing beneath me.

"Hailee, fuck . . ." He gasps, his head tipping back as his eyes screw shut.

I lower myself, pressing kisses along his clenched jaw as he pulses inside me.

"Thank you," I whisper, stroking my fingers through his dark hair.

Opening his eyes, he searches my face. "Don't."

He pushes up onto his elbows and claims my mouth. I know our time is running out. We'll have to get dressed and get back to Carter soon. I'm not sure just how much of myself I can give them—how much truth I can stomach to share—but I'm going to try. I'm going to enjoy the rest of the trip as much as I can before we arrive in Las Vegas, and reality inevitably crashes down around me.

21

It's fucking hot. Swiping the sweat from my forehead, I squint up and down the long empty road, the sun causing ripples of shimmering heat to rise from the asphalt. I should have kept my fucking mouth shut. A roar of frustration tears from my throat, and I kick the metal barrier until my bones vibrate with the effort.

A yellow-toothed trucker named Keith picked me up in Idaho Falls, with a begrudging promise to take me as far as Salt Lake City. His shitty taste in music had grated on my last nerve by Pocatello, and we got into a fight. He could have at least kicked me out near a fucking town.

Sweat stings my eyes as I glare at the I-15. It's illegal to hitchhike in Idaho, and I'll be damned if I'm going to end up in jail again. Okay. I haven't been to *jail.* I've done two years in juvie, and that's more than enough. I may not follow all the rules, but I keep my head down and get the fuck on with life.

Hoisting my bag on my shoulder, I continue to walk along the never-ending highway. A couple of cars slow, but no one stops. Is it illegal if they stop without me asking them to? Do I actually have to stick out a fucking thumb to break the law?

I'm on edge as I wait for the inevitable whoop of a cop car's sirens. Although, if the cops show up, at least I'll get a ride to civilization, and perhaps a fucking drink. I scowl up at the scalding sun, a thousand silent curses filling my head. My hat got lost several towns ago in some shitty bar. I wasn't bothered at the time, but now, under the sun's relentless heat, I wish I hadn't been so careless. Or wasted.

The last two years in Montana have been fairly steady. A small garage took me on, even though I have no formal mechanic qualifications. I proved myself, though. I poured blood and sweat into Mac's Garage. No tears. I used up all my tears before the age of ten. I didn't even shed a tear when Mac keeled over and died of a heart attack last month. I was fucking devastated, don't get me wrong. Mac was nicer to me than any family member I can remember. I just don't cry.

What should have made me cry, is when the debt companies came calling. Turns out Mac's eldest son took out a stack of loans he can't pay back, and the second Mac's garage went to him in the will, he handed it over. Which meant my fucking job, too.

That's why I'm headed to Phoenix. I have an uncle there somewhere, and I'm hoping he'll let me crash on his sofa until I can pin down another mechanic gig. Fuck knows whether Dave is my biological uncle. I don't know who my dad is for sure, but Dave kept in touch over the years with the occasional text. If he isn't there or says no, I'm not sure what my next move will be. *Survive.* That's what I'll do. It's what I've been doing my whole life.

The low rumble of an engine slowing sounds behind

me, and I sigh, waiting for the clipped blare of a siren to tell me to stop walking.

"Hey! Do you need a ride?"

I frown and slowly turn around, wondering if hearing voices is a side effect of heat stroke.

"You okay, man?"

No. Not a mirage. I walk cautiously over to the silver Toyota Camry. A brown-skinned guy with long hair tied up in one of those ridiculous buns is hanging out the backseat window staring at me. He gives me a friendly smile, but I can't shake my suspicion. I've been walking this highway for an hour, and no one has stopped. What reason do these guys have? Everyone always says not to pick up hitchhikers in case they're murderers, but what about the other way around? What if these guys are going to drive me to somewhere quiet, kill me, and take my stuff?

"Do you need a ride?" he asks again.

"Where you headed?" I ask, my eyes flitting to the road, making sure there are witnesses if this guy tries anything. I'm close enough now, I can see he's pretty ripped. Not as bulky as me, but that only means he'd probably outrun me. I'm aware how paranoid I'm being, but you don't survive as long as I have without second guessing everything and everyone.

"Unless you're an axe murderer, of course."

At the sound of a girl's voice, my eyes snap to the passenger seat. *Damn.* She's cute. I peer past her to the bearded guy watching me from the driver's side. My eyes narrow. This is a good-looking bunch of people. They don't look like they'd gut me and dump me in a ravine.

"No axe," I reply, showing my bag. "Not even a small one."

She smiles, and I have to drag my eyes away from the

sight. She's like some sort of Disney princess or some shit. All huge brown eyes, long curly hair, and pouty lips.

"We're headed to Salt Lake City," Man Bun says. "Any good?"

Fuck it. "Sure."

He opens the door, shuffling over, and I get in. The second the door closes, the bearded guy pumps up the A.C. and I lean my head back with a sigh.

"Hot out there, huh?" Man Bun says.

"It's like the devil's ass crack," I grumble, my eyes still shut.

The car rumbles as it pulls back onto the highway, and I shove my bag down between my feet.

"How come you were out there?" Disney Princess asks.

I shrug. "I had a ride, but we got into a disagreement and he kicked me out."

"What did you disagree on?"

"Music," I say. "He was playing some loud ass techno shit, and I said it was giving me a headache."

"What music *do* you like?" she asks.

"Not that."

Man Bun huffs a laugh and holds out a hand. "I'm Lincoln, but everyone calls me Linc."

He has long, pretty fingers like a piano player, but his grip is firm as we shake hands.

"Jax," I say.

"Unusual name."

It's short for Jackson, but I say nothing.

"I'm Hailee," the princess says with a small wave.

"Carter," the bearded guy says, locking eyes with me in the rearview.

I realize now; it's not so much a beard as sculpted stubble. His eyes are something else, though. They're so blue it's hard not to stare at them. They remind me of one of those ice creature things from Game of Thrones. He doesn't like me, and picking me up was not his idea. After a life spent bouncing from one place to another, I'm pretty good at reading people, and from the set of his jaw, I can tell he's itching to get rid of me already.

The smart thing to do would be to try and make myself seem less intimidating. Sit back and let him do his alpha shit. Problem is, I rarely do the smart thing. The next time he glances at me in the mirror, I let a small smirk play on my lips as I fold my arms across my chest, flexing my muscles. His eyes narrow before looking away.

I can't get a read on these guys. They clearly aren't related, and they're too old to be on some sort of college summer trip.

"Why are you heading to Salt Lake City?" I ask, my curiosity getting the better of me.

"We're on our way to the Four Corners Monument," Linc says. "Bit of a road trip."

A road trip. How fucking quaint.

"How about you?" Hailee asks, turning around to look at me. "Where are you headed?"

There's something so innocent about her, I find myself answering despite my better judgement. "I'm headed to Phoenix."

"You want us to drop you somewhere?" Carter asks. "Like a train station or bus station or something?"

I don't miss the edge of hope in his voice. I flash him my best smile, purely because I think it will piss him off. "Nah, wherever you stop is fine. I'll find another ride from there."

Hailee's eyes grow wider as she looks at me. "Isn't that dangerous?"

I raise my eyebrows. "What? Getting into cars with strangers?"

"Oh." She bites her lip, flicking her eyes to Linc. "Good point."

"Don't worry, princess," I reassure her. "I can take care of myself."

Despite her light brown skin, her cheeks darken as she blushes and looks away. I can feel Carter's attention on me in the mirror, but I stare out of the window instead, purposely ignoring him. He's her boyfriend or husband, then. So, who's the pretty boy in the back? Gay best friend? It wouldn't surprise me if he swung that way. I pretend to check out a road sign and cast a glance his way to find him checking out my arms.

"Like what you see?" I ask.

I expect my question to have him scrambling for excuses, but instead he looks at me with dark eyes and gives me a small, confident smile.

"Just admiring your ink."

I'm no closer to getting a read on him, but I hold his stare. "You got any?"

He shakes his head. "No."

Carter laughs. "Is that because you don't want one, or because of some 'my body is my temple' crap?"

Linc leans forward and playfully shoves him, his fingers lingering on his neck as Carter laughs again. I watch the movement with interest. Maybe Princess is the straight best friend.

"Perhaps I haven't found something I want on my skin permanently," Linc says.

"How many tattoos do you have, Jax?" Hailee asks.

"You'd have to count them, princess," I say. "I lost track a long time ago."

She blushes again and I grin. Making her blush is my new favorite pastime. I watch Carter's grip tighten on the steering wheel and my grin widens. This is going to be fun.

22

I'M NOT AN IDIOT. I CAN TELL HE'S TRYING TO WIND ME UP BY flirting with Hailee. We drove past Jax walking along the side of the road, and both Hailee and Linc pleaded until I came off at the next exit and circled back. It's added almost half an hour to the damn journey.

"But he's hot!" Linc had said.

I fold my arms across my chest and stare out of the window. Hailee has taken over the driving. I mean, he is hot. That much is true. In a scary kind of way. His skin-tight black t-shirt has the sleeves rolled, either to show off his biceps or his tattoos. Perhaps both. Complicated designs cover his arms all the way down to his fingers. There's barely any skin left untouched. I know his chest will be the same. His jeans are well worn, with tears at the knees, and they stretch over his broad thighs. His dark blond hair is shaved close to the scalp on the sides, with a messy length on top that he constantly pushes back off his face. He's tanned in the way that makes me think he spends a lot of time outside, rather than at the beach. I'm glad to be out of the driver's seat because it means I can avoid looking at him. I'm definitely not looking at him.

He's so fucking confident. After a few minutes in the back, he's spread out, legs wide and an arm over the back seat like he's king of the road. Linc is confident, but not in the same way. His confidence is quiet and reassuring. Jax's is as loud as his ink.

I tune out the conversation the three of them are having about Chicago, and stare out of the window, the lights passing in a hazy blur. We left Yellowstone around four o'clock, and it's almost six hours to Salt Lake City. My jaw flexes at the thought of what happened in the park. When Hailee came back with Linc, I apologized for pushing her. She explained about the cash, and even after hugging it out, I still feel like shit. What's worse, is she still hasn't explained her change in mood after the phone call with her sister.

"Carter?"

I blink, turning at my name. "What's up?"

"Dinner?" Linc asks, holding up his phone. "There's a steak restaurant just up ahead. Sound good?"

I shrug. "Sure."

"Jax is going to join, if that's okay?" he adds, watching me carefully.

"Why wouldn't it be?"

Linc's gaze lingers for a second, but then he sits back, falling back into easy conversation with Jax.

"You're quiet," Hailee says, reaching over and touching my leg.

Before she can take her hand back, I cover it with my own, linking our fingers. "I'm just tired," I lie. "It's been a long day."

I feel off balance. Things have been going well. Really well. Heat floods my chest as I recall the fun I had with Linc in the back of the car. Then everything changed. That's why I wish she'd talk to us. If she did, perhaps we could fix it—get things back on track. But now, we have a rugged hitchhiker in the back, which means Hailee isn't going to spill any time soon. Which, in turn, means things are still fucked.

My stomach lurches a little. I know I'm being selfish, but I need this. I want it. Badly.

"I need my hand back, Carter," Hailee says, tugging at my fingers.

I let her fingers slide from mine, and she switches lanes, taking us toward an exit I assume leads to the restaurant. My stomach growls at the thought of a steak dinner, and I frown down at it as though it's betraying me. Our appetites had soured a little in the park and most of the food went to waste. I lean my head back against the headrest and try to rein in my spiraling thoughts. We'll have dinner, ditch Jax, and then, when we get to the next hotel, maybe Hailee will tell us what's wrong. Things are going to be okay. They have to be.

The restaurant is busy. Linc says it has rave reviews online and it looks like it's true. Hailee parks the car, and we make our way to the entrance, preparing to be turned away or told there's a waiting time.

"Table for four?" Linc says, flashing the greeter one of his killer smiles.

The greeter smiles back, but then his face falls into a frown as he looks at the book in front of him. "You don't have a reservation?"

Linc shakes his head. "If you can fit us in, we'll eat quick. We need to get back on the road."

The greeter gnaws on his pen before tapping the list of names. I squint at the scrawl, wondering why so many people are eating at a steak restaurant off the I-15 midweek.

"If you can wait a minute while we clear a table, I can fit you in. You'll have to be out within the hour, though."

Linc looks at each of us, and we shrug in turn. "Not a problem."

We stand awkwardly in the entrance, perusing the menu as the sizzling smell of meat taunts us. Despite being busy, it has a cozy ambience, crammed with worn leather booths and warm amber lighting in green glass lamps. Everything about the place screams, 'I'm a man. Give me meat'. I glance at Hailee to find her squinting at the menu.

"How do you have your steak?" I ask.

Her nose wrinkles in a way that makes me want to lean over and kiss it.

"I don't eat steak," she mutters. "There are a couple of chicken options though."

I raise an eyebrow. "Why don't you eat steak?"

Hailee looks up from the menu, studying me for a second. "Don't go thinking this is some girl thing. It's an environmental choice. I like steak. I just don't eat it anymore."

Before I can reply, a waitress comes over with a huge smile and ushers us towards a booth. Linc slides in beside Jax and I take a spot next to Hailee. As we've already looked at the menu, we order right away, with beers for everyone except Linc, who's going to take the final stretch of driving.

"You can have one," I say.

He shakes his head. "I never drink a drop if I'm getting behind the wheel, and I also try not to drink unless I'm planning on feeling the effects."

I shake my head. "Calories?"

Linc winks at me.

"So, what's the deal?" Jax asks, folding his muscled arms

across his chest. "Are you guys like, college buddies or something? Is this some summer reunion road trip?"

Hailee, Linc, and I share a look. How much should we disclose to our hitchhiker?

"Sort of," I say.

Linc laughs, the low rumbling sound sending tingles up my spine.

"Not even remotely, Carter." He shakes his head, tucking a strand of dark hair behind his ear. "We all met on the road. Hailee's visiting her sister in Vegas and we're just kind of along for the ride."

Jax's eyebrows raise as he looks between us. He has unusual eyes. People always comment on mine—cornflower blue, apparently—but Jax's are different. Intense. They're bright blue, but a darker navy ring circles the outside. When he looks at you, it's like being pinned against a wall.

"You met on the road?" he repeats. "So how long have you known each other?"

"Carter and Hailee have a day on me," Linc says. "But it's been two days?"

Jax's eyebrows rise even further. "Two fucking days?"

My jaw clenches and I fight back the urge to kick Linc. Why is he telling him so much? We don't owe him information, and we certainly don't owe him any explanations.

"You got a problem with that?" I bite out.

Jax holds up his hands. "Hey, man. No problem. I'm just surprised. You all seem really close. I assumed you'd known each other for years."

"It feels like we have," Linc says, reaching across the worn wooden table and squeezing Hailee's hand.

I watch Jax's eyes narrow a little at the gesture and I wait, my hands clenched into fists on my lap, for him to ask the next obvious question. It's none of his damn business, and if

Linc even attempts to tell him, I'll stop him. I don't need Jax's judgement. He doesn't though, instead falling back into an earlier conversation with Linc about basketball.

The waitress brings over our drinks, and I trace the beads of condensation on the outside of my glass as the three of them chat away. Occasionally, I let myself glance at Jax. His natural state is one of 'don't fuck with me'—all hard lines and deep scowls. Combined with the ink that I'm convinced probably covers his entire body, it's an intimidating effect. Every now and again, however, when he's talking to Linc and Hailee, he'll laugh, and his entire face changes. He looks younger, and I hate to admit it, really attractive. I mean, he's hot with the scowls, but without them, he's gorgeous.

It's clear Linc thinks so too. Jax reaches up to push his hair back for the hundredth time, and Linc's gaze lingers on the muscles that flex with the movement. I know exactly what he's thinking because I'm thinking it too. What would it be like to be pinned down by those arms? To trace the swirls of ink with my tongue . . .

I scowl at my beer. Jax couldn't be any straighter if he tried. The way he continually winks at Hailee, despite not being sure if she's with either of us, makes that abundantly clear. Besides, what business do I have checking him out when I have both Linc and Hailee? Linc is, without a doubt, the most beautiful man I've ever met. And Hailee is just . . . My gaze drops to her shorts. Those fucking shorts. I grip my beer tighter to stop myself from sliding my hand along her thigh.

The familiar pangs of worry begin to prickle in my chest. What if this really is the beginning of the end? What if she doesn't want anything physical with me anymore? Sure, I want to be her friend too, but I don't think I'd be able to cope with taking a separate room while her and Linc share. I wince at the thought.

The waitress brings over our food, and I dig into my steak, grateful for the excuse to busy myself. Hailee is leaning across the table on her elbows, listening to Jax talk about fixing cars. I frown. He's a mechanic. The image of him in overalls pulled down to his waist, smudged with engine oil, pops unwelcomed into my brain, and I quickly shove it out.

I haven't said a word in ages, but have they even noticed? The sinking feeling in my gut intensifies. It's so easy to dig a bottomless hole if you let your mind wander far enough into the darkness. For the last half an hour, I might as well have been sitting here by myself. This used to happen a lot with Andrew. On the rare occasions we'd go out with other couples, he'd dominate the conversation, giving my leg warning squeezes if I joined in too much, or laughed too hard at someone's joke. If he decided I'd smiled too much or even looked too long at someone else, he'd make our excuses and we'd go home. Then he'd fuck me until he was all I could think about. I've gotten very good at extracting myself from conversations.

I look up, marveling at the bright, open faces around me. Andrew isn't here. All I have to do is listen for a minute, say something, and I'll be back in. Even though doubt grips my heart with cold claws, I know that's what would happen. I just can't bring myself to.

A lump closes my throat and I swallow. The air is too warm and the smell of food too strong. I slide out of the booth, muttering something about needing air, and stumble to the door without meeting any of their stares.

Once outside, I ease past the loitering customers and walk around to the side of the restaurant. Leaning against the wall, I tilt my head back and take a deep breath. I need to get it together. This pity party is getting out of control. Squeezing my eyes shut, I concentrate on my breathing, running through the laughter, touches and kisses of the past couple of days. Friends first. Even if this whole thruple thing is fucked, we're still friends. I exhale.

"Carter? What the hell's going on?"

Opening my eyes, I find Linc standing in front of me, concern stark across his face. I close my eyes again.

"I needed air."

"Carter," he says, stepping closer. "You've been weird since Yellowstone. What's wrong?"

"You know what's wrong," I say, forcing my eyes to stay closed, so I won't have to see the concern shift to pity. "I fucked things up. I know Hailee accepted my apology, but it still feels different."

"Things aren't different," he says. Fingers trail down my forearm. "You didn't fuck anything up. Hailee knows you pushed because you care."

"I think you should just drop me at the next bus station. The trip will be more fun without me."

I feel the hardness of Linc's chest a fraction of a second before his lips press against mine.

"Snap out of it, Carter," he rumbles against my mouth. "We're not ditching you."

I open my mouth to argue but he kisses me again, stealing my words. He attacks me with his lips and tongue, biting at my lower lip until I groan, my hands lifting to trace the muscles on his back.

"There he is," Linc breathes, pushing his body against mine until I can feel the shape of his hardening cock against mine. "Don't you dare talk about walking away from this again. Okay?"

I open my eyes, raising my hands to touch his jaw. "I just got lost in my own head, you know?"

"I know." Linc presses a kiss to my nose with a tenderness that causes my cheeks to heat. "Talk to us next time and we'll pull you out."

I nod, tilting my head to take Linc's mouth again. It feels so good. Each touch of him seems to ground me, pulling me back from doubts I know will have me cringing for hours later. I'm so lost in the kiss; I don't hear footsteps approaching.

"Fucking faggots."

Linc tenses, every muscle steel beneath my fingers as he turns around, half shielding me. I keep a hand on his arm, my heart pounding, as I realize what's happening.

Three men have rounded the building. One is older, the other two look around our age. They all have matching looks of disgust smeared across their sneering faces.

"What the fuck do you think you're doing?" one of the younger ones says. "It's fucking disgusting."

Linc reaches behind him, taking my hand. He's trembling. *Fuck.* I squeeze his fingers.

"What we're doing is none of your business," I say, willing calm and authority into my voice. "Why don't you carry on with whatever you were doing?"

"What?" the older man snarls. "Walk away and let you two defile this place? There are goddamn children inside."

"For fucksake," I say, standing a bit taller. "We were only kissing. We're going back inside now. I'd say it was a pleasure to meet you but, you know."

Holding tight to Linc's hand, I take a step away from the wall. The three men don't move. My heart pounds in my throat.

"I think me and my boys need to teach you two faggots a

lesson," the older man says, turning to spit on the ground. "Then maybe you'll think twice before partaking in such ungodly acts in public."

My lips press together, biting back my retort. There's no reasoning with them. They have their backwards opinion and that's their problem. My only concern is getting us back around to the front of the restaurant and to safety.

"Look, we don't want a fight," Linc says.

The waver in his usually calm voice has my pulse quickening, and I tug him closer.

"Damn straight you don't want a fight," one of the younger ones spits. "We're going to teach you a lesson you won't soon forget."

They take a step closer, and I frantically run through our options. I'll shout for help. We'll fight our way out. I have a feeling from the way Linc's clammy hand is still trembling in mine, he's never been in a fight before. I haven't thrown a punch since high school, but maybe I can take them on and give Linc a chance to escape and get help.

Before I can choose an option, they close the gap between us, fists raised.

23

It hurts like hell. One of the younger guys' fists connects with my jaw, and before I can react, he grabs my shoulders and brings his knee up to my gut.

I can't see how Carter's doing. Panic pulses through me. I want to keep him safe, but I also need to not die. Stumbling backwards, clutching my stomach, I attempt to gather myself enough to fight back. I've never been more scared in my life. What if they rupture an internal organ? What if they have knives? Or guns? What if they kill us?

A fist connects with my ribs, and I crumple to the ground with a grunt. Shielding my face with my arms, I try to look for Carter. I catch sight of him landing a punch before the older man swings and connects with his jaw. The sound reverberates through me, and I fight through the throbbing pain to get to my feet. A foot collides with my stomach, and I cry out.

"Get up, you fucking queer!"

Gasping, I try to suck air into my lungs as another kick connects with my side. I'm taller than two of them, and almost certainly in better shape, but as I reluctantly curl into a ball on the cold ground, it doesn't matter. I've never been in a fight. I've never thrown a punch. My entire life has been spent modeling, and models don't fight. My body is my job. It was written into my last contract that I wasn't allowed to play contact sports amongst a long list of other things, like rock climbing, kayaking, etc. etc. Cuts and bruises don't sell underwear or cologne.

"What the fuck?"

A voice calls out as the sound of fighting increases, and I prepare for another kick, my eyes burning at the thought of what the punching noises mean for Carter. I've failed him. The kick I'm bracing for doesn't come, and I lower my arms, peering into the shadows. My eyes widen as I push myself up and scramble backwards.

Carter is half laid on the floor, clutching his jaw as he tries to stand. The older man and one of the younger ones are lying on the ground groaning, and I watch, mouth open, as Jax grips the front of the other man's shirt and delivers a punch that has him crumpling to the ground with a grunt.

Jax shakes out his hand and then extends it to Carter, who takes it, allowing him to haul him to his feet.

"You three better get the fuck out of here," Jax snarls, drawing back his foot and delivering a hard kick to one of the fallen men. "You so much as look at one of my friends again and I'll rip your fucking throats out."

His cold words send a chill through me, but then he looks over at me and the hard lines of his face melt into concern.

"Shit. You okay?"

I groan in response, and he jogs over to me, dropping to a crouch at my side.

"Can you walk?" He lays a hand on my shoulder. "Do we need to call for an ambulance?"

My head spins as I look from him to Carter, who stands behind him, his lip bleeding. I scramble to my feet, wincing at the pain, but I need to get to him. Carter opens his arms, and I fall into them, pressing my face into his neck. His arms tighten around me, and I screw my eyes shut, fighting the tears.

"Are you okay?" I manage; the words muffled against his shoulder.

"Jax saved us," he says. "Thanks, man."

I pull back, watching as the three men clamber to their feet. Jax takes a step towards them, shoulders squared, and they retreat behind an onslaught of slurs and hate-filled curses.

"What happened?" I ask. "How did you . . .?"

Once it seems he's certain the men aren't coming back, he turns to us. "You took a while, and Hailee was worried. I offered to come check on you and found those pieces of shit laying into you. Carter had already taken care of one, so I helped with the other two."

"Thank you," I say, shaking my head in disbelief. "If you hadn't shown up . . ."

"Yeah, well, I did. And no worries."

I turn back to Carter, running my thumb against his cheek and below the cut on his swollen lip. "I'm so sorry."

He covers my hand with his. "What the hell are you sorry for?"

"I was useless." I shake my head as cold shame coats my skin.

"Hey." Jax's tattooed hand grips my shoulder. "You got jumped by three rednecks. They outnumbered you. It was never a fair fight. It was also a fight they shouldn't have started in the first place. Fucking assholes."

I nod gratefully, but his words do little to make me feel better.

"Come on," he says, squeezing my shoulder before stepping back. "Let's get back inside. Hailee will be worried. Besides, I got their plate. You need to report those fuckers for assault."

Carter grips my hand as we head back to the restaurant, and I'm grateful for his steadying presence. The cute greeter almost drops a stack of menus when we push open the door. Jax steers us toward the booth while he explains what happened and asks for ice.

Hailee gasps as we approach. She scrambles out of the booth, glancing between us as though she doesn't know who to deal with first.

"What happened?" she asks, her big brown eyes wide and glistening as they skim over our bloodied features.

I can feel the eyes of everyone on our side of the restaurant watching and listening, and I shift uncomfortably.

"Three dumb fucks decided to jump them round the side of the restaurant," Jax explains, coming to stand next to us, his vibrant blue eyes narrowed as he eyes our injuries.

A strangled cry tears from Hailee's throat. Almost falling forward, she throws her arms around us both, and I grunt, wincing at the pain in my side.

"We called the police."

I turn to find the greeter standing behind us, and I offer him a small smile of thanks.

"This is my evening job," he says quietly, his eyes darting to the eavesdropping customers. "I'm training to be a paramedic. I can check your injuries if you want. See if you need to go to a hospital."

My stomach rolls. I really don't want to go to a hospital. I just want to get out of here.

"I'm almost fully qualified."

I decide to put him out of his misery. "That would be great, thanks."

He leads us to a small room through the doors to the kitchen. Although both Carter and I tell them they don't need to, Hailee and Jax insist on coming, too. Judging by the bags and clothes strewn over the benches, it must be some sort of staff break room. He gestures for us to sit and goes to fetch a first aid kit.

"I can't believe it," Hailee says, her hand raising to her mouth. "I just . . ."

She looks away, and Jax puts a comforting arm over her shoulders. I glance at Carter, expecting him to look jealous, but he just looks defeated. His lip has stopped bleeding and there's a bruise blossoming on his cheekbone. I wonder what I look like. I don't think I'm bleeding. They only landed one punch to my face before getting stuck in with their feet. I close my eyes and draw in a painful breath. I won't be able to set up an appointment with the agency in San Francisco until my injuries are gone.

"Here." The greeter hands us each an ice pack and then kneels in front of Carter to inspect his cut. "I'm Brett, by the way."

"Thanks, Brett." I press the ice pack to my jaw. "We appreciate your help."

His face creases into a frown as he dabs antiseptic onto Carter's wound. "It makes me so mad that people think they can do that. My ex-boyfriend got a brick thrown at him once."

I wince. "I'm sorry."

"It just shouldn't happen," he continues, sitting back to inspect his work. He pulls free another wipe and sets about checking Carter's knuckles. "You and your boyfriend should be able to be yourselves in public without closed minded bastards getting physical."

I feel Carter stiffen beside me. My skin prickles. Should I tell Brett that we aren't boyfriends? I don't think a word exists for what we are. Before I can make up my mind, he stands up and tosses the wipe in the trash. I suppose it doesn't really matter, anyway.

"Are you injured anywhere else?" he asks.

Carter shakes his head. "No, I only took a couple of hits to the face."

Brett turns his attention to me. Gripping my chin gently, he inspects my throbbing cheekbone. "He didn't break the skin. Did you get hurt anywhere else?"

I hesitate, but before I can say I'm okay, Jax speaks up.

"They were kicking the shit out of him when I turned up."

I shoot him a look, but he shrugs. Under his arm, Hailee's face crumples. "I'm fine," I reassure her. "Honestly."

Carter reaches out and touches my arm. "Let him take a look at you. We don't want you dying of internal bleeding or something."

I roll my eyes and stand, grimacing with the effort. Grabbing the back of my t-shirt, I pull it off over my head.

"Shit." Carter hisses at my side.

Reluctantly, I look down at my side. Red marks are already deepening into purple just below my ribs and stretching to my hips. I can feel from the stretch that they follow around to my spine, too.

Brett shakes his head and carefully inspects the damage. I glance at Hailee, who's watching with warring emotions on her face. It looks as though she can't decide whether to cry or tear the world a new one. Wincing as Brett presses against one of the bruises, my gaze flicks to Jax. He still has a hand on Hailee's shoulder. His eyes, however, are on me. My body, to be more precise. At first, I think he's looking at the bruising, but as his gaze tracks across my chest and down my abs, I grin despite the pain I'm in. He must sense me watching, because his eyes meet mine, challenging and impassive, before looking away.

"You look okay," Brett says, straightening. "Just keep an eye on the bruising and take it easy."

I grab my shirt and pull it back on. "Thanks, man."

"No problem. I just wish you hadn't needed my help."

Hailee steps forward and carefully wraps her arms around me, resting her head against my chest. I exhale and press a kiss to her curls, stroking her back.

"Let's pay and get out of here," I say.

Brett turns from where he's putting the first aid kit away. "No need to pay; the restaurant is footing the bill. I spoke to the manager already."

Jax scoffs. "Probably hoping you don't sue."

"Great," I say, ignoring his comment. "Shall we get out of here, then?"

"You need to talk to the police," Hailee mumbles against my chest. "You'll need to give them descriptions and stuff."

I almost sink back down to the bench. I just want to get back in the car and pretend this never happened. Hailee releases me and heads toward the door, following Brett.

Carter heaves to his feet beside me. "Come on. Let's get this over and done with."

I start toward the door, but Jax steps to us, lowering his voice.

"Listen. I need to ask you a favor."

Frowning, I lift my shoulders in a shrug, glancing at Carter. "Sure. Whatever. We owe you one."

"I need you to leave me out of things when you talk to the cops."

I raise my eyebrows. "What do you mean? Why?"

Jax shakes his head. "It's nothing bad, I swear. I just don't like cops, and I don't want where I am on record. Can you just say the guys got spooked and ran?"

My jaw flexes and I look at Carter, who's watching Jax with narrowed eyes. I owe him. We both do. It's not exactly lying, and we'll still be reporting the crime.

I sigh. "Sure."

Jax looks at Carter, who gives a half-hearted shrug. "Fine."

As we follow the others out of the room, I try to quell the feeling of unease churning in my gut. Jax saved us, has been fun to hang out with, but we really don't know anything about him. But then, how well do I really know Hailee and Carter? I haven't even told them the truth about me. By the time I step back into the restaurant, my shoulders weigh a ton.

Three hours later, we arrive in Salt Lake City. After a lot of protest from both me and Hailee, Jax drove the final two hours. Carter and I dozed in the back seat, aware of Hailee turning around to check on us every five minutes. Going over what had happened with the police was horrible. Although they were understanding, it still sent ripples of shame through me. It's the same whenever I look at Carter's handsome face. I should have been able to protect him. I was as much use in that fight as a six-year-old.

"Stop it," Jax says, gesturing at me with his bottle of beer. "You're in your head again."

I cock an eyebrow at him and take a sip of whiskey from the plastic hotel cup. I've drunk way too much beer on this trip already, considering I'm not hitting the gym, so when we swung by a liquor store, I opted for spirits. If I'd known I'd be drinking it out of a questionable plastic cup, I might have reconsidered.

We booked a suite, which consists of a double bed, a single and a couch. Carter and Hailee fought about the cost, but I said I wanted the space, and I was happy to pay for it. Playing the invalid card got me my way, at least.

Jax says he's going to head off after a few drinks. Hailee has tried to press him for information, but so far, he's dodged her questions. I suspect he doesn't have enough money for a hotel room, and I know there's no way he'll accept charity.

The bathroom door opens, releasing a cloud of steam into the room as Carter emerges in a pair of sweatpants with a towel draped over his shoulders. I grabbed the first shower, desperate to get the feel of the parking lot off my skin. I hand Carter a beer, shamelessly taking in the sight of him. He accepts the drink with a wink and sits down beside me on the bed.

"Okay," Jax says, leaning back on the couch. "I can't take it anymore."

"What?" Hailee asks from where she's sitting, legs under her, at the other end.

"What the fuck is this?" He gestures at each of us in turn with his drink. "You're all sharing a room like a fourth-grade sleepover?"

I take a long sip of my drink, letting the burning liquor slide down my throat, searing my gut. Hailee looks at me at the same time as Carter, and I huff a laugh.

"Like that, is it? You two are putting this on me to explain?"

Hailee gives me an apologetic smile, drawing her teeth over her plump bottom lip.

"Fine." I hand Carter my whiskey and stand, crossing the short distance to the sofa.

Hailee looks up at me with those beautiful eyes and I bend down, claiming her mouth in a gentle but thorough kiss. Then I straighten and return to the bed, where I repeat the action with Carter, being careful not to hurt his injured lip. When I sit back down and look at Jax, I find him watching us, amusement sparkling in his eyes.

"So, like, the three of you . . .?" He gestures with his beer bottle.

We all nod, awaiting his response. Not that it should matter, but I know if he tells us we're disgusting, especially after what happened earlier, it will hurt like hell.

"Whatever works for you," he says, taking a thoughtful swig of his beer. "So, you're all okay with each other being with . . . each other?"

"Yes," Carter says firmly. "We decided we're friends first. Everything else is secondary."

Jax shrugs. "I mean. Sharing is caring, right?"

We all stare at him for a moment, unsure what to make of his reaction, but then he smiles, shaking his head.

"Your faces. Seriously. Relax. It's none of my business, anyway. I was just curious. If I overstep, just tell me to fuck off, and I will."

My shoulders loosen a little. "You're fine. We just haven't had to explain it to anyone yet. I mean, we're still figuring it all out ourselves."

"But we'll definitely tell you to fuck off if we need to," Carter adds, his lips twitching.

Jax chuckles and takes a drink of his beer.

"In all seriousness, though," Carter continues. "I don't think I've properly thanked you yet for saving our asses."

Jax holds his drink up in a salute. "You're welcome. And you don't need to thank me."

I down my drink and stand to pour another. If I can't make myself stop thinking about what happened, perhaps the alcohol will help.

"Okay," I say, holding up the bottle of whiskey. "Who's in the mood for shots?"

24

Laughter fills the room, and I lean back on the sofa, smiling, my face a little numb from the alcohol. I'm glad Linc insisted on a larger room. It's nice to have the space, and I'm happy that Jax has decided to continue to hang out with us. Linc has produced a Bluetooth speaker from his bag, a chilled playlist the backdrop to our conversations, and someone has turned off the main light, leaving just a lamp on, which gives the room a cozy feel. Despite everything that's happened today, I'm feeling quite relaxed. Or maybe that's the alcohol.

I watch Linc smiling as he listens to something Carter's saying, and my heart swells. When he and Carter walked back into the restaurant, battered and bruised, I was devastated. Worse than the cuts and bruises, it was the look on Linc's face that shredded my heart. Carter and I are forever up and down with our moods, but Linc is our constant. His warm smile is a life raft I cling to, and to see him look so defeated was too much to take.

Jax booms a laugh beside me, pulling my attention. I realize it's something Carter has said, and I can't help but feel relieved. It was obvious he hadn't wanted to pick Jax up, especially when Linc had protested that we should because he was 'sexy'. I'd said there was no way he could possibly tell driving past him at seventy miles an hour, but he was right. Jax is hot as hell.

I sip my Jack and coke and let my gaze drift over his tattooed biceps, moving up to his broad chest and chiseled jaw. His eyes are mesmerizing. I've never seen anything like them. They're as striking as Carter's ice blue ones, but they hit differently. Come to think of it, Linc's dark eyes, with his long thick lashes are stunning, too. Frowning, I look at each of the men in turn, appreciating just how gorgeous they are in their own ways. All different, but equally beautiful. It's enough to make me giggle. How on earth did this happen? It's got to be some sort of cosmic joke. I'd expected a lonely trip of self-reflection for one when I ran away. Not this.

I swallow, the truth trailing an ice cold finger down my spine. I ran away. The thought is never far from my mind. I glance at Carter, who's leaning back on the bed, still shirtless. Things have been strained between us, even though he apologized. I know I have to try and get over it if we want the rest of the trip to go well.

"What's going on in that head of yours?"

I find Jax watching me, his mouth curved in a smirk.

"Just thinking," I say.

"About what?"

I shake my head. "Just about today. A lot happened."

Jax gives me a sympathetic smile and lifts his bottle of beer to his mouth. My gaze lowers to his hand, and my eyes widen. His knuckles are split, already scabbing.

"You didn't tell that paramedic guy about your hand," I say.

"I'm fine." He shrugs. "It's only the one hand. It's not the first time and it won't be the last."

Although I'd pretended I wasn't listening, I heard Carter and Linc tell the cops what happened. I heard them purposefully not mention Jax, and I also noticed that he conveniently disappeared when the cops arrived. What is he hiding? He might not be an axe murderer, but that doesn't mean he's not a criminal.

Jax watches me intently as he sips his beer, as though daring me to push the matter. There's something about the way he holds himself, the way he looks at me, that makes my breath catch.

"What are you two talking about that's got you so intense?" Linc asks, causing me to break the stare.

"I was just pointing out that Jax didn't mention his injured hand at the restaurant."

"Shit," Linc says, lowering his glass of whiskey. "Are you okay, man?"

Jax sits back against the sofa, hooking one ankle over his knee. "I'm fucking peachy. Don't worry about me."

"Why didn't you want the police to know you were there?" I ask, the words tripping from my tongue before I can stop them.

Jax stares at me, his expression unreadable. On the bed, I can feel Linc and Carter watching and waiting. After an impossibly long silence, he sighs and shakes his head.

"I don't owe you a fucking explanation," he says quietly. "But, if you really want to know, it's simple. I had a shitty childhood, grew up in the system and did a stint in juvie when I was a kid. Trusting cops is not something that comes easily to me, and I try to stay out of their way. I'm not a damn criminal, so you can fucking relax. Okay?"

My heart clenches as he downs his beer and reaches for

another one, avoiding our stares. "I'm sorry for asking," I say. "It's none of my business."

Jax shrugs. "If I hadn't wanted to tell you, I wouldn't have."

For a moment, only the sound of music fills the room and I mentally kick myself for killing the mood.

"Thank you for trusting us enough to tell us," Carter says. "I appreciate it."

Jax glances over at him and Carter stands, walking over and knocking his mug of whiskey against his beer.

"Whatever," Jax mumbles. "It doesn't mean we're gonna start braiding each other's hair or anything."

I snort into my drink, and Linc laughs. He winces, hissing, through his teeth and Carter groans, tugging a hand through his hair, making it stick up.

"I'm so sorry, Linc," he says, kneeling on the bed beside him. "You're hurt because I was such a dick. If I hadn't stormed off, it never would have happened."

"Shut up," Linc says, reaching behind him and placing his cup down on the nightstand. "You had every right to take a minute. It's not your fault those assholes did what they did. If you want to blame someone, blame me. I'm the one who kissed you."

Carter scowls. "You know that's bullshit."

"Is it? 'Cause I thought that's what we were doing? Casting blame around?"

I squirm in my seat. Carter stormed off because he was still in a mood after what happened in Yellowstone. Hopefully, they won't remember that I'm really the person to blame.

"Shut up," Carter growls. "Just stop."

Linc drags his gaze down Carter's body before licking his lips. "Make me."

Carter reaches behind him and puts down his mug, his eyes never leaving Linc's. With wolf-like intensity in his ice-blue eyes, he reaches out and grabs a fistful of Linc's t-shirt, pulling him forward. He kisses him hard, his other hand gripping Linc's jaw, and I swallow, my mouth dry as I watch, transfixed.

I saw them kiss the first night we spent together, and I know they fooled around in the car, but I've forgotten just how much I enjoy watching them. My breathing slows, the grip on my drink tightening as I watch Linc's fingers trail over Carter's chest. Carter pushes Linc's shirt up, pulling it up over his head, and my breath hitches. They're going for it. Right here. Now.

I know they'll be okay with me being here, and possibly even ask me to get involved at some point, but have they forgotten that Jax is still in the room? Perhaps they don't care. After all, I suppose he could get up and leave at any point.

Tearing my eyes away from the two men, I glance to my right. Jax is lazing back on the sofa as before, but his eyes are fixed on me.

"You like watching?" he asks, his voice low.

I nod, my heartbeat thundering in my ears.

His eyes flash. I open my mouth to say something, although I'm not sure what, when a moan drags my attention away. Linc has pushed Carter down onto his back, kissing his way down his chest while sliding a hand down the front of his sweats. Carter arches, his eyes closing as Linc grips him.

Heat pools between my thighs, my nipples hardening as I watch Linc grip hold of his waistband and pull down. Carter's cock springs free, and I inhale sharply, mesmerized as Linc stares hungrily at it. He lowers his mouth, running his tongue along the hard length before taking him between his lips. A faint whimper escapes me, and Linc's attention snaps to the sofa.

"Do you like what you see, Hailee?" he asks before sliding his mouth back down over Carter's length, his eyes fixed on mine the whole time.

I suck in a breath, pressing my thighs together as I nod. Carter swears as Linc works him with his mouth, but after a few seconds, he lifts his head again.

"What about you, Jax?" Linc asks, his voice low. His breath catches as Carter slides his hand down his shorts, gripping him.

I turn to Jax, but his gaze is still on me. "I'm enjoying watching what you're doing to Hailee."

"How do you feel about Jax watching you?" Linc asks, his words tight between panting breaths as Carter strokes him.

I think about it for a second, remembering my resolution to throw myself into the experience wholeheartedly. "I don't mind at all."

Carter groans, and I look back in time to see Linc take him into his mouth again.

"Get your fucking cock out," Carter grunts. "I want to taste you."

It's all I can do not to slide a hand between my legs. Instead, I put my drink down, my hand clutching the arm of the sofa as my heart pounds in my throat.

On the bed, Linc shoves down his shorts, releasing his own long, hard cock, and Carter moans as he sits up and takes him deep into his mouth. Linc throws his head back, his abs flexing as he grips Carter's hair, moving his hips. It's so fucking hot, I can't breathe.

I cast a quick glance at Jax to find him watching Linc and Carter, his bottle paused just before his mouth. A fraction of a second later, his gaze snaps to mine and I look away, returning my attention to my men.

"Carter," Linc gasps. "I want you to fuck me."

My breath halts, my grip tightening on the sofa. Carter pulls off Linc, a look of uncertainty flashing across his features, and Linc frowns, pulling him up so they're face to face on their knees.

"I can fuck you if you want," he murmurs against his lips. "Is that what you want, Carter? My big dick in your beautiful, tight ass?"

Carter whimpers, his eyes fluttering closed as he exhales. "Yes."

I take in a breath, my body throbbing. I know they haven't had sex yet and I don't want to get between them, figuratively or literally. But as much as I'm enjoying watching, I need to touch myself or I'm going to combust.

"Hailee?"

I look at Carter, my eyes flitting between his icy gaze, and where he has his hand wrapped around both his and Linc's cocks, stroking them together.

"Are you wet, watching us?" he asks.

"Yes." The word is a rasp.

"How would you feel about Jax confirming that?"

My eyes widen, and I turn to Jax. He licks his lips, a predatory glint like fire in his navy-rimmed eyes.

"I'm game if she is," he says, his voice low and steady.

My head spins. I need to be touched. If the guys are okay with Jax being the one to do it, then fuck it.

"Yes," I manage.

Jax puts down his beer and stands, walking around the sofa and coming to a stop behind me. He brings his mouth down to my ear. "How drunk are you, princess?"

I shudder as his lips brush my skin. "Drunk enough that

I'm not embarrassed, and sober enough to know that I really want you to touch me."

His lips curve into a smile against my ear. "That's the perfect amount of drunk."

Jax slides his hands down my stomach, unbuttoning my shorts, and my breathing quickens. On the bed, Linc and Carter grind against each other as they kiss and claw, the sound of their desperate moans filling the room. Jax presses a kiss to my neck at the same time he slips a hand down my shorts, underneath my panties, and my eyes flutter shut. I lift my hips and he strokes his fingers through me.

"How wet is she, Jax?" Linc asks, looking up from the bed.

Jax presses another kiss to my neck. "Fucking drenched."

Linc's eyes flash, and I look at Carter, who's also watching, his eyes hooded.

"Do you want me to touch you more?" Jax whispers against my neck.

"Yes. Please."

"So fucking polite." Jax chuckles softly as he pulls his hand out to draw up my shirt, exposing my bra. He pushes down the cups and pinches my nipples so hard I cried out.

"You like that?" he murmurs.

I pant, wanting more. "Yes."

He licks his fingers before returning them to my breasts, rubbing and rolling my nipples until I'm arching back against the sofa, writhing.

"Keep looking," he says softly. "I want to watch you."

I force myself to sit up, opening my eyes. My mouth runs dry as I take in the scene on the bed. Carter is on all fours as Linc tears open a packet of lube, rubbing it over his fingers and the condom he's already rolled on.

Jax snakes a hand back between my legs as I watch Linc

grip Carter's hip, inching a finger inside him. Carter groans, bracing on his forearms, and I writhe against Jax's hand.

"Patience," he murmurs against my ear. "You'll get there."

Jax strokes through my center, teasing and swirling, knowing what I want, but holding back.

He gently grips my chin with his other hand. "Do you like watching them fuck?"

I moan in reply, swallowing hard as Linc pushes in a second finger. Carter's pleading noises reverberate through me, and I lift my hips, urging Jax to touch where I need him to so badly.

"Soon," Jax says, dropping a hand to my breast and working the nipple.

His fingers graze my clit before moving away again, and I whimper. I know what he's waiting for. On the bed, Linc tightens his hold on Carter's hip, steadying himself as he grips his cock with his other hand. I can barely breathe, panting as he slowly pushes into Carter. Jax's fingers curl, and I lift my hips, desperate for him to fill me. Just as Linc sinks into Carter, and they both cry out with guttural groans that light me on fire, Jax plunges his fingers into me, pumping hard enough that I gasp, my head falling back.

When I open my eyes, I find Linc and Carter watching, their eyes fixed on where Jax's fingers are working me inside my shorts. I bite my lip as he flicks my clit before continuing his steady rhythm.

"Fuck," Linc mutters, as he starts to move his hips.

The hotel room fills with sounds of raw pleasure, drowning out the music. I drop my hands to my shorts, eager for more, but Jax stops me.

"Keep them on," he says against my ear. "If you decide

you want me to fuck you, we'll be alone, and I'm going to take you so hard, you'll forget your own name."

With a shiver, I move my hands to cover his, grinding as he curls his fingers inside me. The pressure builds, and I writhe, cursing as I come, pulsing against him. Jax nibbles my neck, stroking me until the last tremors of my orgasm fade.

"Hailee?"

I open my eyes, and a breathy moan escapes me at what I see. Linc has Carter up on his knees, an arm wrapped around his chest as he thrusts into him.

"How would you like to help Carter out?" Linc asks.

I stand on shaking legs and walk over to the bed. Carter leans his head back against Linc's shoulder, his sounds of ecstasy spurring me on as I reach for his length. I wrap my hand around him, marveling at how hard he is, and he cries out.

Leaning forward, I take him into my mouth, his resulting whimpers making me more lightheaded than the alcohol.

"Fuck. Fuck . . . Fuck!" Carter pants, one hand stroking my face as the other grips Linc's arm wrapped around his chest. "Fuck. I'm coming."

I take him as deep as I can, swallowing down his release, and when I pull off him, I smile as he leans back against Linc, a sated, sweaty mess. Linc presses a tender kiss to his shoulder and winks at me.

"Fucking hot," he says.

I grin, shaking my head. "Fucking hot."

A click pulls my attention, and I look over to see the bathroom door locking.

"What do you think Jax made of this?" Linc asks quietly.

My cheeks heat as I recall the words he whispered in my

ear. "I have no idea. I honestly thought he'd bolt as soon as you two started getting naked."

"Me too," Carter says, his breathing labored.

I reach up and stroke his chest. "You look well and truly fucked."

He opens an eye and looks down at me. "Hilarious."

Linc grips Carter's chin and gives him a brief but fierce kiss, before pulling out and disposing of the condom in the small bin by the door. I straighten my clothes as Carter pulls his sweats back on.

"What do you think he's doing in there?" Linc whispers, in a way that sounds like he knows exactly what he's doing.

Carter chuckles. "I bet he's twenty shades of confused right now, because you know it's not just Hailee that's going to be popping into his head."

I shush them, my cheeks heating, as Linc pulls on his clothes then grabs everyone a drink. When the bathroom door finally opens, Jax steps out, heading back to the sofa as though nothing has happened.

"The couch is yours if you want it, Jax," Carter offers. "It's really late, and it's the least we could do after today."

Jax takes a swig of his beer, and I watch as he considers the offer.

"Sure," he says. "Thanks."

I exhale. After the events of today, I have no idea what tomorrow will bring, but as I fetch another round of drinks, I smile at the thought of us facing it together.

25

THE FIRST THOUGHT I HAVE WHEN I OPEN MY EYES IS, 'WHERE the fuck am I?' It's not unusual to wake up with that thought, but it's been a while. The room is frustratingly light, in the way hotel rooms get with their cheap ass thin curtains. My mouth is as dry as a crusty sock, and my head a little heavier than it should be after only a handful of beers. Squinting, I reach across to the bedside table and grab a half-empty bottle and take a sip.

For a hotel room, it's pretty comfortable. I close my eyes and lay back on the pillow, tugging the covers half off to let my body cool. They told me I could have the sofa, but eventually they all squashed onto the queen-sized bed, which meant the single had my name on it. What a fucking turn of events. When I accepted a ride from them, I had not expected last night. I smile to myself. *Kinky fuckers*.

It had been hard to rein myself in. Hailee was so hot for Carter and Linc, I've got no doubt she'd have bounced on my cock quite happily. I meant what I said to her, though. If she decides she wants me, I want her alone. So, I slipped off to the bathroom to take matters into my own hands instead.

Turning my head, I look over at their bed. They're all still fast asleep. Linc is on the side nearest to me, the sheet only covering one of his legs. The guy is ripped as fuck. Carter has that outdoor, go for the occasional run look, but Linc's muscles are crafted. I know because I work out hard. My build isn't for fucking aesthetics, though. I've earned this bulk for protection—to survive situations like at the restaurant last night. Despite his god-like physique, it's clear Linc's never been in a fight in his life. Maybe I should teach him to throw a punch before we part ways.

I allow myself to take him in, like a piece of art, but a movement draws my attention. Eyes still closed, Linc slides a hand into his briefs, taking his morning wood in his hand. I raise my eyebrows, a smirk on my lips, as he begins to tug in languid strokes. Stifling a snort, I turn my head and close my eyes. I should probably start thinking about getting out of here. Last night was interesting, but if they start getting up to stuff this morning, I'm getting the fuck out of here.

After a few seconds, I find my head turning back, and my eyes opening just enough to see. I'm just checking to see if he's finished. I'm not *watching*. Linc stretches, his back arching slightly, but I don't look away. His dark, olive skin is so smooth. Other than the huge fucking bruise on his side, it's like he's been carved from fucking marble. His stomach tenses and I watch the grooves between his abs deepen like the Badlands.

"Like what you see?"

My eyes dart up to find Linc watching me through sleepy eyes, a lazy smile curving his lips. They're feminine lips. Full and pouty. Nothing else about him is feminine, though. Well. Maybe his hair.

"No," I mutter, returning my gaze to the ceiling.

"Your dick says otherwise."

Snorting, I resist the urge to adjust myself where I'm tenting the goddamn sheets. "Fuck off. It's just morning wood. I was looking at your fucking bruise."

Linc's laugh sounds like a yawn. "Sure. Whatever makes you feel better. Speaking of which. I can help you out, if you want?"

I turn to look at him, my brain caught somewhere between disbelief and disgust. "What?"

"The others are still asleep, so no one will be watching."

There are no words, so I shake my head and close my eyes.

"You watched me fuck Carter, and I'm pretty sure that image popped into your head when you went to the bathroom to finish yourself off. If I blow you, how is that any different?"

I keep my eyes closed, willing my skin not to heat. That image had popped into my head as I beat one out in the bathroom. I'd tried to focus on Hailee, with her pretty tits and russet nipples, but I just couldn't keep my head there.

"It's very different. Fuck off."

Linc sighs in a way that tells me he's stretching. "Well. The offer is there. Don't get obsessed over labels. If I suck you off it doesn't make you gay. We're both hard as fuck and jerking yourself off isn't as much fun as someone else doing it. It's not rocket science."

Balking at his words, I scoff, "I don't give a shit about labels. I just don't need you to get me off."

Despite my better judgement, I open my eyes and look over at him. His hand is no longer on his dick, thank fuck, but tucked behind his head. He watches me carefully, his eyes tracking over every inch of me. I clench my jaw, trying not to shift under his gaze. If he wants to check me out, he can be my fucking guest.

"Don't get me wrong," he says, locking eyes with me again. "I'm not trying to pressure you or anything, and I'm certainly not going to demand you sit on top of a float at Pride, Jax. It was just a friendly offer to experience the best head you've ever had."

I snort a laugh. "I've had a lot of head. That's a very bold statement."

Linc grins. "I'm very confident."

"Yeah, well thanks for the offer, but I'm good."

With that, I toss off the rest of the sheets, grab my bag and head to the bathroom. I shake my head as I flip on the water in the shower. The fucking cheek. Kicking off my underwear, I step under the spray and unwrap one of the shitty hotel soaps. What would he have done if I'd said yes? Had he been serious? I close my eyes and scrub at myself. Would he have just slipped over and slid my dick into his mouth, with Carter and Hailee right there? My dick perks up further at the thought and I frown down at it. Absolutely fucking not. I've never watched gay porn, and I've certainly never touched myself thinking about a man before. Appreciating a good-looking man isn't something I've shied away from, but that's just because I'm comfortable with my sexuality. I shake my head, and wash myself off. Gritting my teeth, I step out of the shower and grab a towel. I'm not jacking off thinking about Linc's pretty mouth on my dick. If that means I have to walk around with a semi, so be it.

When I emerge from the bathroom, Linc has drifted back to sleep, and I watch the three of them for a moment, feeling like a fucking creeper. This is the point where I should leave and not look back. The hotel is quite central, and I know I'll find another ride sooner or later that will take me closer to Phoenix. As much as it pisses me off, though, I don't want to leave without saying goodbye.

They have a weird ass situation, but they seem happy. And although I wouldn't tell Linc in a million years, it was hot as hell last night. I haven't been that hard in a long time. Stifling a sigh, I root around until I find something to write on, and scrawl my cell number down with a note saying to call when they get up.

My skin heats as I place it down on the bedside table. They aren't going in my direction. What do I even want from them? If they call me, what am I going to do? Suggest we hang out? I pinch the bridge of my nose. I don't have a fucking clue.

Letting the hotel room door close behind me, I head for the exit, already reaching for my pack of smokes. Maybe they won't even call. They might be relieved that I've left. I pull out my phone and look at the time. It's only eight am. I'll give them until nine thirty. If they haven't called by then, I'm not going to answer.

26

It's so hot. Why do I feel like I've been hit by a bus? I peel open my eyes, grimacing at the furry feeling in my mouth. *Shit.* The events of the day before hit me like a freight train. Reaching up, I touch the thin scab on my lip before pressing at the tender spot on my jaw. Although my attacker hadn't landed any hits to my body, he'd knocked me down hard, and my limbs are sore from cuddling the concrete. My pulse quickens as I realize the other cause of my soreness. Linc fucked me last night, while Hailee and Jax watched. I swallow, waiting for the mortification to kick in, but it doesn't.

Turning my head, I smile at Hailee's spill of brown curls across the pillows. I thought I'd fucked everything up, but things seem to be okay. I reach out and trail a finger down Hailee's arm. How is it possible that I've found myself in this situation? It's only been a couple of days, and I care about the two people in bed with me more than almost anyone else I can think of. My stomach drops as I remember our days are numbered.

Pushing the thought from my head before it festers, I lift

my head to check on Jax. The bed is empty. I frown, turning to look at the bathroom door. It's open, with no one in sight. *Shit.* He left. The disappointment that courses through me takes me by surprise. I wanted to get rid of him at the first opportunity, so why am I not happy?

Careful not to wake Hailee and Linc, I slide out of bed to relieve myself and brush my teeth. I inspect my face as I brush, wincing at the redness. It's nowhere near as bad as it could have been, and I'm grateful for the lack of black eyes. I move away from the sink and lean against the doorframe, watching Linc sprawled on his back. The way he'd trembled against me when those men approached had awoken something in me I didn't realize I could feel. The protectiveness that rose, red hot, in my blood had been enough that I think I could have killed one of them.

Even though Linc seemed like he was back to his normal laid back self last night, I know in my heart that those men broke something inside him. His light will always be a little darker, and I hate that. It makes me want to hunt down those three scumbags and make them pay. Hopefully, the police have found them.

Linc stretches, and I step back into the bathroom to spit and rinse. By the time I turn to the door, he's there.

"Morning." He grins.

I reach for him, but instead of kissing him, I wrap my arms around him and rest my head on his shoulder.

He presses a kiss to my temple. "Is this your way of avoiding my morning breath?"

"No." My shoulders shake with a chuckle. "I just wanted to hold you."

Linc seems to relax a little at my words and his arms grip me tighter. The warmth of his body against mine is comforting, and I could quite happily stand here a lot longer, but Linc kisses my head again and releases me.

"Let me brush my teeth, and then I can give you a proper good morning," he says.

"I'll hold you to that."

"I'm counting on it."

I look back out at the room, where Hailee is still fast asleep. "Jax is gone."

Linc turns, frowning around his toothbrush. "I know."

I walk over to the bed to check that his things are gone, but the only evidence that he was there at all, is the queue of empty beer bottles and the rumpled sheets. My gaze snags on the receipt from the liquor store, curled on the table beside our bed. I pick it up and unfurl it.

"Did you find something?" Linc asks, stepping out of the bathroom.

I smile. "Jax left his number. He's said to call when we get up."

Linc's eyes light up, and instead of the twinge of jealousy I'm expecting, I realize my expression is probably not dissimilar. There's something about Jax, and although I know he's not headed to Vegas, I'm not ready to say goodbye just yet.

I take the receipt around to my side of the bed and root in my bag for my phone. By the time I've shot him a text telling him we've just woken up and should be checking out within the hour, Linc has discarded his underwear and climbed back under the covers.

My lips quirk as I stare down at him, folding my arms across my chest. "What are you doing?"

He looks up at me with big, brown, innocent eyes. "What do you mean?"

My resulting laugh causes Hailee to groan.

Before she can lift her head, I follow Linc's lead and shuck off my own briefs and climb in on her other side.

"Why does my head hurt so much?" Hailee grumbles into her pillow.

"Here," I say, handing her the glass of water I poured last night. She'd passed out before she could touch it.

Grimacing, she sits up and takes it gratefully. "Whoever suggested shots, I hate you."

Linc clasps a hand to his heart. "That's a little harsh."

I reach out and smooth a curl from her cheek. She's wearing Linc's t-shirt, and somehow manages to look both ridiculously cute and insanely sexy in it. I can't remember if she kept her underwear on when she got ready for bed, and the thought of her sitting between us in nothing but Linc's shirt has my dick waking up fast.

Hailee squints at me. "Why are you looking at me like that?"

I raise my eyebrows. "Like what?"

"You know," she says, waving a hand in my direction as she sips her water. "You're doing your wolf thing."

Linc barks a laugh. "Oh, my god! Yes!"

"What fucking 'wolf' thing?"

"You get a look in your eyes," Linc explains. "It's like a wolf waiting to rip some small creature's throat out."

I look between the two of them, my eyebrows on the ceiling. "Well, that's just fucking fantastic."

"No," Linc says, reaching across Hailee to trail a finger down my chest. "It's not a bad thing. It's hot as hell."

I'm not convinced. "Sure."

"Look at you all skeptical," Linc says. "You want proof?"

Before I can answer, he whips back the covers to reveal his dick, almost at full attention. "That's what your wolf look does."

Hailee chokes on a mouthful of water. "Please warn me before you do something like that."

"What?" I say, pushing down the laughter building in my chest. "Something like this?"

I pull the rest of the covers back, revealing my own rapidly hardening dick. Hailee presses her hands to her eyes, which is only semi-successful, because she's still holding her glass of water.

I prize it from her fingers and place it on the nightstand. "What I'm dying to know, Hailee, is whether you're wearing anything under that t-shirt."

Her eyes widen, but before she can respond, Linc trails his fingers up her thigh, causing her attention to snap to him.

"I was wondering the same thing," he rumbles. "I also want my shirt back."

Hailee's eyes narrow as she looks between us. "Oh, it's like that, is it?"

I meet Linc's eyes and grin. "I think it is."

"Don't think I don't smell your minty fresh breath," she says. "At least let me brush my teeth."

"We're minty enough to balance it out." Linc holds out a hand. "Now, give me my shirt back."

Hailee rolls her eyes, but the twitch of her lips is unmistakable as she reaches down and grips the hem of the t-shirt, lifting it up over her head.

A low groan leaves my chest as she chucks the t-shirt at Linc, revealing she's wearing nothing underneath. He immediately throws the shirt on the floor behind him, his attention focused on Hailee lying naked between us.

I lean forward, taking one of her breasts into my mouth, as Linc does the same on his side. Hailee gasps, throwing her arms back to steady herself. I glance at Linc to find him watching me. My heart jolts with electricity, and I pull off Hailee's nipple with a pop, leaning forward to kiss him.

As he strokes my tongue with his, I run a hand up Hailee's inner thigh, drawing a shudder from her. I break the kiss, and Linc looks down at my hand, mirroring my long, teasing strokes on her other leg.

Hailee whimpers, her arms trembling, and as she leans her head back, I trail kisses up her neck.

"Lie down," I whisper. "Let us take care of you."

She sinks down to the pillow, and I drink in the sight before me. Hailee's breasts, her nipples darkened and peaked from our attention. Her body slightly arching, urging our trailing fingers closer to where she wants them. And then there's Linc, lazing on the other side of her like a Greek god, his dick now bobbing at full attention between his muscled legs.

I grin. "What do you say we see whose name she screams first?"

Hailee mutters something about 'bastards', and Linc laughs. Holding his gaze, we lower our mouths to her breasts again, licking and sucking in tandem. I trail my hand up her inner thigh, but this time, I continue upward, meeting Linc's fingers at the top. Together, we draw our fingers through her pussy, gaining a gasped curse that makes Linc chuckle. Staying as one, we push our index fingers inside, pumping slowly. It's a strange sensation, and my eyes drift shut as my teeth graze her nipple.

"Which of us is going to fuck you this morning, Hailee?" Linc rumbles, his free hand gripping his cock.

My dick twitches in anticipation, and my eyes flick open. Hailee's head is pushed back into the pillow, her back arched as we work her with our fingers. Linc continues to worship her nipple with languid strokes of his tongue, his dark lashes fanning against his cheeks and I watch, transfixed, until Linc pushes our fingers deeper. I feel him curling against her walls and she swears, grinding her hips against our hands.

"Please," she says, the words no more than an exhale.

Together, we increase our pace, and I angle my thumb against her clit, causing her to cry out, her fingers digging into my bicep. I bite back a smirk. I can tell she's purposefully trying not to say either of our names.

"Who's it going to be?" Linc asks. "It's a shame we don't have more time. You could have us both."

My breath catches at the thought of it. Hailee between us, a thin wall between mine and Linc's cocks as we fuck her in tandem. My dick weeps at the image and I drop my head to Hailee's shoulder. Pushing my thumb harder against her clit, she gasps.

"Fuck," she whimpers. "I need you. Please."

I've had enough. She won't choose, so I'll make the decision for her. "Get on your hands and knees," I command, my voice almost unrecognizable.

Dragging my fingers through her center, I use her wetness to lubricate as I wrap my fist around my cock and stroke.

Linc's gaze fixes on the movement, a low groan rumbling in his chest. His own cock is rock hard in his hand as he reaches behind him for the box of condoms left there from the night before. He tosses one to me as Hailee gets into position, and I tear it open and slide it on. My heartbeat is painful in my chest as I get to my knees behind her, my fingers kneading the gorgeous soft flesh of her hips. I tease her, dragging my cock through her core, pressing against her entrance. She pushes back against me with a noise of frustration, and I run a hand up her spine.

"Patience," I murmur, looping an arm under her and swirling my fingers around her clit.

Behind me, Linc presses open mouthed kisses against my shoulders, his teeth nipping, as his fingers press against my hole. I lean my head back against his shoulder, and he runs his tongue up my neck as he pushes his finger inside me. Exhaling a breathy moan, my eyes drift shut, and he moves, pulsing only a few times, before pulling out and easing in a second.

My body shudders at the overload of sensations, and I can't hold back anymore. I place one hand on Hailee's hip, and gripping my cock with the other, I guide it into her dripping pussy.

"Fuck, Hailee." I moan, my fingers clutching her hips as I slide inside. "You feel fucking incredible around my cock."

Her answering whimper draws a noise from Linc that has my breath catching, and I tense in anticipation as he pulls his fingers out. He drags his cock along my ass, his teeth and tongue teasing my shoulders and neck.

"How bad do you want it, Carter?" he grinds out against my ear.

I struggle to take the breath needed to reply. "So, fucking bad. I need you inside me, Linc."

His head drops to my shoulder with a groan, and I feel the head of his cock press against me. My breath hitches as he pushes in, the sensation sending sparks up and down my limbs.

"Fuck, fuck, fuck," I chant.

Linc's teeth tug on my earlobe as he sinks all the way in. "How does that feel?"

"Fucking amazing."

This isn't real. It can't be. Nothing should feel this incredible. Hailee pushes back against me, begging for me to keep moving. My head spins. I'm not going to last a fucking second. I already feel like I'm burning, or floating, or something I can't quite grasp. Words don't make sense in my head as the feeling of Linc filling my ass, and Hailee clenched around my cock, threaten to make me lose my damn mind.

"You set the pace," Linc pants against my neck.

It takes me a second to process what he means. Then my chest tightens as I realize I'm in control. Hailee sinks down onto her forearms, granting me better access, and Linc runs his fingers lightly over my chest, causing me to shudder. I take a shaky breath and start to move.

My fingers grip Hailee's hips so hard I'm sure I'll leave bruises, but from the hisses and gasps of pleasure each thrust pulls from her lips, I don't think she cares. I watch, fixated, as my dick slides in and out, stretching and filling her. Every time I pull out, I push back onto Linc and the feeling of him inside me has my eyes rolling back in my head. Every move I make is an explosion of perfect pleasure that has me trembling and panting, unable to form a coherent thought.

As my release builds, I thrust faster, causing Hailee's moans to fill the room. The bed thuds against the wall, and the steady rhythm only serves to spur me on as I fuck her harder. As I fuck myself on Linc's cock.

Linc's breathing is labored at my ear, his fingers grasping at my chest as I push back onto him. "I love watching you fuck Hailee," he pants. "Make her come for me, Carter."

Hailee whimpers, clenching around me, and I let my hand slide around, stroking her clit until she cries out. My own release tumbles after, and I grit my teeth as my cock pulses inside her. Linc wraps one hand around my neck and another around my waist, slamming into me with a growling force that has me trembling. Then he stiffens with a groan, his heartbeat hammering against my spine.

We stay there for a minute or two, holding onto each other, the sounds of our breathing filling the room. Hailee moves first, and as I pull out, she rolls onto her back, her eyes closed and her chest still heaving.

Reaching down, I trail my fingertips down between her breasts. "You're so beautiful."

She flings an arm across her face in response, and I chuckle, gently poking the red marks my fingers have left on her hips. Linc presses a tender kiss to my shoulder before easing out.

Stepping off the bed, my head spins a little, and I blink as I steady myself. "That was mind-blowing."

Linc bends down and lifts Hailee's arm from her face, kissing her softly on the lips, before heading to the bathroom with me to clean up. He stops me with a hand on the shoulder, and captures my mouth with his, his thumb stroking my cheek briefly before he pulls away.

I pause, the exhilaration in my chest wavering. How is it possible to enjoy something so phenomenal when you know it's going to be over in a few days? Bittersweet doesn't begin to cover it.

"Did Jax leave?" Hailee calls from the bedroom.

I finish washing my hands and grab the towel I used the night before. "He left his number. I text him to say we'd be out within the hour."

Hailee sits up, her curls a chaotic frame around her gathered brows. "How long ago was that?"

I shrug. "Just before you woke up."

"So, you're saying that all three of us have to get showered, dressed and checked out in the next half an hour?"

The shower flicks on, and I glance over my shoulder to see Linc already lathering up.

"I'm on it," he calls.

I grin at Hailee. "I mean, it would be faster if we showered together."

Hailee throws a pillow at me, and I laugh.

"Do you think it'll be weird?" she asks. "After last night?"

"I don't know. I mean, he seemed pretty cool about it at the time. If he was embarrassed, he wouldn't have stayed. He certainly wouldn't have left his number."

Hailee's teeth tug at her bottom lip. "What if he left his number because he thinks it's going to happen again?"

The water flicks off and Linc steps into the bedroom, dripping over the carpet as he dries himself. "Would you want it to happen again?"

I look between the two of them, my eyebrows raised. "So, what? We're just picking people up like some sort of conga line?"

Linc flashes a brilliant white smile at me. "So dramatic."

"You don't like him," Hailee says.

I hold up my hands. "I'll admit I was wary at first, but he's clearly an okay guy. He saved our asses, and he was pretty cool with what went down last night."

"It was fucking hot," Linc says, pulling on the clothes he's selected from his suitcase. "And I believe you agreed."

"I did," I admit.

"So, if the situation arose again?" he pushes.

Hailee chuckles. "It was a pretty bizarre situation. I doubt it would present itself again."

"What if a different situation presented itself?" Linc asks.

I fold my arms across my chest. "What exactly are you saying?"

"I'm saying, I caught him looking at me a couple of times yesterday and this morning, so I might have propositioned him."

My mouth falls open. "What? When?"

"This morning."

"What?" I glance at Hailee, who looks more bemused than appalled. "When we were all asleep?"

Linc shrugs. "I was testing the waters."

Reaching up, I run a hand through my hair. "What did he say?"

"He said no."

"And if he'd said yes, you'd have what? Sucked him off while we were all asleep?"

Now completely dressed, Linc walks over and places his hands on my shoulders, squeezing. "Are you jealous?"

I open my mouth to reply that, of course I am, but stop. I'm not. Not really. It's not like we're exclusive. Is that even a thing when there are three of you?

"Were you jealous when he touched Hailee?" Linc asks.

I shake my head. "I'm not jealous. Just worried. We've got something incredible here. What if he fucks it up?"

Linc grips the back of my neck and pulls me forward, pressing a kiss to my forehead. "That's why we're talking about it. Hailee? How do you feel about the possibility of being intimate with Jax again?"

I look at her flushed cheeks and know her answer before even she opens her mouth.

"I have to agree with Carter," she says. "I'd be worried about our dynamic."

"Well," Linc says. "I'll go with the majority, but if Jax wants to fool around with either of you two, I'm okay with it."

Hailee blows out a slow breath. "I'm okay if he wants to fool around with either of you two."

They both turn to look at me. Jax is very attractive. Okay. He's hot as fuck. But he's clearly straight. Of course, Linc caught him staring. Everyone stares at Linc. He's stunning. The fact that he turned Linc down is enough evidence to say he isn't going to be fooling around with either of us. The real question is, am I okay with him being with Hailee?

I have no claim over her; not really. We've only known each other for a few days. She's running from a shitty relationship, so who am I to stop her from having sex with a guy that I wouldn't say no to myself?

"No," I say carefully. "I don't have a problem."

Hailee slides out of bed and walks over to me, pressing a kiss to my lips. "Friends first, remember."

I nod, squeezing her hand as she slips past me and starts the shower up again. Friends first. Our whole conversation is likely moot, anyway. Jax might have enjoyed our little 'show' last night, but I have a feeling it was the height of his level of involvement. Either way, after lunch, we'll be back on the road, and he'll be heading to Phoenix.

Moot.

27

"I MEAN, THE MOUNTAINS ARE *RIGHT* THERE!"

Leaning against the edge of the fountain, I hide my grin behind my bottle of water. Traveling is a privilege, and I know I'm more blessed than most, having seen dozens of countries thanks to my career. There are very few states I haven't visited either. Hailee has never left Illinois, and the awe and wonder she finds in the sights around us, fills me with joy.

"I like it here," she says, inhaling as though she can smell the mountain air, even though they're miles away.

Jax leans against a signpost across from us, his mouth quirking in amusement. "Perhaps you should move here instead of Vegas."

"What?" Hailee turns, her features falling into a frown. "No, I have to go to Vegas."

"I'm sure you'll like Vegas, too," he says with a shrug. "It's pretty different from here, though."

Hailee's eyebrows rise in interest. "You've been?"

"A long time ago. Lots of tourists, bright lights, and

booze." He takes a long swig from his bottle of coke. "And sand. Lots of fucking sand."

Carter snorts. "You're going to Arizona. There's a lot more sand there."

Jax raises a dark blond eyebrow before returning his gaze to the mountains behind the city skyline. "I said I was going to Phoenix. I didn't say I was happy about it."

I meet Carter's eye, and he tilts his head, but I shrug. We met up with Jax for breakfast before deciding to wander the city, and in all honesty, it's been fun. Despite my outward confidence that things would be okay, a part of me had expected things to be a little awkward. I even thought I might have scared Jax off with my forwardness this morning. I'm usually pretty good at reading people, but I just can't be sure with Jax. He definitely checked me out at the restaurant, and I caught him watching me and Carter a couple of times last night, too. I'm not an idiot. I know he was hot for Hailee, not me or Carter. But he wasn't repulsed by the idea, and that's what's keeping a spark flickering in the back of my head.

"What if we stayed here for another night?" Hailee says, her teeth tugging her bottom lip in the way that makes my blood stir.

Carter looks up from his phone. "What do you mean?"

"I mean, what if we hang out here for the day and leave for Four Corners tomorrow? It's just over six hours to the monument, so if we leave today, we wouldn't get to see it until the morning, anyway."

"Shame it's not winter," I say, glancing at the mountains. "There's some pretty good skiing around here."

Carter shoves his phone in his pocket. "Is there something in particular you want to do, Hailee?"

"Not really. I just thought maybe a break from driving would be nice. And, mountains."

I laugh. "It's fine with me. There's no huge deadline for me to get to San Francisco."

Carter shrugs. "Same. A vacation's a vacation, right?"

There's something in his tone that pulls my gaze to him, and I try to catch his eye, but he fixes his frown on the people bustling up and down the high street

Oblivious, Hailee exhales, her smile brightening. "Great. I'll let my sister know."

We all know what we're doing. By prolonging the trip, we're desperately trying to cling to whatever this is. When we get to Vegas, I'll carry on to California, and the others will go their separate ways. My heart squeezes at the thought of losing either of them.

"What about you, Jax?" Hailee asks.

His pensive expression shifts into a fierce grin that causes her cheeks to flame. "You want me to stick around, princess?"

I can't help but smile. I figured out yesterday that purposefully trying to make her blush is his go to move.

"When do you need to be in Phoenix?" she asks.

Jax looks away and squints at the mountainous skyline. "I'm heading there, but no one's expecting me. I can catch a bus tomorrow."

A jolt of electricity shoots through me, and I lift my bottle of water to my mouth, taking a long drink to mask my reaction. He's sticking around, but does that mean he'll stay with us tonight? I'm still reeling from the incredible sex of the last twenty-four hours, and desperately trying to steer my mind from flashbacks.

"Are they pointing at us?" Hailee asks.

A chorus of loud giggles sounds nearby, and I turn to see

where Hailee's looking. My stomach folds in on itself, my lungs constricting. A group of five girls, who look like they might still be in high school, are clearly pointing in our direction, giggling as they shove at each other.

"What the actual fuck?" Jax mutters, frowning at them.

I screw the lid closed on my water bottle and stand, angling my back to the girls. "Who's hungry? Does anyone want to go get some lunch?"

"Holy shit." Carter chuckles. "They're coming over."

I swear under my breath. Maybe I'm wrong. Maybe they're going to flirt with Carter or Jax. It might all be a misunderstanding.

"Are you Lincoln Lenzo?"

I wince, disappointment hot and heavy in my gut, as I plaster on a smile and turn around. "Yeah. Hi."

The girls squeal, their eyes wide, as they scramble for their phones.

"I'm such a huge fan," one of them says, her face turning pinker by the second. "I comment on all your posts. Lillyloveslife22. I've been the first person four times this month."

I give what I hope is an impressed smile. "Wow. It's nice to meet you."

"Can we get a selfie?" another asks.

"I can take a photo of all of you," Carter offers, a bemused expression on his face.

Three of the girls shove their phones at him, and they gather around me for a photo, while a piece of me dies inside. I can't bring myself to look at Hailee or Jax.

"You're even more gorgeous in real life." One girl sighs before glaring at Hailee. "Is she your girlfriend?"

"I thought you were a fan?" I say with a wink. "You'd know if I had a girlfriend, right?"

"Right, ladies," Carter says, handing back their phones. "We've got to get going."

Lips pull into pouts as I shoot a grateful expression his way.

"It was really nice to meet you all," I say. "Take care."

Lifting my hand in a wave, I flash them a final smile and walk away. We turn the corner, and Carter reaches out, pulling on my shoulder.

"Woah there, Linc. Care to explain what the fuck that was?"

I suck in a breath, steeling myself, before I turn around. "Fans," I offer lamely.

"Fans?" Carter repeats. "For a photographer?"

"Lincoln Lenzo," Jax mutters, pulling out his phone.

My mouth opens to protest, but I know there's no point. All I can do is watch as Hailee and Carter lean over to view his search. The gig is up. It was fun while it lasted. In a matter of seconds, they'll know who I really am, and things will change. I look away as I await the inevitable.

"You're a model?" Carter says, his voice thick with disbelief.

"You have almost a million followers on Instagram," Hailee gasps. "Oh my god. Your pictures!"

"You can't be that shocked." Jax chuckles as he scrolls. "Have you seen him?"

I glance up at his comment, finding them still poring over Jax's phone as he shakes his head. Before I can turn away again, Hailee looks up and catches my eye.

"Why didn't you tell us?"

I look down at the near empty bottle of water in my hand and pick at the label. "I didn't want you to judge me."

"Why would we judge you?"

"I don't know. Maybe not judge, but treat me differently. That's what usually happens."

"Oh my god," Carter says, looking up. "It all makes sense now. The fruit salad. The water. All those fucking hair products."

I shake my head and turn away, unable to watch them anymore. A hand presses against the small of my back.

"I'm sorry you thought you had to hide the truth from us," Hailee says, moving to stand in front of me. "I have no idea if I'd have treated you differently if I'd known, but nothing's changed now that we do. You're still Linc."

She reaches up and strokes my cheek, her copper eyes shimmering. I tilt my head, leaning into her palm as I close my eyes. More than anything, I want to believe that. What I've found with these people is unlike anything I've ever experienced, and the idea of it being cut short wrecks me way more than it probably should.

"You've had cameos in films for fucksake," Carter continues, pointing at Jax's phone. "You're famous."

"Carter," Hailee snaps. "Stop it."

The air feels too warm and my lungs too tight. Glancing up and down the street, my gaze lands on a bar and I stalk toward it. I'm generally not one to drink my problems away, but I already have a bit of a headache from last night's excess, and honestly, I don't give a fuck.

"Linc, wait up!"

I hear Hailee trotting to catch up, but I don't slow my stride as I reach the door and push it open. There are a few groups of people sitting at tables eating, but the thought of food turns my stomach. I head straight to the counter and sit down.

"Double of the best whiskey you've got," I say before the bartender can open his mouth.

He nods and turns away to fix my drink as Hailee slips onto the seat beside me. I stare at the bottles behind the counter, avoiding her gaze. The door opens behind me, the sound of the street trickling in as the bartender places my drink in front of me. Carter takes the seat on my other side and Jax pulls up a stool next to Hailee.

"Sorry," Carter says quietly. "I didn't mean to make you feel uncomfortable. It's just a shock, you know?"

I take a sip of my drink, relishing the burn as it slides down my throat to my churning stomach. There's no way to talk about this without offending them. How can I explain that most of my life people have used me to get into places or for my money, without implying that I'm worried they'll do the same? I take a longer sip.

"Is that why you're heading to California?" Jax asks, signaling to the bartender. "Modeling job?"

I close my eyes and suck in a slow breath as Jax orders a round of beers. "Sort of," I admit once the bartender has wandered away. "I'm meeting with a new agent."

"Where was your old one?" he asks.

"New York."

When I glance at him, his sharp blue eyes are watching me intently. "That's a big move."

"My last agent dropped me."

I down the rest of my whiskey. I haven't said the words out loud before, and they hurt just as much as I thought they would. Even though it happened a month ago, I haven't gotten around to telling my parents yet. My plan is to secure a new agent first, so they don't freak out.

"Who in their right mind would drop you?" Carter scoffs.

I stand and pull out my wallet, chucking enough money

to pay for our drinks down on the bar. "I need some air. I'll catch up with you later."

Before any of them can protest, I'm out the door and squinting in the summer sun. The last time I visited Salt Lake City, it was ski season, and the mountains were covered in glistening snow. Unlike the cold, crisp air I'd relished then, the air is muggy and thick. Perhaps leaving the air conditioning is a mistake.

Head down, I walk with no particular purpose. I know it's stupid. They're my friends. The thought forces a choked laugh from my throat. I've known them for a couple of days. A couple of fucking days. I'm such an idiot. I think of the times I expected Carter and Hailee to open up to me. Why should they? They looked so damn sincere in that bar. Like they really care. Maybe they do. I know I do. And that's the problem.

I rub my temples, my chest still so fucking tight. Maybe I should have just opened up to them. It's probably better to bare my soul to someone I won't see again after this week, anyway. But there it is. What if they tell people? I've been bitten before. Throw away comments appearing in gossip columns. Despite what Carter thinks, I'm not a celebrity. But mud sticks, and if enough mud gets thrown, you stop getting shoots.

"Linc! Please?"

I reluctantly slow at Carter's voice, letting him catch up. Instead of bombarding me with questions like I'm expecting, he takes me by the elbow and walks me over to an ice cream vendor. I watch with a frown as he orders a couple of cones.

"What are you doing?" I ask.

Carter looks at me with amusement. "Getting ice cream. What does it look like?"

I shake my head. "I shouldn't—"

"Shut up," he says. "I got you sorbet. No fat. Relax."

My heart does a bizarre jump at the thoughtful gesture. It's a weird dance between the two of us. Each taking turns to be the one in control. He hands me my cone, the orange and pink sorbet already sweating in the heat, and points at a bench in the shade.

"Thanks," I say, taking a lick of the orange-colored sorbet on top. It's mango.

Carter groans as he sinks down on the bench beside me. "Maybe ice cream was a bad idea."

"Why?" I shoot him a look as I taste the pink sorbet beneath, happy to find it's raspberry.

"Because I want to talk to you, and I can't think straight when you're doing that with your tongue."

Despite my spiraling doubt, I grin. "What? This?" I ask, taking a long slow lick, sweeping around the top of the scoop.

Carter closes his eyes and sucks in a breath. "Fucking hell."

I chuckle and shake my head.

"Talk to me," he says after a moment. "Please."

"What's there to talk about?"

He sighs, studying his own cone, which looks like mint chocolate chip. "Why did your agent drop you?"

"I refused to sleep with her."

Carter's eyes shoot to mine, the pale blue vivid, even in the shade. "What?"

I look away. "She said that if I wanted to stay on her books, I'd have to work for it. I refused and she didn't renew my contract."

"Surely that's illegal?" Carter says, his hand finding my thigh. "Can't you report her or something?"

I shake my head. "The modeling community is close-knit. If I ratted her out, she'd bad mouth me to enough agencies that I'd never work again."

"So, you're fleeing to the other side of the country instead?"

I raise my eyebrows. "Don't talk to me about running."

"I'm not running. I'm on vacation."

He takes his hand back and we eat our ice creams in silence. I'm not sure what else there is to say. My mind runs over the events of the last half an hour again and again, wondering whether I could have handled things differently. Whether I *should* have handled them differently.

"Is that why you were hanging out with all those retired folks?" Carter asks after a while. "Because they wouldn't know who you were?"

I sigh. "Yeah."

"I just don't get it." He fixes me with his intense stare. "I can tell you're thinking about ditching us, so please do me a favor and explain why it's such a big deal that we know."

I stare at my empty cone for a minute before tossing it in the trash at the side of the bench. *Fuck it.* "Fine," I say. "You really want to know?"

"Yes!" he says, throwing his hands up. "Please."

"Because when people find out you're a model, all they see is a pretty face. No one tries to get to know you, no one cares about how you're feeling, or what you want to do. All they see is a fancy lifestyle, money, and something nice to look at. You stop being a person."

The words spill from me, the weight of them pressing heavy on my chest as I wait for Carter to respond. I've never told anyone that before, and I feel more exposed than I have in my entire life.

"You're a lot more than a pretty face, Linc," Carter says slowly. "I mean, you've got a really pretty cock too."

"You're a dick."

"Seriously, though," he says, turning on the bench to face me. "What you do for a living doesn't change anything. If you'd told us from the start, I think we'd still have wanted to get to know you, but it's impossible to know that. What I do know, is the last few days have been some of the best of my life, and you and Hailee are equally responsible for that. I'm not just talking about the sex either, although that is pretty fucking incredible."

I huff a laugh, placing my hand over his, where it's come to rest on my thigh once more. "Pretty fucking incredible is a good summary. Thank you."

"For the sex?"

"No." I shove his shoulder with mine. "Well, yes. But no. Thank you for coming after me."

"You're welcome."

I frown down at our hands, a niggling thought pushing to the front of my brain. "Speaking of sex—"

"Yes."

"Stop it." I bite back a smile at his deadpan expression. "I'm sorry if I made you uncomfortable last night."

Carter frowns and flips his hand, linking his fingers with mine. "What are you talking about?"

I squeeze his hand. "I mean, we never discussed what would happen, and I forget sometimes that other guys aren't as open to swapping as I am."

Carter's eyes widen as he realizes what I'm talking about. "Oh. No. It wasn't that," he says, his eyes shuttering as he looks away. "It wasn't you."

I squeeze his hand again, willing him to look at me. "Hey. You just made me spill my guts. Talk to me."

He takes a deep breath, his brow crinkling. There's something in his expression that makes me worry I've picked open a wound that runs much deeper than I thought.

"I've already told you a little about my ex," he says, staring at our linked hands. "My sexuality made Andrew very insecure. He was convinced that I was going to run off with a woman the first chance I got. I spent most of our time together convincing him I wouldn't."

"That sounds intense," I say. "I'm sorry."

Carter shrugs. "That's one of many reasons I left."

"He sounds like he was pretty controlling."

"Yeah. It got worse toward the end. When Hailee sucked me off that first night, it was the first blowjob I've had in almost two years."

My mouth falls open. "Seriously?"

He huffs a laugh. "Yep."

"No wonder you've enjoyed the last few days."

Carter throws his head back and laughs. Pride warms my chest at the thought that I'm responsible for lifting the pain in his eyes and making that wonderful sound erupt from his lips. I want to do it again. And again.

"Well, it's more than that," Carter continues, his expression sobering. "I kissed a few guys before Andrew, but he was the first one I slept with."

My eyes widen. "Oh."

"Yeah," he shifts a little on the bench, the lines reforming between his brows. "Like I said. It wasn't you. It's just I've never been given a choice before. It threw me, and I sort of panicked."

My heart speeds up as I gather the nerve to ask the question. "So, if I gave you time to think about it . . .?"

Carter's frown smooths and he looks up, pinning me to

the bench with his glacier-blue eyes. "Are you asking whether I'd like to fuck you, Lincoln?"

I shiver at the sound of my full name as it rumbles from his lips. "I am."

He leans forward, his lips brushing my ear. "Yes, Linc. I want nothing more than to hear the sounds you'll make when I bury my cock in you. I want to hear you moan my name as I pound your ass so hard you see stars."

My breath hitches and my eyes drift shut. "Fuck. I want that."

Carter sits back and takes a loud bite of his ice cream cone. "You'd better not ditch us, then."

I open my eyes to find him with one arm slung across the back of the bench, looking very pleased with himself. "Bastard," I say, looking pointedly at my hardening cock.

He grins. "Good things come to those who wait, right? There's a zoo around here somewhere. Wanna go?"

"A zoo?" I repeat, shaking my head. "I can think of somewhere else I'd rather go."

Carter gives me a disapproving look that has the opposite effect of what he's probably intending, and pulls out his phone. "Oh, I've got a message from Jax."

"Are they okay? I feel bad we ditched them."

Carter grins and shakes his head. "He wants to make sure we're not making out in an alley."

"Cheeky fucker."

Carter taps open a browser and starts searching for the zoo. "He's a dick. I'll tell them our zoo plan."

I exhale and smile at the lightness spreading through my body. Although things have felt great with Hailee and Carter—and even with Jax—the weight of my secret has been heavier than I realized.

"Thank you," I say, leaning over and kissing him on the cheek.

Carter glances at me, his eyebrows raised. "You should probably save that thank you for later."

A laugh tears, loud and booming, from my chest and I sit back, shaking my head, feeling lighter than I can remember.

28

“So, what’s your deal?”

I put down my beer and meet Jax’s teasing stare. “My deal?”

“Did you just wake up one morning and decide to trek across the country, picking up men?”

I stare right back, refusing to rise to his teasing. “Yes. And there’s room for one more. I’m hoping to find one at the Grand Canyon.”

Jax chuckles and shakes his head. “Seriously, though. Why are you headed to your sister’s? Just a visit?”

Frowning at my beer, I consider my answer. I’ve told Carter and Linc most of my story, and after today, I’ll probably never see Jax again. Is there any point in hiding anything? Picking at the label on my beer, I decide to give him as much truth as I can handle.

“My ex-boyfriend isn’t a nice person,” I start carefully. “He emotionally abused me for years. When he didn’t come back from a poker night, I packed up everything I own and took off. My sister is my only living relative. She’s going to give me somewhere to stay while I figure out what to do.”

Jax pauses with his beer bottle halfway to his lips. "No shit?"

"No shit."

"So, your ex just came home at some point and found you gone?"

My stomach rolls. "I guess so. Yeah."

Jax takes a swig of his beer. "Has he tried to contact you?"

"I've blocked him on everything I can think of."

"Good."

I tip my beer in his direction. "What about you? Why are you heading to Phoenix?"

His jaw ticks, as though he's considering how much to tell me—if anything at all. I can't imagine he's the kind of guy that shares his thoughts easily.

"I never stay anywhere very long." His eyes fix on a spot behind the bar. "It's been that way my whole life. My mom was a drunk, and she had no idea who my dad was, so when she died, I bounced from foster home to foster home until I was old enough to make my own decisions.

"I've been in Montana for the past couple of years. When the owner of the garage I worked at died suddenly, I got laid off. I have a sort of uncle in Phoenix, so I'm headed there to take advantage of his sofa while I figure out what's next."

My eyes widen. I wasn't expecting him to give quite so much, and I scramble to find words that won't make him regret confiding in me. Jax doesn't strike me as the pity party type. "That's really shitty."

"It is what it is."

We sit in amicable silence for a moment, sipping our beers. The lunch crowd is slowly filling the bar, the chatter of customers competing with the music filtering in through the speakers. Glancing at the door, I wonder where Linc and Carter are. I hope Linc is okay. The look of mortification on his face when those girls recognized him is enough to turn my stomach. It wasn't far off how he looked after the attack outside the restaurant. Defeated. I know there's a part of him that thinks us finding out will ruin things. If anyone can set him straight, it's Carter. I just hope he's not too late.

"What's the deal with Carter and Linc?"

I turn to Jax, my eyebrows raised. Talk about a loaded question. "What do you mean?"

"They've clearly got some shit going on."

"That's for them to tell you."

He tilts his head in understanding. "Fair enough." He frowns in a way that almost looks like he's uncomfortable, and it's the first time I've ever seen him look anything other than perfectly at ease. "Can I ask about what you three have going on?"

I swallow, my heart beating a little harder in my chest. "That depends on what you want to know."

He turns to face me, his eyes narrowed as though trying to figure out a puzzle. "The three of you are together."

"Until we go our separate ways, yes."

Jax scratches the faint scruff on his jaw. "How does that work?"

My lips twitch. "I think you saw how it works last night."

"I saw a *lot* last night," he says, his eyes glinting in a way that makes my skin heat. "What I mean is, do you always have to be together, all three of you? Like, what if you just wanted Carter, or Carter and Linc wanted some alone time?"

"Then it's fine." I shrug. "It's weird. There's no jealousy between us. I left them alone for twenty minutes to make a phone call the other day, and they steamed up the damn car, sucking each other off."

Jax's eyebrows raise. "It seriously doesn't bother you."

"No." I shake my head. "Friends first. It's really hard to explain. Things just . . . clicked."

It's Jax's turn to shake his head as if I just told him I thought Santa Claus was real. I turn back to face the bar. There's no point trying to explain what we have to someone else when I barely understand it myself.

"What about last night?" he asks. "They were okay with someone else touching you."

My skin heats at his words. Things haven't been awkward, and we've spent the day so far as though we didn't watch each other have sex last night.

"It's all about mutual understanding and respect," I explain. "Everyone was okay with it, and if someone hadn't been, it wouldn't have happened."

Jax nods thoughtfully, then his lips curl back into a smile. "You're a strange one."

"Excuse me?"

"Do you know why I call you 'princess'?"

I stare, my heartbeat in my ears. "Why?"

"Because you have those big brown eyes like a Disney princess, or Bambi, or some shit, but you're nowhere near as innocent as you look."

I open my mouth to protest, but laugh instead. Before I met Carter and Linc, I *was* innocent. I've had three boyfriends, and everything has been fairly beige. There's no point trying to insist I'm still vanilla when he's fingered me while I watched two men fuck, before sucking one of them off. My breath catches at the memory.

It's easy to forget that the very sexy man sitting next to

me had his hands in my underwear twelve hours ago. I shiver as I recall his whispered promise and try to rein in thoughts of what he might look like without his fitted t-shirt; of just how much of that tanned skin is covered by ink. I draw in a slow breath. I already have two incredible men, but I can't stop thinking about Jax. It isn't that I'm bored or fed up with Linc or Carter. If anything, I find myself growing more attached with every passing hour. Not knowing where they are right now has me on edge. It's ridiculous that I'm missing them.

That's what makes it worse. I'm torn up about Linc, but I can't stop my senses being set alight by Jax's sexy smirk and throat-hold of a gaze. I know Linc feels it too, and I've caught Carter checking Jax out several times today. The thought of Jax with either of them has my pulse racing and my breath catching. *What is wrong with me, for fucksake?*

"Did *you* enjoy last night?" I ask, the words tumbling from my lips before I can stop them. It must be the beer.

Jax grins. "It was a surprise. Definitely not where I expected things to go."

I finish my beer, placing it carefully down in the center of the coaster as I avoid his eyes. "I honestly thought you'd run as soon as Carter and Linc started stripping."

"I'm not into guys," he says. "But I can appreciate attractive bodies."

I turn to look at him. "Attractive bodies?"

"Oh, come on." Jax raises his eyebrows. "Linc's body is insane."

Smiling in agreement, I consider his words. I'm not sexually attracted to women, but I can definitely appreciate when someone is attractive. I've most certainly looked at breasts and legs and admired them.

"Fair enough," I concede. "If you had to, though. Who would it be? Carter or Linc?"

Jax laughs loud and hard. "We're not playing *that* game, princess."

I roll my eyes playfully. "Fine."

"You know, I'm glad you stopped and gave me a ride." Jax frowns at his beer bottle and shakes his head. "The last couple of days have been weird as fuck, but they've been fun."

I smile. "I'm glad we picked you up, too. This trip has been nothing like I thought it would be."

Jax's shoulders shake with his answering chuckle. "I'd bet my last dollar on that, princess."

My cheeks heat again, and I reach out and shove him hard enough that he almost falls off his stool.

"Do you want another drink?" he asks, nodding at my beer.

I almost go to check my phone to see if the guys have messaged, but remember I haven't switched it on today. "Have you heard anything from the guys?"

Jax pulls his phone from his pocket, swiping to wake up the screen. He shakes his head. "Nothing."

"Can you send them a text and check they're okay?"

Jax nods. "Sure. But don't worry. They'll be fine."

I watch as he types out a message, anger bubbling in my veins at the thought of what happened to them at the restaurant. If only I'd just come clean to Carter about everything. To both of them. I swallow hard. Glancing down at the backpack at my feet, I swear I can hear my phone buzzing, even though I know it's switched off.

At the restaurant, when I turned on my phone to call my sister, I discovered I had a text from my old boss at the grocery store. At first, I thought it was something to do with my paycheck, or I'd left something behind. It wasn't. Sal had messaged to tell me that Brent has been in every day demanding information and threatening to turn him in for paying his employees in cash. Sal's message begged me to contact Brent before he followed through on his word. He said it was my fault—that I let him pay me in cash—so calling Brent off was the least I could do. The words are like frost down my spine. *The least I could do.* How many times did Brent use those words on me? Sal was always good to me, but at the end of the day, he'd throw me under the bus to save his ass.

I haven't replied. I blocked his number like a fucking coward. That's what I am, after all. That's the type of person who runs from their problems. A coward.

"Hey, princess? What's wrong?"

I blink, turning to find Jax watching me with narrowed eyes. "Nothing. Sorry."

His eyes narrow further, clearly not believing me, but he doesn't push it. "Carter says they're thinking of going to the zoo."

"The zoo."

"Shall we go and tell them it's a shit idea?"

I laugh. "I like the zoo."

Jax shakes his head as he slides off his stool. "We are not going to the fucking zoo."

Still chuckling, I pick up my bag and follow him out into the sunshine. I really do like Salt Lake City. There's something about the contrast of the newer parts of town with the older buildings, all against the backdrop of the mountains.

It turns out Carter and Linc haven't gotten far at all, and I relax when I see that Linc's usual easygoing smile has returned. They stand from the bench as we approach, and I head straight for Linc, wrapping my arms around his waist.

"Hey," he says, kissing the top of my head.

I squeeze a little tighter, still cautious of his bruising. It's only now that he's in front of me, that I realize how worried I was that he might have left us.

"It's only a fifteen-minute drive to the zoo," Carter says. "I can book our tickets online."

Jax snorts. "No."

Carter looks up from his phone. "No?"

"Jax isn't a fan of the zoo idea," I explain. I release my arms from around Linc, but he reaches down and threads his fingers through mine, holding firm.

Carter stares at Jax, and Jax stares right back. After a few seconds, he rolls his eyes and turns to me. "Well, this is officially your trip and your car, so it's your call. What do you want to do?"

"It really is a shame it's not ski season," Linc says. "You'd love the view from the mountains. Not to mention the cabins."

"That does sound lovely," I say, turning to admire the mountains in the distance. "I bet the city looks great from up there."

"Why don't we do that, then?" Jax says. "If Princess wants mountains, let's go to the mountains."

Linc shakes his head. "Most of it will be closed over the summer."

"Great. We'll have the place to ourselves."

I frown. "Wait, what?"

"Let's go see this view." Jax shrugs. "What's the worst that could happen?"

Over my shoulder, Carter snorts. I glance up at Linc, who's staring at the mountains pensively. When I look back at Jax, his eyes are gleaming with challenge.

"What do you say, princess? Shall we have a little adventure?"

My heart speeds under his piercing gaze. There's something about him that makes me want to push myself—to take risks.

"Sure," I say, anticipation tingling in my limbs. "Let's do mountains."

29

Breaking in is a piece of cake. Avoiding the curious glances from the others is a whole other deal. Most of the hotels spread across the mountains are still open, offering hikers and families summer activities and shit. The best part is, it's a lot fucking cooler up in the mountains than down in the city. For the first time all day, I'm not sweating.

We drove up quite far into the mountains, with Linc pointing out different sights and resorts he knows from visiting before; but when we drove past a small resort that looked a little run down, with a massive 'for sale' sign on the gates, I told Hailee to stop.

Adrenaline had pumped through my veins as I worked the lock over on the gates and pushed them open. Hailee had taken a little convincing, so in the end, we ditched the car at a viewing point and walked up. I assured her that if anyone questions us, we'll just say we're hiking and wandered onto the property by mistake.

I'm fortunate enough to have friends that offer sofas when I'm in between places, but there have been a few times since walking out of my last foster home that I've found myself searching for shelter at the last minute. Because of that, breaking and entering abandoned properties is one of my many life skills. I reckon this place has been for sale for a while, because the path is broken up by weeds and the sides are overgrown. It's a little creepy, which only confirms I've made the right choice.

"What if there's surveillance?" Hailee mutters. "What if someone calls the police?"

"I'll say I'm looking to buy the place," Linc says, taking her hand and giving it a kiss. "Don't worry. You're not going to get in trouble."

"It's not like we're causing any damage," I add. "We're just exploring and taking in the view. No one will ever know we've been here."

I give her a reassuring smile and a wink that causes her cheeks to color and my grin to grow. I understand why she's worried. Linc mentioned that her shithead ex-boyfriend is a cop, and from what she told me in the bar, she's scared of him enough to block him and run away. It bugs me she's so nervous. To be honest, a lot of things are bugging me. The fact that I feel so damn protective over these three near strangers is a huge fucking problem.

I figure I feel this way about Linc and Carter because I saved their asses from those redneck fucks. And it makes sense to feel this way about Hailee because she has that whole wide-eyed Bambi thing going on. I know she's tougher than she looks, though. It takes guts to do what she did. Even so, I shouldn't care. Not really. They're random people who have entertained me and given me somewhere to sleep. That's where it ends. Not my circus. Not my monkeys. I look out for myself, and that's it. It's how I've survived this long, and I'm not looking to change any time soon.

Shaking my head, I concentrate on the steep path ahead. The main lodge sits at the end of the trail, built with classic dark wood and a slanted roof. Behind it, several wooden cabins are dotted amongst the trees. I veer off the path, bypassing the main building. If there are any security cameras, they'll be in the lodge, and it isn't like we're checking in or anything. I half expect the others to question, but they follow me in silence. It's calm up in the mountains. Hiking and nature shit isn't really my thing, but I can appreciate the fresh air and the sounds of birds having a blast in the trees. Idyllic. That's the word.

"Is it just me," Linc muses, "or is anyone else creeped out?"

I glance at him over my shoulder. "What? You expecting a deranged murderer to jump out from behind one of these lodges and start chasing you with an axe?"

Linc stops. "Well, I *wasn't*."

"The only dangerous thing around here is those fucking nettles. Watch yourself, we're going off-road."

Stepping off the overgrown path, I pick a lodge that looks like it might have a good view. I turn my back to the others as I jimmy the door. It opens pretty easily, and I peer inside before standing back and gesturing for the others to step inside.

Linc grins, slapping me on the shoulder, but Hailee and Carter look wary. It annoys me more than it should. I don't care what they think of me. Frowning, I pull the door shut behind us.

It's a nice place. The sun illuminates the dust motes hanging in the air as we step into the large living room. The fireplace is empty and an overstuffed sofa is covered by a dust sheet. Linc starts opening the three doors leading off the main room, and I catch a glimpse of a bathroom and a bedroom. I scuff my sneaker over the edge of a discolored rectangle on the floor where a rug must have been.

"Oh wow!" Hailee squeals, as she steps up to a large window taking up most of one of the walls. "Look at this."

I grin. Looks like I was right about this cabin having a decent view. The mountainside sweeps down in all directions, with the city sprawled out below, before moving up into mountains on the other side. A door beside the window looks like it leads out to a deck, and it only takes a little effort before it opens, and I step out.

"You're good at that," Carter says as he steps past me.

I stare him down. His eyes are so damn intense. They're the exact same color as the cloudless sky behind him. I wrinkle my nose. *What the fuck?* It must be the lack of oxygen up in the mountains, because I know I'm not writing fucking poetry about some dude's eyes.

"Thanks," I say, forcing a smirk.

He shakes his head and turns to peer over the railing. If he wants to ask me how or why I'm so good at breaking into buildings, he can fucking ask me. Things are okay between us, but I can tell he's still a little wary—protective. I get it, but it pisses me off. What annoys me the most is that I want to prove to him he's got nothing to worry about. I've never given two shits about what people think of me before, though, and I'll be fucked if I'm going to start now.

"Who's hungry?" Linc asks, taking a seat on the floor of the wooden deck.

He had the bright idea of picking up some food before heading up into the mountains, and I bite back a snort as he unloads chips, sandwiches, and snacks from the bag. How long has it been since I've had a picnic? A fucking picnic. I'm not sure I ever have.

Hailee pats the space beside her, and I drop down with a sigh. Reaching into my bag, I pull out my contribution.

"Fucking A," Linc exclaims. "Nice!"

Inclining my head, I place the bottle of bourbon down in the center of the feast.

"When did you get that?" Carter asks.

"This morning, when I was waiting for you guys to stop fucking, and get up."

Linc coughs around a mouthful of sandwich and Hailee makes some sort of adorable squeak. Twisting off the cap, I help myself to a swig before offering it to Carter. Judging by the frown that seems to have taken up permanent residence on his face, he looks like he needs it most.

"I'm driving next," he says.

I shrug, handing it to Hailee. "Suit yourself."

"This is really nice," she says, taking a small sip and wincing at the burn. "The view, not the drink."

"Hey, this is a really nice bourbon," I reply, taking the bottle from her. "I'm glad you like it here. If Princess wants mountains, she gets mountains."

Hailee rolls her eyes, but her skin flushes, and she looks down to avoid my teasing grin. I know I shouldn't, but I can't help thinking about the night before; the way she responded to my touch. The image of her leaning over the side of the bed with her plump lips wrapped around Carter's dick, her nipples still hard from my touch, will forever live rent free in my brain. My eyes flit to her mouth. I want those lips. I want to taste them. Suck them. Bite them. I want them wrapped around my cock.

I take a deep swig of liquor before handing the bottle to Linc.

"Why don't we play a game?" he says as he takes it.

Carter groans. "Oh god. What?"

"I don't know. Something fun." Linc wiggles his dark eyebrows. "What about 'never have I ever'?"

"I'm not drinking. What's the point?"

Linc gives him a playful shove. "The point is to get to know each other better, not get wasted. We're not fifteen."

"Whatever," Carter mumbles, shaking his head.

Linc looks at me, challenge gleaming in his dark brown eyes. "You game?"

I lift a shoulder in reply. "Sure."

"Hailee?" he asks.

She's pulled her lip between her teeth again, biting down in a way I'm realizing means she's nervous.

I lean into her, knocking her gently with my shoulder. "If it makes you uncomfortable, we can do something else."

"No." She shakes her head and sits up a little straighter. "Go for it."

Linc laughs. "It's not an interrogation. It's supposed to be fun."

"I'll go first," Carter says, sitting back and resting on his hands. "Never have I ever been arrested."

My fingers move to tighten into a fist, but I force them to stay loose, reaching for the bottle of bourbon instead. It's a dick move on his part and from the way Linc's smile has fallen to a frown, I'm not the only one who thinks so. Carter can go fuck himself if he thinks I'm going to be ashamed of my past. Holding his icy gaze, I swig back the burning liquor. No one else moves to take it, so I place it back in the middle.

"My turn," I say. "Never have I ever had a dick in my mouth."

Linc throws his head back as he laughs, and my annoyance at Carter melts away at the sound. A grin finds its way to my lips, and Carter rolls his eyes. He grabs the bottle, tipping it toward me in a salute before taking a very small sip. I sit back as everyone takes a drink, feeling rather pleased with myself.

"My turn," Hailee announces. "Never have I ever posed nude for a photograph."

Linc groans and takes a swig while Hailee giggles. My eyebrows rise when Carter reaches for the bottle and takes a token sip.

"Don't ask," he mumbles, grabbing a handful of chips.

"My turn," Linc says, rubbing his hands together. "Never have I ever had a tattoo."

"Oh, fuck off," I mutter, taking another swig while he laughs.

Carter reaches for the bottle again, and Linc slaps his hands against his thighs. "Wait. What the fuck?"

"Where?" Hailee demands.

"I've seen you completely naked a few times now, and I've never seen a tattoo," Linc says, pointing an accusatory finger at him. "Where is it?"

Carter gives him a sly smile as he places the bottle back in the center. "Maybe you'll have to look harder next time."

I look away at the lust that darkens Linc's face. The heat between the three of them is tangible. It's weird. Especially when one of them throws a little of that heat in my direction. Lust hasn't played a big part in my life. I learned at sixteen that if I wanted to get my dick wet, all I had to do was hang around bars, and flash my smile at women until one took the bait. It wasn't rocket science, but it got the job done. It was always an alcohol infused scratching of an itch. It was never the breath-halting, heart-racing attraction that thrums in the air between these three. My fingers itch as I eye the bottle of bourbon.

I tried a relationship a couple of times, but things never

worked out. The first time, I was nineteen. The friend I was crashing with was a pothead, and I got sucked in. I don't remember a lot of that year, and I'm not even sure when Julie left.

The next time, I was twenty-three. She was a waitress at the diner I was the delivery guy for. We lasted eight months. I found her fucking the assistant manager out back by the trash and smashed his face in. That was the one time I've been arrested as an adult. I left town not long after that.

"I've got another one," Hailee says, her eyes bright, and her smile wide. "Never have I ever left the country."

Linc groans and grabs the bottle. "I feel like you're ganging up on me."

He places the bottle back in the middle and I grab it, taking a bigger drink than I probably should.

"Mexico," I say, wiping my mouth on my shoulder.

"My turn," Carter says.

"I can't stop thinking about your mystery tattoo," Linc mutters, his eyes narrowed as he looks him over.

"How old were you when you got your first tattoo?" Hailee asks, popping a chip in her mouth.

I raise my eyebrows. "Fifteen."

"Do you have them everywhere?" she asks, staring at my shirt like she might be able to see through it.

"You wanna check, princess?"

She looks up, her eyes widening into the Bambi expression that does strange things to my dick. Is it possible to want to hold someone and stroke their hair at the same time as fucking them senseless? Maybe I'm just messed up.

"I think you should show us," Linc says. "It might inspire Carter to show us his mystery ink."

"Not fucking likely," Carter mumbles.

I smirk. "You want to see?"

Linc swallows and I watch his Adam's apple bob in his long throat. When my eyes flick back to his, I still at the desire there. I don't think I've ever had a guy look at me like that. I'm not sure how to feel about the way it makes my heart speed up a little, so I look away, turning my attention to Hailee's eager expression. It must be the alcohol.

"I think you need to go easy on the drink," I say, shaking my head. "You're getting giddy."

Raising her eyebrows, she reaches out and grabs the bottle, taking a large gulp. "Shut up and take your shirt off."

My mouth falls open a split second before I burst out laughing. I'm vaguely aware of Linc and Carter laughing too, but it's hard to tell over my own mirth. Tears sting my eyes and I gasp for breath. I can't remember the last time I laughed so hard.

"You're something else, princess," I say, shaking my head.

Before she can reply, I reach back and grab a handful of my t-shirt, pulling it off over my head.

"Well, shit," Linc whispers.

I turn a little, letting Hailee see my back. "Want to count them?"

"I'd be here all day," she murmurs.

She probably would. I have a lot of ink. It's the only thing I spend my money on. Occasionally I've made friends with someone training, and offered up my skin as a canvas to practice on. I've been quite lucky. There's nothing on me that I want to get rid of. No regrets.

My neck is clean, but my shoulders, chest, stomach, arms, legs, and back are covered. My legs still have a few patches left, but not for long. Thirteen years of tattoos add up to quite a lot. I flinch as fingers touch my arm, and I turn, watching as Hailee traces the ink.

"They're beautiful," she says, her eyes travelling over my body with such intensity, it gives me goosebumps, despite the heat.

"They really are," Linc says.

I look away from Hailee, to find him raking his gaze over me with the same lust-filled expression on his face. I watch him for a second, curiously aware of my quickening pulse. Turning to Carter, I expect a look of disdain or anger—I almost hope for it—but instead his expression is unreadable. His mouth presses into a firm line, his eyes slowly taking in every damn inch of me. I suppress a shiver.

"Okay," I announce, grabbing my shirt. "That's enough. I feel like a fucking steak."

Linc chuckles, grabbing the bottle and taking a drink. "You're a whole fucking meal, man."

Carter groans.

"You jealous?" Linc says. "Why don't you man up and show me your ink, then?"

Carter holds up his hands. "It's not my fault you don't pay attention."

"It's hard to pay attention when you've got no fucking clothes on," Linc says, his voice lowering as he leans closer. "It's hard enough to concentrate when you're fully clothed."

"Aw," Hailee says, grabbing the bottle from him. "Get a room."

I laugh. "Tipsy Princess has an attitude."

Linc leans over to Hailee and runs his hand up the inside of her thigh. "There are a couple of rooms. Want to check them out?"

I take the bottle from Hailee before she spills it. "There might not even be beds in them. It's not like this place is functional."

Linc stands and dusts himself off, completely at ease

with the fact he's tenting his shorts. "There's definitely beds. I'll go investigate properly, though."

I watch, eyebrows raised, as he strides back into the lodge, opening doors. My blood thrums in my veins. Are they seriously going to go off and have sex? While I sit out here on my own? Do they think I'm going to be joining in? Watching again? *Fuck.* I'm not sure how I feel about that. Raising the bottle to my lips, I take a deep drink.

"Beds in two rooms," Linc calls. "They're okay, even with the dust sheets on. Unless you have an allergy."

I look from Carter to Hailee. "Are you serious?"

"Who's coming?" Linc calls.

"I'm going to stay here with Jax," Hailee calls back. She grins at Carter. "Go show him your tattoo."

Carter shakes his head as he gets to his feet. "He's going to be really disappointed."

Hailee stands and wraps her arms around his neck, which means she has to rise onto her toes. "Neither of us are ever disappointed when it comes to you," she says.

He gives a small smile before kissing her softly. I take another swig, the burning feeling steadying me. Whatever is going on, I can get up and leave at any time. Although, with the amount of alcohol simmering in my veins, it might be hard stumbling down the mountain. It doesn't matter, though. I know I'm not going to leave. Curiosity might kill the cat, but I'm planning on buckling up and enjoying the ride.

30

Every time I kiss Hailee, I marvel at how soft and full her lips are—how touching her melts away the rest of the world, ensnaring me in a blissful bubble of contentment. She reaches up, winding her fingers in my hair, and I hum as I pull her closer.

"Go on," she says against my lips. "Linc's waiting."

I pull back and stroke my knuckles down her cheek. As much as the idea of having Linc to myself has me as hard as a rock, I don't want to let go of Hailee. My fingers drift to her waist, slipping under her tank top and stroking the soft skin there. "Are you sure you don't want to join us?"

"And leave poor Jax out here by himself?" she says.

Poor Jax, indeed. I look down at where he's sipping from the bottle of bourbon. He still hasn't put his shirt on. My eyes flit over the inked dips of his muscles, and my jaw clenches. Why does he have to be so fucking hot? I know Linc seems to think he can convince him he's not as straight as he thinks, I don't see it happening.

"Hey, I'm fine, princess," he says. "I can entertain myself while you guys have fun."

"You're always welcome to get involved," Linc calls from inside the cabin.

Jax leans back, resting on his elbows, so he can see Linc through the open door. I watch his tattoos rippling as his muscles shift with the effort. "Thanks for the invitation, but I'll pass."

Part of me wants to say something to him. I feel bad for judging him when he broke in here, and I know he read the look on my face. He told us he had a shitty childhood, and he's done nothing to make me doubt him since we picked him up. Giving him a small smile, I decide to tell him as much the next chance I get. After all, he's not the only one who's done things he's not proud of. I squeeze Hailee's hand before letting go and head into the cabin.

Linc has disappeared from view, and as I make my way across the bare wooden floor, my heart starts to race. I know where this could go, and I'm not sure if I'm ready. I want to, though. Fuck, I want to. I exhale as I push the bedroom door open and freeze. Linc is completely naked, sprawled on the bed with one leg bent, and his cock in his hand, stroking.

"Fuck," I choke out.

Linc smirks. "Yes, please."

I can't make my feet move. He's too much. I don't think I'll ever not be in awe of the sight of him. He's perfection. Even with the yellowing bruise on his side. What the fuck is he doing with me? The same goes for Hailee. They're both gorgeous and so fucking nice. My stomach twists. They're not with me, though. Not really. This is just a really, really weird fling.

"Are you going to come in, or are you just going to stand there?"

I let my hand fall to my side and the door clicks shut.

"Come here," Linc says, his hand continuing to pump his dick in a slow, steady rhythm.

I step forward, and he must sense my hesitation, because when I reach the bed, he pushes up onto his knees and takes my face between his hands.

"What's wrong?"

"Nothing," I say. "Nothing's wrong."

Linc presses his lips to mine and I feel the tension leave my shoulders, melting like butter in the sun.

"If nothing's wrong," he says, pulling back to press kisses to my throat as his hands push up under my t-shirt. "Why does your face look like you walked into the wrong room?"

I sigh, my hands tracing over the firm, warm skin on his chest. "Sorry. It's just . . ."

"Just what?" Linc straightens and it takes all my self-control to ignore his hard cock pushing against my stomach. "We can do whatever you feel like doing. I'm not going to pressure you. You know that, right?"

"It's not that," I say.

"What is it, then?"

I capture his face with my hands and look at him, taking in every perfect inch of his face. His long, dark lashes. His pouty lips and sharp cheekbones. How many more times will I get the chance? "Thank you."

Linc half smiles, confusion in his dark eyes. "I haven't done anything yet."

I lean forward, resting my forehead against his, as I draw a breath. "You have. You do it all the time, without even realizing. I've spent so long feeling . . . less. Like I could never be enough. You make me feel like I'm not broken."

Linc reaches up and takes hold of my chin, dragging his thumb across my lip. "That's because you're not. I hate that you were made to feel anything less. I think that's why

Hailee and I like your wolf so much. It only appears when you let go. That's when you're really yourself—without the doubt and second guessing."

I snort. "My fucking wolf."

He surges forward and sucks my bottom lip, his teeth clamping—claiming. "Where is it?"

His hand pushes down my chest, fingers dipping beneath the waistband of my shorts, and I suck in a breath. "Linc."

"What?" He freezes, his fingers clutching the material of my shirt in his fist.

Reaching around, I pull out his hair tie, sinking my fingers into his thick, dark locks. I want to savor the look on his face. The image of him naked and hard, wanting me. *Me.* The thought that every time we're together could be the last time is enough to gouge a hole in my battered heart. "Just . . . You take my breath away, Linc."

Linc's eyes widen, his lips parting a little as though my words have surprised him. Before he can say anything, I lean forward and kiss him. He moans against my mouth, his hands still clutching fistfuls of my shirt, tugging me closer.

I let go of him just long enough to pull my shirt off over my head, toe off my sneakers, and tug down my shorts and underwear. For a second, we stare at each other, naked, and breathing hard. Then we slam together in a tsunami of desire, a clash of grappling hands and desperate mouths.

I pull away first, working kisses down his hard chest and stomach, sliding my tongue in the grooves between his abs. He tastes a little salty from a day out in the sun, and I love it. The mix of sweat and his cologne is intoxicating. By the time I reach his cock, I'm lightheaded.

Sticking out my tongue, I lap at the bead of precum at the tip and Linc sighs deeply, lacing his fingers in my hair. I wrap my fingers around the base and wrap my lips around him, working my tongue along the sensitive underside.

"Fuck, Carter." Linc moans. "I wish you could see how fucking hot you look with my dick in your mouth."

His words settle, burning flutters, in my chest, and I swirl my tongue, sucking and swallowing him deeper until his groans turn to whimpers. Only then do I pull off him and stand up, swiping my mouth with my arm. Breathing hard, Linc watches me with such awe and desire, I almost want to look over my shoulder to make sure it's really me he's looking at. I press my palms against his chest and push him back onto the bed. Climbing over him, I moan at the feeling of his warm, hard ,body under mine.

"I want you so fucking bad," I whisper, dipping my head to tease his chest with my teeth. My hips roll, pushing our dicks together, and I swear under my breath.

"You've got me, Carter," Linc says, his fingers digging into my back. "Take me."

My gaze falls on the condom and packets of lube Linc has stashed, ready on the window ledge, and I groan.

"Roll over," I order. "On your hands and knees."

Linc melts beneath me, his breath catching as he looks up at me, his eyes hooded with desire. I have no idea what the fuck he and Hailee are talking about with my fucking 'wolf', but if he gets off on me telling him what to do, I can get on board with that.

I grab a packet of lube and tear it open with my teeth, smearing it over my fingers. Reaching down, I wrap an arm around Linc and pull him up so his back is flush against my chest.

"How long has it been?" I ask, dragging my mouth along his broad shoulders in a pattern of sucking, nips and strokes of my tongue.

"Just over a week," he says, his voice breathier than I've ever heard it as he rolls his head back against my shoulder.

His answer tears me in two. On one hand, it means I don't need to spend quite so long prepping him, but on the other, I want to punch whoever had their hands on him. I wrap my dry hand around his throat as I drag my lubed fingers between his ass cheeks. Before the thought can fester, I slowly work a digit inside him and he groans, pushing back against me. He's mine now and I'm going to enjoy every second. I bite down on the muscles flexing along his shoulder, fucking him with my finger.

"Carter," he breathes. "I don't want to sound like a dick, but please don't mark me."

Burying my nose in his hair, I inhale him. I barely touched the bourbon, but I swear I could get drunk on the smell of him. "No worries," I promise.

Linc doesn't need to explain. I'd hate to be the reason he doesn't get a job once he gets to California.

"More," he pleads. "Give me more."

I push a second finger in, and he groans loudly, reaching for his dick.

"That's mine," I snarl, knocking his hand away.

Linc moans, pulling against the arm holding him up, and I let him fall forward onto his forearms. My body is humming with anticipation, my heart like machine gun fire in my chest. I reach out and grab his hair, pulling as I fuck him harder with my fingers.

"Carter," he pleads. "Please."

The need in his voice literally makes me weak in the knees, and the world seems to tilt as I reach for the condom and tear it open, sliding it on. My breathing is shallow, my lungs not taking in enough air, as I tear open another packet of lube and work it over my dick, which is hard as fucking stone. Maybe that's why I feel dizzy. I need to breathe.

"Carter," Linc moans. "Fuck. I need you inside me. Please."

My eyes shut as I suck in as deep a breath as I can manage. How is it possible that this god of a man is on his hands and knees begging for me? It doesn't feel real. I push the head of my cock against his hole, and he presses back against me, urging me on. I steady myself with a hand on his back as I push a little deeper.

"Fuck, Linc," I gasp.

"That's it," he moans. "Give me more."

I push in further, electricity flickering over my senses as I roll my hips, working myself deeper. "You feel incredible," I rasp. "So, fucking tight."

"Fuck me, Carter," Linc pleads. "I want you so bad."

I pull out slowly, the sensation almost making my eyes roll back in my head, before pushing back in, drawing a breathy moan from him as I bottom out.

"No," I say, pulling out and gripping his hips. "Get on your back."

Linc does as I say, his dark eyes searching my face for a reason, or explanation. I take hold of his wrists and hold them above his head, lowering my mouth to his ear.

"I want to see you," I whisper, biting down on his earlobe. "I want to watch your face when I come inside you."

Linc trembles, turning his head to catch my mouth. He kisses me hard, his teeth tugging on my lips. "You are so fucking hot."

I fight to roll my eyes, instead sliding my slick cock between us until I find my destination. Easing in, a little faster this time, I watch, enthralled, as Linc's mouth falls open, his pupils dilating and his hips lifting. He tries to reach my mouth again, but I pull back, watching his face as I begin to move my hips in a slow, steady rhythm.

"I told you," I say. "I want to watch."

Linc stares up at me, breathing hard. He tries to break out of the hold I have on his hands, but I grip them tighter, thrusting into him a little harder.

"Oh, my fucking god, Carter," he moans. "Fuck."

I lick my lips. "You like it hard?"

Linc bucks beneath me, his breathy noises punctuating my thrusts. "Yes."

I pull out slowly, pressing kisses along his sharp jaw and on his cheekbones. Then, I watch his face as I slam back into him.

"Fuck. Yes!" he cries out, his face crumpling with pleasure.

My jaw clenches as I concentrate, making sure each punishing thrust swipes over his prostate, causing him to writhe beneath me. I wish more than anything, I could make this last for hours, but I know I won't be able to last much longer. He's so fucking tight, and so ridiculously hot. Even if I could make this last for hours, it still wouldn't be enough. I don't think I could ever get enough of him.

I let go of one of his hands, reaching between us to grab his rock-hard cock. He inhales sharply, his lips pressing together, as I work him in time with my thrusts.

"Oh my god," he gasps. "Fuck. Carter. I . . ."

The words are lost as he throws his head back in a moan that has my balls tightening. Warm cum coats my fingers, spurting onto his chest, and I let go of his wrists and cock, to brace myself on either side of him as my own release follows so hard, my limbs tingle, and the edges of my vision blur.

With his hands finally free, Linc reaches up and grabs my face, pulling my mouth to his. He kisses me, alternating between tender and savage to where, when I pull away, I'm grinning.

"You okay?" I ask.

He pushes his hair back off his face and closes his eyes. "That was . . ."

"All right? Acceptable?" I suggest.

Linc's eyes fly open, and he grabs my face again, this time pulling us together, so we're nose to nose. "You are incredible," he says. "*That* was incredible. What about you? Are you okay?"

I nod. "More than okay."

Linc reaches to the window ledge and grabs a pocket-sized pack of tissues he must have stashed there at some point. As I pull out and we clean up, I'm still trembling a little.

"Hey," Linc says, shifting so he's right on one side of the small double. He holds his arms open. "Come here."

I climb back onto the bed and into his arms, resting my head on his chest. As my hand traces the dips and grooves there, he presses a kiss to my head, and I smile.

"What do you think Hailee and Jax are up to?" I ask.

Linc chuckles softly. "If they're not in the other bedroom, I'll eat my sneakers."

I lift my head. "Seriously?"

"Uh, yes. Have you seen him? Have you seen her? Just imagine how fucking hot the sex will be."

I frown. Surely, I should feel jealous at the idea of Jax with Hailee. I mean, I am a little, but it feels weird. Different.

"Doesn't it bother you?" I ask.

"No," he says without pause. "I mean, I kind of wish they'd wait until we were there too, but that's it."

I lay my head back down on his chest and Linc massages

my scalp, tugging on my hair. That's what it is. I'm not jealous of them together. I'm jealous that it's without me.

"He's straight," I say.

Linc huffs and I press a kiss to his chest. My mind is already conjuring images of what Hailee and Jax might be up to in the next room, and I don't hate it. Why doesn't it bother me, though? I think of Hailee with her ex, even though I have no idea what he looks like, and the thought has my jaw and fists clenching. I exhale. He's a dick, though. It doesn't count. I picture Hailee in Vegas after we've gone our separate ways, going on dates, hooking up. My stomach rolls.

"What's going on?" Linc asks, shifting so he can look at me.

I consider lying, but curiosity gets the better of me. "I was just thinking. I'm not jealous of Hailee being with Jax, if she even is, but the idea of her being with someone else makes me feel sick to my stomach."

Linc's brow creases into a frown as he considers my words. "You're right. Same. But also, same for you. The idea of you and Jax together has my dick waking up like Christmas morning, but the idea of you with anyone else makes me want to hit something."

His gentle honesty tightens my chest, and I reach out and take his hand, kissing his knuckles. My intake of breath is prepared to carry the words to tell him not to worry—that there isn't going to be anyone else. I don't want anyone else. But I swallow the breath and the words with it. Two more nights. That's all that's left. Whether he's thinking the same or not, I don't ask, but we both hold each other a little tighter.

31

My cheeks are numb. I close my eyes and smile as I tilt my face up to bask in the amber-hued rays of the sun. The stifling heat of midday has faded to a comfortable warmth, and I don't know whether it's the alcohol, the mountain air, or a little bit of everything; but I feel free. Despite the complete shit show that is my life, being up here with the guys feels like none of that stuff matters.

I open my eyes to find Jax watching me, his expression more serious than it was when I closed them. He hasn't put his shirt back on, and I'm certainly not going to bring it up. Between his muscles and the beautiful sprawling black and grey art that covers his body, I could stare at him for hours without getting bored.

"What are you thinking?" I ask.

His frown deepens and my brain must be slowed by the liquor, because I reach up and smooth the line between his eyebrows with my thumb without thinking.

He takes hold of my hand, his thumb stroking, as he stares at me with enough intensity that I swallow hard. His hand feels different from Carter's and Linc's. The skin isn't smooth like theirs. The pads of his fingers are rougher. I turn his hand over, inspecting.

"What?" he asks.

"Your fingers are rough," I say, tracing the hardened skin. He moves to pull his hand away, but I tighten my grip. "I didn't say it was a bad thing. I like it."

He raises an eyebrow. "Oh?"

"Is it from working in a garage?" I ask. I half expect his fingernails to be stained with motor oil, but they're not. I guess it's been a while since he left.

"I suppose," he says, his eyes still watching me curiously. "And I play guitar."

I run my fingers over the tattoos lining the back of his hand and the sides of his fingers. They must have hurt like hell. "You never said."

"That I play guitar?"

I look up. "No. What you were thinking."

"Oh, that." He flips our hands, inspecting mine. "I was thinking I want to kiss you."

"Oh."

He grins. "Which is funny, because you've already come on my fingers."

My cheeks burn and I look away, causing Jax to chuckle.

"That's fucking adorable," he says, shaking his head. "The stuff I've seen you do, and you blush at the mention of coming on my fingers."

It's not just my cheeks that heat. A tingling warmth coils in my belly at the memory of the way he's touched me, the feel of his mouth on my neck. What he watched me do to Carter. Knowing the guys are probably naked in the room next door doesn't help.

I reach for the bottle of bourbon, but Jax takes my hand again.

"What?" I ask, forcing myself to look in his eyes. They remind me of a lagoon, right where the water shifts from dark to light as the depth changes.

"Can I kiss you?"

God, I want him to do a lot more than that. "Yes."

Jax reaches forward and threads his fingers through my curls, drawing me toward him. My head swims at the soft, gentle press of his lips, but as he deepens the kiss, his grip tightens on my hair and my breath catches.

"I haven't forgotten," he says, pulling back to drag slow, sensual kisses along my jaw to my neck. "How your body responded to me in that hotel room."

My eyes close, and my head tips back as he nips at my ear.

His voice is a growl against my skin. "Do you want me, princess?"

"Yes," I say, the word an exhale.

Jax pulls away and stands, holding out a hand. I stare up at him, silhouetted by the late afternoon sun, and for a second, doubt clouds my mind. What if he only wants me because he knows he can have me? I'm a woman who's actively sleeping with two other guys. Is that the only reason he's with us? Does he just think I'm a sure thing? An easy lay?

I let myself look at him; at his low-slung jeans and his sun-bronzed body covered with ink. I want him. I know in my bones the sex will be amazing. Does it matter if those are his reasons? They're mine too, right? This isn't a relationship. Linc's words from the first time we met come back to me. Would I feel bad about dessert? Jax is chocolate lava cake, doused in alcohol and set alight.

I grab hold of his hand.

He keeps my hand in his as we step back into the cabin, heading toward the other bedroom. My body feels lit up from the inside as Jax pushes open the door and steps aside to let me in. He closes it behind him and I can barely breathe, my skin vibrating at the thought of what I'm doing. What we will be doing. Every inch of me burns for his touch.

"Take off your clothes," he says.

I stare, frozen.

One side of Jax's mouth lifts. "Didn't you hear me, princess? Take. Off. Your. Fucking. Clothes."

My hands trembling, I reach for the hem of my top. As I do, he kicks off his shoes and unfastens his jeans. By the time I've pulled the top off over my head, he's stepping out of them. As he's already shed his shirt, he's in nothing but black boxer briefs. I stare at the ink covering the length of his legs. Only the tops of his feet are untouched.

"Don't keep me waiting, princess," he says, dragging my attention from his skin. "If you keep me waiting, I'll do the same to you."

My eyes narrow, and I toe off my sneakers and unfasten my jeans, wondering what he means. The room is warm from a day of summer sun, but standing in my underwear as Jax fixes me with a look filled with promise, I shiver.

"I told you to take your clothes off," he says.

I shrug. "I did. This is underwear."

A smile breaks slowly across his face, his eyes flashing. "Are you sassing me? I'll make you pay for that."

I swallow. "Oh?"

Jax takes a step towards me, and I stop breathing. His dark blond hair falls over his forehead, mussed from dragging his hand through it one too many times today, and the way he looks at me has me frozen to the spot.

He walks forward until we're almost toe to toe, and my lips part as I look up at him, waiting for him to continue the searing kiss we started on the deck. But he doesn't. Instead, he leans forward and kisses the base of my neck, trailing kisses along my shoulder. I reach up to touch him, but he steps back.

"No touching," he says. "Not yet."

I suck in a breath as he continues, his teeth taking hold of my bra strap and dragging it off my shoulder. Instantly I regret not taking off my underwear, too. My breasts are aching for his touch, and as he repeats the action on the other side, my body arches in a silent plea.

Jax kisses his way down between my breasts, his tongue licking lazily, and as he sinks to his knees, my hands clench at my sides, resisting the urge to slide into his hair. His fingers hook in my panties, pulling them down slowly as he kisses my hips. When he drags the tips of his fingers up my legs, his warm breath caresses my skin, and I tremble.

"What do you want, princess?" Jax asks, his searing gaze tracking down my body. He stands, reaching behind me and unfastening my bra, letting it fall to the floor.

"I want you," I breathe.

Jax hums his response. Is this what he meant about making me wait? I'm not sure I can take much more, and I'm about to tell him as much, when he bends and takes one of my nipples into his mouth, sucking hard enough to make me gasp. He rolls it with his tongue, flicking, before repeating the action with the other. My legs are shaking, the heat between my thighs unbearable.

"Get on the bed."

I stumble backwards, climbing up onto the bed and

laying down on the dust sheet, my thighs pressed together. Jax kneels at my feet, shaking his head in a silent reprimand, as he slides his hands between my legs and spreads them apart, baring me to him.

He rolls his neck, cracking it with a groan, as his fingers dig into the soft flesh of my thighs. "Look at you," he rumbles.

Lowering himself between my legs, he pushes them further apart, and my breathing is more like panting as I wait, eyes closed, for the first touch of him. But it doesn't come. His hands are on my legs, his breath on the inside of my thighs. I open my eyes, confused, to find him watching me.

A smirk curves his lips. "This is what happens if you keep me waiting."

I push my head back into the bed with a groan.

"Do you want my mouth on you?" he asks, his fingers trailing feather light touches up and down the inside of my thighs. "My tongue?"

I moan in response, my hips lifting.

"Words," he says. "Tell me."

"I want you, Jax," I say, each syllable edged with desire. "I want your mouth."

Before I can take another breath, he dips his head and drags his tongue through my center, and I gasp, my hands clutching the sheet. His fingers grip my thighs as he devours me, licking and sucking with such ferocity, he has me writhing and panting in seconds.

Jax sits up, and my body sags at the lack of contact. When I open my eyes, he holds my gaze, replacing his tongue with his fingers as he swirls and strokes.

I lift my hips. Urging. "Jax," I plead.

He shakes his head, that teasing smile still on his lips.

"You want my cock inside you, princess? You're going to have to come for me."

I gasp, my cheeks heating. He taps his thumb against my clit, and I writhe. I want to touch him. I want his skin under my fingers. I want his mouth on mine. I want him inside me. Having him so close, denying me, is a forest fire in my brain. I can't think straight, and the flames are burning me alive.

"That's it, princess," he says, his voice soft and low.

My hips lift, pleading for him to fill me, but he places a hand against my stomach, pinning me to the bed as he swirls relentlessly around my clit.

"You want me to fuck you, don't you?" he rasps. "You want my cock inside you so badly, you could scream. Isn't that right, princess?"

All I can do is whimper as he rubs against the bundle of nerves, causing me to arch up off the bed. He leans over me, his lips against my ear as he slips a broad finger inside me. I exhale, my body flaming at the feeling.

"You like it when I talk dirty, don't you?" he asks, nipping at my neck.

I nod as he draws his finger out, adding a second. I groan, urging him deeper. He pumps his fingers slowly, and my knuckles ache from gripping the sheets. I want to touch him so badly, but I don't want to risk him stopping.

"Let me tell you exactly what's going to happen," he says, resting his forehead against mine as he works his fingers inside me. "You're going to come all over my fingers. Then you're going to take my big, hard cock. But only once. I'm going to coat myself in you, and you're going to lick me clean, princess." He squeezes my clit between his fingers, and I gasp. "Then, when I'm nice and clean, I'm going to fuck you harder than you've ever been fucked in your life."

I whimper, my brain mush as he pumps his fingers, his

thumb working my clit. He captures my moan with his mouth, and I'm done for. As he strokes my tongue with his, my orgasm wracks my body, until I'm trembling beneath him.

Jax sits back, his eyes dark, holding mine. "Good girl."

I lie there, breathing hard, as he stands and pushes down his underwear. His cock springs free, bobbing, thick and hard. I swallow, my mouth dry, as he climbs back over me, and I don't have time to wonder whether he meant what he said, as he settles between my legs, pushing into me. The moan that tears from my throat is far too loud, my body singing at the sensation of him filling me like I've been craving. He leans forward and flicks my nipples with his tongue until I whimper. Then, he pulls out, and rises onto his knees.

"Come here, princess," he says, his voice a commanding purr. "Clean up this mess you've made."

My heart slams in my chest as I sit up, moving forward until his glistening cock is in front of me. He grips my chin, gently but firmly.

"Let me see that pretty tongue," he says, squeezing my jaw a little.

I open my mouth, and he groans. Shifting his hips, he places his cock on my waiting tongue, and I curl it against him.

"Fuck," he breathes, his head falling back.

Spurred on by his moans, I drag my tongue along his length, tasting myself. His fingers sink into my curls, and I work my mouth over every hard, thick inch of him.

When he groans, I open my mouth and take him as deep as I can, sucking and teasing. He lets me for a few seconds, his breathing quickening, and I can tell he's holding back from moving his hips.

Hissing softly, Jax gently pulls me off him, tugging me up so we're chest to chest. I stare up at him, wondering if I did something wrong, but he just shakes his head a little before crushing my mouth with his. His kiss is searing, all restraint from before eviscerated, as his hands grip at my body.

I don't wait for permission as I let myself touch him, stroking and kneading the firm planes of his body. I'm desperate for the touch of him, and my hand slips down between us, wrapping around his length. He groans against my mouth, breaking the kiss to rest his forehead against mine.

"Fuck, princess," he says, the light blue of his eyes eclipsed by his pupils.

Shifting off the bed, he fishes a condom from his jeans pocket, and I watch, panting slightly as he rolls it on. Stepping back to the bed, he pushes me gently backwards. I can barely breathe as he moves over me, positioning himself between my legs, and when he eases into me, my head falls back, a deep groan emanating from my chest as he fills and stretches me.

"Do you like the feeling of my cock inside you?" he asks, dipping his head to tease a nipple with his teeth and tongue.

"Yes," I breathe, bucking beneath him, desperate for him to start moving.

Jax sucks at my breast, his fingers finding my other, teasing and flicking. "Do you want me to take you hard, princess?"

I whimper, putty in his hands. "Yes."

He pulls out, and thrusts back in. "Like that?"

"Harder," I moan.

His head drops against my chest, and I open my eyes, my fingers twisting in his hair.

"You're killing me, princess," he whispers.

I pull him up, pressing my lips to his, and as he kisses me back, he starts to move. My fingers tighten in his hair, and the desperate want built by all the teasing and talk explodes as I whisper against his mouth. "Fuck me, Jax. Fuck me hard."

He snarls, slamming into me like an animal, and I wrap my legs around him, pulling him deeper. All the control he used to taunt me with is gone as he pounds into me, over and over. I dig my nails into his back, feeling his muscles shift beneath my fingers, and even as I feel my release building, I don't want it to end.

My mind is addled with pleasure, his strong arms gripping me to him, as I near the edge. Jax slows, drawing out my release until I'm panting, and I cry out, clenching around him, as my orgasm throbs through me. Jax's teeth grip my shoulder as he chases his own release, following seconds later, his body stiffening as he sucks at my flesh with a rumbling moan.

"Jax," I whisper.

He presses a kiss to my shoulder and briefly against my lips. Sliding a hand against my spine, he lifts my chest to his mouth, running his tongue between my breasts, and lapping up the tiny beads of sweat with a groan.

I reach for him, pulling his mouth back to mine, and kissing him deeply. We lie there, hands and tongues stroking, until he pulls back.

"I need to clean up, princess."

The room has a small bathroom attached, and as he pads across the room, I admire his muscled ass, noting the lack of ink. My body is completely spent as I lie, sprawled on the bed, basking in the afterglow.

"You should message the guys and see what they want to

do," Jax calls from the bathroom. "Unless you want to go check on them."

I have no plans to leave this bed anytime soon, unsure if my legs will even work. So, I reach for my discarded jeans, pulling my phone from the pocket. It's usually in my bag, but since the message from Sal, I've felt the need to have it near me. When I turn it on, the battery is almost dead. I'll have to charge it when we check into the hotel. I scroll for Carter's number, realizing that I don't have Linc's at all. I send him a message asking him if he's done, and what the plans are.

The toilet flushes, and I'm considering whether I can be bothered to put my underwear on, when my phone vibrates. I pick it up, but it's not Carter's number on the notification. I frown. It's a number not in my contacts. Perhaps it's Linc. Swiping my phone open, I click on the message.

Call me. Now.

I stare at the screen, my heart pounding in my throat. It's not Linc. I know it's not. It's Brent. He's using someone else's phone. To be honest, I'm surprised he didn't do it sooner. Before I can click off it, another text comes through.

Hailee. Call me. NOW.

I drop the phone as though it's burned me. I'm such a fucking idiot. He saw that I read that first message. My eyes burn.

"What's wrong?" Jax is standing over me, his brow furrowed.

I force a smile. "Nothing. They haven't replied yet. Must still be busy."

Jax's eyes narrow; but if he doesn't believe me, he doesn't push it.

"We can go and watch if you want?" I tease.

He laughs and climbs onto the bed, lying down beside

me and pulling me to his chest. “You’d like that, wouldn’t you, princess?”

My smile is genuine as I tilt my face to his and kiss him. As his hands stroke my warm skin, his mouth worshipping mine, I push the texts as far from my mind as I can.

32

My first thought when I wake is how fucking comfortable I am. Two consecutive nights waking up in a hotel room. Stretching out my arms and legs, I savor the warmth. There's no point getting used to it, though. Tonight, I'll be sleeping on a bus. Probably the next night, too. After that? Fuck knows. Most likely a sofa. I have enough cash to spring for a motel room, but I'd rather not spend money on shit like that, unless my only other option is a doorway, or under a bridge.

Yesterday was . . . I smile, my eyes still closed, as I run through a highlight reel of sex with Hailee. It was fucking incredible. *She's* incredible. My dick is already hard, and I move my hand toward it before I stop, opening an eye, as I remember I'm not alone.

Turning my head to the right, I find Hailee still sound asleep, her plump lips slightly parted. I resist the urge to touch her. She looks like a fucking angel. Taking care not to tug at the covers, I sit up. Carter has an arm draped across her waist, and Linc is spread out on his back, like yesterday. I smile to myself and shake my head.

It's not the same room, although it's the same hotel. This time, we pushed the beds together. Linc insisted it was just for comfort's sake, while we ate pizza and watched a movie. I honestly hadn't intended on spending the night—unsure whether they'd be getting up to their threesome shit again—but by the time the pizza was gone, and the movie finished, everyone just sort of crashed. It felt weirdly natural. Maybe it was just all the mountain air.

Sliding out of bed, I head to the bathroom to relieve myself, then grab my pack of cigs from out of my bag and head to the small balcony. The sky is still a little pink around the edges, and a glance at my phone tells me it's just after seven. I've always been an early riser. There's never been much call for lazing around in my life.

I light the cigarette and take a deep drag. The more I think about it, the more I realize, the last two days have been the most fun I've had in forever. Especially yesterday. I can't remember the last time I spent a day just hanging out with friends. I don't really have friends. I have drinking buddies. Work buddies. No one I expect to keep in touch with from Montana. Even though I spent a couple of years there, I still struggled to put down roots. Perhaps on some level, I always knew I'd end up leaving. Even if it wasn't by choice.

Hailee and I had lain in bed at the lodge, talking and kissing for a while, and it had been really nice. Eventually, Linc had knocked on the door and shouted that they were going back out to finish the food. We'd joined them not long after, and the weirdest fucking thing was, it wasn't awkward. Even though, we'd paired off to have sex in opposite rooms, we continued chatting and hanging like before.

I blow out a stream of smoke and lean against the railing. Last night, I laughed so hard my sides hurt. Has that ever happened before? I take another drag, then put it out, flicking the butt down into the parking lot below. It's been a great couple of days, but it's over now. Fond memories and all that shit.

When I walk back into the room, sliding the door shut behind me, Linc is awake.

He yawns, stretching his arms above his head. "Morning, sunshine."

"Morning."

"You're up early," he says, keeping his voice down to avoid waking the others, as he glances at his phone on the side table.

His voice is even deeper on waking. His hair is down around his shoulders, and I can't help but admire his body as he stretches again, stifling another yawn. He's pretty. Which is weird. Because he's not feminine at all. Can someone be masculine and pretty? I'd have said no before meeting Linc.

I look away and shrug. "Never been one for sleeping in."

"Maybe you just haven't had the right people to sleep in with." Linc drags his gaze slowly down my body, his tongue darting out over his bottom lip. "I can give you several reasons to come back to bed."

"Yeah, yeah." I shake my head. "We've had this conversation."

"And the offer to receive the best blowjob of your life still stands." He folds his arms behind his head, his eyes still tracking across my body.

I think back to yesterday, when I deprived myself of release in the shower to avoid the risk of thinking about him. It feels stupid now. After spending the day with him and Carter, things have shifted a little. My answer is still a hard no, but the thought isn't as jarring.

"You're thinking about it, aren't you?" Linc says, his eyes

flashing. "Me, on my knees, and my lips wrapped around your cock. Maybe your hand gripping my hair as you fuck my mouth?"

My eyes snap to his, and fuck if my dick doesn't wake up at that image. Linc's eyes drop to my crotch, his pouty lips curving into a smile.

"Fuck off," I say, but I'm smiling. "You wouldn't be able to handle my dick. You'd choke."

"I'd certainly hope so." He pulls back the covers with a grin, and stands up, his dick tenting his briefs.

"What are you doing?" I ask as he walks toward me.

He stops right in front of me, close enough for me to feel his 'just got out of bed' warmth.

"I'm going to take a shower," he says. Reaching out, he raises a finger to my chest, pausing right before contact, as though waiting to see if I'll push him away. Contact doesn't scare me, so I meet his gaze, and he continues, dragging his index finger slowly down my chest, dipping briefly into my belly button, before dropping to his side. "I'm going to leave the door open, in case you change your mind."

He steps past me to the bathroom, and I watch, confused, as to what the fuck just happened. The line he drew down my chest is burning like he used a blowtorch on me, and my dick is stone. The water turns on and, just as he said, the door is open. Not fully, but enough. Enough that I catch glimpses of Linc's brown skin as he steps under the spray. I swallow, and before I know what I'm doing, I've stepped closer.

I'm not going in. He's ogled my body enough. I know he won't care if I return the favor. I smirk to myself. Who am I kidding? He'd love it. Besides, it's not like it isn't anything I haven't seen before. I watched him fuck Carter. My dick twitches. No, I didn't watch him fuck Carter. I was just in the room. I was watching Hailee. The whole time.

I step closer, my heart pounding in my chest. I can see half of his back as he stands under the spray, his hands in his hair. His muscles shift as he works some shampoo in, and I watch the suds trail down his back and over his ass. It's a great ass. I can admit that. It makes sense. His body is his job.

I step closer. *I'm not going in.* I can see almost all of him now. He turns, and I freeze, waiting for him to see me watching like a fucking creeper, but his eyes are closed, his face lifted to the spray. *Fuck.* Linc's a good-looking guy. One of his hands drops from his hair and I track it downwards. He grips the base of his dick and pulls. My own dick strains. I've seen Linc touch himself before. Heck, I've seen him fuck someone. But this is different. My hand moves to my cock, palming it over my briefs. I can't fucking help it. I'm so hard.

I glance over my shoulder at the bed. Hailee and Carter are still sound asleep. Oblivious to what's going on a couple of feet away. What *is* going on? I turn back to the shower and lock eyes with Linc.

He pushes his dark hair from his face, before pointedly looking at where my hand is still resting on my dick. *Fuck.* What do I do? Walk away. That's what I should do. Walk away and wait for my dick to calm the fuck down. Or maybe I can wake Hailee. Linc pushes open the shower door, and my heart kicks up a gear. *I'm not going in.*

Linc's words from the previous morning loop in my head. If he sucks me off, it doesn't make me gay. Not that there's anything wrong with being gay. I'm just not into guys. I can practically hear Linc laughing in my head, telling me that my dick clearly disagrees with me. It's not like I can even blame it on being hard up. I had the best sex I've had in . . . probably ever, yesterday.

The past couple of days have been the most ridiculous of my life—and I thought my life was already off the charts. They've also been two of the best days. Linc's still staring at me, but the gleeful look at finding me palming my dick has been replaced with one of concern. I can only imagine what my face looks like as I war with myself.

"Jax?"

I take a deep breath. *Fuck it.* In an hour, I'll be gone. I'll never see these guys again. Curiosity has thrown the cat from a twenty-story building and then dropped a fucking piano on it. I step into the bathroom and close the door.

My hands are trembling as I pull down my underwear, my dick springing free, as eager as anything, clearly not caring about the conflict raging in my brain. Linc is still standing there, his hand on the shower door, keeping it open.

"You okay?" he asks.

I nod, pulling myself together. "Don't make this fucking weird. Just put your money where your mouth is."

Linc grins and steps back, letting me into the shower. "I'd rather put something else where my mouth is."

My cock jumps at his words, and I silently tell it off, but before I can say anything else, Linc drops to his knees. I don't know what I was expecting. Did I think he was going to kiss me? I'm the one who told him not to make it weird. Even as I look down at him, I realize a part of me hadn't quite believed he was going to do it. I watch, wide eyed, as he closes his fingers around my cock and wraps his lips around the head. *Fuck.* I lean back against the tiled wall, cold against my skin, despite my body being on fire. He was right to be confident. It's incredible. My head drops back against the wall as his tongue works me, swirling and licking, while he pumps me with his fist. It's fucking perfection.

When Linc releases his grip on me my eyes fly open. He reaches up and takes hold of my hips, looking up at me through dark lashes, his face dripping with water. I hold my breath as he opens his mouth and flicks out his tongue, running it along my slit before taking me into his mouth. Holding my gaze, he takes me deeper, his cheeks hollowing out as he sucks. My breath catches, a strangled moan escaping my throat, as he works me further down his throat, until his nose presses against my crotch. My hips buck automatically, and when I hit the back of his throat, I groan. After a few seconds, he sits back, working me with his hand.

"Did you like that?" he asks, even though the answer is pretty fucking clear.

I'm breathing so hard; all I can do is nod.

He flicks his tongue out, lapping at my crown. "Do you want to fuck my mouth, Jax?"

I groan, sagging a little against the wall.

Linc grins and takes me into his mouth again. This time, I reach out and grip his head, threading my fingers through his thick hair. Moving my hips slowly, thrusting in and out of his mouth, I'm transfixed by how my cock looks sliding between his lips. I hold back. I know Linc thinks he can take it, but I don't want to hurt him.

When he reaches up and grips my hips, urging me to move faster, my restraint crumbles. My hands tighten their hold on his hair, and I buck my hips, fucking his pretty mouth. Every time my dick hits the back of his throat, my eyes roll back in my head. My heart is pounding so fast it hurts, and when Linc's moans vibrate against my dick, I gasp as my balls tighten.

"I'm going to come," I grunt, making to pull back.

Linc digs his fingers into my hips, sucking and sliding on my cock until I shoot my load down his throat so hard, I draw blood biting down on my lip to keep in my cry of pleasure. He swallows every last drop, swirling his tongue around my tip, before getting to his feet. I'm mush. I can't even form words.

"I told you," Linc says, giving me a wink as he gets to his feet. "Now, I'm going to take care of myself. You're welcome to stay and watch if you want."

My legs are jello, and I couldn't walk if I wanted to. What the fuck just happened? My head spins, the water deafening as it splashes around us. A guy just sucked me off. No. Not a guy. Linc. I swallow, watching as he squirts some shower gel into his hand, gripping his dick and stroking. It feels wrong. Not that I let him blow me. This. I feel like I used him. I know he probably doesn't see it that way. He offered, after all. I just don't like feeling like I owe him one.

Before I can think better of it, I step behind him, my chest against his back, and place my hand over his. Linc freezes for a second, then continues his stroking. I grip his dick lower, pushing his hand off, and Linc makes a breathy noise that makes me smile. He reaches out, bracing himself on the wall, and I stroke him with long, firm movements. I'm sure it should feel strange jerking another guy off, but weirdly, it doesn't. Maybe it's because he just sucked my cock. Maybe it's because it's Linc. I try not to overthink it.

He pushes back against me a little, and there's a split second of hesitation before I relax into it, allowing myself to enjoy the feel of his hard, warm body against mine. Reaching out, I place my left hand against the wall beside his, as I quicken the pace with my right.

Linc's head falls forward, and he moans, the sound rumbling against my chest. I smile again, wondering what other noises I can wring from him. Leaning closer, I gently bite down where his neck meets his shoulder, and Linc trembles, his breath hitching. I like this. I like being in control. Whatever shampoo he used smells like some sort of forest. It's nice. I nuzzle my nose against his neck, breathing it in, and he makes the same breathy whimper. I decide that's the noise I want, and I chase the sound, taking his earlobe between my teeth.

"Fuck. Jax," he gasps. "I'm coming."

His dick pulses in my hand, and for a second, I think about letting go, but I don't. Instead, I continue to stroke, wringing every last drop from his dick, before pressing a quick kiss to his neck, and rinsing my hand off under the spray.

Linc turns to me, his brown eyes wide.

"What?" I shrug, stepping under the water and reaching for the soap. "I didn't want to owe you one."

When I finish rinsing and turn off the spray, Linc is still standing there, watching me with a strange expression on his face. It looks almost sad.

"What's up?" I ask, as though two guys sharing a shower is the most normal thing in my life.

Linc steps closer, his eyes flitting over my face, lingering on my mouth. My chest tightens. I know what he wants. My gaze dips to his lips. He's got a great mouth. The only person I know with better lips is asleep on the other side of the door.

I know he won't step closer. He's putting the ball in my court. What's a kiss? The guy just had my dick in his mouth. If I'm worried about what messing around with a guy means, that ship has already sailed. *Fuck it.* I reach out and grip the back of his neck, pulling him toward me. My intention is for a brief kiss, but as our lips meet, his hand mirroring mine behind my neck, I find myself leaning into it instead of pulling away.

My grip tightens on his neck, my other clutching his shoulder, as our tongues battle for dominance in a war fought with lips and teeth. It's urgent and claiming and I don't want it to stop. It feels different, his body, broad and hard against mine, and to my surprise, I don't hate it. He breaks away first, breathing hard, as he rests his forehead against mine. My fingers curl in his hair.

"Jax," he murmurs.

"Yes." I sigh. "You give incredible head. Don't go thinking you're getting anywhere near my ass with that monster cock, though."

Linc laughs before shoving me away. Grabbing a towel, he throws it back to me before getting another for himself. I towel off and wrap it around my waist, following him out into the bedroom. Carter is still asleep, but Hailee is awake, flicking through muted channels on the small television.

I freeze, my heart in my throat. It's not like we're dating or anything, but I just showered with someone else with her in the other room. I'm not sure what the rules are, if any. She glances between us as we step into the room, her eyes lighting up.

"Good morning," she says. "Conserving water?"

Linc laughs and whips off his towel, bringing it up to dry his hair.

"Jesus, man," I bark, turning away. "A bit of warning."

Linc snorts and walks over to his bag. "Not like you haven't seen it before."

Hailee looks fucking gleeful. It's weird. Does she just get off on guys together? She pushes back the covers and climbs out of the bed, heading past me to the bathroom. She pauses as she passes me, rising on her toes to press a kiss to my lips. I'm so confused, I let her pull away.

Then I snap to my senses and pull her back to me, kissing her hard. She wraps her arms around my neck, and I slide my hands under the t-shirt she's wearing, gripping her ass.

"Stop it." She bats my chest and pulls back with a grin. "I need to get rid of my morning breath."

"I don't care," I say truthfully.

Hailee rolls her eyes. "Yeah, well, I also need to pee. You two were in there for ages."

On the other side of the room, Linc chuckles, and I fold my arms across my chest as Hailee closes the door to the bathroom. "What's so funny?"

"Did you find out?" he asks, pulling a dark blue t-shirt on over his head.

I raise my eyebrows. "What do you mean?"

"Kissing Hailee like that. Are you still straight?"

"Fuck off." I roll my eyes and root in my bag for clothes.

Even though I know he's joking, the words still stay with me. Is that what I was doing? If someone had told me a couple of days ago that I would have fooled around with a guy—kissed a guy—in a shower, I'd have punched them in the face and called them a liar. I should be spiraling. I should be freaking out. Pulling on clean underwear under my towel, I glance over at where Linc is combing his hair, expecting to feel the onslaught of shame or doubt, but it doesn't happen. I don't regret a thing. Hailee's phone pings with a text, pulling me from my thoughts.

"You got a text," I say, as she steps out of the bathroom.

When I look up from where I'm trying to find clean socks in the bottom of my bag, I find her face has paled, all the joy that was shining in her eyes earlier evaporated. I open my mouth to ask what's wrong, but she plucks up her phone and steps out onto the balcony, closing the door behind her.

"That was weird," Linc says, watching her through the glass.

"What's weird?" Carter asks, sitting up and stretching.

His hair is even messier than usual and there's a line down his cheek from the sheets. I chuckle and his eyes snap to me. They always surprise me. How fucking blue they are.

"Hailee got a text that made her act weird," Linc explains.

Carter's face falls into a familiar frown. "Who's it from?"

"I don't know," Linc says with a shrug. "Probably her sister."

"Why would a text from her sister make her act weird?" Carter presses.

I sit down on the bed to pull on a pair of socks I'm fairly certain are not clean. "She got a text yesterday at the cabin that did the same."

"It's something to do with Brent," Carter says, flinging back the covers and marching over to the balcony. "I know it is."

I reach out and grab his arm as he passes, and he whirls on me, his blue eyes blazing.

"Give her a minute, man," I say, letting him shrug out of my grip. "She's a grown woman, she can handle her own shit."

Carter steps to me, his chin raised. "Yeah, she can. That doesn't mean she has to do it on her own, though."

"She's not on her own," Linc says, tying his hair up into the neat bun he prefers. "She's got us. And we'll be here, when and if she needs us. Let it go, Carter."

Carter looks between us, his eyes narrowed, before

turning back to Hailee on the balcony. I watch him, ready to step in front of him, but he shakes his head and heads to the bathroom instead.

"What's his deal?" I ask once the door locks.

Linc shakes his head. "He's fiercely protective. His ex was a controlling asshole like Hailee's, and I think he's projecting a little."

"Dude needs to chill," I grumble, shoving stuff into my bag.

When I grab my phone and pull up a browser, my heart sinks. The last visited page is the bus timetable. Frowning at the screen, I search the listings until I find that the next bus heading to Phoenix leaves at half ten. After breakfast I'll have to split. My chest is tight enough that I rub it. Maybe I should leave now. Well, after I've brushed my teeth. Prolonging it is only going to make it worse.

The balcony door opens, and Hailee steps in, her frown melting into the most fake ass smile I've ever seen, as she finds Linc and me watching her.

"What's up?" she asks.

"That's what we were going to ask you." Linc nods at the phone in her hand. "Everything okay?"

Hailee shoves the phone in her back pocket and closes the door behind her. "Yeah. Just my sister asking for an update. I told her we're about three days out."

"Where did you guys say you were headed next?" I ask, perching on the bed. "Somewhere random, wasn't it?"

Hailee puts her hands on her hips. "We're going to the Four Corners Monument. That's not random."

"I don't think you understand what random means."

"It's famous," she says, fighting a smile. "Just because you haven't heard of it."

I raise an eyebrow. "Who said I hadn't heard of it? What else is around it?"

"It doesn't matter what else is around it," she says. "We're going for the monument."

"Stop winding her up," Linc says, tossing a pillow at my back.

I catch it, throwing it right back, and he grins. My heart fucking skips. *What the fuck?*

I turn to Hailee, who's smiling again. "My bus is in a couple of hours. Any chance you could drop me off at the station on your way to the middle of nowhere?"

The smile falls from her face, and she glances at Linc, tugging her bottom lip with her teeth. It's something that shouldn't look cute, but it does.

"You're leaving," she says, not quite a question.

"I mean, I was never supposed to stay." I hate how sad she looks. I hate how tight my chest is.

"You should come with us," Linc says.

I turn, but he's not looking at me. His attention is fixed on his phone as he leans against the dresser. When I look back at Hailee, her big brown eyes are wide with hope.

"Ah, princess." I shake my head. "Don't go pulling that Bambi shit on me."

The bathroom door opens, steam spilling into the room, as Carter steps out with a towel around his waist. He's got a good body. The kind of build where I bet he played sports in college. He's got a little hair on his chest, darker from the shower, and it trails down his stomach. I look away, scrubbing a hand over my face. One blow job, and now I'm checking out guys? What the fuck is wrong with me?

"What did I miss?" Carter asks.

"We're trying to convince Jax to come to the Four Corners with us," Linc says.

I watch Carter, unsure of what he'll say. I still can't get a proper read on him.

He looks at me, considering. "I mean, there are four corners. One state for each of us."

"Good point," Linc says. "You can stand in Arizona, Jax."

Hailee sits down beside me, looking so nervous it's adorable. "We can totally drop you off at the bus station, but if there's any chance you could come with us . . ."

I take Hailee's hand and thread my fingers through hers, squeezing as I weigh up the pros and cons. There really aren't any cons. My 'uncle' isn't even expecting me. I haven't worked up the guts to call him yet in case he says no. I've learnt from experience that it's harder to turn someone away when they're standing on your doorstep with a bag.

Carter's back is to me as he pulls a t-shirt on and when I turn around to look at Linc, his phone is down, and he's watching me, waiting.

"You know you don't want to get rid of us just yet," he says.

His words sound light, but there's a softness to his eyes that tells me he wants me to stay. I mean, I *want* to stay. I just don't usually get to do what I want.

"Fine," I say, the weight on my chest shifting as I exhale. "I'll come to your stupid monument."

Hailee squeals and wraps her arms around me. I hug her tightly, and when Carter catches my eye, he smiles in a way that lifts the last of the weight from my heart. They want me. All three of them. Warmth spreads through my chest, and I close my eyes, pressing a kiss to the top of Hailee's head. It's a feeling I could easily get addicted to, and I'm going to have to tread carefully to make sure that doesn't happen.

33

"Do you want anything?"

I look up from where I'm filling the car with gas. As Linc walks backwards across the concourse, he flips his sunglasses up onto his head and winks at me. Even in basketball shorts and a plain blue t-shirt, he looks like a goddamn snack. "Grab me a Coke?"

"What about you, Hailee?"

She turns from where she's walking to the restrooms. "Just a water for me, please."

I watch as he gives her a thumbs up and follows Jax inside. My heart is pounding so ferociously in my chest, I might vomit from the force of it. I know I shouldn't do this. It's a bad idea. A seriously bad idea. I'm still going to do it, though.

As soon as they're all out of sight, I reach in through the back window where Hailee's backpack is resting on the seat. It's the third time we've stopped today, but it's the first time she's left her phone behind. I've watched a few times as she's unlocked it, and now I tap the digits to open it with confidence.

I finish fueling and turn my back to the station. I have to be quick. Clicking on her messages, I frown. There are only three recent threads. One is between her and Brent, but the last text was a few days ago. It's from her, asking him if he's coming home. What an asshole. She must have blocked him after that.

The other thread is from someone named Sal. Glancing over my shoulder to check I'm still okay, I quickly read the last couple of messages. My stomach rolls. Brent's been threatening her old boss? A glance at the time stamp tells me the text is from when we were at the restaurant, and my jaw clenches as I stare at the screen. This is what made her go weird and quiet. There are no more texts.

The most recent thread is from an unknown number. I open it up and my blood boils. It's clearly Brent using a different number. They start out quite tame, just demanding that she call him. The most recent one, though . . . The one she got on the balcony . . . My grip tightens on her phone.

YOU FUCKING THIEF.

I'M COMING FOR YOU.

I stare at the message until my eyes blur. He must be talking about the money in her backpack. Unless she took something else that's his. My teeth crack, my jaw is tensed so tight. She owes him nothing after what he did to her. She left him. It's over. Can't the guy take a fucking hint? My blood is lava in my veins as I dig my own phone out of my pocket and type the mystery number in. Laughter sounds over my shoulder, and I almost drop both phones. I turn, slipping Hailee's phone back where I found it, just as Linc and Jax reach the car.

"Here you go," Linc says, handing me a bottle of Coke.

"Thanks, man." I put it on top of the car and type out a message before I lose my nerve.

Leave Hailee alone.

If Brent wants to harass her, he'll have to go through me. A sense of calm floods through me as I grab my drink and walk back around to the driver's side. Ever since Hailee went all weird, I've been at a loss. The feeling of helplessness has gnawed away inside me, stretching the scars on my heart into deep gaping caverns. I doubt my text will do anything, but at least I've tried. At least he knows she's not alone anymore. That she has someone in her corner.

"What are you doing?"

My head snaps up at Hailee's tone, my skin ice cold as I watch her stride toward the car. *Does she know?* "What do you mean?"

"It's my turn to drive," she says, pointing at where I've got one foot already in the car.

Relief floods through me. "You sure?"

"Get in the back."

I do as she says and join Jax in the back. He's moved Hailee's bag, so it sits between us. I try not to look at it.

Jax looks up from his phone as Hailee starts the engine. "How much further?"

"Just under two hours," Linc says, holding up the map open on his phone. "Last leg."

Spending six hours in a car with three other people should sound like hell. It should *be* hell. Somehow, it's been fun. Things seem to have reached a comfortable middle ground with Jax, and now that I've managed to do what I've been planning since this morning, I can finally relax into the conversation buzzing around me—the discussion that's been going on since we stopped for lunch a couple of hours ago.

"There's nothing wrong with classic rock," Jax says,

leaning forward and resting his forearms on the back of Linc's chair.

Linc groans. "Please don't. 'Carry On Wayward Son' is not going on the ultimate road trip playlist. Veto."

"Hailee?" Jax pleads. "Please tell me you don't agree with this idiot?"

Hailee shakes her head. "Not getting involved."

"What about 'Hotel California'?" Linc suggests.

"I knew it!" Jax squeezes his shoulder before giving the headrest a triumphant thump. "You can't hate all classic rock."

I watch as Jax sinks back into his seat with a grin. This is the third day he's spent with us, and I've never seen him be so tactile. Linc turns around and winks at him, before continuing to flick through a list of songs he's pulled up on some website.

"Something happened, didn't it?" I say, more to myself than anyone else. But of course, everyone hears.

"What do you mean?" Linc asks, glancing back at me.

Curiosity has the better of me, so I plough forward, pointing between him and Jax. "Between you two. Something's different."

Linc's smile falters, and my heart clenches as I realize I'm right. I didn't quite believe that I was.

"They showered together this morning," Hailee says before Linc can speak.

My mouth falls open. "What?"

"You were dead to the world," Hailee continues, oblivious to the quiet that's fallen over the rest of us. After a second, she swears under her breath. "Sorry. Was I not supposed to say anything?"

"It isn't a secret," Linc says, his eyes fixed on me. "We said that from the start. I just wasn't sure how to bring it up."

"It's not hard," I say, wrestling with the emotions warring in my chest. "You say, 'Carter, I showered with Jax this morning'. It's actually pretty fucking easy."

Linc twists in his seat and reaches a hand back, placing it on my knee. "I'm sorry. I'm a dick."

"Speaking of which," I say, turning to Jax. "It's apparently something you like now. When did that happen?"

Jax looks the picture of unease, and for a second, I feel bad. He's been sucked into whatever the fuck we have going on, and he didn't agree to the rules we did when we set out on this trip.

"Carter," Hailee warns.

"Were you involved?" I ask. "Did you three have a good time fucking around while I was asleep?"

"Hailee was asleep, too," Linc says. "She was awake when we got out of the shower."

A large part of me wants to give into the pouting child inside me; to knock Linc's hand away and stare out of the window, ignoring them. I know it's pointless, though. All it would do is make everyone miserable, and things awkward. I don't want that. Besides, I'm not upset that it happened. I'm annoyed that we've spent all day together and no one thought to mention it.

Ever since Jax joined us, I've been keeping a wall between us. I know Linc's been shamelessly flirting with him, but that's not me. It's not something I've been allowed to do for a very long time. Plus, I know better than to waste time on a guy who's clearly straight. My lips press together. Not so clearly, it seems.

"So, what happened exactly?" I ask.

Jax sits up a little straighter, his jaw clenched, as he refuses to shrink under my scrutiny. "Linc gave me a blow job, and then I jerked him off."

My eyebrows lift, impressed that he would admit it so confidently. I cut my gaze to Linc, who's still looking at me with big puppy dog eyes.

"Oh, stop it," I say, taking his hand and squeezing it. "If anyone was going to turn the straight guy, it would be you."

Jax makes some sort of grunting noise, and although I want to press it, I let it drop.

"Highway to Hell," I say. "If you're going to do classic rock, do it right."

Jax's tense expression lifts, and I swear I see a flash of something like gratitude in his eyes as he smiles. "You can't go wrong with AC/DC."

My breath catches a little, and I mentally kick myself. *Fuck.* I find out he's not entirely straight, and within seconds, the carefully crafted wall I've built is crumbling. I've tried hard not to acknowledge the attraction I've felt since the second he got in the car, both out of loyalty to Linc and Hailee, and self-preservation. Now, I can't help but wonder, is it just Linc that he's into? Does he feel anything for me at all? No. There's no point starting down this road. It won't lead anywhere. I take a breath and try to piece the wall back together.

"What about 'Sweet Home Alabama'?" Hailee asks, and the car fills with groans. "What?"

"What's with the old guy rock, anyway?" I ask Jax. "Are you secretly in your fifties or something?"

"It's nothing to do with age. I appreciate good music."

"How old are you?" Hailee asks. "I just realized I don't know. Did we ever ask?"

"No, you didn't, princess," he says. "And I'm twenty-eight."

"Oh," Linc says, twisting around to look at him. "You're officially the daddy of the group."

"Gross," I say, reaching forward to shove him. "Just, no. And if we're doing that, I'm pretty sure that makes you the baby."

Jax looks between us. "Why? How old are you?"

"Calm down," Linc says, his white smile beaming. "I'm legal, if that's what you're worried about."

Jax barks a laugh. "No one was worried about that, man. You don't look seventeen."

"He's twenty-three," I say. "I'm sure he told us earlier, but I remember because I saw it on his Instagram profile."

At that thought, I unlock my phone and bring up the app. I followed him the day we found out that he was a model, and my eyebrows raise as he appears in my stories.

"Have you been posting on the trip?" I ask, clicking on the circle.

Jax leans over, and I angle the phone so we can both see. The first picture is one of Linc lying in bed looking sleepy, his dark hair spread out on the pillow. The second is in the mountains. He's standing on the deck with his shirt off, staring out at the view, his muscles on full display. I turn the phone around and show him.

"Who took that?" I ask.

"I propped my phone up and used the timer."

I look back at the picture. It looks damn professional. "It's a great photo."

Linc chuckles. "I've had a lot of practice."

His bruise, although faded to yellow, isn't visible at all, and I wonder whether he photoshopped it out. If he did, I can't tell.

"Shit," I say, clicking out of his stories to his grid, where he's posted the picture from the lodge. "It's got seventy thousand likes."

"Stop it," Hailee whines. "I want to see."

Linc reaches out and tugs on one of her curls. "You don't need to see. You've got the real thing right in front of you. The guy in that photo isn't real."

I glance at Jax to see what he makes of the cryptic comment, but he's frowning at Linc with what looks like as much concern as I'm feeling. The words Linc used back in Salt Lake City echo in my head. 'You stop being a person'. My gaze drops back to the profile still open on my phone. It's the first time I've looked at it since those girls asked for his photo, and it's strange. He's insanely beautiful, and the photos from his modeling shoots have my chest swelling with pride, and my cock hardening with lust. At the same time, I can see what he means. The gorgeous man in the pictures looks like Linc, but it's not him. None of these photos show the teasing sparkle in his eye, or the fierce protectiveness that burns inside him.

I unbuckle my seatbelt and slide forward, reaching for him. He turns, eyes wide, as I take his face in my hands and kiss him.

"Carter!" Hailee scolds. "Sit back and put your seatbelt on."

Pulling back, I look into his dark brown eyes. "I see you, Linc."

His eyes flutter shut, and I brush a kiss against his lips before letting him go. Giving Hailee a kiss on the cheek, I settle back in my seat and grab my seatbelt. Once it's fastened, I look over at Jax and grin. "You want a kiss too?"

"Fuck off."

He rolls his eyes, and I laugh. As Linc starts working his way through a blog on best road trip songs, I sink back against the seat and exhale. For the first time in a very long time, everything feels . . . right.

34

"Stop it!"

I cover my mouth to hide the laughter bubbling beneath the surface. Hailee shoves Jax, her hands smacking his back, as he literally doubles over with laughter. I was worried things would be weird after outing our morning activities to Carter, but if anything, he and Jax have been getting on better than ever. It's like whatever protective, alpha bullshit they had between them has evaporated.

"This is the middle of fucking nowhere," Jax gasps out between barks of laughter.

"It doesn't matter," Hailee says, whacking at him again, and forcing him back against the car. "We only came here to see the monument, then we can leave."

"Let's get to it, then," Carter says, tugging Hailee away from Jax. "Before it gets dark and we can't see the damn thing."

It's only five o'clock in the afternoon, with a couple of hours until sunset, but his words do the trick and Hailee sticks her tongue out at Jax before heading toward the payment booth.

"It's only five dollars per person," I say, fishing a twenty out of my wallet and handing it to Carter.

He looks at the money in my outstretched hand and raises his eyebrows. "Exactly. I'll pay."

It takes all my self-control not to roll my eyes. "I know you can pay, but I've already got it out, and it's literally right there."

His jaw tightens, but he takes it and hands it to the guy behind the counter. It's quiet, with only a handful of cars in the parking lot. No tour buses or anything. I suppose late afternoon toward the end of summer will do that to a random tourist attraction in the middle of nowhere.

The monument does exactly what it says on the tin. Benches surround paving stones lined with metal markers showing where the corners of Arizona, New Mexico, Colorado, and Utah meet. A small group of what sound like Italian tourists are taking selfies, so we loiter by the benches to wait.

"Which state are you going to stand in?" I ask Hailee.

She frowns. "Utah, I think."

"Really liked Salt Lake City, then?"

"I did." She looks up at me and grins. "I think we all did."

My skin heats a little, and I knock her shoulder with my arm. Damn right I enjoyed it. My pulse kicks up at the thought of Carter claiming me at that lodge. Fuck, if it wasn't incredible. I glance over at where he's talking to Jax. He's wearing jeans, with rips at the knees that look like they've been caused from genuine wear and tear rather than fashion, and an olive-green t-shirt, that hugs across his chest just enough to show off his build. I lick my lips, picturing my hand gripped in that messy brown hair, his bright blue eyes lit with desire as he pounds into me. *Fuck.* I look away, trying to stop my dick from getting too excited. Unfortunately, my gaze lands on Jax.

He's watching the tourists as they goof around, his arms folded across his chest. It should look menacing, but the warmth on his face as he laughs at something Carter says tells a different story. I smile as he nudges Carter with his elbow and grins. Seeing them like this makes my heart happy. There have been glimpses of it over the last couple of days, but this feels different. My gaze dips from his face, taking in his perfectly crafted form. I think he only has one pair of jeans, and every shirt I've seen him wear has been either black or white. Today's is white. Don't get me wrong, it's a strong look on him. His bag isn't much bigger than Hailee's backpack, though, and I realize for the first time that it must contain his entire life.

The thought settles in my stomach like a stone. He'd hate that I was thinking like this. He's so independent and proud. It doesn't stop me from worrying, though. He must sense my attention on him because he turns and looks at me, raising an eyebrow. I wink, and he shakes his head, turning back to Carter.

Jax is another reason Salt Lake City will be forever burned into my memory. When I told him I'd leave the bathroom door open, I hadn't in a million years thought he'd actually join me. Maybe take a sneak peek . . . but to come in? A full body shiver runs through me as I recall Jax leaning back against the shower wall, his inked skin glistening, mouth parted, and eyes half closed, as he came down my throat. Even though I'll happily relive that moment a million times before the end of the year, I'm not sure if it's my favorite from our brief encounter. I felt his smile as he teased my neck and shoulders with his mouth. And that kiss . . . I swallow hard. I really want to kiss him again. After the shower, I was worried he'd freak out, but he's been really chilled about it. I'd be a liar if I said I haven't been enjoying the little squeezes and touches he's bestowed on me throughout the day, treasuring each one like a fucking gift. I'd bet my last dollar that he's ridiculously dominant in the sack, and my heart aches a little at the fact that I'll probably never find out. This morning was almost certainly a one-time thing. Which sucks.

Hailee threads her fingers through mine and squeezes, pulling me back to the present. I look down at her and she leans into me, her head laying against my chest. There's something melancholy about the gesture, and it has me wrapping my arms around her, resting my chin on her hair. It's so hard not to think about the inevitable: that I'm going to have to say goodbye to these incredible people. In just a couple of days, I'm going to have to walk away.

I've thought about it a lot. Sure, we could exchange numbers, even meet up. But it wouldn't be the same. It wouldn't be all of us. The days of all four of us being in the same place are numbered. I press a kiss to Hailee's head. The symbolism of the monument seems more poignant than ever.

"Right!" Jax claps his hands together. "Let's do this, people."

The Italians are moving back toward the car park, so we step forward onto the triangular slabs. Hailee claims Utah, Carter takes Colorado, and Jax takes Arizona, leaving me with New Mexico.

"There," Jax says, his lips twitching as he looks at Hailee. "Are you happy?"

"Yes," she says, wrinkling her nose at him.

She reaches out and takes Jax's hand in her right and Carter's in her left. Immediately, Jax and Carter reach for mine, and we stand there, looking at each other as the late afternoon sun paints the desert a mellow golden color. It's so damn bittersweet. I squeeze the hands holding mine, and they squeeze back.

"Well, this was worth every cent," Jax says with a sigh.

I tug his arm as Carter laughs. "You're such a dick."

"What now?" he asks.

I stare at the metal circle in the middle of the monument, an idea forming. "Everyone, lie down in your state with your head in the middle."

Carter and Jax shoot me curious looks, but Hailee seems to have caught on to my plan and is first in position. Once we're all on the ground, our heads in the center of the monument, I pull my phone from my pocket and hold it above us.

"You'd better not drop that fucking thing on my face," Jax grumbles.

"Shut up and say cheese."

We haven't taken any photos together yet, and the weight in my gut feels like a ton as I take what might be the first and last.

Even though a few people are chatting nearby, waiting their turn, none of us move. Fingers find mine again, and I close my eyes, trying to savor every second of this moment.

"I'm so glad I met you all," Hailee says quietly. "Thank you."

A lump forms in my throat, and I choke it down, not trusting myself to say anything. The fingers laced with mine squeeze a little tighter.

"Come on," Carter says with a sigh. "Let's go get some food and a room for the night."

It's a simple statement, but it holds a lot more weight than it should. A room. Singular. Jax says nothing to correct him, and I grab onto the thrill that runs through my chest with both hands.

As we get to our feet and dust off, heading back to the car in silence, I pull up the photo on my phone and smile. It's perfect. Hailee's curls spill out around her head, her big brown eyes crinkled as she grins at the camera. On her left, Jax is smirking, amusement flickering in his sapphire and navy eyes. On her right, Carter is smiling, looking more relaxed than I've seen him in a while. It suits him. I don't even bother looking at myself. This photo isn't going on Instagram. It's mine and mine alone. Well, sort of. I forward it to Jax and Carter, smiling when their phones buzz, and they pull them out at the same time, giving me very similar smirks. I grin, scrolling for Hailee's number, but it's not there.

"Hailee," I mutter. "I don't have your number. Can I have it so I can send you the photo?"

"Sure," she says, pulling it from her pocket.

As she does, it vibrates in her hand and her face freezes. Carter tenses beside me, and I take a step closer.

"Everything okay?" I ask.

She nods. "Yeah. Fine."

"You don't look fine," Jax says, stepping to her side. "Is this to do with the message you got this morning?"

Her head snaps up. "What?"

"The message you got this morning and had to deal with on the balcony," he presses. "If you're in trouble—"

"I'm not," she says. "It's fine."

"It's him, isn't it?" Carter seethes.

The hatred in his voice surprises me, and I turn to find him glaring, not at Hailee but at the phone in her hands.

"It's Brent."

He almost spits the name, and after a moment, her shoulders sag as she nods her head.

"I thought you blocked him," I say, stepping to her side.

"He's using a different number," she explains. Her hands are trembling. "He wants me to call him."

"Don't," Jax says without hesitation.

I raise my eyebrows, wondering how much Hailee's told him about her situation. "What does he think calling him will do? Is he trying to get you back?"

She shakes her head, and I hold out my hand. Hailee's gaze flits between my outstretched fingers and the phone, then biting her lip, she hands it over.

There are only four texts from the unknown number, but the threat is as clear as day. Texting in all caps like a psychopath.

"He's going to 'come for you'?" A cold laugh of disbelief bursts from my lips as Jax takes the phone from my hand. "How would he find you?"

"He's a cop," she says, her eyes fixed on the ground. "I'm sure he has ways if he really wants to."

"What does he mean about you being a thief?" Jax asks, scowling at the phone.

Hailee shifts uncomfortably and I open my mouth to offer her a way out of explaining, but she shakes her head.

"I had some money saved," she says. "I didn't think he knew about it, but it's the only thing I can think of. It's my money, though, I swear."

I pull her into my arms; the fact that she's trembling breaks my fucking heart. "It's going to be okay. We know you're not a thief. He's just an asshole."

Jax switches off the phone and slips it into her pocket. "Next town we get to, you should get a new phone."

"Jax is right," I say, my hands stroking her back. "Ignore him like you have been doing. You're safe with us."

Jax traces her cheek with the backs of his fingers. "We won't let anything happen to you."

She holds me tighter and as I turn my head; I find Carter staring into space, looking as though he's seen a ghost. His earlier anger has dissipated, and he looks pale. "Carter? What's wrong?"

Carter swallows, his glazed expression clearing. "Nothing. Just pissed at Brent."

My eyes narrow, but I let it drop as he steps to us, completing the wall of strength we've built around Hailee.

"Linc and Jax are right. We've got you," he says.

"Until Vegas."

Hailee says the words so quietly, I'm not sure if she meant us to hear. I glance at Jax and Carter, and their furrowed brows tell me they did. The stone is back, weighting my heart into my stomach, and it takes all my strength to paste a smile on my face.

"Come on," I say. "Let's go and find some food."

"There's a town forty minutes away." Carter squints at his phone. "Cortez."

Jax takes Hailee's hand as he heads toward the car. "Sounds good to me."

"He even sounds like an asshole in his texts," I say, as Carter falls into step beside me. "I can't believe he's threatening her."

Carter shoves his hands in his pockets, his voice barely more than a whisper. "What if he follows through? What if he finds her?"

"He's not going to find her. I'll make sure of it."

He raises eyebrows. "*You* will?"

I smile, knocking Carter with my shoulder. "*We* will."

He smiles back, but it doesn't reach his eyes. I wonder whether Hailee's whispered words are haunting him, too. We can't protect her forever.

The air is bittersweet in my lungs as we meander back to the car, and I reach out and take Carter's hand in mine. I open my mouth to ask what food he's in the mood for when Hailee's pained gasp sounds out across the parking lot, setting my heart racing.

"What is it?" I ask, jogging to her side. "Are you okay?"

She points, her face crumpling, and I follow the gesture.

"Some fucker's slashed the tire," Jax says from where he's crouched by the wheel.

"Are you sure?" I ask.

Jax raises his eyebrows, looking pointedly at the clearly deflated tire.

"No, I mean, could it just be a flat? How do you know someone did it on purpose?"

"He's a mechanic," Hailee says, her voice filled with such disappointment, it pains me. "He'd know."

She's right. I turn and look around the parking lot, as if I might be able to find who'd do something like this. We were in there for all of forty minutes.

"Is there a spare?" Jax asks.

Hailee nods and walks around to open the trunk. I start toward them, to help empty out the bags, but stop when I realize Carter hasn't moved. His phone is in his hand, his fingers gripping it so tight, his knuckles are white.

"Hey," I say, stepping in front of him. "You okay?"

He looks a little pale as he stares through me at the slashed tire.

"Carter?" I try again.

His jaw clenches. "What if it's him?"

It takes me a second to realize what he means. "What?

Brent? How would he know where we are? He's just bluffing with Hailee. Everything's okay. It's probably just bored kids."

He nods, but as I take in the hardened look in his eyes, I know my words have had no effect. I press a kiss to his cheek and turn away to find that Jax is already halfway to getting the tire off.

I push my concern to the back of my mind. This is what Carter does, he worries. I told him everything was okay, and I meant it. Swallowing a sigh of frustration, I step forward to see if Jax needs help.

35

We eat somewhere called the Lazy Salamander. As soon as the first round of cocktails was ordered, any lingering annoyance about the slashed tire evaporated. Good food and laughter round off a pretty great day, and by the time we check into the hotel, we're all a little buzzed. Hailee seems more relaxed than I've seen her, and I wonder how much keeping those texts to herself was weighing her down. The corridor echoes with laughter, Hailee trying and failing to shush us as we make our way to the room.

"What?" I ask in a stage whisper.

She gestures to the closed doors around us, some with 'do not disturb' signs hanging on them. "People are trying to sleep."

"Sleep?" Carter says, bringing up his wrist and squinting at his watch. "It's only nine thirty."

Hailee shushes him again, but she's smiling.

Linc swipes the key card and opens the door, stepping aside to let us in. It's a suite again, and we've barely dumped our bags before Carter is between the beds, hauling a bedside table out of the way. I know what he's planning to do, so I move over to the twin and start pushing it together with the double.

"The people below are really going to love us," Hailee groans.

Linc chuckles, coming over to help me push, and I try not to think too much about what this means. Last night, we all shared a bed, and just fell asleep. But last night was before I put my cock in Linc's mouth. The thought of any sort of repeat has my dick waking up. What the fuck is up with that? Do I like guys now? *What the actual*... I'm just not going to think about it. Yeah, right. I've been thinking about it all day.

Frowning, I crouch by my bag, and pull out what's left of the bottle of bourbon we shared in the mountains. There's just over a third left. By the time I stand, Linc has dug out the plastic cups he picked up at a gas station earlier today, and Carter is already sitting on the bed, connecting his phone to Linc's Bluetooth speaker. I head over to the desk that lines one end of the room, and unscrew the cap, pouring out generous measures. When I turn to hand Hailee her cup, I find her by the door, her bag on her shoulder, and a strange expression on her face.

"Princess?"

She blinks, her attention focusing on me.

"Are you okay?" I ask, taking a tentative step toward her.

"Of course I am," she says, half laughing. "Why wouldn't I be?"

"Because you're still standing by the door with your bag on your shoulder."

She looks at her bag as though she forgot it was there. "Sorry, I just got a bit carried away watching you all." She drops the bag to the floor and kicks off her shoes.

Linc grins. "Oh?"

"Not like that." She laughs. "It just . . . it all looked so natural. Like you've been sharing hotel rooms for years."

Carter snorts from where he's sitting on the bed, and she hops up next to him. He wraps his arm around her, and presses a kiss to her temple.

"It does feel natural, though," Linc says, toeing off his sneakers and climbing up on Carter's other side. "I feel like I've known you all forever."

I study them for a second. There's room on Linc's other side, but I don't take it. Instead, I stretch out along the foot of the bed, propping myself up on my elbow. "I've got to admit," I say. "When you guys picked me up on the interstate, this is not where I imagined things going."

"Are you disappointed we're not axe murderers?" Carter asks.

I reach out and flick his foot. "You might still be. Lulling me into a false sense of security, then slitting my throat while I sleep."

"Oh, well, that's a nice image," Hailee says, screwing up her nose. "Thanks for that."

Something catches my eye, and I cough around my mouthful of bourbon. "What the fuck is that?"

Linc and Hailee frown, but Carter knows exactly what I'm talking about, his face paling.

"What?" Hailee asks.

I reach out to grab Carter's foot, but he pulls it away, tucking it under him.

"Nothing," he says.

"Oh, it's not nothing," I say, feeling positively fucking gleeful as I watch him squirm. "Show everyone your tattoo, Carter."

"What?" Linc gasps. "Where is it?"

I laugh. "On his fucking ankle."

Carter groans, barely putting up a fight as Hailee and Linc tug his foot free, peering at his ankle. It's a small stick man, about an inch tall. He tries to glare at me as Hailee and Linc poke at it, but his mouth twitches, and I grin back in response.

"No wonder I never saw it," Linc says, shaking his head as he settles back against the pillows.

Carter tugs his leg back underneath him. "Yeah, well. I was eighteen, and it was a dare."

"Sorry, man," I say, still grinning. "Someone was bound to spot it sooner or later."

"Later would have been preferable," he grumbles.

I shrug. "I wouldn't have been around later."

"Are you not sticking around, then?" Carter asks bluntly.

Hailee chokes on her mouthful of bourbon. "Carter!"

I'm not an idiot. I've been gatecrashing their threesome for a couple of days now, and after what happened between me and Linc yesterday, I knew this was coming. It was fucking awkward in the car when Hailee outed us. It wasn't that I was embarrassed or anything. I just didn't want Carter to be annoyed. To be fair, he genuinely only seemed to be annoyed that we hadn't told him straight away.

The whole thing fucks with my head. I'm not a jealous person, but the fact that Carter is fine with the idea of me getting physical with both Linc and Hailee, when he clearly cares a whole lot about them, is bizarre. If this thing they have going on was purely sexual, it would make sense. But it's clearly more than that. Hell, I already care more about these fuckers than people I've known for years.

"Do you want me to stick around?" I ask.

Carter stares at me as he takes a sip of his drink. I swear Hailee and Linc are holding their breath. Even though my heart kicks up a nervous pace in my chest, I know what his answer will be. Ever since he found out what happened between me and Linc, he's relaxed around me. It's like he finally let his guard down, and I've found myself doing the same.

"Yes," he says, his ice-blue stare fixed on me. "I want you to stick around."

"I mean, it depends on where you're headed next," I say, swirling the amber liquid in my cup. "If it's somewhere shit, you can count me out."

Carter's mouth twitches.

"Grand Canyon is the next stop," Hailee says, her eyes flitting between us. "Last stop before Vegas."

"I haven't seen the Grand Canyon," I say, peering at my drink as I contemplate. "Wouldn't mind seeing it."

"Are you sure?" Carter deadpans. "It's in the middle of nowhere, and there's not much around. I mean, it's literally a giant hole in the ground."

The playfulness dancing in his piercing blue eyes causes a grin to spread across my lips. "Sounds like you're trying to talk me out of coming."

"Not at all," Carter says without hesitation, all teasing vanishing from his voice.

The bourbon is fire in my stomach. I don't remember it feeling this strong in the mountains. Maybe it's not the bourbon at all. I know where this conversation is going. The room is thick with it. When I came with them to the hotel—when I helped push the fucking beds together—I knew. Even though my head still can't quite wrap itself around what's going on with these three people, I came here knowing, wanting, what it means. I hold Carter's stare, my heart pounding so loud, I'm surprised they can't hear it.

"So, you're coming to the Grand Canyon?" Linc asks, pulling my gaze to him.

I take another sip of the amber liquid, the burn lighting up every inch of me. "If you'll have me."

We're skirting around the issue, but I don't know how to bring it up. Do I just come out and fucking say it? All day, I've been in my head, trying to sort out how I'm feeling. I'm not sure how successful I've been, but I know a few things for sure. I really like hanging out with all three of them. I instantly clicked with Linc and Hailee, but today things fell into place with Carter.

I want Hailee. If it came down to it, I'd sell my left nut to hear her moan my name as she clenches around my dick one more time.

Linc is still watching me, as though he doesn't quite know what's going on. *Fuck*. Neither do I. I've wrestled with the fact all day, but the truth is, I want Linc, too. What happened in the shower was hot as hell, and my curiosity is a throbbing beat in my blood.

My attention flicks to Carter, whose intense fucking stare is still focused on me. I realized today; I've been misinterpreting that stare this whole time. It doesn't mean he's pissed off at all. In fact, I suspect it means quite the fucking opposite. He's a good-looking guy. Not in the same way as Linc. But then, who is? I think that's what makes me hesitate. Linc is very much a man, I mean, the guy is packing. But he's so fucking pretty. With those pouty lips, long hair, and not a hair on his body. Carter, on the other hand, is different. He's got hair on his chest, for one. He's also got a beard. It's only a little more than stubble, but it's there.

What would that be like? Kissing someone, and feeling stubble against my skin? What would it be like to be up close, with those intense blue eyes fixed on me? The thought sends a small tremor through me, and I frown as I take another sip of my drink. That damn curiosity again. I should just get my stuff and go. I tell my feet as much, but they don't move. I've never run from anything in my life. Especially not something I want.

"What are you saying, Jax?" Carter asks.

I swallow. "I'm saying, I want to come with you to the Grand Canyon."

"Is that it?" Linc asks, staring at his drink.

My heart kicks up a gear. "What else is there?"

Fuck. The room is hot. Most of my hookups since high school have been simple. Go to a bar. Have a drink. Talk to a girl. Have sex with girl. There have been no contracts or rules. There have also been no guys. I take a gulp of liquor, savoring the burn as it tracks down my throat. This isn't a hookup. This is . . . I don't know what this is.

"I know you feel it," Hailee says quietly. "When we met you, it felt just like when I met Carter, and when we met Linc. You clicked. It feels right, Jax. Complete."

I freeze. She's put it right out there. It's the fucking truth, too. I'm not the life and soul of the party, and it takes a long time for me to relax around people. It hasn't been like that with Hailee, Linc and Carter, though. I roll off the bed and walk over to the bottle of bourbon to top off my drink, if only to get a minute to get myself together.

"You have to say it, Jax," Linc says. "What do you want?"

I can't bring myself to say the words. That I want them. My skin burns, and I turn, staring out of the window through a crack in the curtains. Part of me screams to take the easy way out, and just leave. That way, I don't have to make this choice. But they've sucked me into this situation, and the naked fucking truth is, I'm not ready to give it up. I haven't laughed or smiled so much in my whole damn life. It makes me wonder if this is what most people's lives are like.

Linc swings his long legs off the bed and walks over to

me. I watch him, my cup in my hand, and my expression still as neutral as I can manage. He comes to a stop right in front of me, close enough that I can smell his aftershave mixed with sweat. I kind of like it. My grip tightens on my cup, making a cracking sound.

"This is one hundred percent your call," he says, his voice soft, as though he's trying not to spook me. "But what I know is, I like having you around. What Hailee said is completely true. It feels right with you here. Sure, I'd really, *really,* like to repeat what happened this morning, but if things have to go back to just being friends, then I'll take it."

He reaches out and touches the tips of his fingers just below my collarbone. I look up at him, remembering how it felt to have him pressed against me in the shower, his hands on my skin. Linc traces his fingers, barely touching over my chest, before dropping his hand back to his side. "If you wanted something more, though, we could discuss what you'd be comfortable with."

I put my drink down and suck in a breath. "I do."

"Do what?"

"Want more."

Linc's eyes close as he inhales, and my heart skips at seeing just how much he wanted me to say those words. I look over at the bed and Hailee's grin pulls my own mouth into a smile. Beside her, Carter looks seven shades of relieved, but the smile he gives me looks unsure.

"Anyone else feeling awkward as fuck?" I ask.

Nervous laughter fills the room, and Linc grabs the bottle of bourbon from beside me, topping off everyone's drinks.

"So," he says, returning to my side. "As you know, our rule is friends first. Pairing off is fine, but be honest about it. If things aren't working, say so."

I nod. "You realize what a weird ass conversation this is, right?"

"Oh, for sure," Carter says, smirking. "Just wait until you have to explain it to someone you pick up at the side of the road."

Chuckling, I shake my head. "Fine."

Linc leans against the desk beside me. Close, but also not close enough. "As for what you'd be comfortable with. No one is going to force you to do anything you don't want to do. That's not what this is. Especially when you're still figuring things out."

His words have me opening my mouth to tell him there's nothing to figure out, but I press my lips together. I am figuring things out. Fuck. I'm the definition of confused. Is it possible to want something and be terrified of it at the same time?

I look between the three of them and know nothing has ever felt so right. How can I fear something that might just be everything I've been looking for my entire life?

36

My eyes widen, my heart leaping in my chest. I honestly thought he was going to leave, and I can't process the emotions I'm feeling fast enough. I'm so relieved I could cry, but I'm also nervous and excited about what his words mean. The room now feels a lot smaller, the air a lot thicker.

"What I'm comfortable with," Jax says slowly, his eyes fixed on his drink. "Kissing and touching are fine, but I don't think I'm ready for anybody's dick in my mouth. I also don't want anything near my ass."

I swallow, my heart slamming against my ribcage. This is happening.

"What about putting your dick in someone else's ass?" Linc downs his drink and sets it on the desk.

Jax turns to face him, his eyes narrowed. "Are you saying you want my dick inside you?"

Linc's eyes half close, and he sucks in a shaky breath that has heat building between my thighs. "Fuck, yes."

"Fuck," Carter breathes beside me.

"Let's stick a pin in that idea, okay?" Jax chuckles and places his drink down beside Linc's empty cup. "Princess?"

His authoritative tone has my body lighting up. "Yes?"

"I think you should call the shots."

I frown. "What do you mean?"

Jax smiles slowly, and it's so damn sexy, my heart kicks up another notch. At this rate, I'm going to have a heart attack before we even get our clothes off.

"I mean," he says. "You tell us what to do. This is your trip, right?"

Linc grins. "I like this idea. A lot. What do you want us to do, Hailee? We're yours to command."

I narrow my eyes at him before looking back at Jax. He's watching me in that predatory way that tells me, even though he's putting me in control, I'm not actually in control at all. I know why he's doing this. He knows it will push my boundaries, but he also knows how much I like seeing the guys fool around. I suspect it's also a little bit to do with taking the pressure off him. Even though he's said he's in, I know he's nervous. It's a dangerous game he's playing. I drink in the challenge in his eyes and make my decision.

"Fine," I say, taking a sip of my drink. "Linc and Jax, take each other's shirts off."

With that simple sentence, tame as it might be, the atmosphere shifts. I've pressed play. Linc's grin disappears as he turns to Jax and grips the bottom of his t-shirt. Jax holds his gaze as he lifts his arms, letting him pull it up and off, then smirks as he returns the favor. They both turn and look at me expectantly.

I'm not sure what the boundaries are. Jax said he was okay with kissing, and I know he's kissed Linc before, but I don't want to make anyone uncomfortable. My indecision must be written all over my face, because Jax gives me a reassuring smile.

"If you ask me to do something I don't want to do," he

says. "I'll give you a thumbs down, okay?" He holds his hand up, thumb down, in demonstration.

"Okay," I say, trying to calm my nerves.

"Don't overthink it," Linc says softly. "Tell us what you want."

I down the rest of my drink, wincing at the burning sensation. Carter takes the empty cup and places it on the bedside table beside his own. "I want you two to kiss." I turn to Carter. "And I want you to get undressed."

His blue eyes flash at the command, and he reaches back and grabs the back of his shirt, pulling it off and dropping it on the floor. I smile and turn back to Jax and Linc, my breath catching in my throat as I find them kissing already. It's not a gentle kiss, but one of gripping hands and eager tongues that has me pressing my thighs together, a moan gathering in my throat. There's something aesthetically pleasing about the contrast of Jax's tanned, ink-covered skin, intertwined with Linc's smooth, deeper brown skin. I tear my eyes away to glance at Carter, and find him lying naked beside me, his hand wrapped around his cock as he watches Jax and Linc. *Fuck.*

I must say it out loud, because Carter's gaze snaps to me, pure blue flame. He sinks a hand into my hair and pulls me to him, capturing my mouth with his. I let my hands move over his chest and shoulders as he strokes my tongue with his, getting lost in his warmth.

"You're wearing too many clothes," he murmurs against my lips.

"Take them off, then." I sit forward onto my knees, allowing him to pull my top off over my head. The guys are still kissing, but Linc's fingers are teasing the waistband of Jax's jeans. "Right," I announce. "I want everyone naked and on this bed in the next thirty seconds."

Carter rises onto his knees, facing me, and kisses me again as he reaches around and unhooks my bra. I shiver as he slides it off, desperate for his hands on me. The bed dips, and two hands slip around my waist from behind, moving up to cup my breasts. I moan against Carter's tongue as two thumbs brush against my nipples. I can't tell if it's Linc or Jax, which only excites me more. Fingers unfasten the buttons on my shorts, and I realize, with a jolt, that there are at least five hands on me. Carter's mouth leaves mine and I open my eyes. My breath catches in my throat as he takes one of my nipples into his mouth.

Linc is behind me, and as he presses kisses to my shoulder, one hand teases my breast while the other sinks into Carter's hair. My skin is on fire, and I look to my left to find Jax easing down my shorts and panties. Hands push gently at me until I'm lying down against the pillows, and Jax tugs the rest of my clothes free.

"What's next, princess?" Jax asks, running his fingers down the inside of my thighs.

Linc and Carter each take a nipple in their mouths, and I push my head back into the pillows with a gasp. I can't form a thought. I want everything. I close my eyes and take a deep breath, my hands grasping Linc and Carter's hair, as their tongues work me.

"I can't." I writhe as Jax teases me with barely there touches. "Please don't make me—"

My words are stolen by a gasp as Jax runs his tongue through my center. I moan, my back arching, and I tug Linc from my breast. He gives me a questioning look, but I pull him to my mouth and kiss him.

Breathing hard, as Jax swirls his tongue over my clit, I whisper against his lips. "I want you in my mouth."

Linc's eyes close, and he groans, a deep rumble from his

chest. He rises to his knees, a hand around his hard length, as he guides it to my waiting mouth. The second I close my lips around the tip, Jax eases two fingers inside me, and I whimper. Linc moans at the vibration, and I take him deeper, stroking him with my hand, as I work him, sucking and teasing, with my tongue.

Lying at my side, Carter nips at my throat, his fingers stroking my body as his gaze flits between my mouth and my thighs. Jax's fingers pulse in time with his tongue, flicking and sucking on my clit, and I pull off Linc, crying out, as he tips me over the edge. Carter moves, capturing my whimpers with his mouth, as rolls of pleasure shudder through me.

Jax rises from between my legs, his lips glistening, and as Linc trails kisses down my jaw to my neck, Carter moves to his knees. He traces a finger along Jax's lips, bringing it to his own, and tasting me. At my side, Linc pauses, his breath on my ear, and I know he's watching, too. Carter reaches out again, but this time Jax grabs hold of his wrist, stopping him. I can barely breathe as they watch each other, the silent conversation between them, somehow deafening. Then, Jax grips Carter's neck with his other hand, and pulls, closing the gap between them.

Linc groans, and I gasp, watching as their tongues battle for dominance. After a moment, Carter places a hand on Jax's stomach. Waiting. Testing. When Jax doesn't stop him, he begins to slide it down until his fingers close around his cock. My breathing is nothing more than shallow pants as I watch, my own hand trailing down Linc's body, and gripping his hard length in my fist.

He drops his head against my shoulder with a sigh, then twists, reaching for something behind him. I tear my eyes away from Carter and Jax, to admire the way Linc's body stretches, the muscles defined, as he rummages in a bag on the floor. When he shifts back, he brings the bottle of lube and a handful of condoms with him. Taking my hand from around him, Linc squirts a little lube onto my palm. When I return my grip, he moves his hips, slowly fucking my fist, as he kisses me.

The bed dips with movement, and I open my eyes to find that Carter and Jax have broken apart. Carter settles behind Linc, and Jax lies down beside me, pressing a kiss to my jaw. Linc pulls away, but Jax grips his chin, giving him a brief but fierce kiss, before turning to me.

"Can I fuck you, princess?" he murmurs against my ear. "I want inside you so bad."

I've forgotten how to speak. The sheer amount of heated flesh, sensual mouths and teasing fingers has my head spinning—every inch of my body alight with pleasure.

Jax pinches my nipple, and I gasp. "Yes."

As Jax plucks a condom from the bed, Linc's thrusting into my fist increases, and I flex my fingers around him.

"Carter," Linc gasps. "Fuck."

I turn to him, but his eyes are closed, dark lashes against his cheek, as his head presses into the pillow. Carter's wintery eyes watch me hungrily over his shoulder, his arm moving in time with Linc's thrusts. My eyes track the movement causing Carter's bicep to flex, and I realize his fingers are inside Linc. My breath catches.

"Don't let go," Carter says to me, his eyes blazing.

All I can do is stare, my mouth dry, as the throbbing builds between my legs.

Linc groans, burying his face in my neck. "Please," he pants. "I need you, Carter."

Teeth close around my nipple, and I turn to find Jax

watching me. "I thought that might get your attention," he says, flicking out his tongue across the hard peak.

I grip his hair with my spare hand, pulling him up to my mouth. "I thought you were going to fuck me."

Jax chuckles. "There's my dirty little princess."

Before I can respond, he settles himself between my legs and pushes inside me. A cry of pleasure tears from my lips as he fills and stretches me, and I arch into the movement. When his lips find mine, he kisses me deep and slow, his thrusts languid and teasing.

At my side, Linc rolls onto his back, and I open my eyes in time to find Carter easing into him, his head dropping back with an ecstasy-laden sigh.

"Fuck, fuck, fuck," Linc chants, his hands clutching his hair as I tighten my grip around him. "That feels so fucking good."

Jax bites my neck gently, and I cup his face, bringing his mouth back to mine. My heart is pounding like I've run a marathon, and my brain is a mess of sparks and fireworks. It's sensory overload. Jax's broad tattooed shoulders flexing as he thrusts into me. Linc's slick, hard length in my hand. Carter's heated gaze flicking between Jax and me, and Linc beneath him. The sight of Carter's cock sliding in and out of Linc. A low moan builds in my chest.

"Fuck," Linc gasps. "I'm close."

Jax reaches down and hooks an arm around my leg, his eyes like blue fire, and his jaw clenched. He pounds into me, pushing deeper, and my answering gasp melts into breathy pants. He and Carter match each other's pace, steadily increasing, harder and deeper as the sound of sweat-slicked skin on skin, and moans of pleasure fill the room. My pants turn to whimpers as my core tightens, and the edges of my vision darken.

"Yes," I gasp, fireworks erupting in my brain, as my body pulses around Jax. "Oh my god, yes."

Jax's thrusts quicken, then he stills with a groan. His breathing is labored as he rests his forehead against mine, and I tilt my head to press a kiss to his lips.

Beside us, Linc cries out, his cock pulsing in my hand as cum shoots out onto his stomach and chest. Seconds later, Carter swears repeatedly under his breath, falling forward onto his forearms.

For a moment, the only sound is of ragged breath. Then Carter leans down and kisses Linc, who still has one arm slung over his eyes as he catches his breath. He grins at me, reaching out and running a hand up Jax's spine. Jax pushes back onto his knees and Carter tugs him forward, pressing a kiss to his lips. It's a lot gentler this time, and only brief, before Carter bends down and kisses me.

I feel like I should say something, but I don't think I could if I wanted to. Carter and Jax both climb off the bed to clean up, and seconds later, Jax throws a towel through from the bathroom. I take it gratefully and clean my hand and Linc's stomach.

"Thank you," he says, lifting his arm from his eyes. "I would have done that."

"It's fine." I kiss his cheek, and he turns toward me, catching my mouth with his lips.

It's a soft, lazy kiss, and I roll toward him as he drags his fingers up my side, stroking. I'm so lost in his touch, and the gentle caress of his tongue, that I pull back in surprise when the bed shifts.

"You two going for round two already?" Carter teases, lying down behind me and wrapping his arms around my middle.

I swat at him, but he pulls me tighter, pressing a kiss to

my neck. Jax climbs onto the bed behind Linc, propping himself up on an elbow, and I reach out and touch his cheek. He smiles and presses a kiss to my fingers. My heart is on the verge of bursting in my chest.

"Any regrets?" Carter asks, his thumb caressing my ribs with slow strokes.

"No." Jax shakes his head, his face still flushed. "That was . . . I'm not sure there are words."

"I thought you were going to put your dick in my ass," Linc says, rolling to look up at him. "Don't threaten me with a good time if you're not going to follow through."

A snort of laughter escapes me, and Jax raises his eyebrows as he looks down at Linc. His lips part as though he's going to give some sarcastic comeback, but then he dips his head and presses a kiss to Linc's mouth. Linc reaches up, gripping the back of Jax's head as he deepens the kiss, but only for a minute.

"I'm pretty sure I said we were putting a pin in it," Jax says, pulling back and draping an arm over Linc's chest. "Maybe next time."

Linc groans and closes his eyes, rolling forward to rest his head against mine. "How is it possible for something to feel this good?"

"Right?" Carter sighs, his breath warm against my skin.

Closing my eyes, I try to savor everything about this moment. Carter's body tight against my back, Linc's rhythmic stroking, his head against mine. Jax's sated smile as he stares down at me. It's not just the afterglow of sex, though. I feel lighter than before.

I should have told the guys about the texts sooner. Keeping the worry and fear bottled up inside has been a burden I didn't need to carry alone. Even though I know the problem is far from being solved, and Brent's threats are very real, I feel better now that they know. Their anger and disgust have helped too. I was starting to wonder whether I was overreacting. Of course, I haven't told them about Sal. Guilt turns my stomach, and I hate that it sours the moment, even if the guys don't know.

"Princess?"

I open my eyes and find Jax watching me.

"You're frowning. What's wrong?"

My teeth tug at my bottom lip as I consider whether I should tell them. If they knew I'd hung my poor old manager out to dry—that I was a coward—would they still be so supportive?

Linc lifts a hand and strokes his thumb over my bottom lip, releasing it from my teeth. "Tell us."

I exhale and look up at the ceiling. "The texts. There's something I didn't tell you."

Carter's grip tightens around me. "What is it?"

"My old manager, Sal, messaged me. Brent's been threatening him and his business. He was begging me to get in touch before Brent did something." I take a breath and close my eyes. "I ignored the texts. I blocked him, like a fucking coward."

"Just when I think I can't hate that guy any more than I do," Jax grunts. "You're not a coward, princess."

"I am." I open my eyes and look at him. "I didn't think that by running away I'd affect anyone else. But I did. That shop is everything Sal has." I shake my head. "Maybe I should just call him."

"What?" Linc says, turning my face to him. "Brent? No."

"But—"

"This is not on you," he says, his eyes fierce. "Your boss shouldn't have been paying you in cash in the first place. If

Brent decides to turn him in out of spite because his girlfriend left him, it's his own fault."

"Linc's right," Carter says at my ear. "He's just bitter because he lost you. That's not your fault."

Jax huffs in agreement. "Biggest fucking mistake of his life."

"Thank you," I whisper. "I wish I'd told you all sooner."

Their words don't completely rid my heart of the cold guilt that's draped over it, but they help. I just wish there was a way I could erase Brent from my life without having to see or speak to him ever again.

"I have a confession," Carter says, his voice so quiet, I'm not sure if the others hear.

I turn in his arms, stroking the frown line between his brows. "What is it?"

"I lied."

"Well, it wouldn't be the first time," I tease, trying to lighten the tension that's fast filling the room. "Let me guess. You're actually straight."

Carter smiles at me, but there's no humor in his pale blue eyes, only sadness and guilt. Worry hooks in my gut.

"Carter?" Linc says, his voice laced with tension. "What is it?"

He groans and unwraps himself from around me, rolling onto his back. "I'm such a dick. It's the same as the bisexual thing. It's not an outright lie, it's just that I haven't corrected you. I've had the chance so many times, but I didn't take it."

"Carter," Jax says. "Spit it out."

He scrubs a hand over his face and stares at the ceiling. "I quit my job. I'm not headed back to D.C. in a couple of weeks."

Relief and confusion roil in my stomach. "Why wouldn't you tell us that?"

"I don't know," he says with a sigh. "I didn't want to sound like a loser."

"But you *are* headed to Vegas?" Linc clarifies.

Carter nods. "Yeah. That's a coincidence. I wanted a fresh start, so I threw a dart at a map."

Jax laughs. "What if it had landed in the middle of the fucking desert?"

"Las Vegas *is* in the middle of the desert." He turns his head to me, his face lined with regret. "I'm sorry, Hailee. All this time, I let you think you were the only one running, but I've been running too."

I stroke his face, tracing my fingers through his stubble. "Did you pack up and leave Andrew without so much as a note?"

Something flickers across his face, but he shakes his head. "No."

"This isn't a big deal," Linc says. "I hope you haven't been letting that eat at you."

Jax chuckles. "Is that the reason you're such a grumpy motherfucker?"

"Fuck off." Carter shoots him a glare, but it doesn't hold, and they grin at each other.

"Anyone else got any confessions?" Jax asks, flopping down onto his back.

"I already told Carter," Linc says. "But I'm going to California because my agent in New York dropped me when I wouldn't sleep with her."

I sit up, looking down at him, my eyes wide. "What the fuck?"

He shrugs. "It happens. I've got a few agencies interested, though."

"Fuck, man," Jax breathes. "That's messed up."

I think about what Linc said in the car, about people not

seeing him as a person, and my heart breaks for him. How could anyone not see him as more than his beautiful shell? I trail kisses along his sharp cheekbones and down his jaw.

"I'm sorry you had to go through that," I say. "You're the most beautiful person I've ever met, and I'm not talking about on the outside."

Linc wraps his arms around me, pulling me into a hug. "Thank you," he murmurs against my ear.

The bed shifts, and Carter drapes an arm over us both, as Jax does the same on the other side. We lie there, as one, just being. My heart aches for them. Carter running from his jealous ex. Linc having to start again, wrestling with the mistrust that people don't really see him. Jax drifting from place to place with no friends or family to rely on. Tears sting my eyes.

Apart, we're jagged broken pieces of a neglected puzzle, but we fit together somehow to make something new, and beautiful, and whole.

37

Everyone's asleep. Listening to their steady, rhythmic breathing, I lie on my back and stare at the ceiling. It felt good to tell the truth, but there's so much more. I swallow the guilt down and wince as it cuts at my throat. No one said much more after my confession. We held each other for a while and then fell asleep. I can't sleep.

I wonder whether Hailee has put two and two together yet. I'm going to be staying in Vegas. I'm not sure it matters, though. Would she even want a relationship with me? Without Linc—without Jax—I know it would feel a hundred shades of wrong. *Fuck.* I might have to go somewhere else. Maybe I'll head to Seattle or Portland. Just because the dart chose Las Vegas, doesn't mean I have to stick with it.

Jax is snoring a little. It's not loud. It's actually a little adorable. I sit up and look at them; the people I'd honestly do anything for. The streetlights cast enough orange glow beneath the thin hotel curtains that I can make them out easily. Jax is on his back, one arm above his head, his tattoos merged in the dim light. My gaze tracks to his parted lips.

Fuck, he's a good kisser. Bruising, demanding. The memory of his fingers gripping my hair as he fucked my mouth with his tongue has my dick waking up. I resist the urge to slip my hands beneath the covers, picturing the rough and wild way I'm sure he'd take me if he wanted to.

Swallowing my moan, I turn my attention to Linc. Hailee's right. He's the most beautiful person I've ever met. He wouldn't lie. He wouldn't do the things I've done. Make the choices I've made.

Hailee mumbles in her sleep, and I reach down and brush the curls from her face. The covers have slipped down, exposing one of her breasts and I tug it back up, resisting the urge to stroke the soft curve.

I did the right thing, messaging Brent. He isolated her, took everything from her. Andrew would have done the same thing to me if he could have, but my family are too present in my life. He'd have had better luck shaking off one of my brother's rescue dogs than my little sister. Hailee doesn't have that privilege. She has us, though. I exhale. I did the right thing.

When I saw that slashed tire, my stomach had plummeted to my sneakers. Even though I know it's almost certainly nothing to do with Brent, a thin layer of doubt coats my chest.

My eyes are heavy, but I feel like I drank a gallon of coffee. My limbs are twitchy. As a last resort, I carefully climb out of bed and grab my phone. Maybe some mindless scrolling will finish me off. I get back under the covers and flick through social media, tiredness finally pulling at me as I peruse the twenty-five pictures of cakes my mom has posted on her Instagram.

My phone vibrates with a text, and I frown, clicking on it before I even read the name. It's an unknown number.

Hello Carter.

I frown at the screen. Is it Andrew? I blocked him, but it makes sense he'd try to reach me through another number. To be honest, the fact that he hasn't has made me more nervous.

My thumb moves to block the number, but three dots start bouncing at the bottom of the screen. I hold my breath, waiting for the second text to come through.

Having fun with my girlfriend?

My heart slams in my chest. This isn't Andrew. Of course, it isn't. In my sleepy state I hadn't even noticed my own text at the top of the thread. The one where I told him to leave Hailee alone. *Fuck.* How does he know my name? I stare at the screen, my mouth dry, as the three dots begin bouncing again.

Don't bother blocking me. I know where you are.

My blood runs cold. What the actual fuck. *Shit.* He's bluffing. He can't possibly know. I realize too late that he knows I'm reading the messages he's sending. The dots start up again, and I dart a look at the people sleeping beside me, oblivious to the dumpster fire I've started.

Did you have fun in Tremonton? How are those bruises?

The phone falls from my fingers. Tremonton is where we stopped at that steak restaurant. Where Linc and I got jumped. *Shit. Fuck.* How does he know about that? I pick up the phone with trembling hands. He's a fucking cop. I lean my head back against the wall, my skin ice cold.

Linc and I gave our names when we reported the assault. Hailee gave her name, too. *Fuck.* He must have had some sort of alert on her name or something. Or maybe he just ran my number. I claw a hand down my face and rub my jaw. What have I done? There's no point ignoring this. I just need to try and make it right. If he finds her because of me . . . I take a deep breath and type out my message.

What do you want?

For the longest time, there's nothing. Then the three dots start bouncing, and I can barely breathe.

Andrew wants his money back. And so do I.

I stare, unblinking, at the phone. The room spins, and I shove the covers back. I get to my feet and I'm not even sure why. I just . . . *How?*

Brent knows my biggest secret. The one I haven't been able to bring myself to tell them. It's the most shameful thing I've ever done in my life. I sink down to the floor and rest my head on my knees, the light of my phone illuminating the carpet in an eerie blue glow.

Andrew convinced me we should buy a bigger place together. He wanted us to move away. We saved for over a year. Mostly my money because I earned more than him, which wasn't a lot to boast about.

When I realized what he was doing to me—when I realized that our entire relationship was unhealthy beyond belief—I broke up with him. Everything we'd done together, everything we were building towards was painted in a new light. The reason he wanted us to move away was to isolate me more. Fuck. Andrew and Brent would get along great.

I'd wanted a fresh start. Away from Andrew. Away from the places that would remind me of how fucking clueless I'd been. How I'd thought we had a good relationship. I screw my eyes tight and swallow my frustration. When we broke up, I quit my job. I didn't have enough money to start over, so I emptied our joint account.

My stomach rolls. Eleven thousand dollars. Not a huge amount. Not enough to start over, but enough to rent a shitty apartment in a shitty part of town and work my ass off before it runs out. It's not stealing. Not completely. At least seventy percent of it is my money, anyway. Maybe sixty-five. My eyes sting, and I swallow the bile rising in my throat.

I've been waiting. Waiting for him to find a way to contact me. Waiting for the police or something. *Fuck.* I should have given a fake name. We should have left without filing a report. *Fuck.*

I lift the phone to see that the three dots are bouncing again.

20K Carter. Or lose everything.

I drop the phone on the carpet, making it into the bathroom, just in time to empty my gut into the toilet.

38

I WAKE UP WITH LINC'S FUCKING HARD ON PRESSED AGAINST my thigh. I groan and rub a hand over my face.

"Morning, gorgeous," Linc says with a yawn. "What you thinking?"

Raising an eyebrow at his perkiness, I turn to look at him. "I'm thinking, I can't remember the last time I woke up, and your dick wasn't the first thing I saw."

Linc fucking beams. "You love it."

"I most definitely do not." I try to frown, but can't quite pull it off and Linc laughs.

Last night was one of the most bizarre, and hottest, nights of my life. If I wasn't already sporting wood, the flashbacks would be doing the job. I still can't quite cope with the fact that, apparently, I'm kissing guys now. Closing my eyes, I try to picture my friends, or guys from work. I never got fucking hard over any of them. I mean, sometimes at the garage in the summer, we'd take our shirts off, and I'd admire some of the guys. It was just appreciation of their bodies, though. I hadn't thought about sucking them off. *Fuck.* No. I'm still not thinking about sucking anyone off.

I open an eye and look at Linc. He's half turned toward Hailee, gently stroking her arm. She's beautiful. When she's asleep, she looks like she should have those little blue cartoon birds fluttering around her.

From where I'm lying, I can't see Carter. Kissing him last night had been interesting. I'd been wary of the stubble, but I definitely didn't hate it. My heart kicks as I remember the way he dragged his finger over my lips, that intense stare slicing right into my fucking core. His whole bossy teacher thing makes me want to take control—to show him who's in charge. I remember the way Linc took him on the bed, the first time I watched them fuck, and I can't stop myself from imagining doing the same. Fucking him into submission, until he cries out my name.

I reach under the covers and wrap my fingers around my dick. It's tenting the sheets, and one hard stroke has me pressing my lips together so hard it hurts. *What the fuck is up with that?* Last night, Linc joked about me taking his ass, and the thought had caused my stomach to flip. At the time, I'd thought it was fear, but now, I'm not so sure.

Letting go of my aching cock, I open my eyes and sit up. No one's noticed. In fact, Carter isn't even in the bed. I look around, and his stuff's gone, too.

I poke Linc. "Where's Carter?"

Linc sits up, looking around. "I thought he was in the bathroom."

The bathroom door is wide open. I get out of bed and head to where I left my jeans last night.

"Fuck," Linc breathes. "I hope you're not planning on wasting that."

Pulling my phone from my jeans, I look at him in confusion. His heated gaze is fixed on my very hard cock. I roll my eyes and swipe open my phone.

Gone to find somewhere for breakfast.

I read the text aloud, and Linc shrugs, falling back on the bed. It's weird. Why would he not wake any of us? I place my phone down on the nightstand and shake my head. Why do I even care? It's not my problem. There's something about Hailee, Linc and Carter. They're like some sort of weird addiction.

A moan pulls my attention back to the bed, and I freeze. Hailee is awake, although her eyes are still closed, and Linc has two fingers inside her, pumping slowly as he sucks at her nipple. My hand drops to my dick before I can stop it. I don't think I'll ever get used to this. Linc turns his head toward me, his eyes dropping to where I'm stroking my cock. He licks his lips.

"I want you both," he says.

Hailee writhes against his hand, her eyes fluttering open. She looks up at me, and then drags her gaze down my body, her eyes darkening with lust as she watches me touch myself. I grip harder, my heart pounding.

My mind whirs with possibilities of what Linc means by having us both. "What are you thinking?"

He pulls his fingers from Hailee, and she moans in a way that has my breath catching in my throat. Locking eyes with me, he shifts a pillow behind him, slouching against the headboard.

"Sit on my cock, Hailee," he says.

He holds out his hand to me and my brain is so fuzzy with lust, that it takes me a second to figure out that he wants me to give him a condom. I grab one from the nightstand and tear it open. Linc's barely rolled it down to the base before Hailee straddles him.

The noise she makes as she sinks down onto him almost has me blowing my load right there and then.

"Jax?" Linc says, pulling my gaze from where Hailee is moving up and down his slick cock. "Get in my mouth."

My breath halts in my throat. I'm almost in a daze as I kneel on the bed, still fisting my cock. Linc's hands grip Hailee's hips, but he turns his head to me and opens his mouth like he's expecting a fucking treat. I steady myself on the wall as I bring my hips to his mouth. His eyes are like goddamn melted chocolate as he looks up at me, and I drag the tip of my cock over his bottom lip, painting it with precum. Keeping his eyes on mine, he flicks out his tongue and licks it off. A groan builds in my throat, and Linc leans forward, taking me into his mouth, his cheeks hollowing as he sucks and licks.

My hand clenches into a fist against the wall. It feels fucking amazing. Hailee's moans force my eyes open, and I lick my lips as I watch her ride Linc, her tits bouncing with the movement. Gripping her chin, I tilt her face toward me, and she looks up at me, eyes half lidded with pleasure. I dip my head, silencing her moans with my mouth. Kissing someone while another mouth is on your dick is something I've never experienced before and, fuck me, it's everything.

I drop my hand from her chin and take one of her breasts in my palm, pinching at her nipple hard enough that she yelps against my tongue. My dick hits the back of Linc's throat, and I pull back from Hailee, a curse on my tongue. Twisting my fingers in his hair, I watch in awe as he takes me so deep, his eyes water. I reach out and stroke his throat, feeling high as a fucking kite.

When Hailee whimpers in a way I've already learned means she's close, I flick her nipple as Linc moves his fingers to her clit, and she swears loud enough that I raise my eyebrows, a smirk lighting my face. A smirk that is wiped from my face as Linc does something with his mouth that has me falling forward against the wall, one hand gripping the headboard. He moans, and it vibrates against my cock in a way that pulls me right to the edge.

Hailee cries out a string of words that make no fucking sense, her head falling forward, and Linc grips her hips, pulling her down, as he empties inside her.

"Fuck. Shit." I groan, Linc's moan trembling against the length of my dick as it nudges the back of his throat. "I'm coming."

Linc swallows down my release, just like in the shower, and I lean against my arm, resting on the wall, as my breathing evens out. Linc pulls off me, and when I reach out and wipe the spit from his chin, he looks up at me in a way he really shouldn't. No one should look at me that way.

"Next time," he says as Hailee eases off him, collapsing on her back. "Hailee can ride me backwards while sucking your dick, Jax."

Hailee groans, and my dick twitches despite its deflating state.

"You're a fucking liability," I say, as he rolls off the bed and heads to the bathroom to clean up.

"Or," he calls through the half open door, "I could fuck Hailee while you fuck me. The possibilities are endless."

I shake my head, even though he can't see me, and Hailee chuckles from where she's lying, spent on the bed. My eyes fall on my wallet, half hanging out of my jeans, and I remember what I meant to ask last night but got distracted by a fucking foursome.

"Linc? I need to pay you for the room."

"No, you don't," he calls over the sound of the toilet flushing.

I wait until he appears in the doorway. "Yes, I do. I'm not a charity case."

Linc stares at me as though I'm speaking another language. "I never said you were."

"You paid for the last one, and that was bad enough. I have the money."

"I'm sure you do, Jax." Linc shakes his head and folds his arms across his chest. It's difficult not to look at his half-hard cock. "Look, I'm happy to pay for the hotel. I enjoy spending time with you."

My skin heats as my blood boils beneath my skin. "I'm not a fucking whore," I grit out.

Linc's mouth falls open. "I didn't say you were. Stop overreacting."

I stride across the room until we're face to face, my fists clenched at my side. "I'm not overreacting. Let me pay for my share."

Linc grabs the back of my neck, pulling me until my forehead touches his. "I'm not going to argue about this. I like spending my money on people I care about, okay."

My chest tightens, and I shrug out of his hold, taking a step back. "You hardly know me."

"So, what? That doesn't mean I can't care about you."

There's a roaring in my head. I'm vaguely aware of Hailee sitting up to my right. "What the fuck is it with you people?"

Linc arches an eyebrow. "You people?"

I turn around, breathing hard. "It's like some sort of mindfuck cult."

"What the hell are you on about, Jax?"

I grab my boxers and jeans and start pulling them on. "You picked me up on the side of the road, and now you've roped me in to this fucking sex circus."

"Sex circus," Linc repeats slowly.

His voice is so calm, it only riles me up more. I snatch up my shirt, not caring that it stinks of sweat, and pull it on.

Linc watches me like he's scared I'm going to turn on him. "Who are you right now?"

"Exactly." I laugh, cold and harsh, as I shove my feet into my sneakers. "You don't fucking know me."

Snatching my bag up off the floor, I storm out, the roar of my blood deafening in my ears. By the time I find myself outside, I'm a fucking mess. What the fuck just happened? I shove a hand through my hair and stare at the quiet high street. What the ever-loving hell am I doing here? I should be in Phoenix. I should be starting over.

"Jax?"

I close my eyes at the sound of Hailee's tentative voice. "What?"

"I wanted to see if you were okay."

The concern in her voice tightens my chest further and my shoulders sag. "Are any of us okay?"

She huffs a laugh and steps closer, running a hand up my back until it rests on my shoulder. I turn to look at her. She's scraped her curls back into a messy ponytail, and it's the cutest fucking thing I've ever seen.

"I've never seen you with your hair up," I say, tracing her ear.

"Jax? What was all that about?"

"I don't know." I rub a hand over my face and lean against the wall of the hotel. "I don't know why I said those things."

"It's more than the money, isn't it?" she presses, her hand rubbing soothing circles on my shoulder blade.

Exhaling loudly, I stare up at the bunting lining the high street as it flaps in the warm morning breeze. "I don't know."

Hailee moves to stand in front of me, her hands on my chest, as she looks up at me with those eyes that slay me.

"I don't want you to go," she says quietly.

I shake my head. "Don't look at me like that."

Her eyes only widen further. "Like what?"

"Like this is something more than it is," I say. "You say you don't want me to go, but we're all going the day after tomorrow."

Hailee's face crumples, and I groan.

"I'm sorry," she says, her hands sliding from my chest.

It takes all my self-restraint not to grab hold of them and pull her to me.

"It's hard to explain," she says, her eyes fixed on the floor, "the thing between us."

You're telling me. "I know."

"I hate it." She looks back up at me, unshed tears glistening in her eyes. "Linc is going to San Francisco. You're going to Phoenix. Even though Carter's apparently staying in Vegas, it's not the same. It'll never be the same. I'm trying not to think about it, but it's always there. I know this has always had an expiration date, and I let myself get too attached."

My gut twists. "That's the problem. I didn't want this. I don't get attached."

Hailee studies me for a moment, like the answer is written on my fucking forehead. "Why?"

I stare down at her as if there's an easy answer; a way to explain how I'm twenty-eight and have nothing permanent in my life besides my name. The way she's looking up at me is too much. The way Linc looked at me, too. Like I'm their missing piece. I'm nobody's missing piece.

"Because of this," I relent. "Nothing ever lasts."

Hailee shakes her head, her mouth opening to dispute, but then she closes it and wraps her arms around me, pressing her face into my chest. There's nothing she can say. It's the cold, hard truth. I fold my arms around her and hold her tight.

39

By the time Hailee gets out of the shower, my hurt has morphed into anger. She came back from talking to Jax, saying he was going to stay down there. He isn't leaving, though. She managed to convince him to stay. Fuck him. Maybe it was a bad idea to bring him in on this. Maybe we should have left him in Idaho. Maybe we should never have picked him up. My hands curl into fists on my lap.

"Hey," Hailee says, sitting down beside me. She's washed her hair and it smells delicious.

"What?"

"Don't be angry with him." She takes hold of one of my hands, unclenching my fingers.

I stare at her fingers as they intertwine with mine. "Please don't tell me how I should feel."

"I'm not," she says gently. "I just want you to remember that this is an unusual situation, and Jax is trying to deal with it his own way. I mean, he probably thought he was straight until yesterday."

I huff. "Yeah, apparently not so much."

"So, give him a minute." She squeezes my hand. "If you

care about him like you say you do, you'll give him some space to figure it out."

I shrug, feeling like a sullen teenager.

"He didn't leave. He could have, but he didn't."

Hailee stands, and I flop back on the bed. She's right. He could have left. The sad fact is, I can count on one hand the people in my life I truly care about right now, and three of them are going to the Grand Canyon with me today. Sure, I have hundreds of thousands of followers. I have dozens of 'friends'. But it took this trip to realize that I have no one I could call if I needed help. That's been one of the best parts of this trip—aside from the mind-blowing sex. Talking. Telling someone how I feel and having them understand. I've forgotten what it feels like to be validated. I close my eyes, remembering the way Carter looked into my damn soul in the car, and told me he 'saw' me.

"You ready?"

I sit up with a groan, then stop. "That's new."

Hailee's scraped her hair up into a neat ponytail, the curls cascading down her back, still a little damp from the shower. She watches me through narrowed eyes as I stand and walk over to her. Reaching up, I take hold of the ponytail, wrapping it around my fist and tugging until she's looking up at me, then I kiss her. Her fingers slide up under my shirt as I stroke her tongue with mine, and it takes a lot of willpower to step back.

"I like this," I say, giving her hair another tug before letting go.

Hailee shoves my chest, and I grin. Then I remember. We're about to go downstairs and face Jax. I hope he doesn't make the car ride awkward.

"I'll take first shift," I offer. If I'm driving, I don't have to worry about talking as much.

Hailee opens her mouth to protest, then shakes her head and heads to the door. Jax isn't by the car. I glance up and down the street, but there's no sign of him. As much as I hate to admit it, my heart sinks. Carter is already in the car, and as we approach, he pops the trunk.

"Where have you been?" I ask, sliding into the passenger side. Carter turns to look at me, and I halt. He looks like shit. His grey t-shirt is wrinkled, and his eyes are bloodshot, with dark circles under them.

"I couldn't sleep," he says with a shrug.

"Like, at all?" I open the door and swing my legs out. "You shouldn't be driving. Get out."

Ignoring his groaning protest, I walk back around the car to find Hailee standing with Jax. He at least has the decency to look sheepish, but at the sight of him, my anger bubbles back to the surface. He hasn't told me to care about him—he hasn't made me—but it happened. When he threw it back in my face after last night and this morning, it cheapened what happened between us, and I don't like the sour feeling it's left in my gut.

"Hey," he says.

I hold his stare, my jaw tight. "I thought you'd left."

He frowns. "Sorry to disappoint you."

A disgusted noise rumbles in my throat, and I make to walk around him, but he reaches out and grabs my arm. I whirl on him, snatching my arm back. "What?"

Jax holds his arms out to his sides like it's obvious. "I'm sorry."

"Whatever."

"Linc, please." He snags the sleeve of my t-shirt, and I stop.

"What do you want me to say?" I ask. "I forgive you?"

"Yeah. Pretty much."

I shake my head. "You said some really shitty things."

Jax stares at me, his lips pressed together. His eyes look darker today. Almost navy blue. I focus my attention on the butterfly tattoo by his neck, because if I keep looking in his eyes, I'll fold. I'm too fucking soft.

"I'm sorry, Linc." He takes a step forward. "I don't know what else to say."

"Whatever. Don't feel like you have to stay with this 'sex circus' if you don't want to." The words taste as bitter as they sound, but I don't care.

"Stop trying to push me away," he says, taking another step forward. Our chests are almost touching, and I can feel his warmth. "I said, I'm fucking sorry, okay?"

I look at him then, drinking in the fire in his eyes, the anger tensing his shoulders. Every word that rises in my mind is too sharp and jagged to speak without cutting myself in the process.

"Linc." Jax reaches up and clasps a hand to the back of my neck, pulling me toward him . "I want to stay. I'm sorry for fucking things up. I got spooked, okay?"

I exhale, leaning my forehead against his. "No. It's not okay. You can't tell me who I'm allowed to care about."

Jax shakes his head, his hair rubbing against my skin. "I'm not used to people caring."

Fuck. The last of my resolve dissipates and I wrap my arms around him, holding him as tight as I can without cracking his ribs. It takes him a second, then he returns the gesture. It feels nice. Really nice.

"If you're going to stay with us," I mumble against his shoulder. "You're going to have to be okay with me caring about you."

Jax hugs me a little tighter, then turns his head and presses a kiss to my neck.

"Everything all right back there?" Carter calls from the passenger seat.

We pull apart, and I squeeze his shoulder before heading to the driver's seat. I buckle up and turn to Carter. "Where we going?"

He looks at me in confusion. "What do you mean?"

"You said you were scouting places for breakfast."

Carter blinks. "Oh. Yeah. Erm—"

"I'm on it," Jax says from the backseat, his phone in his hand.

"What's going on?" I ask Carter.

He frowns. "Nothing. Like I said. I couldn't sleep."

I shake my head, but let it drop as I pull out of the parking lot.

There's an accident, and we end up stuck in traffic for two and a half hours. The August heat is stifling, and we kill the air conditioning to save gas. The temperature doesn't help the atmosphere, and even though Jax and I have hugged it out, there's still a weird tension in the car. Carter tried to fall asleep, first in the front, and then in the back, but woke up grumbling that it was too hot each time. It's not worth going to see the Grand Canyon by the time traffic starts moving again, so we head to a nearby town called Tuba City.

There are only two hotels in the town, both quite nice. I bite my tongue and let Jax pay. I understand why it means so much to him, but I still hate it. He's got nothing. I stand to the side in the lobby and watch him hand over the cash, knowing that it's hurting him. I've got more money than I know what to do with. Yeah, it won't last forever, but I'm sensible. My parents have been investing the earnings from my big contracts since I was twelve. The cost of a hotel in the middle of the Arizona desert wouldn't even touch the sides of my bank account. The fact that we're in Arizona hasn't escaped my attention either. While we were stuck in traffic, I checked. We're only three and a half hours from Phoenix. Too close.

"They've only got a twin room," Jax says, holding up a key.

I shrug. "We've made it work before."

We skipped lunch because of the traffic, and I'm starving. At the same time, I'm desperate for a shower. My t-shirt was stuck to my back when we got out of the car.

It's eerily quiet and no one talks as we make our way toward our room. The hotel is only one story, with a long corridor of plush green carpet that muffles our steps. Jax opens the door and steps aside to let us in.

"Oh," Hailee says, turning a slow circle as she enters. "This is nice."

It is. Green like the corridor, the room is clean and fresh looking. I dump my bag by the door and start to tug on the nightstand, but it doesn't budge. I crouch down, only to discover it's bolted to the floor. A hard shove of the bed confirms the same.

"Well, fuck," I say, getting to my feet. "Looks like we're pairing up tonight."

Carter kicks off his shoes and collapses on the nearest bed. "Do you guys mind if I try and sleep?"

"What about dinner?"

Carter's eyes are already closed. "Bring me back something."

"Do you mind if I grab a quick shower?" Hailee asks. "I'm not washing my hair, so I'll only be five minutes."

"Sure," I say, as Jax shrugs.

I kick off my shoes and socks, and flip through the leaflets spread out on the desk. By the time I'm halfway through, Carter's soft snores can be heard over the sound of the shower.

"They've got a laundry service," I say, holding up a leaflet. "I'm going to see how long it takes. Do you want to throw in some stuff with mine?"

The words are out of my mouth before I realize I've probably offended him, but when I turn with an apology already on my lips, I find Jax sitting on the bed, scrolling through his phone.

"Yeah," he says, not looking up. "Thanks, man."

I lean against the desk and watch him. Whatever he's looking at causes his face to fall into a slight frown. I don't like it.

"What's the plan when you get to Phoenix?" I ask. "Will you look for a job at a garage?"

Jax locks his phone and puts it down on the nightstand. "I guess."

"Do you enjoy it?"

Jax stares at me for a minute, then shakes his head. "What are you trying to do, Linc?"

"Why do I need to be doing anything? I'm talking."

"Fine. Yeah. I enjoy it. I like cars, and I like figuring out what's wrong with something and fixing it."

I nod thoughtfully. "Do you wear those all-in-one things?"

Jax raises an eyebrow. "Coveralls? Sure."

I can just picture him, sliding out from under a pickup truck, grease smeared across his tattooed pecs.

"Hey," Jax says, throwing a pillow at me. "Stop looking at me like I'm a fucking snack."

I catch the pillow and laugh. "Stop looking like one, then."

Jax shushes me, nodding toward Carter, but a smile has replaced his frown. "Do you enjoy modeling?"

Although I should have been expecting it, it pulls me up short. "I guess," I say slowly. "I've been doing it my entire life. There's never been anything else."

Before Jax can respond, the bathroom door opens, and Hailee steps out fully dressed in different clothes.

"You got dressed in the bathroom?" I ask.

She shrugs. "I didn't want to risk waking Carter up."

"Liar." Jax chuckles. "You didn't think we'd be able to keep our hands to ourselves, did you, princess?"

Hailee gives us both a knowing look, and I bite back a laugh. "You're fucking animals," she says. "I'm going to check out the restaurant at the hotel. If it's open, I'll get us a table and meet you down there."

"Oh," I say, holding up the leaflet. "Will you find out about the laundry service? If they can do it by tomorrow morning, I'll organize it."

Hailee gives me a thumbs up and opens the door. "Don't wake him up and don't take ages."

I hold up my hands in mock surrender. "We'll be quick and quiet. Promise."

As she rolls her eyes and steps out into the corridor, I turn and stare at Carter, face down on top of the covers. He really should have gotten changed or had a shower first. Although, I suppose a shower would have woken him up.

"Do you want first shower?" Jax asks, getting up from the bed.

I shrug. "I don't mind. You didn't have one this morning, so you can go first if you want."

Jax nods and heads toward the bathroom, pulling his

shirt off as he goes. When he reaches the door, he stops, but doesn't turn around. "You know, we could always share. If you want?"

I raise my eyebrows. "Oh?"

He turns around, looking so nervous, I fight to keep the smile from my lips. "Saving water, time, and all that stuff."

"Only if you're sure."

Jax lifts his shoulder in answer and takes his jeans off. I grip the edge of the desk, writhing in indecision. I really want to go in there, but I'm also still a little pissed at him for this morning. That said, maybe he just means we could share the shower. He might not want anything to happen.

"Is that a no, then?"

I look up to find Jax watching me from the doorway. "I'm just trying to decide what's best."

"You're still annoyed about this morning."

It's not a question, so I don't answer.

Jax sighs. "Well, if you'd like me to attempt to make it up to you, come join me in the shower. Either just bring yourself, or bring lube and a condom. Your call."

My mouth falls open as he steps back into the bathroom and out of sight. His words have my dick standing to attention. If he wants me to bring a condom . . . I swallow hard. We're only a few hours from Phoenix. Tomorrow is our last day together. My heart thuds loudly in my chest as I stare at the bathroom door. Maybe it's better to not take this last step.

When the water turns on, I stand up and grab the supplies from my bag.

I strip off before heading in, closing the door behind me. Jax is already under the water, and I dump the lube and condom on the side of the bath and step in while he watches me. I'm not sure why I feel so nervous. He asked me to join him, and judging from the way his dick is pointing at me, he's happy about it.

I reach out, taking the bar of soap from his hand and turn him around, lathering his back. I work the suds over his arms before circling round to his chest and stomach. He sighs, his head falling back, and I press a kiss to his neck.

Jax turns, his eyes flicking down as our dicks rub against each other. He takes the soap from my hand, and I stand there, barely breathing, as he works the suds over my chest and stomach, never once touching lower than my hips.

"Turn around," he says, soft but commanding.

I do as he says, and he runs his hands over every inch of my back. Just when I'm convinced all he wants to do is clean up, his hand slides down to cup my ass, squeezing. My breath catches in my throat.

"Do you want me?" he asks at my ear.

I exhale with a groan. "Yes."

He puts down the soap and runs both hands down my ass. "Are you still angry with me?"

I turn around, brushing wet strands of hair from my face. "I was never really angry. I was hurt. This isn't just new for you, Jax. It's not something I do all the time. It's new for all of us." I take a breath, gathering my thoughts. "What you said. It cheapened it. I love sex, and I don't ever feel guilty about it. I've never felt bad about it. Until this morning."

Jax closes his eyes, and I watch the droplets of water trace his chin. "I'm so sorry. I freaked out. The way you looked at me this morning. I just couldn't handle it."

I reach up and cup his face. "Why?"

"Because it's always just been me. You looked at me like I was something special. Something good for you." He opens his eyes, and they're filled with sadness. "I'm neither of those things."

My heart squeezes in my chest, and I lean forward and kiss him softly. "You are special," I say. "So fucking special. And you don't get to decide if you're good for me or not. If anything, it's the other way around. I've clearly corrupted you."

Jax laughs and I smile, pressing another kiss to his lips.

When I place a hand on his chest, I can feel his heart hammering like mad beneath his skin. "Are you sure you want to do this? We're clean. We can just stop now."

Jax kisses me hard enough that I lean back against the tiles. When he reaches down and wraps his hand around my cock, I moan against his tongue.

"Show me what to do," he says, the words breathy against my lips.

I consider for a second, then reach out and switch off the water. Jax looks at me questioningly, and I smile. "This will be easier without all the slippery surfaces."

Stepping out of the bath, I grab the lube. I pump some onto my hand, aware of Jax standing right behind me. His breath caresses my shoulder, making the hairs on the back of my neck stand on end. Turning around, I take his hand and smear the lube on his fingers. He swallows, and I track the movement, leaning forward and licking a slow path up his throat.

"Say stop at any time," I murmur against his ear. "Promise."

Jax nods.

I face the mirror, gripping the edge of the sink with one hand, and taking his in my other. I guide his finger between my cheeks and ease him inside. He drops his forehead to my shoulder, wrapping an arm around my middle, as he begins to pump in a steady rhythm.

"Add another," I say after a minute, my words breathier than I expect.

"Does it feel good?" he asks.

"So good." My head hangs forward as I push back against his hand. "Not as good as your cock is going to feel, though."

Jax groans, and his teeth clamp down lightly on my shoulder.

"More," I pant, gripping my dick and stroking.

He adds a third finger, and my head falls back with a moan.

"It's so fucking tight," Jax whispers against my neck. "You're going to strangle my cock."

"That's the plan." I pant, my heart racing. "I'm ready."

Jax pulls out, and I whimper, squeezing and stroking my dick as I watch him roll the condom down over his thick cock, and coating it with lube.

He positions himself behind me, teasing the head of his cock against my hole, and I push back hungrily.

"Greedy," he growls against my neck.

"Get inside me," I say. "Now."

I think for a second he's going to tease me for the order, but he pushes in, a gasp escaping his lips, as the head of his cock passes the tight ring of muscle.

"Fuck," he breathes. "Fuck, Linc."

He moves his hips in gentle thrusts until he bottoms out, resting his forehead on my shoulder as he catches his breath.

"How does it feel?" I ask, trying to be patient, when all I want is for him to start moving.

Jax meets my eyes in the mirror, and they're wide with wonder. "Fucking incredible," he says.

"Good." I push back against him, and his eyes flutter closed. "Fuck me, Jax."

A low rumble sounds in his throat, and he wraps his arm around my chest, his other hand gripping my hip. Then, he pulls almost all the way out, before thrusting back in, and I groan. The way his thick cock fills me is heaven and I love the feel of his muscled, tattooed arm, wrapped around my chest, holding me as though he might fuck me so hard, I'll fall over.

"You won't break me," I manage, between gasped breaths. "Don't hold back."

Jax exhales and scrapes his teeth along my jaw. "Hold on tight, baby."

My heart explodes at the term of endearment, but before I can process it, he slams into me fast and hard enough to make me cry out.

"You'll wake Carter," he pants at my shoulder.

I moan. "I don't fucking care."

Jax grins over my shoulder, moving his hand from where it's pressed against my pec, and covering my mouth. The sight of his tattooed hand pressing against my mouth, his dark blue eyes wild with desire as he pants at my ear, is too much. I clutch the sink, my knees weak.

"Harder," I mumble against his fingers.

Jax growls against my neck, and I whimper against his hand, working my dick in sync with his relentless pounding. A tingling sensation, like imploding stars, works its way from my toes, along my limbs. I bite my tongue, Jax's name a deep guttural groan in my throat, as my orgasm jolts through my entire body, my knees buckling as I come.

"Fuck," Jax gasps. "Linc—"

His words are stolen by a ragged moan that reverberates against my back as his dick pulses inside me. He drops his hand from my mouth, his forehead resting on my shoulder, as he pants like he's just finished the Boston Marathon. After a few seconds, he pulls out and throws the condom in the trash, before turning me around.

"Linc," he murmurs, his eyes wild.

I study his face, looking for signs of spiraling regret. "You okay?"

He lifts a hand, running it through his damp hair. "That was . . ."

"Mind blowing?" I supply. "Because it certainly was for me."

Jax nods slowly, his eyes darting between mine.

"Don't overthink it," I say softly. "Don't try and label it. It was incredible. That's all you need to know."

"Incredible," Jax repeats on an exhale.

I smile and press a kiss to his lips. "Come on. We need another shower. Hailee is going to be pissed."

40

CARTER DIDN'T WAKE FOR FOOD, SO THE ROOM STILL SMELLS of the pasta we brought back for him. It's the first thing I smell when I wake up. I shared his bed because, as the smallest, I could fit in beside him without disturbing him. Linc and Jax shared the other one.

Even though they kept me waiting last night, I'm beyond relieved that things are back to normal between them. I knew they'd end up fooling around in the shower, but I was surprised to find out they'd had sex. So much for giving Jax time to figure his shit out. Though, I know no one could force him to do anything he didn't want to.

When I open my eyes, I find Carter gone. I'm not surprised. He fell asleep at five yesterday. I sit up, prepared to smile at the sight of Linc and Jax in the next bed, but Linc's alone. A yawn shudders through my body as I frown. Maybe they're together. Throwing back the covers, I grab a shower and brush my teeth, mulling over the bittersweet feeling that encompasses today.

Today we're going to the Grand Canyon, which is something I've wanted to see since I was a little kid. The thought sends butterflies fluttering in my stomach. On the other hand, it's our last day together. Tomorrow, Jax will head south to Phoenix. I'll take Linc as far as Vegas, and then he'll make his way across Nevada to California. My lungs are tight. I always knew this was coming, but it doesn't make it any easier.

When I emerge from the shower, Linc is sitting up in bed, his dark hair loose around his shoulders as he scrolls through his phone.

"New followers?" I tease.

He holds up a certain finger, without looking up from his phone, and I laugh. I haven't had any more texts from Brent. I'm not sure whether I'm relieved or worried. Part of me wants to know why he needed to speak to me so badly. I refuse to believe it's because he wants me back. I don't think he ever actually loved me. Well, maybe in the beginning, but certainly not for a long time.

I wrap a towel around my hair and head to my bag.

"Our laundry should be outside the door," Linc says. "I don't care if Jax pitches a fit, I paid for an express service and shoved everything I could find in."

"Well, I appreciate it, even if he doesn't," I say. The laundry isn't outside the door, though, it's already been dragged in and opened. Carter and Jax must have taken their stuff already. I spot one of my favorite t-shirts on the top of one of the piles and pull it free.

"Ugh, it smells so clean. I forgot what that's like."

Linc chuckles and heads to the bathroom. "You're welcome."

By the time he gets out of the shower, I'm dressed, and I've organized our laundry into piles. There's still no sign of Jax or Carter.

"Have you heard from the guys?" I ask.

"No. Have you?"

I go to fetch my phone from my bag and stop short. My heart vibrates in my throat. My backpack is open. Not just the main pocket where my clothes and toiletries go, but the one holding all my cash. I can see, even from a meter away, that it's empty, but I still drop to my knees beside it, pushing my hand into every available space just the same.

"What's wrong?"

I look up to find Linc staring down at me, his jeans unfastened, and a t-shirt in his hand. His eyes flit between my distraught expression and my ransacked bag as he puts two and two together.

"It's gone," I whisper. "All my money."

Linc frowns. "How? This room has never been empty."

I might throw up. I clutch at my stomach, sucking in the air. Linc's right. Which means something I really can't think about. With shaking hands, I grab my phone and unlock it. There are no new messages.

Linc shoves on his t-shirt and takes my elbow, hauling me gently over to one of the beds. "Was it definitely there when we arrived?"

"Yes. I took some out to pay my share of dinner." Tears sting my eyes.

Linc squeezes the top of his nose, his dark hair hanging in wet tendrils around his face as he processes. "I can't believe . . ."

I swallow. I don't want to believe it either.

"Call them," I whisper.

Linc stands and fetches his phone. I watch, a tiny shimmer of hope flickering in my chest. They'll answer. They'll explain. It's going to be fine.

After a few tries, he puts the phone in his pocket and

shakes his head. "Jax's is switched off or out of range, and Carter's is going to voicemail."

A sob bursts from my lips, and I clap a hand to my mouth. It doesn't make any sense. Carter wouldn't do this. He can't have done this. Why after all this time? Even as I think the words, I realize how ridiculous they are. It's been no time at all. A week. My eyes burn with tears.

Jax would have the most reason to, and I feel dirty for thinking it. Why would he do something like this after what happened yesterday? Surely, he would have been happy letting Linc pay for stuff if he was planning on robbing us?

"Check your wallet," I choke out, hating the words.

Linc sits down heavily beside me, and flips open his wallet. "Everything's there."

I'm not sure whether that makes things better or worse.

"Do you think they're together?" he asks.

My hands are trembling. Could they be? Tears track down my cheeks. This was supposed to be our last day together.

"Hailee?" Linc says.

The seriousness of his tone has me swiping at my tears and sitting up. "What?"

"Where's the car key?"

My heart slams down into my stomach. "No."

We tear the room apart, searching for the key, but it's nowhere to be found.

"Maybe we're jumping to conclusions," I say, my voice trembling. "Their bags are gone, so it would make sense they took the key to put them in the car, right?"

Linc runs a hand through his hair, and exhales slowly. "Yeah, I guess."

With nothing else to do, we pack our own bags in silence and check out. All the while, Linc keeps trying to call the guys. Every time I look at him expectantly, he shakes his head.

The desert sun is already blazing hot when we step outside, and we don't speak as we cross the parking lot to where I left my car. Even though we can see it's not there before we're halfway across, we keep walking until we're standing in the empty space.

"Why would they do this?" I ask, knowing full well Linc has as many answers as I do. I sink to the asphalt and cross my legs.

"Hailee?" Linc says. Even though he's got his Ray-Bans on, the sun is bright enough that he has to hold a hand up to shield his eyes. "Is that your car?"

I look up, the distant rumble of a car engine sounding in the distance. Linc helps me to my feet, and I squint at the road. It's a silver car for sure, but as it pulls into the parking lot, fresh tears spring to my eyes. It is.

It pulls into a space beside us, and Jax gets out, a worried look on his face. "Hey guys."

I want to throw myself into his arms, the relief is so overwhelming, but I don't. There are still so many questions, and the pain carved into my chest is still raw and bleeding.

"Where the fuck have you been?" Linc asks, the stress and worry of the last half an hour filling every space between syllables.

Jax stares at us. "I'm sorry. I woke up early and went to get the tire replaced. It's dangerous to keep using the spare. I thought I'd be back before you checked out."

I glance at my watch. He's right. If we hadn't panicked, we'd still be in the room. We'd probably be having sex.

He locks the car and walks around to us, his expression tightening. "What's going on?"

"We woke up and both you and Carter were gone," Linc explains.

Jax raises his eyebrows. "Carter was still asleep when I left."

My stomach rolls. "You didn't answer your phone."

He reaches into his pocket and holds it up. The screen is black. "It ran out of battery. I forgot to charge it last night and it didn't charge enough in the car to turn on. It's a piece of shit."

The tension between us is thicker than the humidity. Jax hands me the key, and I shove it in my pocket. I can't bring myself to look at him. Guilt and disgust are cold and damp against my skin. How could I have thought that he would . . .

"You thought I'd done a runner, didn't you?" Jax says, his voice tight.

I don't answer.

"Hailee's money is gone," Linc explains quietly. "We didn't know what to think."

Jax stares between the two of us. "What money?"

I press a hand to my mouth as bile rises in my throat. *Fuck.* Jax didn't even know about the cash. Only Carter and Linc did. *Carter.* My legs start to tremble.

"Hailee had her life savings in her backpack," Linc says. There's something in his tone to suggest he's reached the same conclusion as me. "It's all gone."

"So, you figured I'd stolen the money and the car, and left you high and fucking dry?"

I shake my head, but it's a lie and he knows it. That's exactly what we thought. Linc's hand rubs my back as tears track down my cheeks again.

"I can't fucking believe it," Jax seethes. "What was all that caring bullshit? How could you think I'd do that?"

I want to say more than anything that I didn't think that,

but I can't. I can see everything crumbling, falling like sand between my fingers, and there's absolutely nothing I can do to stop it.

"It's not like that," Linc tries.

"Oh?" Jax snaps. "What is it like, then?"

Linc's hand tightens on my shoulder. "Come on, you can't blame us. We wake up and you're both gone, and Hailee's been robbed. Anyone would have jumped to the same conclusion."

"No." Jax shakes his head and opens the passenger door, grabbing his bag from the seat. "I would have thought there was a reasonable fucking explanation."

"I'm sorry," I choke out.

Jax looks at me, but his eyes are cold. "I thought you were different."

Linc takes a step forward. "Jax—"

"Stay the fuck away from me," Jax barks. "You with all your caring crap. Did you say that shit just to get me to fuck you? Was that your fucking plan all along?"

"No!" Panic rises in Linc's voice. "I meant everything. I swear—"

"Fuck you."

I can hardly breathe as Jax strides across the parking lot.

Linc swears under his breath. "Come on," he says, tugging at my hand.

We follow him back to the hotel and into the lobby. The dark-haired woman behind the desk looks between us in concern, and I can't blame her. Between the anger rippling from Jax, and my tearstained face, we probably look suspicious as hell.

"Can you give me the local bus info, please?" Jax asks. "And a taxi number if you've got one."

"Jax, please," Linc pleads.

He ignores him, and the woman frowns as she hands him a bus leaflet and a business card with a taxi number on it.

"Do you have a phone I could use please?" he asks. "Mine's dead."

The woman picks up the receiver from behind the counter. "I can call you a taxi if you'd like?"

Jax nods. "Thank you. To the nearest bus station, please."

I reach for him, but he shrugs me off. "Leave it."

"Don't do this," Linc says. "Jax?"

"We're sorry," I say, tears choking the words. "Please? Let us make this right."

"Taxi will be here in ten minutes," the woman says.

Jax thanks her and walks back outside, pulling a packet of cigarettes from his bag. We follow, watching from a distance, as he lights up.

"Jax," I try again. "Please don't leave. Not like this."

He shakes his head. "Damage is done, Hailee."

I gasp a breath as my heart cracks. I don't think he's ever used my proper name before. Looking at him hurts too much, so I turn and walk back into the lobby. Nothing makes sense. Where is Carter? Why would he take my money? My head is pounding.

"I don't understand," Linc says, following me. "Carter was acting weird yesterday, but I would never have thought . . ."

"Do you think it's something to do with Andrew?"

Linc sighs. "I have no idea."

I watch the woman behind the desk tapping away at her computer for a minute. "Linc?"

"What?"

"Carter would have had to take a taxi, right? This place is in the middle of nowhere, and Jax had the car."

Linc nods slowly. "And?"

I walk over to the woman behind the desk and give her a smile. "Good morning. There was another man with us last night. Did he book a taxi this morning?"

The woman's eyes are wary as she takes in my tear-stained cheeks. "Yes. He booked a taxi."

"Could you tell us where he was going?"

She looks between me and Linc, who's come to stand at my shoulder. "I shouldn't really—"

"Please?" I beg. "We think he might be in trouble. Please."

Indecision wars on her face, but then she sighs and shakes her head. She reaches into the small trash can at the side of her desk and pulls out a scrap of crumpled paper. "This is the address he gave me."

I take the piece of paper. "Thank you so much."

"I don't understand," Linc mumbles, reading it over my shoulder.

Neither do I. The address is for a hotel in Phoenix.

I shove the paper in my pocket and head back outside. Jax is still leaning against the wall. He flicks the cigarette to the floor, stamping it out with his foot, but doesn't look up as we approach.

"Carter is headed to Phoenix," I say. "We think he might be in trouble. We're going there now. I know you're angry with us, and I know there's nothing we can say or do to change that. But we're heading to Phoenix, which is where you're going. So, if you want to ride with us, you can. You don't even have to talk to us. When we get there, you can get out and never see us again."

Jax stares out across the carpark, his arms folded across his muscled chest.

"We'll be in Phoenix in a couple of hours," I say. "If you take trains and buses, it'll take you a lot longer. The choice is yours."

I stare at him, wondering if it'll be the last time I see him, and it physically hurts. Of all the ways I thought we'd be saying goodbye, this is not a way I imagined. Linc's fingers intertwine with mine and squeeze. Blowing out a shaky breath, I turn around, heading back across the parking lot to our car. I've done everything I can.

"Why would Carter be in trouble?" Jax calls after us.

I turn around. He hasn't moved, but his eyes are fixed on me. "I don't know. There's got to be a reason he stole my money and ran. We're going to find out."

When Jax doesn't move, I turn back around and continue to the car. Linc takes the driver's seat, and I'm grateful, because I'm still trembling. I try not to think about how weird it feels not having anyone in the backseat.

"Ready?" Linc asks.

I have no idea what being 'ready' means. Am I ready to chase Carter across the state? No. I'm definitely not ready to leave Jax behind. I take a deep breath. "Sure."

Linc turns the ignition and puts the car in reverse, but then the backdoor opens, and I jolt. Jax slips onto the backseat, dumping his bag beside him. He doesn't say a word. Linc's jaw is clenched, his knuckles white on the wheel. I glance over my shoulder, but Jax just stares out of the window, ignoring me. After a second, Linc sighs and pulls out of the parking lot. The car has never been so silent.

41

I'M A DICK. I'M A COMPLETE PIECE OF SHIT. LOWEST OF THE fucking low. Watching my pale, clammy reflection in the taxi window, I scrub a hand over my face, drowning in regret. Jax woke me this morning when he took a shower, but I pretended to be asleep until he left. My phone vibrates in my hand, and I look down to see Jax's number flashing on the screen. I stare at it until it goes to voicemail. Every time my phone vibrates, my heart leaps into my throat.

I called Brent that night. Standing outside in the freezing parking lot, I'd told him to fuck off. I'd told him there was no way I was going to give him any money. It had felt great telling him exactly what I thought of him and the way he'd controlled Hailee. He'd listened too, letting me get it all off my chest, without saying a word. Of course, he had. Because the fucker knew he had the upper hand the entire time.

After a moment of smug, calculating silence, Brent had calmly laid out his threats. If I didn't bring him the cash, he'd make sure I was arrested for taking Andrew's money. I told him I didn't care. I'd have to pay it back, and we'd probably lose most of it in fees during drawn out court proceedings, but whatever. It's not like I'd go to jail for emptying a shared bank account. I'm not an idiot.

Then he'd brought Hailee into it. She thinks Brent doesn't know where her sister is, but he does. He knows everything. He knows where Stacey's bar is, where her apartment is . . . Everything. This whole time, Hailee was never going to escape him. In a voice that made me shiver more than the icy desert climate, he told me how Stacey has been fudging her taxes for the last couple of years. Enough, that if Brent pulled the right strings, she'd lose everything. Which means Hailee would lose everything. Even though I'd hope she wouldn't, Brent was confident she'd fall right back into the safety of his arms.

My stomach gurgles at the memory. His words had knocked me sick then, and the thought still does. The idea of her back with him, paying for his gambling habit. That's all she is to him—a meal ticket. He doesn't love her. Hailee is a fucking gem. She's sweet, and funny, and beautiful. She deserves the world.

He had me. Hailee is a better person than me. Even if I didn't care about her so damn much, I would have made the choice to help her any way I could. But Brent doesn't know how much I care about her. Not for sure. So, before I could answer him, he dropped his final threat.

He'd been in touch with Andrew. I knew that much from his texts. What I didn't know was that they'd worked together to hammer the final nail into my coffin. Brent had told me, with a voice so fucking smug, to check my messages. I'd sunk to the asphalt, almost dropping the damn phone. Sweat beads my forehead at the memory. Andrew gave him the photos we'd taken. Naked, fucking sex photos. While I'd stared, gasping for air, Brent had told me how those photos would find their way online, and to any employer I approached for the rest of my damn life.

I screw my eyes shut, and tears burn behind my lids. Fuck Andrew. Fuck Brent. Fuck them both. I'd tried to bargain with him. Tried to explain that there was no way I could get ahold of that amount of money. He told me to find a way and hung up.

After an hour of fruitless conversation with the bank this morning discussing loans, it left me with one painful, awful option. An option I know Brent was counting on me taking the whole fucking time. My stomach clenches and I lean my forehead against the window. It's warm. I'll pay Hailee back.

For the hundredth time, I go to my messages and scroll to the last one I got from Linc. The photo of us all lying down on the Four Corners Monument. Looking at it is the worst form of torture. I knew I'd be the one to fuck it up. Hailee should have ditched me back in South Dakota. A glance at the clock in the top corner tells me we should be heading to the Grand Canyon by now. I hope they still go. Linc and Jax will make sure Hailee gets to her sister's place in Vegas. It's not like she'll be homeless or anything. She had eight thousand in her bag. If I all but empty my account, I'll just have enough.

"Are you okay back there?"

I look up from my phone to find the taxi driver eyeing me warily. "Yeah. Fine, thanks."

He doesn't look convinced. Then again, I probably look like I'm about to vomit all over his car. I might. My gaze drops back to my phone. Maybe I should send them a message. I could explain to Hailee that I'm sorry, and I'll pay her back. I don't care how long it takes. My fingers hover over the button. After a minute, I turn it to silent, lock the screen, and shove it in my pocket. What's done is done. There's nothing I can say to explain. Nothing I can say to make what I've done okay.

A quick internet search told me that my bank has a branch eight minutes from the hotel. I'll go in, withdraw my cash, and still have plenty of time to meet with Brent. I wipe my clammy palms on my jeans.

"Bank is just up ahead," the taxi driver says. "It's got a drive through ATM."

I shake my head. "No. I need to go in. Will you wait?"

He eyes me in the rearview. "I'll keep the meter running."

"Fine."

The taxi is already costing me around five hundred dollars, what's a little more? I bite my tongue and stare out the window as he pulls into the parking lot. I'd pitied Jax for not having anywhere to go, but with every passing mile, I'm closer to the same fate. I wonder how many days it will be before I find myself sleeping under a bridge, or in a shelter.

The taxi parks up and I pull my bag out with me. The driver gives me a weird look, like I don't trust him to keep my stuff in his car. Or maybe, he thinks I'm going to do a runner. Either way, I'm not leaving Hailee's money out of my sight.

Sweat trickles down my back on the way into the bank, and by the time I find myself standing, fidgeting, waiting for the teller to complete my request, I'm drenched. I answer the questions, sign the release and then, I wait for someone to come and tell me that I'm under arrest. Surely, either Andrew or Hailee have called the police. I try not to look at the security cameras. Even though it feels like it, I'm not robbing a bank. I'm taking out *my* money. The money in my bag is stolen. I shift the bag to my other shoulder, the air conditioning cooling my sweat to ice.

"Mr. Willet?"

My heart pounds in my throat as I head to the teller. After this is done, I probably won't have enough to make it to Vegas. Maybe I should stay in Arizona. What if I ran into Jax, though? The chances are slim, but I'm not sure it's worth the risk. If he saw me, he'd probably knock me out for doing this to Hailee. Hell, I want to knock myself out. I picture the look of disappointment on Linc's face and clutch at my churning stomach.

"Would you like me to count it out for you?" the teller asks.

Shaking my head, I'm painfully aware of the sweat beading at my forehead, despite the air-conditioned building. "No. Thank you."

I watch, my mouth as dry as the Arizona desert as the teller, a young auburn-haired woman, shoves the money into an envelope and pushes it through the slot. My stomach is in knots.

"Is there anything else we can help you with, Mr. Willet?" she asks, smiling as though my world isn't crashing down around me.

I shake my head and force a smile. "No. Thank you very much for your help."

"Have a great day!"

Fifteen minutes. That's all it takes to practically empty my account. And now, I'm going to just hand it over to some fucking asshole. Bile stings my throat as I push open the door and head back out into the stifling heat.

As promised, the taxi driver is still waiting, and he doesn't say a word as he pulls out of the parking lot, heading toward the hotel. I take out my phone and text Brent like he told me to. I ignore the four new missed calls.

Got the money. Five minutes away.

Taking shallow breaths, I watch the screen. Almost instantly, the three dots start bouncing in their hypnotic rhythm.

4th floor. Room 407.

Five minutes feels like five seconds, and autopilot kicks in as I pay for the taxi and step through the automatic doors of the hotel. Holding my head high, I walk to the elevators as though I've already checked in, but no one even looks my way. Why would they? The neon sign above my head, telling people I'm a thieving piece of scum about to betray the sweetest person on the face of the planet, is one only I can see. Someone should stop me. Someone should tackle me to the ground. I'm disappointed they don't.

Static buzzes in my ears all the way up to the fourth floor, and with every muffled step I make along the corridor. I can't believe I'm doing this. By the time I find myself standing outside room four oh seven, I'm ready to turn and run. What then, though? Get a taxi back to the others and give Hailee her money back? Beg for forgiveness? Wait for Brent to carry out his threats? I could take the money and run. Go somewhere else. I could change my name. No. I should go back to Hailee and the others. Tell them the truth—what's been going on this whole time. The thought has my heart slamming against my chest, the clarity painful.

Brent had told me, if I didn't bring him the money, I'd lose everything. It's almost enough to make me laugh. By stealing Hailee's money, that's exactly what I've done. She is everything. Her, Linc, and Jax. Anything Brent could do to me pales beside the idea of losing them. I need to go back. They'll help me figure it out. I trust them. It's what I should have done in the first place, and no one is more disappointed in me than myself.

Before I can lift a foot to turn, the door opens.

42

THE SILENCE IS PAINFUL. I'M GLAD. I'M SO FUCKING disappointed. Both at myself, and Linc, and Hailee. When I was the first to wake up, as usual, I thought it would be a nice thing to do, to go get the tire replaced. I know how excited Hailee was about seeing the Grand Canyon, and I wanted to take the pain of finding and waiting at a garage out of her day. I wanted to make today special. I frown out of the window. Maybe I should have left a note. They shouldn't have been up. I've spent the last few nights in hotels with them, and every morning we barely make it out before checkout. The one fucking time . . .

I know why they thought it was me. If money is missing, and the choice is the high school geography teacher or the unemployed tattooed mechanic, it's a no brainer. It shouldn't have been, though. Hailee and Linc aren't just anyone. They should have known.

I can't believe Carter would pull such a dick move. He always seemed so straitlaced. There's got to be more to it. That's the only reason I got in this fucking car. I feel Linc's eyes flick to me in the rearview, but I refuse to meet them. *Fuck.* I had sex with him yesterday. It takes everything I have not to smash the back of his seat with my fist. It's not that I regret it. It was insanely hot. I just wouldn't have gone through with it if I'd known things were going to end this way. I wouldn't have given so much of myself to him. To any of them. Not when the betrayal hurts so much.

I close my eyes and lean my head back against the seat. Last night, Linc fell asleep wrapped around me, and honestly, that might be worse than the sex. Either way, it fucking hurts.

"Jax—"

"You said you weren't going to talk," I snap.

"Actually," Linc says, measuring his words carefully. "Hailee said you didn't have to talk to us."

I fold my arms across my chest. "Well, if you're going to keep talking, you can just pull over right now."

"It's the middle of the fucking desert, Jax." Linc laughs dryly. "You'd die."

As if that's not what's already happening right now.

Hailee doesn't say a word. She's practically curled in a ball, her feet up on the seat, and her head against the window. As silence fills the car again, she sniffles. *Great.* She's crying. Linc reaches out and squeezes her shoulder, but she curls tighter into the little cocoon she's formed. I open my mouth to say something, but I don't even know where to start.

"We'll get your money back," Linc says. "If we don't find him, we'll go to a police station and tell them what happened. You don't need to worry. I'll get you to your sister's place. Okay?"

"It's not the money," she says between sniffs.

I root around in the back and find the stash of napkins that's been building over the course of the trip. Grabbing a couple, I lean forward and drop them into her lap.

She looks over her shoulder in surprise, but I look away. I don't want to see her tears.

43

Brent is exactly as I imagined him. Broad and square, with dirty blond hair in a close-cut military style. Everything about him screams high school jock. If I had any money left, I'd bet he shoved his fair share of kids into lockers in his day. He stands back to let me into the room, and I try to hold my head high, and not look like I'm shitting myself, but I'm sure he can smell the fear. This is such a bad fucking idea. I step through the narrow entrance, into the main room.

"Hello, love."

My heart leaps into my throat, and I almost drop my bag. *Andrew*. I look back at Brent, to find him grinning like he's just pulled off the best prank in history. My brain can't process what's going on. Andrew is sprawled out on one of the twin beds, like it's the most normal thing in the world for him to be here.

All I can do is stare. "What the fuck is going on?"

Andrew smirks. "Are you not happy to see me?"

The endearment twists in my gut, and my hand tightens around the strap of my bag. I'd forgotten what it was like to be around him. Shame slides, cold, down my throat, as I remember all the times I let him shush me, control me . . . I hadn't realized how much he'd made me feel like I was less, until I met people who made me feel like I was more. My heart aches as though a nine-inch nail has been hammered through it. *What have I done?*

"Why the fuck would I be happy to see you?" I ask, the words not nearly as fierce as they sound in my head.

Andrew gets up from the bed, dragging his gaze slowly down me. "Are you mad at me, love?" he says, licking his lips in a way that makes me shudder. "You shouldn't be."

He looks different. It's only been a couple of weeks since I last saw him, but he looks thinner. Meaner. Maybe he always looked like this. His short brown hair is longer than he usually wears it, but it doesn't suit him. It looks like he's trying to hide the fact that his hairline is receding. Which it is. Any attraction I used to feel toward him is long gone. When I look at him now, all I feel is cold, hard, disgust.

"Of course, I'm fucking mad at you," I grit out. "Why the fuck did you give those photos to him?"

Behind me, Brent chuckles. "Trust me, I did not enjoy seeing that shit. Very useful, though."

I turn to him, seething. He's standing, blocking the way to the door, his arms folded across his chest. My heart is pounding so hard it hurts, and I clench my hands into fists, to stop myself from rubbing my chest.

"I had to, love," Andrew says, taking a step closer. "You took my money."

"It's not your money." The words spill from my lips before I can stop them.

Brent coughs. "It's not yours, though, is it? Just like Hailee isn't yours."

I turn to him again. I have never wanted to hit someone

so badly in my life, but assaulting a police officer in a hotel room is not something I plan on adding to my list of poor decisions today.

"At least five grand of that money is mine," Andrew says, pulling my attention back to him.

I stare at him in disbelief, and he steps closer, stopping close enough that I can see the faint freckles on his cheeks. He's shorter than I remember. How is that possible? To remember someone so differently after years of being together. I try to find something recognizable in his light brown eyes. I loved him. For over three years, I let him rule my world. Dominate it. Now, when I look at him, all I feel is sadness and regret.

"I'm still listed as your emergency contact," Andrew says, his eyes flitting over my face as though he's searching for something. "When Brent contacted me to tell me that you were with his girlfriend, we discovered we had an awful lot in common. Both of us have been betrayed by people we thought loved us as much as we loved them."

"We broke up," I say, trying to keep the exasperation from my voice.

Andrew wrinkles his nose, looking me up and down with disgust. "And now I know the real reason why. I always knew you were craving pussy."

"Don't you fucking talk about Hailee like that," I spit. "You know what? Both of you can fuck right off."

Brent unfolds his arms and shoves his hands in his pockets, leaning against the wall, which somehow manages to look even more menacing.

"You know, Carter," he says. "I was worried about her. It was so out of character. Hailee's never left Illinois before. She's such a shy, timid thing."

My jaw clenches. He hasn't got a fucking clue. Hailee

was only shy and timid because that's all he allowed her to be. That's what he told her she was.

"I tried so hard to keep her safe," Brent says, his eyes burning holes in my skull. "There are predators out there. Devious, perverted motherfuckers, like you, who can't wait to prey on a poor innocent girl."

"You don't know what the fuck you're talking about," I snap.

He pushes off the wall, taking a step toward me and I back up and smack into the desk, the corner slicing into the back of my thigh.

"I know exactly what I'm talking about," he says, his voice low and calm. "And you know what? You're welcome to her. I don't want her after you've had your filthy fucking dick in her. Which you have, haven't you?"

My skin burns as I grit my teeth, staring back at him. I know he's trying to rile me. It's working, but I'm not going to give him the satisfaction of knowing.

"Was it just you?" he asks, taking another step closer. His breath smells of coffee. "Or was it the other guy, too? Now, *he* is an interesting guy. Not sure what a fucking model is doing, slumming it with Hailee. Does he know about you? About what you've done?"

I'm sweating again. It was stupid to think this would be as simple as handing over the money and walking away. I knew what a dick Brent was. I fucking knew.

Squaring my shoulders, I move to push past him, but he puts out his beefy arms and shoves me back into the room. Staggering backwards, I just manage to stop myself from falling to the carpet. We're around the same height, but he's got at least forty pounds on me in bulk. Right now, it feels like a hundred. Panic rising in my chest, I turn to Andrew.

"You know," he says, placing a hand against my pounding heart. "I didn't just come here for the money."

Blood roars in my ears. "What the fuck are you talking about?"

"I thought I'd see if you'd come to your senses. Whether you'd gotten it out of your system." His eyes soften. "Come back home with me, love."

I stare at him in disbelief, stepping out of his reach. "Are you serious? What we had wasn't a relationship, Andrew. It wasn't healthy. Do you know what? You and Brent have a whole fucking lot in common. You isolated and controlled me, until I didn't even know what normal was anymore. You're messed up, Andrew. I just can't believe it took me so fucking long to figure it out."

Andrew holds my stare for a long minute, then shakes his head. I watch, my head spinning, as he turns and returns to the bed, stretching out like he's about to watch a movie or something. He gestures to Brent.

"He's all yours."

My jaw is slack with confusion as I turn to Brent, and I barely have enough time to focus before his fist collides with my face.

44

He still cares. I know he does. Ever since I handed him the phone charger cable and he reluctantly accepted it, I've watched him calling Carter every twenty minutes. My fingers are sweaty from gripping the steering wheel so hard, and I wipe them, one by one, on my jeans. I still don't understand why Carter would do this. Everything was going so well. My eyes flit to the rearview for the ten thousandth time, and just like every time before, Jax is staring out of the window.

My heart is a dull ache in my chest as I torture myself, thinking of how we all shared a bottle of wine over dinner last night. We laughed until our faces ached. The only thing that could have made it more perfect was if Carter had been there, too. What happened? When did things change? Something had stopped Carter from sleeping. Was it knowing that he was going to do this? Has this been the plan all along? I refuse to believe it.

Last night, I fell asleep wrapped around Jax, with a shit-eating grin on my face. My breath catches as I think of his hand over my mouth, his breath hot on my shoulder, and his beautiful blue eyes wide with wonder, as he fucked me against the bathroom sink. Remembering the way he called me 'baby' makes my chest tighten, and the thought of never getting the chance to hear it again, hurts like hell. I look in the rearview one more time, but he's still not looking. He never is.

The closer we get to the hotel, the more nervous I feel. I have no idea what I'm planning to do. Camp out in the lobby until Carter walks past, I suppose. What's worse is I don't think there's any explanation he could give that would make this right. This whole thing between the four of us was always too good to be true. It was never made to last. How could it?

"That's it there," Hailee says, pointing at a tall building further down the street.

My heart kicks up another notch, and I exhale, trying to calm myself. I look in the rearview again. "Are you okay if we drop you off at the hotel, Jax?"

He grunts in response, and I look at Hailee, but she's watching him over her shoulder with red-rimmed eyes. Anger is starting to trickle into my sadness again. I understand why he's so angry, but he's hurting Hailee, and that's not okay.

Gritting my teeth, I turn off into the hotel parking lot. There's an ambulance by the entrance, the siren silent, but the red and blue lights illuminating the glass front of the building. I park up and turn off the engine.

"Come on, Hailee." I open the door, trying to force confidence into my voice that I don't feel. "Let's go and get some answers."

Carter only had a couple of hours head start on us at best, so unless he changed his mind, he should still be here. Hailee gets out and closes the door behind her, leaving her bag on the floorboard. There's no point bringing it now the money's gone, I guess.

When she reaches my side, I take her hand, and start toward the hotel. Forcing myself not to look at Jax, I lock the car remotely over my shoulder when I hear his door close. I refuse to say goodbye and be ignored. We're halfway across the parking lot when I realize Jax is following just behind. I say nothing.

The automatic glass doors slide open before we reach them, and two paramedics rush out, pushing a gurney in front of them. I step back out of the way, tugging Hailee with me. The person on the stretcher is a mess. I stare, wide eyed, at the blood covering the man's face. Well, what's left of it. I'm aware I shouldn't be staring, but I can't look away as they open up the back of the ambulance, calling out in medical jargon to each other. One of them takes hold of the man's wrist and my breath freezes in my lungs. I know that watch. I know that hand.

"Carter?" I croak.

Hailee's grip tightens on my arm, a strangled cry ripping from her throat. I can't move. I'm frozen to the spot as I try to find any sign of Carter's face amongst the mangled mess in front of me.

"We know him."

Jax steps forward, calm as a fucking cucumber, and the paramedics look up from loading Carter into the ambulance.

"His name's Carter," he says. "Carter Willet. What happened?"

The paramedics share a look. One is all worry lines and streaks of grey, while the other is younger and Hispanic looking.

The grey one shakes his head. "We can't share that information without—"

"He's my boyfriend," Hailee says, stepping forward. "Please, tell us what happened. We were coming here to meet him."

The Hispanic paramedic relents with a sigh. "We got an anonymous call telling us that someone was injured in the stairwell. He's been beaten badly."

My eyes burn as I stare at his face, each faint rasp of his labored breathing like a kick in the gut. "Is he going to be okay?"

They finish securing him, and the grey-haired paramedic stands to close the doors. Ignoring my question, he looks at Hailee. "You can ride with us if you want."

She stares up at me, her red eyes glistening with fresh tears. I want to kiss her and tell her it's going to be okay, but as she's just told the paramedics she's Carter's girlfriend, it's probably not the best idea. I settle for squeezing her shoulders instead.

"Go," I say. "I'll follow."

"Central Hospital," the paramedic calls out as Hailee climbs in.

I nod my thanks and watch as the siren starts up, and they pull out of the parking lot and into traffic. *What the fuck just happened?*

My hands are trembling as I turn to Jax. "Do you want to come to the hospital?"

He turns, and I'm expecting the same mask of irritation and indifference that he's been wearing since this morning, but it's gone.

"Who the fuck would do that to him?" he asks, his eyes wide. "*Why* would someone do that?"

Dragging a hand over my face, I can still hear the siren

in the distance. "I don't know. It's got to have something to do with the money. Right?"

"Andrew?"

"Or Brent."

Just the thought of his name turns my stomach. I've been thinking about this the entire drive. There's no way Carter would just steal the money and run. It makes no sense. He's been acting weird for a while. Something was worrying him. I know in my gut he was taking the money to someone. And there are only two people I can think of.

Jax stares at me, perhaps waiting for me to explain, but I'm too tired, and I can't quite connect the dots myself. It's like the answer is just out of my reach.

With a heavy sigh, I turn and head back to the car. I haven't even buckled up when Jax slides into the passenger seat and closes the door. My eyes close for a second as a wave of relief slams into me.

"What the fuck."

I turn to Jax, thinking he's talking to me, but he's not. He's glaring out of the window at two men walking across the parking lot. I don't recognize either of them. One is built like a linebacker, with short blond hair and flat features. The other is short and lean, wearing a t-shirt tight enough to restrict blood flow.

"What?" I ask.

Jax is already opening the door. "That's Carter's fucking bag."

He's right. The blond guy has Carter's bag slung over his shoulder, another in his other hand. It could be a coincidence, of course, but I know in my gut it's not. I've looked at that fucking bag every day for the past week. I know it's Carter's. Jax is already halfway to the men by the time I snap out of it. *Shit.* I scramble out of the car and jog to catch up.

"Hey," Jax calls.

Everything about him in that moment is menacing. His voice, his posture, and definitely his face. He looks ready to tear someone apart. The men slow their walk, but they don't stop. Not until the blond guy sees me. Then, he comes to a halt, a huge grin lighting his square face as he turns to us.

"Lincoln fucking Lenzo, as I live and breathe."

My blood runs cold. This guy is not a fan. As we come to a stop a few feet away from them, I realize the smile lighting his face is the kind an alligator might give before it pulls you under the water and snaps your spine.

"Give me the bag," Jax barks.

The men ignore him, although the shorter guy looks nervous as fuck, shifting from one foot to the other. The blond guy hasn't taken his eyes off me.

"You're taller than I expected," he says, cocking his head to the side. He looks behind us, scanning the parking lot. "Where are you hiding her, then?"

The pieces slam into place with painful clarity. "Brent."

His smile widens. "Indeed. I'd say nice to meet you, but it's not. Have you enjoyed fucking my girlfriend across the country?"

My hands clench into fists at my side. "She's not your girlfriend."

He raises his eyebrows, looking like this is the most amusing conversation he's ever had in his life. "She never broke up with me. Not even a fucking text. I'd say that makes her still my girlfriend."

"Give me the bag," Jax says again, each word sharpened steel.

Brent ignores him. "Not that it matters. I told Carter he was welcome to her. I have no interest in damaged goods."

Jax takes a step forward, but I reach out and place a hand on his chest.

"He's a cop," I say quietly.

"Not in Arizona, he's not," Jax grinds out.

I keep my hand on his chest, pressing gently. "It doesn't matter. It's not worth it."

The smaller guy is eyeing me curiously, disgust stark on his face. Disbelief bubbles in my chest, and I laugh as the final puzzle piece falls into place.

"You're Andrew," I say. "Aren't you?"

The smaller man folds his arms across his chest. "Carter told you about me, then?"

I snort derisively. "Yeah. He told me what a controlling asshole you are."

Andrew's teeth grind together, hatred blazing in his eyes. "Did he also tell you he stole from me? Emptied our fucking joint account and ran?"

No. He didn't tell me that. My stomach rolls, but I keep my expression blank. *For fucksake, Carter.*

"Did you just stand by and watch while this asshole beat him up?" Jax asks Andrew, his voice dripping with disgust. "Or did you help?"

"Okay," Brent says, with an exasperated sigh. "Who the fuck are you?"

"It doesn't matter who I am," Jax spits. "Give us Carter's bag and maybe I can convince him not to press charges."

Brent laughs. "Press charges? He won't. That fucking faggot knows he deserved every second of it."

Disgust roils in my gut. "You're sick."

"No," Brent says, stepping closer. "*You're* sick. What did you have to do to convince Hailee to join your perverted freakshow?"

Jax reaches into my pocket and pulls out my phone. I

stare, open-mouthed, as he snaps a photo of Brent and Andrew before handing it back to me.

"What the fuck was that?" Brent barks.

Jax grins, and it's like a shark. "I needed a photo to go with the audio."

Thunderclouds roll across Brent's face. "What did you fucking say?"

Jax's smile grows even more vicious. "I've recorded this whole conversation. When we convince Carter to press charges, it'll make things a lot easier. What did you call him? A 'fucking faggot'? Pretty sure that makes what you did to him a hate crime."

The grinding of Brent's teeth is audible. "Delete that fucking recording."

Jax rolls his shoulders and cracks his neck. "Sure. As soon as you give us the bag."

I can hardly breathe as I watch, waiting. My eyes catch sight of Brent's knuckles, and the world tilts a little. They're cut and bruised, and the sight lodges in my throat like a rock.

A movement pulls my attention, and I look up as Andrew turns and sprints across the parking lot. He barely stops to check for traffic, before darting across the road and disappearing down a side street.

"Fucking queer," Brent spits.

I shake my head in disbelief. "You're a delight, aren't you?"

"Last chance," Jax says. "Or we can add theft to the charges, too. I'm pretty sure the hotel surveillance will show Carter entering the hotel with that bag, and you leaving with it."

"Fuck you." Brent growls.

Jax all but growls back. "Drop it."

I swallow, my throat drier than the desert. Glaring daggers, Brent lowers the bag and drops it to the ground.

"Pick it up," Jax says to me. "Check it."

Grabbing Carter's bag, the pure hatred in Brent's eyes chills me to the core. I can't picture Hailee with this guy, but I do understand why she was so scared of him. He's a fucking monster. Unzipping the bag, I find an envelope stuffed full of cash amongst Carter's clothes. The bag smells so strongly of him, and my chest aches as I continue to root around his things. A little more digging turns up Hailee's cash, still bound in piles by purple hair ties. The sight fills me equally with relief and despair.

Looking up, I nod at Jax. "It's all there."

"Delete the recording," Brent says.

Jax pulls his phone from his back pocket and holds it up. Sure enough, he's been recording the entire conversation on the voice memo app. I'm beyond impressed. But just as Jax lifts a hand to stop it, a thought slams into me with enough force that I reach out and grab his arm.

"Wait!" Ignoring Jax's questioning look, I focus on Brent. "What did you have on Carter?"

Brent narrows his pale blue eyes. "What? Other than the fact he's a fucking thief?"

My heart pounds in my throat. It's not enough. I know it isn't. "That money wasn't all Andrew's. It was a joint account." I turn to Jax. "For him to betray Hailee like this, there must have been something else."

Jax's jaw tightens, and he turns to Brent. "What was it?"

"Nothing." He sneers. "It took barely any convincing to get him to bring me the cash."

My hands clench into fists. It's not true. Earlier today, I made the mistake of underestimating Jax—of not trusting what we had together. I'm not making that same mistake again. I know there has to be more.

"Tell us what the fuck you have on him, or I'm not deleting this," Jax says. "Linc, get your phone out and dial 911, just in case this fucker tries anything. Although, I'm pretty sure there's surveillance in this parking lot, so consider your next move carefully, asshole."

Brent's nostrils flare. He looks between us, calculating, considering his options. I straighten my shoulders, trying to look as menacing as Jax beside me. It's two against one.

"Fuck you," Brent spits.

I watch as he digs his phone from his pocket and taps at the screen. After a second, he holds it up to face us, and the blood drains from my face. It's a photo of Carter and Andrew. Andrew has him tied up and gagged, while he fucks him. I want to vomit. When I meet Brent's eyes, they're wild with delight.

"There's more," he says, proud as fuck.

The anger radiating from Jax is palpable. "Give me your phone."

Brent snorts. "Fuck off."

"You think I trust you to get rid of them?" he sneers. "Give me your fucking phone."

Jax hands me his phone, the recording still going, and I take it, grateful for an excuse not to see the rest of the photos. Instead, I force myself to watch Brent as Jax takes his phone and scrolls through the photos, deleting them. It takes ages and I know Jax is checking every single folder and app to make sure they're gone for good.

Eventually, Jax throws Brent's phone back at him. He catches it and clicks through, annoyance seeping into his features as he realizes Jax got everything. Relief weakens my knees, but I force myself to stand tall as I hand Jax his phone back.

"Your turn," Brent snarls. "Delete the fucking recording."

Jax holds up his phone, and Brent watches like a hawk as he stops the recording and chooses not to save it.

"There," Jax says. "Now fuck off."

Brent looks like he's about to say something, but instead, he steps forward and spits in my face.

Jax rushes forward, his fist raised, but I push him back. "No. It's not worth it."

"I hope you're fucking happy together." Brent turns and stalks across the parking lot, and around the corner, disappearing out of sight.

I still have my hand wrapped around Jax's forearm, and when I let go, he turns to face me. Shaking his head, he reaches up and wipes the spittle from my cheek with such tenderness, it might just finish me off.

"Are you okay?" he asks.

"I don't know."

"Brent is a fucking peach," he says, glaring over his shoulder in the direction he disappeared.

I draw in a shaky breath. "You were incredible."

Jax doesn't respond. Instead, he turns and heads towards Hailee's car. "Come on. Let's get to the hospital."

Swallowing the myriad of emotions slowly suffocating me, I hoist Carter's bag over my shoulder and follow.

45

The coffee is beyond shit. The watery brown liquid trembles in the paper cup, and I watch the ripples for a full minute before I realize it's because I'm shaking. It's been half an hour since they took Carter through the double doors and told me to take a seat. Who would do that to him? What the hell happened?

"Hey."

A hand squeezes my shoulder, and I almost crumple with relief to find Linc standing over me. I place the cup on the floor and stand on shaky legs, wrapping my arms around his waist and burying my face against his solid chest.

"Any news?" he mumbles into my hair.

I shake my head against him. "Nothing."

"He's not going to die. Don't worry."

I pull back from Linc to find Jax standing just behind him. All I want to do is to throw my arms around him, but I know I can't. It aches, standing here, staring at him like he's a stranger. My lip trembles, so I clamp it down under my teeth. The fact that I have any tears left to cry is a surprise.

Jax's shoulders sag, and he blows out a slow breath. "Bring it in, princess."

He lifts his arms, and tears are already streaming down my face by the time he closes them around me.

"I'm so sorry, Jax," I mumble against his chest. "I'm so sorry."

He squeezes tighter and presses a kiss to my head. "I think the reason I was angry is more to do with me than you and Linc."

"What do you mean?"

A long sigh leaves Jax's chest. "I was pissed that you assumed I'd stolen the money, thinking it was just about where I'd come from, but I know that was only part of it. Linc was right. Anyone would have come to the same conclusion."

"So." Linc folds his arms. "You're saying you overreacted?"

Jax chuckles, the sound warm, as it vibrates against my ear. "Don't push it, pretty boy."

A second later, Linc's arms wrap around us both, and I breathe for what feels like the first time all day.

"Hailee Powell?"

We pull apart to find a doctor watching us, clipboard in hand. My stomach flips as I search his face, looking for some clue to what he's going to tell us. Jax wraps an arm around my shoulder, and Linc takes my hand.

"Is he okay?" I ask.

The doctor gives us a tight smile. "He has two fractured ribs. Luckily, there's no internal bleeding. We've given him something to help with the pain, but we want to keep him overnight to monitor. If all goes well, he should be able to go home tomorrow."

"Can we see him?"

The doctor hesitates, then sighs. "There's thirty minutes left of visiting hours. Just take it easy with him, okay?"

I nod, trembling with relief. "Thank you."

"Nurse Ramirez will show you to his room." The doctor gestures to a male nurse, who beckons us toward a set of double doors.

No one speaks as we walk down the corridor. Ever since I saw Carter getting stretchered out of the hotel, I've been going out of my mind with worry. Sitting in the back of the ambulance, listening to him groan in pain as the vehicle moved through traffic, I'd felt numb. So many feelings had rushed through my mind, I couldn't process them, so I'd shut down. Now that I know that he's going to be okay, the truth is beginning to bubble to the surface. Carter stole my money. He violated my trust. I honestly have no idea what I'm going to say to him.

When the nurse opens the door to a small room, standing to the side to let us in, I'm not sure I'm breathing. Linc thanks him as we step inside, which I'm grateful for, because I can't seem to remember how to speak.

My stomach rolls at the sight of Carter lying on the hospital bed. In the ambulance, he'd been an oozing, bloodied mess, but now he's been cleaned and stitched, somehow, he looks worse. The blood must have hidden a lot of the damage. It's hard to tell if he's awake or not, his eyes are all but swollen shut.

"Fucking hell," Jax says, stepping to the bed, his voice tight. "You shouldn't have held me back, Linc."

Linc drags a hand over his face, covering his mouth, as he stares at Carter. "Trust me, I'm regretting that decision. If I'd known it was this bad, I'd have killed him myself."

I look between the two of them in confusion. "What are you talking about?"

Jax drags a chair over and gestures for me to sit. I eye him warily as I sink down into it.

"Are you awake?" Linc says softly. "Carter?"

He doesn't stir. For a moment, the only sound is the steady beat of the heart monitor.

"We were in the car, ready to come to the hospital," Linc explains. "When Jax spotted two men carrying Carter's bag."

"It was Brent and Andrew," Jax says, the words peppered with barely contained fury.

My hands fly to my mouth, my heart dropping to my feet, as I look at Carter's battered body again. "Brent and Andrew did this? Why?"

Carter groans, his face crumpling a little, and we all rush to him.

"I'm so sorry," he croaks.

"You're a fucking idiot," Jax says, but there's no real anger in it.

Carter turns his head, seeking me out. "Hailee. I'll pay you back. I promise. I'm so sorry."

My eyes sting with fresh tears, and I swear under my breath. I'm so done with crying today. "Why, Carter? Why did you do it?"

"I looked at your phone," he explains. Each word is a struggle, and he winces with every intake of breath. "I saw the messages Brent was sending you. I sent him one from my phone telling him to back off."

Linc groans.

"He found out who I was through the number. From Tremonton."

I frown at the name, looking at Linc and Jax in question.

"The attack," Linc says after a moment. "At the restaurant. We gave our names and numbers when we spoke to the police."

Carter wheezes. "He threatened you, Hailee. He said if I didn't bring him twenty grand . . ."

He struggles for breath, and Jax places a hand on his chest, calming him.

"Brent was blackmailing him," Linc explains.

Between the dehydration, and the fact that none of this is making a lick of sense, my head is pounding. "What? I don't understand."

Linc sighs. "When Carter left Andrew, he emptied their savings account without telling him."

I look down at Carter, and he turns his head away.

"You should have told us," I say softly. Even as I say the words, I realize we've all kept the whole truth back to some degree.

"I'll pay you back," he says quietly. "I promise. I know you'll never forgive me, but I'll make it up to you."

He's getting worked up, the heart monitor beeping faster, and I take his hand. It's the only place that's not bruised or bloodied.

"Breathe, Carter," Linc says, taking his other hand. "If you get worked up, they'll kick us out."

Carter groans again. "I'm so sorry."

I shush him, bringing his hand to my mouth and pressing a kiss to his fingers. "It's okay."

"No," he says. "It's not. I was an idiot."

Jax snorts. "You can say that again."

"Wait," I say, piecing things together through the thumping haze in my head. "How do you know Brent was blackmailing him?"

"We confronted them in the parking lot," Linc says. "Brent was threatening to turn him in for stealing Andrew's money. But he also had photos . . ."

Linc trails off, wincing, and I look at Jax. His jaw is

clenched, and there's something dark in his eyes that I can't read.

"What?"

Jax looks at me, then stares at the floor. "Andrew gave Brent a load of photos of him and Carter having sex."

A strangled noise comes from Carter's throat, and he closes his eyes.

Staring between the three of them, I'm unable to find words. "Oh Carter..." I shake my head. "You should have told us."

Jax shakes his head. "Brent is a real fucking treat."

His words tighten my lungs. This is my fault. I brought Brent into their lives. I spent so long in the bubble he created for us; I don't know if I ever really saw the real Brent. If you asked me a week ago, whether he was capable of almost beating a man to death, I'd have said no.

I force my gaze up from the bed. "What happened?"

"Jax blackmailed him," Linc says, a flicker of pride on his face. "Recorded the conversation, and said we'd get Carter to press charges."

"Yeah," Jax says, his face falling into a frown. "The choice words he used to describe Carter would have made it an open and shut hate crime. We traded. I deleted the recording and the photos, and he gave us back the money."

My heart jumps into my throat. "You have the money?"

Linc smiles. "Yeah."

"You could have fucking led with that," I say, swatting him.

Carter makes a noise that might be a sob, and I bring his hand up to my lips again. "Hey. It's all going to be okay. Don't pull your stitches."

"There's more," he says.

Jax groans. "Of course, there fucking is."

Carter tries to sit up, but Linc gently puts a hand on his shoulder, stopping him. He sighs. "Brent knows where Stacey is. He said she's been messing with her taxes. He was going to report her."

The blood drains from my face. All this time, he knew. I thought I was escaping, but I hadn't been free for a single second.

"She wouldn't," I whisper. "He must have been lying."

Carter turns his head to look at me. "I couldn't take the risk. If you lost her, you'd lose everything. And if you ended up back with him, I couldn't live with myself."

A sob builds in my throat, and I swallow it down.

Carter grunts. "I deserve this. You don't have to stay."

Jax full on laughs, and I shoot him a warning look.

"We're not going anywhere, Carter," I say. "You fucked up. It happens."

"Just don't steal from any of us again, okay?" Jax says, poking his foot and getting a groan in response.

"I forgive you, Carter," I say softly. Before we walked into the room, I wasn't sure if I'd be able to, but the words come easily. He fucked up. Majorly. But he was trying to protect me. I bring his fingers to my mouth again, kissing his fingers, one by one. As soon as I get out of here, I'm going to call Stacey and make sure she hasn't been stupid enough to risk her bar.

"Do you want us to call your parents?" Linc asks.

Carter shakes his head. "No. They'll want to fly out, and I don't want them to see me like this. I'll be fine."

"Oh, yeah," Jax scoffs. "You look fine."

"You need to rest," I say. "Try to sleep, okay? We'll see you in the morning."

Carter exhales and squeezes my hand. After a few

minutes, his breathing evens out, and we all stand, heading to the door.

"Sorry, princess," Jax says as we head back down the corridor. "But your ex-boyfriend is a fucking dick."

I shoot him a withering look. "Why do you think I left him?"

He slings an arm around my shoulder and presses a kiss to my temple. "I'm sorry you didn't get to see the Grand Canyon."

"There's always another day, right?" I smile up at him, but I know it doesn't reach my eyes. I don't want to see it without them. Without all of them.

No one speaks as we walk through the hospital to the parking lot. With every step closer to the car, it's a step closer to the end.

"Is there somewhere you want us to drop you off?" Linc asks, pulling the car key from his pocket.

Jax shrugs. "Don't worry about it. I can find my way from here."

Everything we've built over the last week is swirling around the drain, and panic grips my chest. I don't want this to end. I don't want to let go. We've only just started to get to know each other. My skin heats as I make the decision to leap from the ledge and grab onto the threads of what we have with both hands, hoping it's strong enough to stop me from falling. If they say no, it will be mortifying, but at least I'll have tried.

"Don't," I say, my pulse deafening in my ears.

Jax raises his eyebrows, glancing at Linc. "Don't what?"

"Don't stay in Phoenix."

He sighs and leans against the car. "This was always the plan, princess."

"Why, though?" I ask, hating the desperation coloring my words. "You don't have a job or anything, right?"

Jax snorts. "Thanks for the reminder."

I step forward and place a hand on his chest. "What I mean is, there are garages in Nevada."

He stares at me, his expression unreadable. Ignoring the trembling sensation shaking my limbs, I turn to Linc. "I know you have to go to San Francisco, but once you've met with the agencies, could you not come back to Vegas? Modeling jobs happen all over the world, right? Does it matter where your base is?"

The silence is enough to choke me, and doubt starts to fill in through the cracks in my resolve as I drop my hand from Jax's chest. I should have just taken the hit like a big girl—walked away with my head high, and my pride intact.

"Sorry," I say. "I didn't mean to make it awkward. I just—"

"Hailee." Jax reaches for my hands. "Are you sure?"

My heart skips as I look up at him. "Of course, I'm sure. You, and Linc, and Carter, mean the world to me. Maybe I'm delusional, but I want to see where this goes. I don't want to let you go if I don't have to."

I'm too scared to look at Linc. If he says no—if he looks at me like I'm being ridiculous—it'll destroy me.

"We'll need to talk to Carter in the morning," Linc says.

I look up to find him looking more unsure than I've ever seen him. "Does that mean . . .?"

Linc nods. "If everyone's in. I'm in."

Jax lifts my hands to his mouth and kisses my knuckles. "Same here."

My heart feels so full it could burst. There's still so much to figure out, though. We can't all stay at my sister's place.

"Hailee?"

My spiraling thoughts screech to a halt as Linc comes to stand beside Jax, brushing his fingers against my cheek.

"We'll figure it all out," he says, a knowing smile on his full lips. "Shall we go and get some food?"

I nod, remembering that I haven't eaten all day. No wonder my head is pounding. I go to open the car door, but Jax wraps his arms around me and pulls me to his chest. Smiling, I sink into the embrace, breathing him deep into my lungs. Linc drapes his arms around the both of us, pressing a kiss to my temple, and one to Jax's neck. My skin thrums with happiness. I try not to let my relief settle, though. After what happened today, there's every chance Carter will say no.

The bruising is worse, but Carter is sitting up when we file into his room the next morning. Linc's brought a change of clothes for him, and some toiletries.

Carter looks at us, his eyes slightly more open today. "I wasn't sure you'd come back."

Jax leans against the wall and folds his arms. "Don't make me punch you, man."

I sink into the chair beside his bed. "Why wouldn't we come back?"

He stares at the pale brown blankets pooled in his lap. "You know why."

I sigh and take his hand, squeezing until he looks up at me. "I told you yesterday. I forgive you."

He grimaces, but it might be a smile. "I don't deserve your forgiveness. Any of you."

"Well, I can think of more than a few ways you can make it up to us," Linc says. "Once you're recovered, of course."

Carter looks between us, confusion clear on his face, despite the injuries.

"Come on," Jax says, pushing off the wall. "Let's get you dressed and out of here. I'm starving."

I pull the change of clothes out of the bag as Linc reaches around to unfasten Carter's hospital gown.

"Fucking, fuck," Jax barks.

My head snaps up, and I grip the bed as my legs threaten to give way. Carter's torso is almost entirely red and purple, a darker circle on his left side, where it's clear he's been kicked.

"Who wants a road trip to Illinois?" Jax growls.

Linc carefully pulls the t-shirt over Carter's head, apologizing as he winces. "There's no point and you know it."

"I fucking hate him," Jax seethes.

I press my lips together. This is my fault. If Carter hadn't gotten in the car with me in Sioux Falls, he wouldn't be in hospital right now. There's no way around that stark, horrible truth.

"Don't," Carter says, reaching for my hand. "I know what you're thinking, and none of this is your fault."

"What?" Jax says, eyes blazing as he looks between us. "No way. This is all Brent's fault. And fucking Andrew. They're the assholes. You two just got caught up in their shit."

I open my mouth to argue, but Jax and Linc stare at me until I close it. It takes both of them to ease Carter into the sweatpants they brought, and my nails dig into my palm to stem my tears. I hate seeing him in so much pain.

"Right," Linc says, as we wait for the nurse to arrive with the wheelchair. "We need to talk."

Carter looks between them, but it's hard to read his expression. "What about?"

"We talked last night," Jax explains. "If you want in, we're thinking of keeping the team together."

"Fucking team," Linc scoffs. "What are you? The coach?"

Jax raises an eyebrow. "Damn straight."

I roll my eyes and he winks at me. "What we're trying to say is, we want you to come to Las Vegas. With us."

Carter stares at me. "Are you sure?"

"We're all sure," I say.

Carter looks at each of us in turn, and I really wish I could tell what he's thinking. His ice-blue eyes are bloodshot, and it makes my heart spasm in my chest. It physically hurts to see him like this.

After what feels like an eternity, he reaches out a hand, and I take it. "Yes," he says, his voice thick with emotion. "Let's do it."

"Five hours to Vegas," Linc says, relief clear on his face as he smiles. "Plus stops for food. Lots of time to figure out the details."

I smile back. We worked out most of the details last night, but I love that he's making Carter feel included. I'm not sure how much he'll be able to contribute in his condition, anyway.

"Right," Jax says, clapping his hands together. "I'll go chase down the wheelchair for the invalid, and then, let's hit the road."

Linc smacks his arm, and I laugh. I set out on this trip, hoping to find myself—to find the person I'd been before Brent. When I invited Carter to join me, I'd thought I was chickening out. Using him as a distraction, so I didn't have to face the sharpest, darkest parts of myself. I realize now, each of the men in this room have played a part in helping me find myself.

Carter made me feel like I was worth something for the

first time in years. Knowing he was going through something similar gave me strength to keep going.

Linc opened my eyes. Not just by encouraging me to embrace my sexuality, but by living life to the fullest. His lust for adventure, and his positive attitude, make me feel like I could do anything—like I should aim for the stars.

And Jax . . . Jax gave me back control. He pushed my boundaries, forcing me to make decisions. I wonder whether he even knows what he did. Since meeting him, I feel more confident than I have in years. I think back to the forest with Carter, when I fell to pieces at the prospect of making a decision by myself. It feels like a lifetime ago, and the person I was in that moment, like a weaker, faded, copy of myself.

I got into my car in Chicago, a mess of fragmented pieces, with no clue how to piece myself back together. Carter, Linc and Jax haven't fixed me. They've given me the strength and confidence I needed to do it myself.

Looking between the three of them, my heart swells at the thought of what lies ahead of us. It's not the final leg of the journey I imagined, but in some ways, perhaps, it's actually the first.

EPILOGUE

6 and a half years later

I STOP AT THE BOTTOM OF THE STAIRS, LISTENING. PHOENIX IS going through a phase of resisting his afternoon nap. When I hear nothing, I breathe a sigh of relief. Even still, I keep my footsteps light as I move through the house to the living room. I love this house. After staying in Las Vegas for just under a year, it was too much for Linc when most of his work seemed to come from L.A., so we moved to the Los Angeles suburbs, where we've been ever since.

Around eighteen months ago, I fell pregnant, despite being on the pill. Although it was a huge surprise, the guys didn't miss a beat when I told them; and ever since Phoenix was born, they've doted on him. He's the most loved little boy on the planet.

I smile to myself as I turn the corner into our living room, my gaze landing as always on the huge canvas print on the wall. It's the photo we took at the Four Corners Monument. Every time I look at it, my heart swells.

Jax is sitting on the sofa, but he doesn't look up as I enter. He's usually at the garage, but today, at midday on a Tuesday, he's not. A magazine is open on his lap, and my heart pulls when I realize what he's looking at. On one of the pages is a full-page advert for a big-name cologne, and Linc stares up from a pool of purple water, white petals clinging to his torso. He's been in Peru for a month, and it's the longest he's been gone for years. We're all feeling it. Linc too. Especially when a month makes so much difference in Phoenix's life right now. That's the reason Jax is home. Linc's flight should get in at any minute.

"I miss him too," I say, leaning down and kissing his cheek.

Jax puts the magazine down on the coffee table and sighs. "It doesn't get any easier."

He's right. It doesn't. I walk around the sofa and sit down next to him, but he wraps his arms around me and pulls me onto his lap.

"Where's Carter?" I ask.

"Here," a voice calls from the study. "Almost finished!"

Jax presses kisses to my neck as I squint at the open door. "What's he doing?"

"Grading papers or some shit."

Carter's voice calls through again. "Swear jar!"

Jax groans and reaches into his pocket, pulling out a five-dollar bill. "Fucking, bastard, motherfucking shit."

"You could have just taken change from the jar." I smack his chest, and he grins at me.

Carter walks in from the study wearing a white t-shirt and grey sweatpants, his new glasses perched on his nose. "Did I just hear five-dollars' worth of swearing?"

The schools have closed for winter break, but I know Carter will have been trying to make his way through the mountain of papers he has to grade before Linc gets home. I'm starting back in January.

Once we moved to L.A., I completed a teaching qualification and was able to get a job teaching art at the same high school as Carter. I've been off since last summer looking after Phoenix, and even though I'll miss him like mad, I'm excited to go back.

Carter pokes at the magazine lying open on the coffee table. "Have you been pining again, Jax?"

Jax holds up a finger. A loophole to the swear jar. "I'm allowed to miss my husband."

The word still sends a thrill through me, even though it's been three years. Of course, it's not legal. We had a party with our friends and family, exchanged vows and rings, and legally changed our surnames. Now all four of us, and Phoenix, are the Willen-Bradwells. A combination of all our surnames. As if reading my thoughts, Jax picks up my hand and kisses my ring finger, his matching band of four different colored intertwined golds catching the light.

It hasn't all been sunshine and roses. There have been a lot of times over the years where people have voiced their unwanted opinions. Although we're not ashamed of what we have, we find it easier to not correct people. Most people at Saint Jonas High think Carter and I are married, and when Linc and Jax come to events, they assume they're a couple. We don't bother correcting them. We've learned it's easier that way. The important thing is, we're stronger than ever, and incredibly happy.

Carter sits down on the sofa and moves to take off his glasses, but Jax slaps his hand away.

"Leave them on," he says.

Carter rolls his eyes. "You almost broke them last night. So, no."

Jax huffs, and I stroke his chest, my fingers slipping between the buttons of his shirt.

"Do you have to go back in later?" I ask.

He shakes his head. "No. I told the guys to close up shop today. Perks of being the boss."

I smile and lean forward, pressing a kiss to his lips. When the garage Jax was working for went up for sale, Linc offered to help him buy it. It took a lot of convincing, but eventually Jax agreed. It's now his pride and joy.

"I've asked Sally next door if she'll take Phoenix for a few hours when he wakes up," Carter says.

I raise my eyebrows. "The house to ourselves? Child free?"

Carter grins. "Yes."

"What time does Linc's flight get in?" Jax asks.

I move from Jax's lap to grab my phone. "I'll see if there are any updates."

"I'm sure I can think of something to distract you, if you want." Carter says, sliding off the sofa and between Jax's legs, hooking his thumbs into the waistband of his pants.

Jax slides a hand into Carter's hair, his eyes flashing. "Oh, yeah?"

I frown at my phone. I've got the page saved, but it doesn't look right. "It says his flight got in early. Like an hour ago."

Before either of them can respond, the front door opens.

"Don't wait for me or anything," Linc says, raising his eyebrows at Carter on his knees.

We're all on our feet, and wrapped around him, before he can put his luggage down.

"I missed you all so much," he says, his voice muffled by the three of us, but still clearly laden with emotion.

I reach up and pull his face down, claiming the first kiss. "We missed you too."

"Where's Phoenix?" he asks.

"Asleep."

He nods, but then Jax's mouth is on his.

"How did I draw the last straw?" Carter says, huffing in mock annoyance.

Linc laughs and reaches for him, pulling him in for a kiss. "Well, this is a welcome I could get used to."

Jax snaps his fingers. "Ditch the clothes and the luggage. Everyone upstairs in thirty seconds."

Linc chuckles. "Wait a minute. I need to tell you something first."

I place a hand on his chest, searching his face for answers. "What is it?"

He gestures for us to move into the living room, so we do. There's more than enough room on the sprawling corner couch, but we all sit close enough that we're touching.

"I didn't tell you sooner because I didn't want to get anyone's hopes up," he says. "I had a meeting while I was gone. I'm not getting any younger—"

Jax snorts. Linc is the only one of us still with a toe in his twenties.

Linc narrows his eyes, reaching out and tweaking Jax's nipple through his shirt. "As I was saying. Modeling is a fickle business, so I want to have a backup. I've been testing the waters to see whether I could set up my own agency."

"Linc!" I gasp. "That would be amazing."

"Where?" Carter asks, ever the practical one.

Linc grins. "Here. I'll still book occasional jobs until things start moving, but if it takes off, it means I won't have to travel. I can be here for you and Phoenix."

"That's brilliant," I say, pressing a kiss to his lips.

Jax wraps a hand around the back of Linc's neck and trails kisses along his jaw. "Best news I've heard all year. I'm so proud of you, baby."

Carter stands up and pulls his t-shirt off, dropping it on the coffee table. "What was that about upstairs in thirty seconds? Because I think we need to celebrate."

I laugh, my heart so full and happy it could burst. "Race you."

ACKNOWLEDGMENTS

I like to keep my thank yous short and sweet. So here it goes.

Thank you to my BEST ladies. Without you, this story wouldn't have been what it is. You are my harshest critics and my loudest cheerleaders and I would be lost without you.

Thank you to my readers—the enthusiasm for my men and my smut is what drives me to write. I hope you have fallen in love with Hailee, Carter, Linc and Jax as much as I did writing them.

And to anyone who has a Brent or an Andrew, I wish you the strength to find yourself. Remember, it doesn't matter how long you stayed—it only matters that you left.

ABOUT THE AUTHOR

Addison Arrowdell is an adult romance author. Born in New York, she has spent most of her adult life in London, where she likes to people watch, hang out in coffee shops, and daydream about the perfect man.

If you like a touch of magic with your romance, check out the Man of Magic trilogy!

facebook.com/addisonarrowdell

twitter.com/arrowdell

instagram.com/addisonarrowdell

Made in the USA
Columbia, SC
16 September 2022

67431923R00245